Anonymous

Western Border Life

Anonymous

Western Border Life

ISBN/EAN: 9783337345143

Printed in Europe, USA, Canada, Australia, Japan

Cover: Foto ©Andreas Hilbeck / pixelio.de

More available books at **www.hansebooks.com**

WESTERN BORDER LIFE;

OR, WHAT

FANNY HUNTER SAW AND HEARD

IN

KANZAS AND MISSOURI

Philadelphia:
PUBLISHED BY JOHN E. POTTER,
NO. 617 SANSOM STREET.
1864.

PREFACE.

THERE are scenes in every life's history which, if artistically portrayed, would not only excite the imagination or please the fancy, like some strange passing dream, but would teach an earnest beholder many a lesson of wisdom and truth, and give fresh vigor and strength to the humble aspirant after good, in his wearisome struggle with contending foes. Where is the heart that is not moved to sorrow as the eye falls upon the sad, sad picture of mental deformity and ignorance. Where is the hand that will not grasp more tightly the "sabre's-hilt" with which humanity battles with wrong, as the vision rests upon injustice and oppression ?

But there are lights as well as shadows in every representation of historical interest ; and in no part of our national drama are they more closely blended or more strongly interwoven than in those two eventful years which cast a pall of gloom over a heretofore happy and prosperous people. There were also prophetic rays darting out from behind the clouds, through which the discerning eye might behold the rocks and quicksands that impede the progress of "great events."

While the life of our great nation shall be prolonged, there will hang in the gallery of time a picture so full of political teachings that every beholder cannot fail to read in it a lesson of progress and reform. The writer of this little volume lived among them, noted their sudden changes, and has sketched as well as she could a few scenes from beneath the sunshine and the clouds; and she doubts not there were many hearts that joined with hers in a fervent and earnest petition that God would save our beautiful country from a repetition of those fearful events which followed each other in such quick and rapid succession over the beautiful fields of Kanzas, sprinkling them with noble blood, and blotting the sunshine of prosperity from many an otherwise happy home. But, alas for the happiness of our great nation! this prayer was not answered; and to-day there are bitter, bleak winds howling through the wide-spreading branches of our much boasted "tree of liberty."

But we will not forget, while listening to the requiem-notes which fill the air, that Kanzas felt the angry blast before us; and it may be, in looking back over the track of this sweeping tornado, we may discern some method of impeding its progress.

This book, kind reader, will not lead you through dark, gloomy shadows only. There is much to amuse and please; as of course there must be when we take a peep into the social and domestic scenes of frontier life. Such commingling of characters, such diversity of sentiments, such clashing of interests and contention for "rights,"—each with his own peculiar idea respecting it,—could not fail to fill up a glowing picture. This the Authoress has endeavored to do in her present sketch of the three years she spent in Kanzas.

CONTENTS.

CHAPTER XV.

CHAPTER XXXI.

CHAPTER XXXII.

CHAPTER XXXIII.

CHAPTER XXXIV.

CHAPTER XXXV.

CHAPTER XXXVI.

CHAPTER XXXVII.

CHAPTER XXXVIII.

CHAPTER XXXIX.

CHAPTER XL.

CHAPTER XLI.

CHAPTER XLII.

CHAPTER XLIII.

CHAPTER XLIV.

WESTERN BORDER LIFE.

CHAPTER I.

SETTLING A CLAIM.

" Look here, Turner, ever since Atchinson telegraphed to the borders, I have had my eye on this piece of ground, three or four hundred acres of as pretty land as you 'll find in Kanzas, with that beautiful growth of timber yonder; hey, neighbor, do you hear ?"

" Well, now, Squire Catlett, that 's just like you. You are always speaking first," rejoined Turner, reining up his horse by his neighbor's side, and reconnoitering the ground with his eye; " only a day or so before we started on this tour, I crossed the river to pick out my diggins, and sure as life I settled on this same identical spot. But it 's no use now. The man that says first ' It 's mine,' owns these new lands, and you are the chap this time. So just nail up your claim to yonder tree, and we 'll ride on and find one for Joe Turner."

" Where on earth is that smart sprig of our young gentry, Tom Walton ? You, I say, do you hear ?"

" What 's wanted, Catlett ?"

" Hurry back here, can't you, and do a little writing for a fellow. My fingers are clumsy, and I never was much used to handle pen and ink. Can scrawl Jack Cat-

lett at the end of a receipt so that it will go, but I did n't
have much schoolin', any how. You see, Turner, I mean
my brats shall know more than their father, so I have sent
for a Yankee pumpkin, near by the leeks and garlics, to
train 'em. If she's as smart as they make out, there'll be
times there, I reckon. By the way, she's coming about
these days. Won't the young ones kick up a fuss,
specially Maud? Halloa, Tom, you've come back, have
you, on that Arabian courser by which you manage to
keep always ahead of us. Now down from your painted
saddle, and while Turner holds the rein, help me write a
claim and nail it to this tree."

"Jimminy! Tom, if that don't beat Turner. How like
a French dancing-master you came off Bucephalus. With
your ruffled shirt and tight pants and glittering gimcracks,
blow me, Tom, if you ain't a sight for these new lands,
such as they never saw before. Whoa! what do you
champ the bit so furiously for, Bucephalus; did you
know Turner had got hold of you?"

"Hold your tongue, Turner, don't you see Tom has
got his little pocket ink-stand out, and gold pen, and the
paper on his hat; now what shall he write? that's the
question."

"Write? why, This two hundred and forty acres is
Jack Catlett's, of La Belle Prairie. That's it; right to the
pint, you know."

"Don't quite like that, neighbor; don't look official,
you see. It oughter begin in law style. What is it,
Tom? Something about presents. Come, you stayed in
St. Louis there a week with old Squire Stanton, the big-
gest lawyer in Missouri. Of course, though, he kicked
you out of doors for a lazy lummux, as you are."

"Tom's got too many niggers for his good, Catlett,
He's an all-fired shirk."

"No lazier than the rest. Turner and Catlett don't do a whit more than is good for 'em. But just shut your head. I've got the ticket drawn up in shape."

"Read it, then."

"Hold on, can't you? Let me nail it to the tree, and you can all read it, for it's writ in thunderin' big letters. It's the thing, any how, and I shan't write no more. There, now, what do you think?"

Tom had nailed it to the tree, and there it stood, staring at them in large characters, thus:

Kno al men bi these presents,

that I,

JACK CATLETT, ESQ.,

OF LAR BEL PRAYRY.

hav taen possesshion of this lot of lan, of as mani akres as the lor purmitz, mezurin' from this tre as the south-east cornur, and in sixty days I shal send hither my son Dave with a lot of harty niggers. So kep ure distance.

"Ha! ha! ha!" roared Catlett, "that's it! that's it! Tom, you are a trump. Wonder who'll see that first. No rascally abolitionist owns this land. It's Jack Catlett, Esq.'s. Not the worst man in the world, neither. Now if Kanzas will only grow like Illinois! Whew! would n't Tom Walton here have to haul in his horns as the richest dog on the prairie. Hang me, but don't I wish Chicago was growing here like 'taters in a hot-house!"

"Look here, Catlett, you are talking treason. This allusion to the free States taints the air."

"They work in Illinois," chimed in Tom, "and that's what makes 'em rich. But I'll be hanged if I had n't rather laze about and be little short on't, than tear round like a Yankee for a bit."

"Now, Turner, did you accuse me, Jack Catlett, of treason. I say, and say it again, that the free States are a heap the best off, and I'd like Chicago just here, but I've got niggers, and I'll stick to 'em."

"Well, neighbor, now Tom's mounted, and the claim's up, I reckon we'd better make tracks. We must clear twenty miles before dark, for I want to settle on my own claim mighty quick, or all the best will be taken up. We are a leetle ahead, though. Even old Marm Gamby hasn't stirred yet, as nigh as I can find out. She won't wait long, though, before she gets her paw on some of these acres."

"That Gamby is a case, sure enough; but how on earth will she work it? She's no boy to send over, and them great strammin' girls of hers ain't of much account in managing a farm," said Catlett, as they rode along.

"Leave her alone for that," said Tom; "she knows a thing or two. But, neighbors, I came off to have a tour through these new regions, and not to be botherin' over claims. Pooh! I would n't snap my finger for all Kanzas."

So saying, away flew the beau of La Belle Prairie, and his neighbors rode after at a more quiet pace.

CHAPTER II.

"What in the world keeps Dave so long at the office to-night?"

"Lor, Nan, what makes you bother yourself about Dave all the while? You know he always stays till the last minute, if he gets chatting with the boys at the store."

"Nanny is right," said Mrs. Catlett, laying down her pipe with a concerned air; "it's time the boy was at home. Martha, run out to the kitchen and see if big William has put out Massa David's horse; he may have stopped at the quarters. Tilla, don't toat that child so nigh the fire—you'll both be in. O! there he comes!"

As she spoke, the subject of her anxiety made his appearance, and after kicking over two or three stools and ruthlessly demolishing a cob-house the children had spent half the evening in building—they only escaping destruction by the most surprising agility in scrambling out of his reach—he finally made his way to the fire, commanding every body to get out of his way, for he was cold.

"Any thing from the office, Dave?" said his sister, as he settled himself comfortably in the warmest corner.

The young gentleman fumbled in his pockets and brought out a letter, which he handed to his mother. It was addressed in a delicate female hand to "Jack Catlett, Esq., La Belle Prairie, —— Co., Missouri."

"O, ma, let me read it," said Nanny, as Mrs. Catlett leisurely examined the envelope, "it always takes you so long."

"Don't be in such a strain, Nan," said her sister; "you act like you never saw a letter before."

"Well, it's from the new teacher, I reckon, and I want to know when she's comin', that's all."

"She sha'n't come at all," said one of the children from the corner; "we don't want a teacher, anyhow."

"Ma, just hear those young ones; you'd better smack 'em for their impudence."

But Mrs. Catlett was too intent upon her letter to attend to any thing else. "Well," she said at length, tossing it over to Nanny, "the new teacher will be here to-morrow, sure enough; so now, children, there will be an end to your romping for one while, I reckon. Dear me, how glad I should be to get quit of your noise."

"O, ma!" said little Cal, "we don't want to go into school. Why couldn't the old teacher stay at home in Connecticut? It just spoils all our fun."

"Yes, indeed," echoed Maud; "we can't go over the prairie after persimmons now, I suppose."

"Nor down in the wood lot after grapes," said Joy; "the Barker boys will get them all. O dear, it's too bad."

"It's too bad," cried all in chorus, while even the baby set up a sympathizing yell.

"Now, children, hush! every one of you," said Mrs. Catlett, angrily. "Don't let me hear another word. You ought to be ashamed of yourselves to make me so much trouble, and your father off in Kanzas. What do you think he would say if he heard you talk so after he had taken so much trouble to get you a teacher? But, there! nobody ever had such a troublesome set to manage. Tilla, quit rocking the cradle, and go to rubbing the sideboard directly. Maud, what in the world are *you* about? That girl will burn us all up some day."

The child's occupation was evident. Having rebuilt the cob house, she had conceived the idea of illuminating it by means of a bonfire, and providing herself with materials from a pile of chips and rubbish on the hearth, and making the letter of her future instructress serve as a torch, she had set fire to the whole, and was watching the conflagration with looks of great satisfaction. One would naturally expect that this discovery would occasion some excitement, but, with the exception of two or three loud calls for Martha, a stout black girl who had fallen asleep across the door-sill, nobody troubled themselves about the matter. A few lazy strokes of the broom swept the whole burning mass into the fire, leaving traces of its progress in the shape of long smutty lines; and the child, unreproved for her mischievousness, looked about for something else to do.

"I'm right glad for my part that she's coming," said Nanny, resuming the conversation for a moment interrupted. "The young ones have run wild long enough. How will she get here, ma; the stage leaves her at the store, you know?"

"O, David will ride down for her, of course," said Mrs. Catlett.

"No he won't," said that young gentleman in a surly tone. "He's got something else to do. You can send big William down with the farm-wagon to toat up her and her traps. I am not going to spend my time in waitin' on her. She may as well learn first as last to go about by herself."

"David Catlett, I'm ashamed of you," said his mother; "when your father told you, just before he went away, to be polite to the new teacher. What an example you set the children! Of course you'll go for her. Big William can't be spared anyhow, we want all hands to-morrow to strip tobacco. As if I had n't enough to pester me with the charge of this great place on my hands, but you must set up and show how mighty smart you are. Martha, bring me a shovel of coals and my pipe off the sideboard. You don't know half the trial you are to me, David."

"No, ma, nor half the blessing, I reckon," said her hopeful son. "Come, Othoe," to a beautiful hound, crouching at his feet, "we'll go to bed."

"You too, children, all of you," said Mrs. Catlett. "Here you, Martha, drag out the trundle, and get these children off to bed. Viny, is there a good fire up stairs?"

"Yes, Miss Car'line."

"Come, then, girls, you had better be off; it's after nine o'clock. I'll just give out breakfast, and see to the house, and then go myself. Viny, you bring in a fresh log for the fire."

A general scampering ensued, the doors were locked, the fires mended, and the house became at length quiet for the night.

"Nan," said Maria, in a half whisper, as soon as the regular breathing of her neighbors betrayed their unconscious state, "how old do you reckon the new teacher is?"

"How should I know? Why?"

"Because Dave says all teachers from Connecticut are dried up old maids who can't get husbands, and so take to teaching for a living."

"Nonsense, 'Ria, Dave was just joking you."

"I wonder if she will set her cap for the old bald-headed schoolmaster over the creek. Would n't it be funny if she should?"

" 'Ria, you must n't talk about such things.   Children hav'n't any business with nonsense of that sort."

" Well, I just hope she won't wear a cap and spectacles, and a coat with a short body and scant skirt, like old Miss Barker over the prairie."

" I don't care so much for that, 'Ria, but I do hope she will know how to set up in company.   I don't reckon she will though, for those folks from the back States are mighty green, they say."

" O dear, I wish she was n't coming, Nan."

" Hush ! there 's ma knocking for us to go to sleep."

CHAPTER III.

THE next day, notwithstanding his expressed determination to consign the new teacher to the care of a servant, Massa David was to be found in company with half a dozen loungers, watching from the porch of Belcher's store, for the arrival of the semi-weekly stage from the city.

"The Store," a low, narrow, log-building, standing on the edge of the prairie, had for many years performed the duties of private residence, post-office, tavern, variety store, and general gathering-place for the whole neighborhood. Its proprietor was an old bachelor, Tom Belcher by name, who by his long residence here in the capacity of post-master, had given his own name to the establishment. Shuffling about in his loose roundabout and slippers, his shining bald head partially covered by a red silk handkerchief, he was to be found in a dozen different places in as many minutes, carrying on in his own person the duties of post-master, clerk, host, and chief cook and bottle-washer with wonderful expertness.

A couple of negro servants, whose cabin stood a few rods from the house, constituted his entire household, but the jolly-tempered old bachelor was seldom without guests, his own good company, and excellent tobacco and whisky, furnishing irresistable attractions to all the loafers of the prairie. On mail days especially, a motley company assembled to watch for the stage, and to while away an hour or two in talking over the news of the neighborhood, and to pick up such scraps of intelligence from the busy world beyond, as those who were fortunate enough to take a city newspaper felt disposed to impart.

In no very amiable mood was "Massa Dave," as he awaited the arrival of the stage on this particular afternoon. He had resisted manfully before ever he consented to escort the expected stranger to her new home, only yielding at last because, as he said, "the women made such an everlasting fuss about it," and resolving to perform the task with as ill a grace as possible, and "let the woman see that she would get no palaver from him"—a discovery that no lady could be long in making, judging from his unpromising appearance. As he stood sulkily in the doorway, his cap slouched over his eyes, and both hands thrust in the pockets of an out-grown coat, he presented any thing but a graceful figure. True, he possessed length of body and limb sufficient to constitute a full-grown man, but nature had not yet supplied him with a corresponding breadth and thickness, and whatever she might do for him in future, had left him at present a lank, ungainly, overgrown boy. His temper was not improved by the laugh raised at his expense by the loungers at the store, who joked him unmercifully on his new character as a lady's man, and advised him to practice all his airs and graces, and astonish "the Connecticut school-marm." Dave chafed under it all like an enraged cur, inwardly cursing all women in general, and the new teacher in particular. In this pleasant frame of mind he awaited the arrival of the stage, and when at length it drew up in front of the establishment, and the driver assisted a lady to alight, he might have been the most unconcerned per son present, for all the notice he took of her arrival. A slender, girlish figure, arrayed in a close-fitting traveling-dress, and a little straw hat with green ribbons, stood upon the platform, and throwing back her vail, gazed timidly round, as though expecting some one to address her.

"Now, then," whispered a flashy-dressed young fellow, standing at Dave's elbow. "Come, Dave, don't be bashful, speak to her, or I'll do it myself. By George, she's worth it, any how."

Thus admonished, Dave stepped forward, but never in his life had he felt so much at a loss for words. It had not occurred to him in what way he should address the stranger, or indeed that it would be necessary to address her at all, except to indicate to her in as few words as possible, that she was to be honored by his escort over the prairie. When, therefore, it flashed across him all at once, that he must make himself known to the young girl standing there alone, and say something civil to her, he was quite at a loss how to proceed. Something must be said, however, and making a desperate effort, he dashed into the subject at once.

"You are bound for Catlett's place, I reckon," he said, approaching her.

"Yes," said the stranger, raising a pair of large brown eyes to his face. "They were to meet me at the store, I think."

"I've come for you," said Dave, blushing to the roots of his hair. "How do you do?"

He stretched out his arm as straight as a pump-handle, and touched the little gloved hand she extended, as though it had been an egg that he was afraid of crushing, then letting it drop, stood awkwardly enough twirling his fingers.

"Have you waited long for me," said the young lady, breaking an embarrassing pause.

"Well, no; a middling while, though," said Dave; "yonder's the horses, if you are ready. They'll send for your traps after night."

"Yes, I am quite ready; let us go at once," said the lady, and her color rose as she met the curious glances of the loungers in the porch.

Mounted on his good horse, on the open prairie, with a yard or two between himself and his companion, "Massa Dave" began to feel a little more at his ease, and was wondering what in the world had put him so out of sorts, when the stranger broke the silence by inquiring the direction they were to take.

"The road yonder over the prairie leads us straight to the house," said Dave. "The pike goes on to Cartersville, and the little horse-path to your left, takes you to Barker's Ferry. You've rode before, I reckon."

"Yes, I am fond of it, and you have given me a beautiful horse," she said, patting his neck with her gloved hand.

Filly was Dave's favorite horse. "She *is* an easy-footed beast," he said, proudly, "and she's a real staver to go— there ain't her beat on the prairie."

"Kind?" inquired the lady.

"Kind? there ain't a better-natured beast in Missouri; and as knowin' as she is kind. She all but talks, I tell *you.*"

"I love a good horse," said the lady, enthusiastically.

"You can have Filly while you stay here," said her companion. "We all ride our own horses on the prairie."

Dave had forgotten what he had said that very morning about "Old Poke Neck" being just the horse for the "Connecticut school-marm."

"A horse to myself," said the lady, "to ride over this ocean of land. O how delightful! I shall never tire of it, I am sure."

Dave smiled at her earnestness, but as he glanced at her flushed face, animated by an expression of girlish delight, he inwardly pronounced her a mere child. "A pretty teacher she'll make for our young ones," he thought. "They will run over her head in a week."

The remainder of the ride was taken in silence, the young lady appearing to be engaged with her own thoughts, and Massa Dave finding it difficult to shake off his newly-acquired bashfulness.

"Yonder's the house," he said at length, indicating its direction with his riding-stick.

She looked eagerly in the direction he pointed. It was a substantial log-house, two stories in height, with an outside chimney at each end, and a porch in front. The coat of whitewash it had received in the spring had nearly disappeared, but the porch in front, and a part of the house itself, was covered with a luxuriant vine, which even at this late season retained a portion of its freshness. There was a yard in front, with a common rail fence surrounding it, and a large round log for a horse block just before the gate. A little behind stood a small log building, which it was easy to perceive by the various utensils in front, was the kitchen, and further to the right, its low chimney peeping out from among the branches of a large beech-tree, another, which Dave pointed out as the school-house. Still further on, and partially hidden by the yellow corn which was yet standing in the field, a dozen or more log-cabins stretched away in a row behind the house.

There was ample time for these observations as they rode slowly up the lane, which branching off from the main road, led directly to the gate; but the stranger soon

found more engrossing objects of attention in the group
who were awaiting her arrival in the porch.   The whole
family had assembled to receive her, while two or three
black women with brooms and dish-towels in their hands,
stood in the yard, and any number of little woolly heads
were darting backward and forward, peeping at her from
the corners of the house.

A sallow-faced woman of forty, or thereabouts, dressed
in a faded calico, and smelling strongly of snuff, stepped
forward, and introducing herself as Mrs. Catlett, gave the
new teacher a cordial shake of the hand, and welcomed
her to her family.   "My daughter Nanny," a tall girl of
nineteen or twenty, came next in turn, and then the stranger shook hands with a group of children, whose names
she could not remember, but whose rude staring and
ruder whispers she found it impossible to forget.

"Maud, shake hands with the lady, and say how dy'
dear?" said Mrs. Catlett to a child with black eyes and long
sandy hair, who was too busy examining the stranger
from head to foot to return her salutation.   "And Miss
Hunter, we had better come into the parlor, I reckon you
are tired after your ride."

Conducting the stranger across a wide passage, dividing
the house into two parts, Mrs. Catlett led the way to the
parlor, a large room occupying nearly half of the lower
floor.   A fire had been kindled upon the hearth, though
doors and windows were both open, and the cracks between the logs admitted a free circulation of air.   The
room was scantily furnished, but the few articles it contained were of a motley character.   A home-made carpet
covered the floor, while before the fire, its soft colors contrasting strangely with the coarse green and yellow stripes
of the other, was stretched a rug of the finest Brussels.
Wooden seated chairs, scanty in number and dilapidated

in condition, were placed here and there about the room, while in the corner stood a rosewood piano of elaborate workmanship, and upon an old-fashioned sideboard there was quite a display of silver plate. A canister of shot and a few wax flowers under a glass case, stood upon a small pine table, against which leaned a gun, while a pair of stag's antlers ornamented the doorway.

"So this is one of my pupils," said the new teacher, turning with a smile to one of the children, who was slyly fingering her dress to find out its material; "I hope we shall be good friends directly. Do you like to go to school, dear ?"

"No, indeed," was the prompt reply. "I'd a heap rather be down to the stable, or off on the prairie all day. Quit winkin' at me, ma. The teacher asked me herself, and I said I would tell her if she did."

"Maud, I'm ashamed of you," said Mrs. Catlett, something like a blush rising to her sallow cheek; "go right up stairs this minute, and stay there till you can behave yourself. She's the worst child I've got, Miss Hunter," she continued, as Maud left the room with a careless, unconcerned air, "but you'll find 'em all hard enough to manage."

This was not encouraging, and the stranger's face lost its bright expression, as she glanced at her future charge, who were amusing themselves in one corner of the room. She felt wearied with her journey, and longed to be alone, but just as she had found courage to ask to be shown to her room, a shout from one of the children announced that Martha was bringing in supper, and a moment after the bell rang.

The appearance of the room in which the family usually resided, and where the evening meal was spread, did not serve to raise spirits which had been rapidly sinking for the last hour. It was low and dark, scantily, even meanly furnished, the walls without paint or plaster, but hung round with hanks of yarn, red peppers, articles of clothing, and strings of dried apples. A bed in the corner, and the long table in the center of the apartment, filled it up so completely, that there was scarcely room to move about; and it was only after a confused scrambling and quarreling among the children that all at length found seats at the table.

"Viny, lead Madam Hester to her place," said Mrs. Catlett, after the tumult had subsided.

The girl approached an old woman who was seated in the chimney corner, wrapped up in a large cloak, and endeavored by touching her arm to attract her attention.

"Come, Madam Hester," said Mrs. Catlett, "supper is ready."

The old woman looked up, displaying a yellow, wrinkled visage, with thin, sharp features, and a pair of bleared eyes.

"Two silver tea-caddys and three dozen spoons," she said, in a cracked voice, "in the corner cupboard in the keepin' room."

"Yes, yes," said Mrs. Catlett; "no matter about it now—don't notice her, Miss Hunter; her mind just runs on the past the whole while."

With the assistance of Viny, the old woman hobbled to the table, and grasping her knife and fork with her trembling hands, every thing else seemed forgotten in the food before her.

The table was bountifully spread with a variety of good things, while black Martha was kept running to and from the kitchen for fresh supplies. A side of cold bacon, the "staff of life" with all westerners, loaves of delicious-looking batter bread, fresh from the dutch-oven, hot coffee

and biscuit, with a huge pitcher of buttermilk, these com-
prised the entertainment, a saucer of preserves being
passed round at the close, from which all helped themselves with a teaspoon.

The new teacher was too anxious and weary to feel
much appetite, and soon after supper requested permission to retire to her own room.

" Viny, show Miss Hunter up stairs," said Mrs. Catlett ;
and following the girl up an open, uncarpeted staircase,
leading from the apartment where they sat to one of the
same size above, she discovered to her dismay that it was
designed for more than one occupant. It contained three
beds, a bench with its bucket of water, tin wash-basin and
gourd shell, a small table, a broken looking-glass, four
trunks, and a stool. A calico curtain fluttered in the
night air before one of the small windows, the other was
destitute of even this poor protection.

Declining Viny's proffered assistance, and dismissing
her for the night, the new teacher gave one long, melan-
choly look round the room, and then sinking upon the
stool before the fire, she buried her face in her hands and
burst into tears.

Fanny Hunter was the daughter of a clergyman, who
for twenty years had been pastor of a church in one of
the smaller cities of Connecticut. His ministry had been
greatly blessed, and it seemed a mysterious providence
when in the prime of life, and in the midst of increasing
usefulness, he was suddenly removed from his labors on
earth to his everlasting rest above. His loss was deeply
mourned, not only by his own afflicted people, but by the
neighboring churches, and wherever his influence as a
minister and as a Christian had been felt.

To those nearer and dearer ones who were thus de-

prived of a husband and a father, it was a stunning blow,
and the pleasant parsonage, where they had spent so many
years in his society, seemed desolate indeed. It was at
this time, and when the widow was so bowed down by
sorrow as to be incapable of any active exertion, that her
eldest daughter, Fanny, displayed a strength of character
and maturity of judgment, of which none had supposed
her capable. She controlled her own grief to comfort
and sustain her mother and young sister, took upon herself the arrangement for the last sad rites, and, after all
was over, though her own heart was bursting with grief
and she longed to weep in solitude, constrained herself to
receive visits of condolence from well-meaning, though mistaken friends, that her poor mother might find comfort
in silent communion with her own heart and with her God.

It is one of the hard necessities of a minister's lot at the
present day, that he is unable to make any adequate pro-
vision for his family, in case of his sudden death. His
salary is not often large enough to allow him to live as a
people expect their minister to live, and at the same time
to lay up any thing against a rainy day. His children
must be well-educated and well-dressed, his house furnished genteelly, and a certain amount of company entertained, his name at the head of every subscription-list,
and his purse open to every call of benevolence, and all
this, perhaps, on a salary of eight hundred or a thousand
dollars a year. If he was permitted to live as a mechanic
or merchant in his own parish, whose income is the same,
he would not so often be found in debt, or his widow in
destitute circumstances.

Mr. Hunter was not a man to study economy in little
things, and he would have found no difficulty in spending
his salary twice over; but through the prudent management of his wife, they had contrived to make both ends
of each year meet, and this was all. The rent of a small

farm somewhere in the State of Maine, which had been left to Mrs. Hunter by her father, was all she could now depend upon for a support, and this was barely sufficient for her own maintenance, setting aside her two daughters, the younger of whom was not yet out of school.

In this difficulty, she applied, without hesitation, to one who was both willing and able to assist her, and who, foreseeing the possibility of this misfortune, had frequently assured her that whatever he possessed, should be at her command if she ever needed it. This was Uncle Peter, an unmarried brother, who resided at the West, where he was doing a fine business, and had accumulated a handsome property.

To Uncle Peter the widow wrote, and received just such a reply as she expected, a letter full of sympathy and brotherly love, and containing the assurance that she and her children should never want while he owned a penny in the world. Fanny must go on with her music, and Mary with her schooling, and as soon as the business season was over, he would come on and see how they were getting along. Meanwhile she must set aside all delicate scruples, accept the people's kind offer, and continue to occupy the parsonage rent free. It was no more than they ought to do for the family of a man who had worn himself out in their service; she was to take it as her due, and not as a piece of charity.

This letter, so characteristic of Uncle Peter, and accompanied by something more substantial than words, was like a ray of sunshine to the widow's heart, and relieved her mind of its one great anxiety, the welfare of her children.

"For myself, Fanny, I can get along with very little; but to think of you and Mary pinched by poverty, oh, it was dreadful! Now we will all keep together in the old spot, and be as happy as we can."

Fanny gave a cheerful response, but her own mind was far from being at ease. Such an entire dependence upon any one save an own parent, was extremely trying to a proud spirit like hers, and again and again the thought presented itself that with her education and various advantages, she could easily earn a comfortable support for her sister and herself. But one look at the pale face of her mother, convinced her that her whole duty at present was to comfort and support the bereaved one, and accordingly all plans that would interfere with this, were given up.

But when a year passed away, and the widow had regained in some measure her accustomed cheerfulness, Fanny felt that the objection was removed, and after talking the matter over with her mother and Uncle Peter, she received their reluctant consent, and Uncle Peter promised to find her a situation. This was speedily done, and through the influence of a friend at the West, the place of teacher was secured for her in the family of Mr. Catlett, represented to be a gentleman of wealth and respectability, who had removed a few years previous from Virginia to Missouri.

"But it's so far," said the widow to Uncle Peter, after the letter was received and Fanny had left the room. "Way off in Missouri! Why, the child never was away from home six weeks in her life."

"The farther the better, then," was the reply, "the further the better. She'll be thrown upon her own resources at once, and will be a deal better off than if she had half a dozen counsellors to go to. Let her go, Mary; Fanny has a brave spirit, if I understand her, and will go through it all like a heroine."

And Fanny went.

2

CHAPTER IV.

WHILE the family below stairs, were commenting freely upon the dress, appearance, and manners of the new teacher, in the room above, the young lady herself was sitting disconsolately before the fire. So startled and bewildered was she at the aspect of her new home, that it was some time before she could compose herself sufficiently to think calmly, and to form any thing like a correct judgment of the real discomforts of her situation. In the first gush of disappointment at finding every thing so rough and strange, with the desolate, loneliness fresh upon her, that one seldom from home feels in a new place, she had sunk down astonished and overwhelmed at the prospect, giving way to the most despairing thoughts.

"*Could* she stay here a whole year?—here!" and she glanced disconsolately round the room. "Had she left the dear old parsonage at N—— for such a place as this? where nobody cared for her, and where she could not even have the comfort of a room to herself? What would mother and Uncle Peter say if they should see her to-night? Could she stay? O dear, dear!" and leaning her head against the chimney, Fanny cried as she had seldom cried before.

Rising at length, and wiping away the tears that blinded her eyes, she crossed the room, and unlocking her trunk, took out a small pocket-Bible. Pressing the well-worn volume to her lips, she returned to her low seat by the fire. "I have still this comfort left," she thought, and once more wiping away the tears that would come, she opened the book at random and began to read: "Not that I speak in respect of want, for I have learned in whatsoever state I am, therewith to be content. I know both how to be abased and I know how to abound: everywhere and in all things I am instructed both to be full and to be hungry, both to abound and to suffer need. I can do all things through Christ which strengtheneth me."

"That's it!" said Fanny, half aloud; "that's just the spirit I need! What right have I to murmur at any thing, if indeed Christ is my friend? O! I can never be alone while I keep near to him."

She felt rebuked for her selfish despondency and want of trust in God, and thinking that it was not by mere chance that she had opened to the passage, she took the lesson it conveyed, home to her heart. She remembered how her pious grandmother, in times of darkness and distress, would sometimes open the Bible in the same way, and lighting upon some cheering promise, would come forth from the cloud with joy and peace in her soul. "Be careful for nothing," she further read, "but in every thing, by prayer and supplication with thanksgiving, let your requests be made known unto God. And the peace of God which passeth all understanding shall keep your hearts and minds through Christ Jesus."

Fanny bent over the little Bible, and breathed an earnest prayer that a larger portion of this spirit might be given her—a simple child-like trust in God—and then, comforted and strengthened, she began to look her situation calmly in the face.

" After all there was nothing so very bad about it. She had come out West to teach school, not to enjoy herself. She had found her new home a log-house in the middle of a three mile prairie; but what then? People had lived in log-houses before, very comfortably too. There was nothing so terrible in this.

"Then, too, though not refined and cultivated in their manners, the family seemed kind and cordial; it would be easy to win their regard, and they would do all in their power to make her happy. Happy! of course she would be happy. Her school would keep her too busy to allow much time for home-sickness. There was plenty to do; all that was needed was courage and patience to do it. The children looked wild and neglected enough, to be sure, but she would try to obtain a place in their hearts, gain some influence over them, and do them good. O! if she could succeed in this, what were the few inconveniences she might suffer in comparison with the pleasure she would experience?"

Fanny was looking on the sunny side now, and soon forgot all her doleful thoughts, in forming plans for the advancement of her school. An hour slipped by, and in the same cheerful frame of mind she retired to rest. Even the discovery that through one or two chinks in the roof, the stars could be seen, only afforded her merriment, and she amused herself by thinking how conveniently she could teach her scholars the science of astronomy.

She quickly fell asleep, and so sound were her slumbers that even the entrance of her room-mates failed to disturb them. Long after their whispered conversation had ceased, the subject of it awoke with a start, and raising her head looked round upon the sleeping group.

The fire was burning brightly, and stretched before it wrapped in an old quilt, a black woman was sleeping.

Fanny glanced at the face of her bed-fellow, but a strange noise in the next room drew her attention that way, and immediately fixed it upon what she discovered there. This chamber, or rather closet, for it deserved no other name, opened out of the principal room, occupying a part of the space over the passage. Fanny had not observed it before, but as she now lay, it was in full view, being lit up by the fire. A narrow bed, a chair, and a large old-fashioned chest studded with brass nails, was all the furniture it contained, and, indeed, all that it would hold. There was nothing remarkable in this, but sitting upon the side of the bed, was a figure so wild and grotesque in its appearance, that Fanny gazed upon it in perfect astonishment. The face was that of the same old woman whom she had seen at the supper-table, but looking infinitely more ghastly and hag-like, by the flickering light of the fire, and from the strange manner in which her withered form was dressed. About her head, from which streamed long thin locks of gray hair, was twisted a wreath of artificial flowers, all crushed and faded by age, while over her night-dress she had thrown a scarlet mantle with rich trimmings of black lace, from which protruded her long skinny arms, ornamented with showy bracelets rattling and shaking at every movement. She was bending over the old chest which stood wide open, and after fumbling awhile in its depths she brought out some faded article of finery, a scarf or ribbon perhaps, and holding it to the light, turned it this way and that way, brought it close to her bleared eyes, and muttering to herself all the while between her toothless gums, smoothed down every wrinkle with her trembling hands, and then laid it carefully away in its place. Behind her on the wall, a huge, grotesque shadow went through the same motions, nodding its head and raising its palsied arms in hideous mockery of the original.

There was something unearthly in the scene, and one could easily imagine the strange figure fumbling with bony fingers in the old chest, to be the ghost of some defunct grandmother, to whom all this moth-eaten finery once belonged, and whose ruling spirit, strong even in the grave, prompted to return at the dead of night, and mutter and grin over its long-lost treasures. Fanny even fancied herself under the influence of some horrid dream, and closed her eyes to shut out the vision, but when she opened them, there it was again as vivid as before.

At length loneliness becoming unendurable, she turned to awaken her companion, but Miss Nanny slept soundly, and at the first whisper, the old woman turned so sharply in the direction from which it came, that the frightened girl sank back on the pillow and did not raise her head till all was quiet.

When she ventured to look again, there was no trace of any disturbance. The lid of the chest was down, the ghost had disappeared, and in its place a little yellow-faced old woman, in a broad ruffled night-cap was sleeping quietly in the bed. Fanny was too weary to look long, and was herself soon fast asleep.

She was awakened the next morning by the sound of the horn, blown a little after daylight to call up the servants. In the twilight of a rainy morning, the low room looked even less cheerful than on the previous evening, and to Fanny's half waking gaze every thing appeared so strange and outlandish, that she with difficulty collected her scattered senses sufficiently to remember where she was, or how she came there.

The black woman who had lain all night before the hearth, was also awakened by the summons, and after a great number of yawns and stretches, slowly gathered herself up, and tossing her bed of quilts into a corner, proceeded to rake open the coals and make up a fire. This proved to be a lengthy proceeding, for the logs being freshly cut, and the pine bark wet through with the rain, they both required a deal of puffing and blowing to coax them into a blaze. They yielded at last, however, and Viny, who for ten minutes had been enveloped in a cloud of smoke and ashes, suddenly loomed up in the midst of a bright blaze, that filled the room with its cheerful glow.

"You Viny," called out a sharp voice at the foot of the stairs, "fly round there, and get the girls up; it's past six o'clock."

"Yes, Miss Car'line," said Viny, and snatching up the empty bucket and balancing it on her head, she turned a broad good-natured face toward the sleepers, and proceeded in earnest to rouse them from their slumbers.

"Miss Nanny, Miss 'Ria, you all get right up, can't sleep no more dis mornin'. Come, scratch. I'll be back wid de water 'fore you half out ob bed."

This was said with a laugh at the end of every sentence, and after lingering long enough to see that all were awake, black Viny disappeared down the stairway.

By the time she returned, the inmates of the room were huddled round the fire, dressing with all the speed that limited space and cold fingers would allow, and she was greeted with loud calls for assistance from three or four different persons at once. Viny did the best she could, flying from one to another, hooking Miss Nanny's dress, tying 'Ria's hair, and hunting up Maud's shoe-string, which she had used the evening previous to tie two of the children's heads together, and which was finally found in the slop-bucket, where one of the sufferers had thrown it out of spite. The pleasantest state of feeling did not exist while the process of dressing was carried on, as an occasional push and some angry words testified.

"I declare, 'Ria, I 'll just tell ma this very day how you carry on, takin' up all my room, and ramming your elbows out both sides. I will so," said little Joy.

"Children, why don't you stand round and let Miss Hunter come to the fire," said Miss Nanny, who herself occupied a goodly space in the corner.

"Lor, Nan, she 's only the teacher," said Joy, in a whisper, "I ain't goin' to give up my place to her."

"Hush, Joy, she 'll hear you."

Fanny did hear, and the words brought an indignant flush to her cheek. No one observed it, however, for at that instant Martha appeared with a gourd-shell in her hand.

"Yonder's Marthy with the drink," cried some one, and there was an immediate rush toward her.

"Give it here, Marthy, it 's my turn this morning," said Maria, reaching up her hand for the cup.

"No it ain't, Miss 'Ria, you all quit now," said the girl, holding it out of her reach, "Miss Car'line say the new teacher was to hab it fust dis mornin'."

Maria fell back, casting a sulky glance at Fanny, who was struggling to subdue the feelings Joy's hasty words had excited.

"Not any, thank you," she said, as the girl offered the cup.

"Why, yes, Miss Hunter, you must take some drink," said Nanny; "we all do here; there 's nothing like it to keep off the chills."

Thus urged, Fanny swallowed a little of the mixture, which tasted slightly of whisky and very strongly of brown sugar. The gourd was then passed from one to another, all drinking with a relish, and little Joy smack ing her lips over the drainings in the bottom of the cup.

"I'm sure I'll be glad when pa comes home," said Maria, after taking her portion, "if it's only to mix the drink. Ma is so scrimpin' with the whisky."

"It goes fast enough though," said Nanny. "A barrel don't appear to last any time on this place. Dave deals it out to the field hands about once a week."

"It's no such a thing, Nan, they haven't one of 'em had a dram since the corn-shucking."

"Yes they have, Miss 'Ria; Big William came up to the house last night, and got one for toating up the teacher's trunk from Belcher's."

"Well, s'pose he did, one dram ain't of much account, any how."

"They all count up, though, 'Ria."

"Now just to hear 'em run on," said Viny, with a giggle. "Miss Nanny, she's a snug one. Lor, when she sets up for her sef, dar'll be mighty tight times, I reckon."

"Viny, you mind yourself," said Nanny; "you are gettin' too smart."

"It's so, any how," said Maud. "I do think Nanny's too awful mean. Aunt Tibby says, when she gives out breakfast, there ain't lard enough to stick the batter-bread together."

"Shut up, Maud," said her sister; "you've no more respect for your betters than Viny there. Come on down to breakfast, all of you. Miss Hunter, are you ready?"

In the room below, they found the bed made, "the trundle" pushed under, the hearth swept, and the cloth spread for breakfast. Mrs. Catlett sat by the fire washing the baby's face with a wet cloth, while the child, in a dirty flannel night-gown and black silk cap, was kicking and screaming in her arms. Massa Dave made an awkward bow to the new teacher, and even pushed his chair a little one side that she might come to the fire.

"Mighty polite, Dave, all of a sudden," whispered Nanny, as they gathered round the table. "I reckon you are struck."

The young gentleman deigned her no reply.

"David, cut a thin slice of bacon for Madam Hester," said Mrs. Catlett, "and Marthy hand me that pone of bread, and quit rolling your eyes all over the room, when they ought to be on the table. Go and get your waiter and carry Madam Hester's breakfast right up to her."

"Is Madam Hester sick this morning," inquired Fanny, remembering the scene she had witnessed the previous night.

"Oh, no, she always takes her breakfast in bed," said Mrs. Catlett; "she don't sleep nights, and—careful, Marthy, you'll have that coffee all over me, yet—can't you keep your eyes on what you are about? You are the most careless creature. There, now, see if you can toat that up stairs without upsetting it. That girl ought to understand her business; I'm sure I've spent time enough teaching her; but I think sometimes you can't learn those creatures any thing."

"Who goes to church to-day?" inquired Nanny.

"Nobody from this house," said her mother sharply. "It will rain right down by noon, and I shan't have the children's clothes spoiled by being out in it, so you may just make up your minds to stay at home."

"Nanny feels bad now," said Maria, "'cause she's just gotten her new coat done on purpose to wear. Ma, you ought to let her go, she's worked so hard on it."

"Don't you fret, 'Ria, the new coat's of no account."

"I don't care," said Maud, in a whisper, to her next neighbor. "I hope I don't want to go to church. We'll go down to the spring and ride our tree-horses, won't we Cal?"

In this kind of talk, breakfast passed off, and the family all left the table except Mrs. Catlett, who remained to give the house-servants their allowance. These came filing in one after another, each with a small pewter trencher in her hand, which she laid before her mistress, who divided the fragments of the meat into equal portions, placing one upon each plate.

"Where's Aunt Phebe's trencher this morning?" she said, missing one from the row.

"Miss Maud's gone to fetch it," said Viny. "I met her on de way."

"That child is always meddling with what don't concern her," said Mrs. Catlett, cutting a piece of corn bread in two. "Why couldn't she let the boy toat it up as usual?"

"Don' know, Miss Car'line; she seem in a mighty big hurry."

Just then the door opened, and the child who had replied so ungraciously to Fanny the evening before, entered the room. Her hair was hanging about her ears, and her frock was wet to the knees.

"Now, ain't you a sight?" said Mrs. Catlett. "There, go right to the fire and dry yourself this minute. You'll have a chill for this to-morrow, as like as not. Who told you to be running down to the women's cabins before breakfast, anyhow?"

"I want Aunt Phebe's breakfast," said Maud, with the most unconcerned air in the world; "and here's a cup for some coffee."

"She can't have a drop," said Mrs. Catlett. "I ain't

goin' to give the servants coffee every day or two; we can't afford it; she had some not three days ago, and she's no business to send for it so soon again."

"She didn't send for it," said Maud; "I found the cup on the shelf, and brought it along. Pa said we were to be good to Aunt Phebe." She laid the trencher and the little tin cup upon the table, and turned away with a quivering lip.

Mrs. Catlett looked very cross as she proceeded with her task, but when, a few moments after, Maud took the things away, the cup was not empty.

"Bring in your tub, Marthy, and wash up the cups," said Mrs. Catlett; "and Viny, hurry your breakfast, and come back to the house. I can't get Aunt Hester up alone every morning; that's a settled thing."

She, however, proceeded directly up stairs, and before Viny returned from her cabin, came down again supporting the old woman to her seat in the corner.

"Now, children, you pack off up stairs; there's a good fire there, and Jinny has just swept up the floor. I want to write a letter this morning, and there's no living in such a noise. Come, off with you; and Tilla, you take the baby out to the kitchen awhile; don't you let her walk a step on this wet ground, neither; you toat her all the way; do you hear?"

The person last addressed, a little negro girl of six or seven years, who was tottering across the room under the weight of a child nearly as heavy as herself, set down her load for an instant, and turned a weary, old-looking face toward her mistress.

"What's the child staring for," said Mrs. Catlett, impatiently. "Are you deaf? I told you to toat Miss Hetty out to the kitchen, and there you stand as senseless as a log. Come, off with you."

Miss Hetty enforced her mother's commands by clambering upon Tilla's back, and seizing fast upon her woolly head, she by several decided twitches gave her to understand that she was anxious to proceed.

" Now, then," said Mrs. Catlett, as the little bent figure with its burden disappeared in the doorway, " you heard what I said, children, go on, all of you. Cal, take Johnny with you, I can't have him here."

There was a general scattering, the children making a rush for the stairway, each pushing and fighting to get there first, and chasing each other up the stairs and through the room above, till a whole shower of dried whitewash rattled down from the rough planks.

" O, dear, dear ! how they do carry on," said Mrs. Catlett. "Miss Hunter, I hope you will teach 'em better manners. Marthy, go up and tell Miss 'Ria to keep 'em quiet, and then bring me a shovel of coals and my pipe."

With this never-failing solace of all her troubles, the lady settled herself comfortably in the corner. Miss Nanny threw herself down in the cradle, which, in Mrs. Catlett's family, was an article of furniture by no means devoted exclusively to the baby's use ; and Dave sauntered somewhere out of doors. Fanny was left sitting alone by the window, and finding that she was in danger of breaking last night's resolution by falling into the state of mind she had determined to avoid, she roused herself and looked about for something to do.

An almanac hanging by a bit of twine in the chimney-corner, and a couple of last week's papers lying upon the shelf, appeared to be all the reading-matter that the room afforded, and as Mrs. Catlett had by this time commenced her letter, and Nanny was taking a nice nap in the cradle, there seemed little hope of carrying on a conversation in either quarter, while Madam Hester, with the cloak drawn close about her, had sunk down into a dreamy unconscious state, from which nothing could arouse her.

Fanny gazed listlessly upon the prospect out of doors. The rain was dripping from the eaves of the house, and from the vine over the porch, while a gust of wind now and then brought a shower of damp, dead leaves to the ground. Little puddles of water were standing here and there in the yard, where the pigs had rooted beds for themselves in the black mould, and two or three of these animals, disgusted with their places of repose, were wandering about the premises, giving utterance occasionally to a discontented grunt. The prairie beyond, looked brown and withered, and the clouds hung heavy above. What should she do with herself this long rainy day?

An answer to the question suggested itself. The children were amusing themselves in the room above. Ought she not to be with them? True, her duties did not strictly commence until the next day, and inclination whispered that it would be time enough then to begin her labors. On the other hand, something might be gained if she could become a little acquainted with them; she might obtain some influence over them; as yet she had done nothing. At least her presence would prove a restraint, and perhaps prevent any open violation of the Sabbath. She would try it, so walking boldly up stairs, she pushed open the door and entered the room. The children all looked up, and it was evident from the expression of their faces, that she was not a welcome guest; but this was no more than she expected, and smiling pleasantly in answer to their sour looks, she sat down quietly by the fire.

Maria, Caroline, and Maud, the three elder children, were seated upon the table, playing a game with marbles, the skill of which appeared to consist in dropping one with sufficient force and accuracy of aim, to displace several from the ring, the person playing pocketing all which she thus moved. They stopped for a moment and held a consultation, but after a good deal of whispering and a half audible " I don't care, she need n't come, then," from Maud, they went on with their game. Meanwhile the little ones, Joy and Johnny, having nothing to do but lounge about the table and watch the rest, were finding amusement for themselves in teasing the players, snatching their marbles and making off with them, or pinching their toes under the table. Angry exclamations and an occasional kick from one of the sufferers, frightened them into good behavior for a few moments, but they soon returned to the charge with renewed vigor.

At last Johnny received a blow from some unknown foot that sent him howling to the other side of the room, and Fanny thinking this a good opportunity to try her powers of amusing, coaxed him to her, and after a little pleasant talk, proposed to tell him a story. The child looked up with a shy, half frightened expression, but seeing nothing in her face to justify his fears, he allowed her to take him in her lap.

Fanny had gained quite a reputation among the little folks at home, by her skill in story-telling, and many an evening had kept the undivided attention of a group of listeners, as she repeated tale after tale from her almost inexhaustible stock. Selecting one that had always been popular, she commenced, adapting her story to the capacities of the older children, though it was simple enough for Johnny to comprehend.

For awhile no effect was produced upon the players. The game progressed steadily, and an occasional glance toward the fire was the only sign given that they heard any thing but the rattling of the marbles on the table.

Fanny grew excited. Her pride was roused, and she determined that they *should* hear. She called all the skill she possessed to her aid, and never before had she tried so hard to make a tale interesting. Joy and Johnny, with mouth and eyes wide open, were staring at her with all their might; but the game continued. At length there began to be pauses. Some one forgot that it was her turn to play, or with marble suspended in the air, waited for the conclusion of a sentence before letting it drop. Fanny went on with renewed courage. The marbles dropped slower and slower, and finally stopped entirely; one, and then another slipped down from the table, until, before the story was completed, not a sound was heard but her own voice.

This was excellent. She complied at once with their request for another story, and still another, and was herself as eager to relate, as they to listen. An hour slipped by before they knew it, and then Fanny rose, and refusing their request for more, left the room as quietly as she had entered.

CHAPTER V.

As the door closed behind her, the children gazed in each other's faces a moment without speaking.

"She ain't so bad, after all; is she?" said Cal.

"I like her a heap better than I thought I should," said 'Ria.

"I, too," said little Joy.

"Did n't you reckon we should catch it, 'Ria, when she found us playing 'tumble top?'" said Cal.

"Lor', no, she did n't seem to care a bit; she just walked in and never said a word."

"I know it, but I reckon she did n't like it for all that, 'cause, don't you know, one of her stories was about a girl that never played Sundays. Did you mind that?"

"She knows a heap; don't she, Maud?" said little Joy.

"No," said Maud, sullenly.

"Why, Maud Catlett, I'd be ashamed," said 'Ria; "you know she knows sights and sights more than you do."

"I don't car'. If you all want to be kept in school these pleasant days, I don't; and I ain't going to like the new teacher anyhow." Maud spoke loud, and grew quite red in the face.

There was a general silence, broken by little Joy, saying, "Well, I do, 'cause she tells such pretty stories; don't she, 'Ria?"

But her sister was too busy at the window to reply.

"I declare," she said, "if there ain't old Miss Gamby coming up the lane on her white horse. Now won't we have fun, listenin' at her brag."

"What brings her here this rainy day, anyhow?" said Cal.

"I reckon she's come to see about Boss an' Biny comin' here to school this winter. You know she talked about it a long time back."

"Did she? Well that's it, then. There, now, she's gettin' down; come let's run down stairs, while ma goes out to meet her, and then she can't send us back."

The guest had already been seen from the window below, and by the time the children found their way down stairs, Mrs. Catlett ushered her in. She was a tall, spare woman, as hollow-chested as a man, with coarse features, and a red face. She was dressed in a scanty, home-made gingham, with a turban of the same material, covering her gray locks. Throwing off her sun-bonnet, and a large cloak, she took the proffered seat before the fire, and carefully folding back her dress, extended a pair of feet on the hearth, that no man in Missouri would have felt ashamed to own.

"I reckon you did n't look for company to-day, neighbor Catlett?" she said. "It ain't the prettiest day to be out, neither, but I had a little business matter to talk over with you, so I told Jerry he might gear up old White, and I'd ride along. I reckoned you'd feel kinder lonesome, too, with the squire over there in Kanzas. Heered any thing from him?"

"Heard any thing? No. It's hard upon six weeks since that man started away, and not a blessed thing do I know about him. He may be dead and buried over there among them wild Indians, for all I know I declare

I wish men would be contented to stay at home a week at a time. It's always gad, gad, with 'em. I should think there was land enough in Missouri, and good land, too, without every body's chasing over to Kanzas after more. I know one thing, it 's hard enough to keep things straight on this place, niggers and all, and if Jack Catlett thinks he 's going to spend half his time over there, fussin' over a new farm, and leave me to worry and fret over things at home, he 's mightily mistaken; and I 'll let him know it, too."

"Lor', neighbor Catlett, he ain't agoin' to do any such thing. He 's only gone over to settle on a claim. Besides it 's for Dave, ain't it?"

"O, I know he says so. Great times for Dave. He thinks he 's a grown man, sure, with his farm and his niggers; but I tell you he needs a deal of looking after yet, and Mr. Catlett will have to be over there the balance of the time, keepin' things straight. Besides, they say there 's awful times just now with the new settlers, and Dave is so hot-headed, he 'll be getting into trouble the first thing, and get his head broke of course. O dear! I do nothing but fret about that boy the whole time."

"The more fool you. The boy 's well enough. He won't be half a man till he shoots down two or three of them sneakin' abolitionists over there. I should want him to fight 'em if I was you. And can't you see what a chance there is for a young fellow, with a snug bit of land and a few niggers. Why, neighbor, if my two daughters was sons—and gracious knows I wish they had been—I 'd send them both over there as straight as a gun—I would so."

"Why how come you to know so much about it, anyhow?"

"How? Have n't I been to take a look myself. Did

you reckon I was goin' to wait till Squire Catlett, and Joe Turner, and all the smart chaps round here, had picked out the best claims. No, no, I wanted a dab at it myself, so off I starts two months ago, and I and old White makes a tour round the diggins. Ha! ha! Some of them wide-awake chaps may find Marm Gamby's name pinned to the post before 'em, if she is a woman. Forehanded, neighbor Catlett, that's my way, you see."

"You don't mean to say you've picked out a claim there 'a-ready, Madam Gamby? What on earth do you mean to do with it?"

"Do with it?" said Madam Gamby, her hard eyes open to their widest extent. "Well, if that ain't a question. Why, work it, to be sure."

"As if you had n't enough on your hands a'ready. A widow woman like you, with a great farm to manage here. Why, what will become of your place, and your tribe of niggers in Missouri, if you start another over the border. Madam Gamby, you are crazy."

The person addressed pushed back her chair from the fire, and crossing one limb over the other, looked up with a cunning twinkle in her gray eyes.

"You wait awhile, neighbor," she said. "Did you ever know me start a thing and not put it through? Come, own up, now."

"O, I know you are powerful smart; but I can't see yet how you mean to manage. I don't trouble my head much about law matters, but I 've heard say you can't own a claim over there, without settling down on it. Now how you are goin' to carry on your place here, and live over in Kanzas, is more than I can make out."

"No more I don't mean to live over there, neighbor. Don't you reckon I can keep two or three niggers there just to see to things, and keep off other people, and ride

over myself now and then to keep 'em straight. That's
my plan."

"But that won't be according to law, will it ?"

"My gracious! Just to hear the woman talk! Fid-
dle-stick's ends! What do you reckon I care for their
laws. We make our own laws over there; and I would
like to see the fellow that disputes mine. Let him show
himself, that's all. The land's mine, and I'll stick to it,
too, if I have to fight for it like a pirate. Laws be hanged,
I say."

"Well, you talk fierce enough, if that's all, and you
are welcome to your land for all me. I'm sure what we
own here, keeps me frettin' the whole time."

"He, he, he," laughed the old woman in the corner,
suddenly starting up in her chair. "There ain't been
such a gatherin' these twenty years. It cost a power o'
money to get up that weddin'."

"What's the woman talking about?" said Mrs. Gamby

"Old times, old times," said Mrs. Catlett, in a low voice.
"You see her mind's always runnin' on those days."

"A lavender silk gown with trimmins so wide," said
the old woman, measuring in the air with her skinny fingers; "real point lace, too; and her father nothin' but a
colonel—he, he, he—there's extravagance for you."

"Never mind her talk," said Mrs. Catlett; "she often
runs on that way; it seems like she acted over every thing
she ever did, sittin' there in her chair. It's real grand
sometimes, to hear her tell about the great dinners and
dances they used to have when her grandfather was Governor Peters of Virginia."

"She don't look much like goin' to such things now,"
said Mrs. Gamby, glancing at the palsied old creature,
who, with a feeble laugh, had sunk back into the dreamy
state from which she had so suddenly awakened.

"You spoke about frettin'," said Mrs. Gamby; "I tell you, neighbor Catlett, that don't work at all; least ways with niggers. You must lay down the law to 'em, and make 'em keep it. That's been my way, and they do say it works, too."

"Well you've got the strength to carry it out, I suppose; but, with my poor health, I have to manage as easy as I can. Mr. Catlett always said I let my women run right over me; somehow I never could keep 'em under. I don't believe any body ever had such a hard set to manage; there ain't more than two on the place that I can trust with any thing."

"Trust a nigger, neighbor Catlett! That's a good one! Of course you can't trust 'em. Did you ever come across one that would n't cheat, and lie, and steal whenever he got a chance? Trust 'em, indeed! I would n't trust one of my gang with a sixpence. No, no, you must keep your eye on 'em; watch 'em so close they can't draw a long breath without your knowin' it. That's my way."

"Some folks can do it," said Mrs. Catlett, with a sigh; "I can't. My servants always did have the upper hand. I've told Mr. Catlett many a time that I was more of a slave than any one of 'em."

"Well, you see it's just because you keep frettin' at 'em all the while. They see how they can pester you, and you don't give 'em trainins enough to scare 'em into not doin' it. Niggers find out mighty quick when they can take liberties. Mine never step over the line. They find me up to 'em, you see."

"There ain't many such managers as you. It don't appear to me to be women's business, any how. It's too hard work."

"Well, now, neighbor Catlett, just let me give you a little of my experience in this matter. You see, when my man died, twelve years ago, we owned a place down in Boone county. Well, every body said I should have to sell out or get an overseer; there could n't no woman manage a great farm with fifteen or twenty hands to work it. Well, I thought differently, and I reckoned on tryin' it awhile, any how. So I got the hands together, and I talked to 'em. I just let 'em understand what I meant to do. If any of 'em thought they was goin' to get along easier with a woman over 'em, it 's my opinion they changed their minds 'fore ever I got through. I laid down the law, and how I was goin' to carry it out, and they see I was in arnest, too.

"Well, I begun with 'em that very day, and I 've kept it up ever since, and I do say, you won't find a better trained set this side of the Mississippi. I never had no overseer. I 've gone into the field many a day, and worked alongside of 'em, and every man hoed his row when I was thar. I 've got three inches more home-made a day out of my weavers than any body else in the neighborhood; and I 've had all my wool picked out by children under ten years. Then my crop of tobacco this fall, why, it beats yours all to smash. You want to know why?"

"'Cause she worked every body on the place down to skin and bone," whispered Cal.

"I 'll tell you," continued Mrs. Gamby, "it 's 'cause I watch 'em so close. I keep right round after 'em; they work smart, 'cause they never know but that I 'm somewhere out of sight lookin' on, and they don't get shet of me after work-hours neither. I 've tracked 'em off to the corn-field many a moonlight night, and crept down to the quarters in my stocking feet, to peep through the cracks, and see what they were up to; that 's my way of doin' things."

"Don't you ever feel afraid nights, Madam Gamby, all alone there?" inquired Nanny.

"Afraid! What should I be afraid of, child? Why, bless you, I keep a loaded gun at the head of the bed, and I'd shoot down the first person that entered my premises just as quick as I'd shoot a squirrel. Let 'em come, if they want to, that's all."

"Well, Madam Gamby," said Mrs. Catlett, "you may talk as much as you please, but it is n't such an easy thing to keep matters straight on a place like this. If ever Mr. Catlett gets home alive, I shan't give my consent to his goin' off again. I'm just wearing myself out here, and things goin' to waste as fast as they can go."

"Why, what's come over you, neighbor Catlett? You are as blue as my checked apron. There's Dave, now, he's got to be 'most a man; can't you fall back on him?"

"Dave's of no account, Mrs. Gamby. He's as easy as an old shoe; lets every thing go at loose ends when he's here, but wants to be off hunting or down to the store half the time. He leaves me with the care of the field hands and the house servants altogether."

"Well, boys will be boys. Just wait till he has his own bread and bacon to get, and I'll warrant you he'll steady down. It brings young sprigs to, about as quick as any thing."

"I hope it will, I'm sure," said Mrs. Catlett, with a sigh. "You are going to set up school to-morrow, I hear?" said Mrs. Gamby; "is this the teacher?"

She turned round square upon Fanny as she spoke, surveying her from head to foot with a broad stare.

The teacher bowed, for the question seemed addressed to her.

"Well, you look kinder young. Have you had any experience?"

"I have never taught before," said Fanny, quietly.

"No! Well, do you reckon you know enough? Where did you get your learnin' ?"

"I graduated two years ago at —— Seminary, Mrs. Gamby, and if I am not competent to teach, it is for no lick of the best advantages."

"Lor', you need n't look so red about it. I reckon I 've a right to ask a question or two. I came over, neighbor Catlett," she said, to Fanny's great relief, turning again to that lady, "to make a bargain with you for my gals this winter. You spoke about wantin' two or three day scholars, did n't you ?"

"Boarders, you mean, Madam Gamby. Of course you would n't think of their living at home this winter ?"

"Of course I should, neighbor Catlett. What's to hinder ?"

"What 's to hinder ? Why the bother of getting here every morning at nine o'clock, and ridin' three miles home every night."

"Bless you, that 's nothing ; a little exercise will do 'em good."

"But you can't do it. Don't you see, these short days they would n't begin to get home before night, and you 'd find it a task to get 'em here by nine o'clock in the morning."

"Why, mercy on me, neighbor Catlett, my women do three hours' work before that time o' day. Don't you fret, I 'll have 'em here bright and early in the morning, and safe home at night."

"But you 'll have to send a servant for 'em. It ain't safe for children to be ridin' through the woods after night, anyhow. Why can't you let 'em stay here ? They can go home Friday nights, you see, and stay till the next Monday."

"'Cause there's no use in payin' out board for 'em three miles from home, where victuals are of no account anyhow. That's why. Then, as to sendin' a servant, I shan't do any such thing. My young ones are too much like me to be scared at a little dark. Jerry will gear up the old lame mare for 'em, and one of your boys can turn her out on the prairie till night. That's the way I should fix it, so if you are a mind to take the two, we'll settle on the terms."

"But I have n't a mind, Madam Gamby. We about made up our minds not to take any day scholars. They are always runnin' in and out of the house with the other children, and make a heap of trouble, and don't pay enough to make it an object."

"I did n't know you reckoned on making money out of your school," said Madam Gamby, tartly.

"No more we don't, but we don't want to lose money on it, do we?"

"If I pay you all you ask for the schoolin', I can't see how you'll lose any thing: but there's no use in talking about it; as to payin' out money for board when we raise every thing on the place, and victuals are of no account, I won't do it, that's flat. If you have a mind to take 'em for day scholars, well and good, I'll send 'em along: if not, they can stay at home. They'll have as much larnin' as their mammy, anyhow."

"Well, Madam Gamby, we won't get riled about it. I see Marthy's bringing in dinner, so we'll eat and talk it over afterward."

The subject was brought up again after dinner, and before Mrs. Gamby left she had carried the day.

"It's too awful mean," said Mrs. Catlett, after her visitor had gone; "any body as well off as she is to grudge her young ones board! But I'm glad she's gone off in a good humor; I would n't have her mad with me for all the world. Miss Hunter, I hope you 'll be careful and keep in with the children. They say she 's an awful crittur when she has a spite against any body. Now we want about three more scholars, and then we are fixed."

Fanny was somewhat surprised to learn from all this, that her school could be increased in number to any extent that her employers wished, without a corresponding increase of salary; but thinking that in this thinly-settled neighborhood she was not likely to be overrun with pupils, the circumstance occasioned her little uneasiness.

About an hour after Madam Gamby left, there was a low knock at the door, and on Dave's opening it, there stalked into the room a tall, gaunt man, with an unshorn face, and dressed in clothes that hung in rags at his elbows and at the tops of his heavy boots. He bowed awkwardly to Mrs. Catlett as he entered, and stood in the middle of the room, twirling his hat, with a half-proud, half-sheepish expression upon his sallow face.

"Poor white folks," whispered Cal.

The man turned sharply round, with a look that caused the child to sink back in the corner.

"Sit down, Mr. Jenkins," said Mrs. Catlett, coldly. "Marthy, why don't you set a chair for Mr. Jenkins?"

The girl slowly advanced and pushed a chair to the stranger, making faces at him slyly for the children's amusement.

Dave had resumed his paper, and Mrs. Catlett showed no disposition to open a conversation, so that after shifting uneasily about in his chair for a moment, the man himself began,

"You are goin' to set up a school here, they say."

"Yes," said Mrs. Catlett; "we have a teacher engaged."

"And you wanted to take in a few scholars, did n't you?"

"We tall ed of it," said the lady, coldly.

"Well, 1 've got a little gal," said the man, speaking rapidly and with his eyes fastened upon the floor. "I wanted to give her a schoolin', and the old woman reckoned you would be willin' to take her six months or so. I thought I 'd come over and see you about it."

Dave looked up from his paper with a rude stare, while Mrs. Catlett seemed speechless with astonishment.

"You see I would n't have come to you," said the man, in a half proud, half cringing manner, "seein' that such as you, don't like poor folks' children over and above, but there ain't another school short of eight miles, and I can't seem to feel easy with the gal—she 's the only one we 've got—growin' up without a bit of larnin'. If you could take her—"

"We 've about made up our number, Mr. Jenkins," said Mrs. Catlett.

"Mebbe one would n't make much odds," he continued, trying to speak carelessly, though his voice shook a little. "The gal's a quiet gal, and the old woman will make her decent for clothes. She won't make you a speck of trouble. We are poor"—a flush rose to his sallow cheek— "but there can't nobody say a word agin our honesty. We—"

"Twelve on 'em in the family," said the old woman in the corner; "twelve in the family, and every soul on 'em died in the poor house. The miserablist, idlist set you ever did see."

The man turned fiercely round, but she had sunk back in her chair, muttering unintelligibly to herself.

"Mr. Jenkins," said Mrs. Catlett, in a freezing tone, "I should be glad to do you a favor, but the fact is, we don't want any more scholars. 'We need all the teacher's time for our own children."

"And ain't there other folks that want their children to know something, but you?" said the man, fiercely. "What's to become of the brats round here, growin' up like the very pigs?" then suddenly checking himself, he continued in a milder tone; "you must n't mind me, marm; I get most crazy times, thinkin' about it. But jest put yourself in my place, Miss Catlett. S'pose it was your child a-growin' up so. My old woman at home loves that gal as well as you love yours; mebbe a trifle better, for it's all she's got. You are a woman, now just think of it; and how can I go back and tell her there ain't any chance? If you could give her *one hour* a day, that ain't much; only one hour; it would be a heap better than none to us. Mebbe you'll think of it."

"Mrs. Catlett," said Fanny, leaning over the lady's chair, "I will teach his little girl an hour out of school, if you are willing."

"The Lord bless you," said the man, whose eager ears had caught the words, softly as they were spoken.

"Nonsense, Miss Hunter," said Mrs. Catlett. "You know nothing about it. It's entirely impossible"—then turning to the man, she said, angrily, "I've told you once, Mr. Jenkins, that we can not take your girl; if once isn't enough, I tell you so again. I'm not likely to change my mind for any thing you can say."

His sallow face grew a shade paler, and rising from the cringing posture he had assumed during the conversation he drew himself up to his full height, and bowing as distantly as the lady herself, left the room, the children mimicking his shuffling gait, and whispering each other to look at his ragged elbows.

"Well, I'm beat this time," said Mrs. Catlett, as the

door closed behind him. "If any body had told me that man would dare to come on such an errand, I should have laughed in their face. I never was so taken aback in my life."

"O, there's no end to such people's assurance, ma," said Nanny. "They think they are as crank as any body."

"My goodness!" said Mrs. Catlett, "to think of my takin' his brat to keep company with my children."

"If I'd been in Dave's place, I'd have cracked him over," said little Johnny.

"Shut up, Johnny; you are gettin' too smart. Ma, did you see how those children behaved. You ought to take 'em down a peg," said Nanny.

"Don't tell me any thing about it, Nan, I see enough. If it had been any body but Tim Jenkins, I should have felt ashamed of their tantrums."

"Why, ma, we behaved beautiful," said Cal. "I'm sure I didn't so much as crack a smile, for all he came shambling in so funny."

"You better talk!" said Maria. "You sauced him right to his face."

"I didn't either, Miss 'Ria. I just giv him his title; that's all."

"You ought to have seen Cal when he glared round at her," said Dave, laughing. "She looked like I've seen a rabbit, when you first scare 'em up: all eyes."

"I thought she'd pitch me over, sure," said little Joy, "she was so fierce to get back in the corner."

"I don't car'," said Maud, "I wish his girl could go to school, if she wants to so bad. I'm sure she might go in my place and welcome."

"Maud Catlett," said her mother, "don't you ever let me hear you say that again. I don't want my children to have any sympathy with those low people."

"I don't car'," said Maud again; "I felt mighty sorry for him."

"Miss Hunter," said Mrs. Catlett, when the children had gone up stairs, "I hope you'll be careful how you treat those low people like Tim Jenkins. When you've been here a little longer, you'll see it isn't best to make any such offers as you did just now."

"What have they done so bad, Mrs. Catlett?" inquired Fanny.

"What have they done? Why they are poor, shiftless, no account, white folks."

CHAPTER VI.

THE CLAIM DISPUTED.

"Holloa, Tom, where in thunder is that plaguy tree you nailed Jack Catlett's manifesto to? Hang me if I did n't think this was the very one. Come, my boy, look about you, and find your hand-writing, do you hear?"

"That's it, squire; that big oak yonder; if it ain't, set Turner down for a man without eyes in his head. Well, that is curis, though. What on earth has become of the thing? Look here, Catlett, some rascally abolition dog has torn it down, as sure as you are a born sinner."

"That's so, anyhow, for here's the bits scattered on the grass. Let's see," says Tom, dismounting; "I vow here's the whole word, 'Jack,' on this very first scrap, just as I wrote it. Here's a chance for a little fun now! We have got to shoot some half a dozen free soil scoundrels before you can own this land, squire, that's clear. And here's the fellow that will pitch into 'em the worst way. Gad! I'll be mighty glad to come across something to stir up my blood a little. I'd just as soon shoot one of them blasted Yankees as I would a squirrel, and a great deal *druther*."

"Where are the villains? Who'll scare 'em up? Just let 'em show themselves, that's all. This old rifle has n't done much on Kanzas ground since we started. Let me just see the white of an abolition eye, and I'll send a bullet through it co-chug. Miserable, vile, murderous outlaws! We'll teach 'em to respect a true Southern gentleman, with the last relic of old Governor Peters, of Virginia, in his house. Tear down Jack Catlett's name! Audacious villains! Turner, Tom, our altars, our firesides, our sacred honors are endangered. Shall we submit tamely to such unpardonable insolence?"

"Jimminy! there's eloquence for you. I say, squire, what a tall one you'd make at stump-speaking. We ought to have him up, Tom, at the next election."

Our three neighbors with whom this tale opened, had accomplished their reconnoitering tour, selected claims here and there with Catlett's and Turner's names nailed to at least fifty different trees, and returning, had now arrived at the identical spot where the conversation occurred, so faithfully chronicled in the first chapter. This claim of Catlett's, out of the whole number which these two worthies greedily hoped to secure somehow, by hook or by crook, to them and their heirs forever, is the only one which concerns our history. We shall, therefore, dismiss the others without another word. Perhaps some other chronicler may hand them down to fame. On arriving at this spot, Catlett was the first to discover that his claim in writing was not where he supposed Tom Walton had nailed it; Turner, to conjecture that it had been torn down "maliciously and by instigation of the devil," by some hot-headed abolitionist, and Tom, to demonstrate that by some hands it had been torn in pieces and scattered to the winds.

Words can not do justice to the torrent of indignation which poured forth in the expression, and overflowed in baths under the clear sky of Kanzas, upon that sublime occasion. We have only attempted to record the conversation up to the time when, upon the discovery, the scald

ing stream of violence began to flow, omitting, we must
confess, the oaths with which even then it was garnished.
Our pen has a pertinacious reluctance to give to profane
words a permanency in our history, and so, for the sake
of humanity, we thus far diverge from the utmost exact-
ness.   For at least fifteen minutes these worthies amused
themselves with darting out the forked lightning of their
words into the balmy air of these new lands, which, in
their unoccupied security had heretofore escaped such a
deadly malaria.   Three snakes stirred up by the keeper's
long pole in a menagerie, is the most like to them of any
thing which now occurs to us.

We resume our narrative at a point of time when their
fury, having become somewhat exhausted by its own violence, was still more chastened by the appearance upon
the scene, of an opponent of no mean proportions, with
rifle and cartridge-box, with a boy of some fourteen sum-
mers by his side, armed also with a revolver and bowie-
knife, seemingly ready and able to rebuke and punish the
intolerable insolence of three windy, noisy, braggadocio
cowards.   Making their appearance from the little patch
of trees on the right, the two walked leisurely toward our
party, apparently in no way discomposed by their loud
words and swaggering mien.   .

"Here, you vile son of perdition," cried out the beau
Tom Walton, who first descried them, his horse being in
advance, as always, of the others, "can you tell us who
tore down the claim of Squire Catlett to these acres, fastened to yonder tree in my hand-writing? We want to
find the dog, and hang him to the first tree for his insolence."

"You do. Well, Sir Ruffle-shirt, let's see you about it.
I am the man."

"What's that? you the rascal? Here, Catlett, Turner,

do you hear what the villain says?" and then looking over his shoulder and perceiving his companions close at hand, the young gentleman went on with renewed energy. "You scamp, you infernal Yankee, hanging's too good for you. We'll cut you in inch pieces, we'll roast you alive, you audacious churl. Did you know who Jack Catlett, Esq., of La Belle Prairie is? How dare you lay your nasty fingers upon such a name. You free soil abolition devil! We'll make daylight shine through you this minute."

Upon this Tom aimed his gun, but upon casting his eye across the piece, suddenly discovered a revolver aimed at his own breast. He lowered his weapon, bawling out,

"Is that your brat yonder? If it was n't for shooting him, too, you would be a dead man before this."

"Had you shot my father, I would have shot *you* in double quick time," said the boy; "I've practiced on turkey-buzzards before now."

"Hold your tongue, Zi," said his father. "Come, come, gentlemen, be cool now, and let's talk a little rational. You can't frighten me; and as for a real fight, I and my boy could whip twice as many such as you. So my advice is, keep perfectly quiet, and let's talk the matter over as it lies. You see I am the rightful claimant to these lands, having squatted here for the last six months, and built a cabin hard by. Coming out the other day with my boy, I saw the notice you speak of, and of course I tore it down, and you would have done just so."

"Would I? you low-lived scamp. What right have you to know what I would do? Blast you! there's some difference between a Virginia gentleman and a wooden-headed Yankee, let me tell you. You talk like a man to his equals. Just think, Turner, of Tim Jenkins talking that way. We teach 'poor white trash' manners over

the borders; hey, Turner? I tell you it's none of you.
business what I'd do, so hold your yop, you cur, upon
that pint. All you've got to do is to hurry up your
cakes, and promise to clear these diggins in less than no
time. Do you hear?"

"Squire, I ain't a man of many words; I don't take it
all out in talking like some folks, but just let me tell you
one thing, if you can't talk to me as an equal, you can't
talk at all. I *am* your equal or any three like you, as I'll
show you when the scratch comes. I'm no Tim Jenkins,
thank heaven, bowed down by your cursed slavery over
the border, but a free-born Yankee! on free soil yet,
and on my own rightful soil, too. You ain't lording it over
one of your niggers now, whom you can haul up to the
whip when you please. No, sirree. You've got the wrong
pig by the ear this time. I shan't leave this claim, which
is justly mine by possession, for you, or a dozen like you.
If you want to try the fun of a fight, here's at you. So
mind your eyes, squire, that's all I have to say."

"Look here, now, you consummate fool!" interrupted
the beau, "you talk about reason, will you hear to it?
Who gives you a right here? Our claim is by Uncle
Sam's law."

"No it ain't. There's no law yet about these new
lands, ruffle-shirt! You can't come it over this child that
way. nohow. I've got friends, who've promised to write
the first mail."

"He! he! he!" roared the chorus, and Tom cried out,
"You fool, you! did you ever hearn tell of the telegraph,
which gives word in less than no time. We, on the borders, have got the news fust, and we are here according
to law. So just quit, or we'll oust you. Uncle Sam backs
us."

"I know Uncle Sam as well as you, you miserable squirt!

lived in his diggins full as long, I guess. And I know he ain't such a pesky fool as to give you, lazy, good-for-nothing coots, the right to drive us, working fellows, right square off our claims. Uncle Sam likes folks on his farm that will work, and he'll hold to 'em, too. No, no, stranger, try again; you don't come it that way."

"It's so, though, and no mistake; and if you've got a grain of sense in your old carcase, you'll give up peaceably, or as sure as my name's Tom Walton, we'll tie you up to yonder tree, and whip you like a nigger, as you are. Hang it if Uncle Tim ain't a heap smarter than you, you abolition cuss."

"Now, ruffle-shirt, if you don't want to get particular fits, just take back what you said about my being a nigger, or I'll haul you off your horse, and shake you till there's nothing left of you. Very well, sir; you won't do it; boy, take aim now. Hit the squire's hat first if he shows fight; don't want to kill 'em, but can't waste no more words."

So saying the Yankee made up to our dandy Tom, and seizing him by his shirt and jewelry, tumbled him in the dust, where he rolled him, and rolled him, and rolled him, till he was tired; while the boy, obedient to his sire, had whizzed a bullet through the hat of the redoubtable squire, which setting all his bones in a shiver, he and Turner both put spurs to their horses, leaving Tom to his fate, stopping at a safe distance, for conscience' sake, to discharge their pieces, lest Tom should say they had not defended him.

When the Yankee had amused himself enough with the rolling process, he put the poor, crest-fallen beau on his saddle, besmeared from head to foot, a sight to be seen, and sent him galloping after his redoubtable companions.

Flying at his utmost speed, not stopping till he joined

company with them, he cried out in a doleful voice as he reined up his horse,

"O! Catlett! I say," etc., etc., etc. We omit sundry expressions with which the young gentleman embellished his speech. "I say but we 'll kill every Yankee in Kanzas."

The claim was some thirty miles from La Belle Prairie, to which delightful retreat our company hurried along with oaths and gesticulations, and great swelling words of wrath, that, saving upon themselves, seemed to produce little effect. The sweet air played among the trees, the grass waved beneath their feet, and the sky above was as bright and pure as before, only in their own hearts was there storm and disquiet. Leaving them on their journey, which they will hardly accomplish before night, we hurry before them to Catlett's house, to bring up the domestic history, which, albeit, it may not seem so to the uninitiated, is all essential to our narrative.

CHAPTER VII.

THAT first day in school! O, what a long, weary day it was. You who in some pleasant village in New England, have gathered your pupils about you, in the airy, well-lighted room, with its whitewashed walls and painted desks, can form little idea of the discomfort to which Fanny was subjected, in her log school-house on the prairie.

Its one window, consisting of a single row of lights, extended the length of the building, a log having been left out for the purpose. The chinks between the logs were filled up with clay, which, falling out piece by piece, left large air-holes, useful for ventilation, but rather inconvenient in rainy weather. A rude bench, without a back, extended across one end of the room, but this not supplying seats for all, a smooth round log stood near, upon which the younger children sat; and being little roly poly things, they were continually slipping off, greatly to the amusement of the rest.

The door, alas! would seldom shut, and when it did, could only be opened by "clawing," a process well understood where latches are scarce, but in which it took our New England girl some time to gain expertness. The teacher's chair was placed in the middle of the room, and seating herself thereon, she succeeded, with the aid of a bell, taken only the day before from the neck of old Brindle, in calling her school to order.

Claiming her right as the eldest, Maria Catlett occupied the head of the seat, and with her rosy, good-natured face, full of smiles and good-humor, seemed not an unpromising pupil. But the two girls who sat next her, dressed in blue cotton homespun, but little better in quality than that worn by the servants, with unmeaning faces and dull gray eyes, seemed the very personification of ignorance and stupidity. Boss and Biny, or Virginia and Albina Gamby, were the daughters of the widow lady who had visited Mrs. Catlett the day before. It was with some difficulty that Fanny ascertained the true name of the eldest—the girl insisting that every body called her Boss, and she liked it a heap better than her other name.

"Why do they call you so?" inquired Fanny.

"O, ma called me so first, 'cause she said I was the head one in every thing, and there don't nobody call me any thing else now."

Fanny, however, preferred the original name, and always addressed her as Virginia or Ginry, though it was long before the rest followed her example.

Caroline, or Cal Catlett, came next, the perfect image of her mother, with the same scowl upon her brow, and the same fretful tone to her voice.

Maud, the wild, elfish-looking Maud, with long sandy locks, brown complexion, and big black eyes, sat upon the log with the children, a little boy and girl of six and eight, and amused herself by pinching their fat necks, bumping their heads together, causing them by a sly push to lose their balance and tumble off the seat, and by various other tricks, which suggested themselves to her fertile imagination. Poor Maud! She spoke the truth when she expressed her decided preference for a run on the prairie, to a lesson in the school-room. Never was it harder for a child to keep still five minutes at a time. "Born to tor-

ment the family," said Mrs. Catlett; "always in a strain to
be cuttin' up some mischief," said Nanny; "a confounded
little plague," said Massa Dave; and so it went on. The
mother fretted and the father swore, but neither made an
effort to correct the child's faults, or to encourage her, if
she happened to be right. As for Maud, she laughed at
their threats, and openly expressed her independence of
them all.

"Lors, Dinah," she would say to her sable friend,
"what you s'pose I car', when ma tells me to keep away
from dinner? I like for her to do it. I just goes down
to Aunt Phebe's cabin, and get hot ash-cake and buttermilk—heap better 'n home victuals!"

. Maud was not alone in her love of mischief. The effects
of her training were evident upon the little ones at her
side, who joined in all her pranks, partly from an innate
love of the same, and partly through fear, for Maud was
the master-spirit, and exercised great tyranny over her
inferiors.

Between the roguery of the younger scholars, and the
listless inattention of those older, Fanny's school was a
very disorderly one that day, and, indeed, it was many
days, before, by patient labor and uniform firmness, she
succeeded in establishing any thing like good order.

To Maud, the restraint seemed unendurable. She fid-
geted and squirmed on her seat, sat first on one foot, then
on the other, combed her hair with her fingers, made up
faces at the children, and, finally, watching her opportunity, darted through the open door, clearing at a bound
the obstacle presented there by a little black urchin, who,
with head protruded like a turtle, blocked up the way.
The little ones would fain have followed; but a word from
the teacher kept them in their seats, and, opening her

book again, she proceeded calmly with the exercises of
the school.

At twelve o'clock the horn sounded, and Martha,
thrusting her head in at the door, called out, "Miss
Car'line say you all break up school and come in to
dinner," a summons the children showed no hesitation in
obeying.

"Where in the world is Maud?" said Mrs. Catlett, as
they gathered round the table.

The children exchanged significant glances.

"Miss Car'line," said Viny, stopping on her way to the
table with a plate of corn bread, "she's been a ridin' de
gray colt on de prairie. Uncle Jo cotch her at it, when
he put out Massa Dave's horse, and Aunt Tibby jawin' in
de kitchen, 'cause she steal de hoe cake 'fore de fire. She
done clar out some whar."

"She's down to Aunt Phebe's cabin," said Johnny;
"I jest see her down thar, throwin' rocks at ma's little
young turkeys."

"She'll have to quit that," said Mrs. Catlett, with more
animation than she usually displayed. "You, Viny, go
down to Aunt Phebe's cabin, and fetch her home di-
rec'ly."

"'Tain't no use, Miss Car'line. Mighty hard work to
cotch dat chil', anyhow, and when you get hold, ki, how
she bite and scratch!"

"You do as I tell you," said her mistress; and Viny
departed, shrugging her shoulders and grinning from ear
to ear.

"What a saucy set of servants," said Mrs. Catlett, languidly. "Marthy, why don't you fetch the crumb-cloth?
If I 've told you once, I 've told you twenty times, to brush
off the crumbs before ever you brought in dessert. You
are so stupid."

"I 's goin' to Miss Car'line. I jest stopped to wait on Miss Hetty."

"O ma, just look at Tilla!" said Cal; "she's drinkin' up the baby's buttermilk."

Mrs. Catlett turned in time to witness the dropping of the empty cup, and instantly administered sundry cuffs, which called forth a succession of yells from the unlucky offender.

Poor Tilla! Standing by the chair on which her young mistress's meal was spread, in her scanty blue frock, from which her bare feet protruded, the tears running down her thin cheeks, she looked a forlorn picture indeed.

Fanny had pitied the poor thing, the first time she saw her, bending under the weight of a stout child, who seemed quite her equal in strength, if not in size. "Miss Hetty's nurse," she was called, and the whole care of a healthy baby, of two years, devolved upon her. "A poor, scrawny, ashy-lookin' nigger," Massa Dave declared, "who it made him sick to look at. Why did n't pa keep her down to the quarters till she was fit for something?"

But Tilla was thought strong enough to toat the baby, and accordingly was kept running hither and thither all day wherever the whim of her young mistress directed. Nothing to do but tend the baby! Every body seemed to think that Tilla had a mighty easy time of it, and cuffed her ears, and called her a lazy, good-for-nothing thing when she fell asleep over the cradle, or snatched a mouthful of food from the baby's plate. "What business had she to be sleepy till Miss Hetty was disposed of for the night, or hungry, till Miss Hetty had eaten her dinner? O! a mighty easy time had Tilla."

"Suppose you and I walk down to Aunt Phebe's cabin, Maria," said Fanny after dinner. "I must look up my truant scholar."

"It ain't any use, Miss Hunter," said Maria, as they walked along. "You can't get her into school. There can't nobody do the first thing with Maud, but Aunt Phebe, she's gotten to be so wild."

"How happens it that Aunt Phebe has so much influence over her?" inquired Fanny.

"Why, you see, Aunt Phebe took all the care of her when she had the fever, and ever since then she takes Maud's part in every thing, and pets her 'most to death; and Maud, she toats up her trencher every day for dinner and every thing nice she gets, down it goes to Aunt Phebe's cabin."

"Does n't Aunt Phebe take her dinner with the other women in the kitchen?"

"O! no marm, not this long time back. Why she can't hardly get out of her chair. She's just the fattest thing you ever saw."

"Is she old?"

"Yes indeed. We don't any of us know how old. Ma thinks she must be nigh a hundred. Long time ago, when Grandpa Wortley lived in Virginia, she was grandma's maid, and when ma was married, she gave her to her. Ma thinks heaps of Aunt Phebe."

"I should think she would. Who takes care of her?"

"O! Viny sleeps there nights, and daytimes she takes care of herself, and minds the babies while the women are at work in the field. Sometimes she spins a little, but only when she takes a notion. Ma gives her a new yarn frock every Christmas, and Nan and I knit her a pair of stockings."

"That's right," said Fanny. "You must take a great deal of pleasure in making an old servant comfortable."

"Yes indeed; pa says Aunt Phebe earned her bread

and bacon a long time back. Why, Miss Hunter, when we first come to Missouri, and I, and Nanny, and Dave, were sick with the measles, Aunt Phebe doctored and tended us three weeks, 'cause ma was so afraid the field-hands would catch it. She knows a heap about doctorin'; and ma always goes to her when any of the women are ailin'. And then she's so pious; she lays it off just like a minister, and—holloa! there's Maud now."

Fanny looked in the direction she pointed. A few rods from Aunt Phebe's cabin, a large hole had recently been dug preparatory to the building of an ice-house, but the late rain had left a couple of feet of water there, and the work was discontinued. Here, under Maud's direction, the little piccaninnies were having fine times. A ladder was placed across the cavity, covered with a board, and on this bridge a little darkey, some six or seven years old, was displaying his agility by various gymnastic feats, while the others stood upon the bank shouting and clapping their hands.

As Fanny and Maria approached, he was crossing by a succession of summersets, in which heels and head followed each other so rapidly as to be scarcely distinguishable, but when about half across, and under full head-way, he suddenly disappeared, a splash below, followed by a scream from the lookers-on, declaring his whereabouts.

They rushed forward, but before they could reach the spot the ladder was pushed down into the water, a wiry little figure sprang upon it, and a moment after reappeared, pushing the dripping Jim Crow performer before her, spitting the mud and water furiously from his mouth, while the same elements dripped copiously from his woolly pate and scanty clothing.

"Bravely done!" exclaimed Fanny, in undisguised admiration. "Why, Maud, you are a young heroine!"

Thus apprised of her presence, the child pushed back her hair and looked up, her eyes sparkling with mirth and excitement.

"Did you see him go in? Was n't it great? There would have been a right smart chance of a drownin', if I had n't been here to fish him out. O! how he looked, when his head first bobbed out of the water."

Maud threw herself upon the ground, and laughed till the tears ran down her cheeks. She was so much excited by her adventure, that she had quite forgotten the morning's offense, and it was not Fanny's policy to remind her of it just yet.

"Never mind *him*," she said, as Fanny attempted with her handkerchief to wipe off a little of the mud from the urchin's visage, " dirt 's of no account, Jake's used to it. Here, you, Tom, take him to the kitchen, and mind you don't tell Aunt Tibby where I am," then suddenly remembering what had occurred, she gave Fanny a knowing glance, and growing very red in the face, said she would go and tell Aunt Phebe about it.

" We were just going to Aunt Phebe's, when Jake's performance took place," said Fanny, with a smile. " Suppose you come, too."

" Was you ?" said Maud, with sudden interest. " What was you going there for ?"

" Partly to see Aunt Phebe," said Fanny. " I want to get acquainted with her."

" Do you ? Do you really want to know Aunt Phebe ?" said the child; the whole expression of her face changing at once. " She 's the best woman in the whole world. Yes, I 'll go with you. Do you want to know her, sure enough ?"

She took Fanny's proffered hand with all confidence, pulling her eagerly along toward the old woman's cabin.

"Maud," said Fanny, stopping suddenly and glancing at her watch, "we must wait till after school. It's past one o'clock. Come, I see the children watching for us at the door."

Maud had previously made up her mind not to go into school again that day, but she was fairly caught, and seeing no honorable way of retreat, suffered the new teacher to lead her to the hated prison-house.

"Maud," said Fanny, as they walked along, "who put the ladder across for Jake to turn summersets on, and how came you to think of it so quick when he fell in?"

"Lors, Miss Hunter, Tom and I toated it all the way from the stable on purpose. I reckoned he'd tumble in, but I knew I could haul him out easy."

Aunt Phebe's cabin stood last in the row extending behind Mr. Catlett's house. A large gourd-vine had covered the low roof, where its yellow fruit now lay ripening in the sun, and the little patch of ground in the rear, showed evident marks of cultivation. The house within was dark and gloomy, light only being admitted through the low doorway, and through chinks between the logs, where the mud had fallen out. There was no floor, but the ground was worn smooth and hard by the tread of many feet. The chimney-place was large and wide, and here, in a comfortable arm-chair, with her foot upon a cradle, containing two little woolly-headed specimens of humanity, Aunt Phebe was generally to be found.

"Aunty, here's the teacher come to see you," cried Maud, as she ushered Fanny through the low doorway.

"She's welcome," said the old woman with dignity. "I hope you are well, missus. Dinah, set a stool, and say how-dy to the lady."

Aunt Phebe did the honors of her humble habitation

with great politeness, assuming an air of consequence that was amusing to behold. Fanny accepted the proffered seat, and gazed at the venerable figure before her with interest and curiosity, while Maud busied herself with the babies in the cradle. Aunt Phebe's face was too plump to admit of many wrinkles, but judging by her woolly head, which was nearly white, and by the tremulous motion of her hands, she was a very old woman.

"Mighty poorly, mighty poorly," she said in reply to Fanny's inquiries respecting her health. "'Pears like de ole body gets weaker an' weaker ebery day. De Lord mos' done wid ole Phebe here."

"O! don't talk so, aunty," said Maud, cheerfully, "you ain't goin' to die this long time yet."

"Do' 'no, honey, do' 'no;" said the old woman, "can't spec' to last always. When de ole house shake, massa say pull him down. 'T ain't no use foolin' in de kitchen, when de work done clared up. I'se done, got through my work, jess waitin' for de Lord's call."

"You seem very happy at the thought of going," said Fanny. "Don't you ever feel afraid to die?"

"Lord bless you, honey, one sight o' glory scared off all de dark. Satan's done tryin' to pester me dis long time back. It wa'n't no use. Ye see de Lord He stood by, and showed me whar I was comin' out."

"Aunty's been up to heaven heaps of times," said Maud, looking as though she firmly believed it. "Tell us all about it, aunty, how you saw 'em all sittin' round so happy, and one prettier than all the rest tellin' over the good people to come up by-and-by."

"And so I did, honey, an' bless de good Lord ole Phebe's name was de fus' ting. O! go way! Don't tell me 'bout dyin'; when de Lord open de door dis chil' walk straight through. De Lord he say, 'Phebe, any more

down dar mos' ready?' I say, 'Don' no, Lord.' Den
dey all begin to shout and sing,

> " ' Glory! glory! room for all,
> Come, poor sinners, great and small.'

O! chil'en, dar's a power o' glory up dar; 'nuff to make
my ole eyes glimmer."

"Come now, aunty, you want to get happy, I know you
do," said Maud. "Don't you want to see Aunt Phebe
get happy, Miss Hunter? It 's real good."

"What do you mean, Maud?" said Fanny, "Aunt
Phebe seems very happy now."

"O! not that kind of happy. She 's so all times. I
mean 'Halleluyah happy,' like they get at camp meetins,
you know."

Fanny did *not* know, but was soon enlightened. Closing
her eyes, and rocking her body backward and forward,
Aunt Phebe commenced singing to a wild and monotonous
strain, words something like the following, accompanying
the music with violent gestures of the hands and head,
while the rocking grew more and more vigorous as she
proceeded,

> " ' Jesus up to heaven has gone,
> I'm mos' dar.
> Bids de pilgrims follow on,
> I'm mos' dar.
> Ole companions fare-you-well,
> T-abbling down to def and hell,
> I wid Jesus Christ to dwell,
> I'm mos' dar.
> No more sorrow, no more sin,
> I'm mos' dar.
> Come, my Jesus, let me in,
> I'm mos' dar.

O ! de angels ! bright as day !
Welcome, sister ! hear dem say ;
Glory ! glory ! clar de way !
I'm mos' dar.'

"Yes, yes. Come, Lord ! come ! Don't wait ! O !
praise de good Lord ! No more sin, no more sorrow.
O ! dear Lord Jesus ! O ! blessed Jesus ! Halleluyah !
I feels him here ! Heaben has come ! O ! glory ! glory !"

These ejaculations were repeated again and again, accompanied by sighs, and groans, and streaming tears. At
length they became less and less frequent, and finally ended
entirely in one long-drawn sigh. Her head sank back,
her eyes closed, and her features grew fixed and rigid.
Fanny would have hastened to her assistance, supposing
her in a fit, but Maud held her back.

"Don't, Miss Hunter, don't touch her. She's lost her
strength, you know. Let her be, and when she comes to,
she 'll talk, O ! so beautiful, about what she sees up thar."

"Up where, my child ?" said Fanny.

"Why up yonder in the sky," said Maud, wonderingly.

"Do you think Aunt Phebe really sees all those things,
Maud ?"

"Aunty never tells stories," said the child, earnestly.
"Never !"

"I know. She believes it to be so, just as she tells us;
but, Maud, did n't you ever dream things that seemed
very real to you, and yet were only dreams, after all ?"

"Aunty would n't say so if it was n't true. She never
tells stories," repeated the child.

"O, no ! I did not mean that, Maud. She thinks a
great deal about Heaven, and so sometimes she dreams
about it, and thinks herself really there. Maud, we can't
go to Heaven while our bodies are here alive on the earth.
It 's only our spirits that fly up to God."

But Maud's faith was not thus to be shaken, and, with crimson cheeks and flashing eyes, she assured Fanny that "she did n't like for her to talk that way about her aunty," and snatching up her bonnet, she hastily left the cabin.

"Well," said Aunt Phebe, opening her eyes, "Well, chil'en, 'tain't for long. 'Pears like a few more, take dis yer ole body right up. What for no, if de Lord say Come?"

"Perhaps the Lord has something more for you to do here, aunty."

"'Pears like ole Phebe's work was all done up," said the old woman.

"When we have done working ourselves, we can help others by our experience," said Fanny.

"Jes so, honey. Jes so! 'Cause too old to trabble, no reason should n't pint out de road to odders. Has young missus sperienced 'ligion?" said Aunt Phebe, timidly; "talks mighty pious, anyhow."

"I hope so, Aunt Phebe. I trust I am in the right road. Your Saviour is, I believe, my Saviour too."

"Bless de Lord for dat, honey. It cheers dis ole heart to hear you say so. So young and bloomin' too."

"And, aunty, we must be friends, and help each other along in this good work. Help each other to do good. Do you know that you can help me a great deal if you will?"

"Lors, missus? What can ole Phebe do? Ain't no 'count. Sing and pray a little. Dat's all. Never had no larnin'."

"You have influence, aunty. More influence over one precious soul here, than any body else in the world. Who is it that will do any thing in the world to please aunty, let her be ever so disobedient to others? And who leaves her play many a time, to come here and sit by the fire, with her old aunty?"

"Bless her heart, and so she do !" said the old woman, wiping her eyes with her apron. "Don't you b'lieve dat's de wust child in de world. I'll be boun' now," she continued, with sudden animation, "they's been a runnin' on to missus 'bout my child. It's de curisest ting ! 'cause cut up shines now and den, no reason won't come out straight by 'n by. Dar ain't no better heart nowhar, dan Miss Maud got, and she's smarter dan ary one ob 'em for all dar chat."

"You love her, aunty," said Fanny, "and you want to do her good, don't you ?"

"Don't I !" said the old woman, with uplifted hands. "Dar ain't nothin' I would n't do for dat ar' child.'

"Well, I want to do her good, too, and I find I can't do it half so easily, and perhaps not at all, unless you help me."

"Lor, what does young missus mean ?"

"Just this, aunty : when little Maud runs away from school, because it's tiresome and dull at first, if she finds a pleasant seat by Aunt Phebe's fire, and a pleasant welcome from aunty herself, she'll be very likely to do it again ; but if instead she should be told kindly, how much better it would be to stay in school, and mind her studies and her teacher, would n't she do it, think ? and would n't there be more chance of her growing to be a good girl, and coming out straight at last, as you say ?"

"Well, now, missus, I did n't go to keep Miss Maud here dis yer mornin', no ways. S'pose she done got through her lessons, you know. But tell you what ! spec' you are right, anyhow, and I reckon de Lord sent you here to do us all good."

The conversation was here interrupted by Maud herself appearing at the door.

CHAPTER VIII.

AUTUMN LEAVES.

"MISS HUNTER," said Maud, "the girls are out yonder waitin' to show you the garden."

"I 'll come directly," said Fanny.

"Well, farewell, honey. You come agin. De Lord bless ye and give ye a work to do here 'mong us all. I shan't forget dat ar hint ob yours; and Maud, honey, you run down about supper-time, an' aunty 'll have a hot ash-cake for ye."

"O, goody! I 'll come," said Maud, and she ran on before, swinging her sun-bonnet in her hand, while her long locks streamed in the wind.

They found the children waiting for them at the garden gate, and, sauntering through its leaf-strewn walks, Fanny listened to their animated description of its past glories.

"Yonder 's ma's rose-tree," said Cal. "O, did n't it look beautiful along in the summer. Why, Miss Hunter, it was jest covered with blows."

"Red roses, them were," said little Joy; "but we had white ones, and a mess of little bits of ones, that grew 'most down to the ground."

"Dwarf roses, she means," said 'Ria. "Yes, and such beautiful pinks, and petunias, and fou--o'clocks, and some yellow flowers that spread all over the garden. And then the cypress-vine; oh, was n't that pretty! It grew up

'most as high as the school-house, and the blows was so
thick, you could n't hardly see the leaves. There! you
can see the poles it run on, out yonder there by the cher-
ry-tree."

"You are all fond of flowers?" said Fanny.

"I reckon we be," said 'Ria. "Pa gave us each a little
garden-patch last spring, to plant and take care of ourselves. There's mine over in that second row. There
ain't much left of it, to be sure."

"And here was mine," said Cal. "This was my bed
of pinks, and here was the ragged-robins and the snap-
pers, only you can't see 'em 'cause the hogs got in the
other day, and rooted 'em all up."

"Jest look at mine," screamed little Johnny. "I had
the tallest marigolds of any of 'em."

The children laughed.

"He did n't have any thing else, Miss Hunter," said
'Ria.

"And whose is this?" inquired Fanny, pointing to an
irregularly-shaped patch, with a huge cabbage in each corner, and an edge of green myrtle.

"O, that's Maud's. You might know by its being so
odd. Instead of planting garden-seeds, like the rest of
us, she must needs go off and dig up roots on the prairie,
and set 'em out. When they blossomed, they was jest
nothing but prairie flowers."

"I don't car'," said Maud. "I like 'em best. They
ain't half so stuck up as garden-posies."

"Did they grow well here?" said Fanny.

"A good many of 'em died," said Maud. "They kinder
drooped and pined away, like they were home-sick for the
prairie."

"Transplanted flowers," said Fanny, softly.

"And one that I liked best of all," said Maud, "with a

beautiful blue blossom like a star. O! I tried so hard to make it live, but it would n't."

"Poor flower, it was pining for its old home," said Fanny.

"I know it, and when I found it would n't live anyhow, I jest took it up and carried it back again, and when I went to look at it, it had raised up its head, and looked so bright and glad-like, that it was home again."

"Come, Miss Hunter, if Maud gets talking about her flowers, she 'll keep you here till night. There 's an arbor down at the other end of the garden; don't you want to see it ?"

"You must have gathered beautiful bouquets from the garden all summer," said Fanny as they walked along.

"Yes indeed. You know those two silver cups on the shelf in the new room? Well, every morning ma filled 'em chock full of flowers, and now they look so empty. It 's such a pity flowers don't last the year round," said Cal, with a sigh.

"I 'm afraid we should n't prize them enough, Cal, if they did," said Fanny; "but your cups need n't stand empty all winter. You can fill them with bright berries, or autumn leaves."

"Autumn leaves! Who ever heard of such a thing! What! these old brown withered things?" said Cal, scattering a whole shower with her foot.

"No, Cal, not those, but the crimson, and gold, and orange that you see on the trees."

"But they all turn this color, Miss Hunter, after awhile."

"Not if they are taken fresh from the trees, and pressed with the dampness yet on them. You can keep all these beautiful colors through the winter just as you see them on the trees."

"What a funny idea! A nosegay of leaves! and do they last all winter, sure enough?"

"Certainly, and look almost as pretty across the room as a bunch of flowers."

"Let's have some, girls, will you?" said 'Ria. "Will you go and get some with us, Miss Hunter?"

"Oh, yes, I should be delighted to go."

"Well, then, we will this very night. There'll be time, won't there, Miss Hunter, before night."

"Hardly," said Fanny. "We can go to-morrow directly after school."

"Yes, yes, to-morrow night. You hear, now, all of you. We are going into the woods after autumn leaves," said Joy, skipping up and down on the garden walk.

"If it's clear," said Cal.

"O, it will be clear enough, old maid Cal," said 'Ria. "It never rains in Indian summer."

The next day nothing was talked about among the children but the proposed walk, and Boss and Biny Gamby, whose horse was waiting for them at the gate precisely at four o'clock, looked back sorrowfully as they rode away, at the little group gathered round the school-house door.

"It's too bad they can't go," said 'Ria. "If old Madam Gamby was n't too mean to pay their board, they might have lived here all winter, instead of poking off every night on that old nag."

"Hush, 'Ria. I would n't talk so," said Fanny.

"Why not, Miss Hunter? She *is* as mean as—"

"Nanny's pie-crust," suggested little Joy.

"Good for Joy," said Cal, laughing. "It's a fact, Miss Hunter, and every body knows it."

"Well, it does n't make her any better to talk about it, does it, Cal? Better say nothing at all about a person, than to speak ill of them."

"If it should happen to get to their ears," said Cal.

"Come, what are you standing here all day for?" said Maud. "If you are ready, we had better be off, I reckon."

"Here's Johnny, he can't go," said Cal. "Come, Johnny, you run back to the house, there's a good boy, and ma will give you a great hunk of cracklin' bread."

"I won't," said Johnny, beginning to cry; "I want to go too."

"Let him go, Cal, he wants to so bad," said 'Ria. "He won't do any harm."

"You know better, 'Ria. I ain't goin' to be pestered with him. I shall just have to drag him over all the fences we come across, and he's certain to fall into every ditch."

"I ain't, either," said Johnny; "I think you are real mean, I do so," with a prolonged howl.

"Hush up this minute," said his sister; "Miss Hunter, can he go?"

"Is it very far?" said Fanny.

"Lor, Miss Hunter, it's no way at all," said Maud. "He can go as well as any of 'em. Come on, Johnny, I'll see to you."

"If he gets in any trouble, it won't be my fault," said Cal.

"No, Miss Prudence, you'd get quit, any how," said Maud, looking back as she started off at a round pace, dragging Johnny after her.

"What are you going that way for, Maud? It's nearest down the lane," said 'Ria.

"I want to stop at Aunt Phebe's a minute, she's got a hot ash-cake for us in the ashes."

"O, goody!" said Joy, smacking her lips.

"You all go on," said Maud, as she disappeared in the doorway. "I'll be up with you."

They waited, however, till she reappeared, tossing a round, thick substance from one hand to the other, as large as little Johnny's head, and about the color of ashes.

"Now, then," said 'Ria, "smoking hot, ain't it, Maud?"

"Hot! I reckon it is," said Maud, with various expressive contortions of countenance, breaking up the cake and displaying its golden interior.

"O, how good it smells," said Joy, hopping round on one foot and snuffing up the savor. "Give me a big piece, quick, Maud."

"I'll jest give the teacher some, and then we'll have the balance," said Maud. "Why here's a piece of collup leaf stickin' on yet."

"What's a collup leaf?" inquired Fanny.

"Why, Miss Hunter, don't you know? How funny; the teacher don't know what a collup leaf is. There's heaps of 'em over in Aunt Phebe's patch. Don't you see 'em?"

"What, those? They are cabbages," said Fanny.

"We call 'em collups," said 'Ria. "They always wrap two or three leaves round an ash-cake, to keep in the sweetness, you know."

"I see I shall learn a great many new things here on the prairie," said Fanny, with a smile.

By this time the ash-cake was divided, and each contentedly munching a piece, they went on their way.

"Somehow Aunt Phebe's ash-cakes taste sweeter than any body's else," said Joy, with her mouth full.

"Of course they do," said Maud. "Every thing aunty makes is better than other folks'."

Crossing a stile by Aunt Phebe's cabin, they walked a little way down the road, and climbing a high fence, passed a narrow patch of plowed ground, and found themselves at the entrance of the wood lot.

"This path leads down to the spring," said 'Ria.
"Will that be the best way to go?"

"Perhaps so, it makes very little difference. We shall
find what we want anywhere about here, I think," said
Fanny. Reaching up as she spoke, she broke off a twig
from a tree that overhung the path.

"Here we have something," she said. "See how beautifully this leaf is spotted with yellow and green, and these
others striped with red and yellow, like the leaves of a
tulip."

"That's a maple-tree," said Maria. "Here! I'll hold
on to this branch, if you can pull it down, Miss Hunter."

"What's that tree yonder, that looks so red?" said
Cal. "It blazes like it was on fire."

"That's a dwarf oak, I reckon. What Dave calls a
black Jack," said 'Ria.

"No, that isn't an oak," said Fanny, looking round to
see. "At least I think not. The oak tree turns a darker
red. More of a maroon. This must be an ash, or a birch,
perhaps."

"I'll go and see," said Cal.

"And Cal," said Fanny, still standing on tiptoe under
the maple branch, "stop and get some of the oak leaves
from the tree where I point with my parasol, just this side
of the tall one that's almost bare. Do you see it?"

"Yes, Miss Hunter," and off she ran.

"Lors, Joy, jest look over dar," screamed little Johnny.

"Whar?" said his sister.

"Children," said Cal, "for mercy's sake don't talk so
flat. I should think black Jake was here, with his 'dars,'
and 'whars,' and all that."

"Jake talks as good as any body," said Johnny, who
had his favorite as well as the rest, "and I *will* say *dar* if
I want to, for all you, Cal."

"I'll tell ma how you behave, and then we'll see," said his sister.

"Here are the oak leaves," said 'Ria, returning with a branch in her hand. "They are mighty ugly, though."

"Do you think so?" said Fanny, stripping off the defective leaves. "See what a pretty contrast they make to the bright colors of my maples. They are dark, to be sure, but how soft the shading is. Some of them look like velvet, they are so smooth and glossy. O! no, we must n't exclude the oak leaves from our bouquet."

"Here's a leaf, with little bumps all over it, just like the warts on old Miss Bradley's face," said Joy.

"See what I've got!" said Johnny, hastening toward them with both hands full.

"O! sumach leaves," said Fanny. "Well, Johnny, they are very pretty indeed. As rosy as your own cheeks. Can you find some more? and Johnny," she called out as he ran off, delighted to be useful, "pick them with longer stems. Ah, now, if there was only some way of reaching that high branch, how beautifully those speckled leaves would look in our bouquet."

"I'll get them," said Maud, and before Fanny could utter a word of remonstrance, she sprang up the tree like a squirrel, and was down again with the branch in her hand.

"O! Maud! how could you?"

"Lor, that's nothing. I hope I've climbed higher trees than that."

"But you might fall, Maud, and besides, it's so unlady-like."

"Lady-like!" repeated Maud, contemptuously, "I don't want to be lady-like."

"Ma wants you to be, though," said 'Ria; "she says she's always ashamed of you before folks."

"I don't car'. I 'spose you call Belle Boynton and Mrs. Pitts lady-like, with their stuck-up, mincin' ways. I'm sure I'd rather scratch round like black Jinny, than be like them."

"You can be easy and natural in your manners, Maud, and yet be lady-like," said Fanny. "I should be as sorry to see you 'stuck-up,' as you call it, as you would yourself. But never mind now, we are in the free woods, and won't talk about the ways of the world to-day. Can't we find some vine that has turned a pretty crimson or yellow, to answer for pendants—our bouquet will look stiff without them."

"The wild blackberry," suggested Cal.

"That is pretty, but the leaves are too large and coarse for droops. We will have a few, though, to mix in with the other leaves. They sometimes turn very richly."

"I know where we picked heaps of berries last summer, Cal," said Maud; "come, let's go and find 'em."

"Here's a little yellow vine runnin' round the roots of this old tree," said 'Ria. "Will this do?"

"Finely," said Fanny. "Careful now, careful, pull it up as long as you can. Ah, yes, that is pretty!"

The girls here returned with some blackberry leaves.

"Now, then," said Fanny, "our collection would be complete if we had some pretty green to set off the other colors. Are there any fern leaves about here? They keep their color very well."

"Heaps of 'em down to the spring," said Maud, who seemed to know where every thing grew.

"O, yes, Miss Hunter, and such beautiful moss growin' round the old stumps; it's just the prettiest place anywhere about," said Joy.

"And in the spring the banks are covered over with

blue violets," said Maud, "you find flowers there before you do anywhere else."

"Well, we will go to the spring if there is time," said Fanny. "Is it far?"

"O, no, Miss Hunter, just down the path yonder, a little ways. Do go, we 'have n't gotten half enough," said Johnny, who was hopping up and down in his delight.

Fanny needed little persuasion. In the beauty of the scene before her, the soft, spring-like air, the gorgeously tinted trees, the rustling carpet beneath her feet, and, above all, in the glorious freedom of the forest, she experienced a kind of wild delight, that carried her back to the days of her childhood. She could have danced about with the little ones, or shouted and sang as they did, in their free-hearted gayety, till the old woods rang again. But though she refrained from any such manifestations of delight, there was a springing lightness to her step, and a flush on her usually pale face, that told of intense enjoyment, and the children, who possessed no such keen perception of the beautiful, wondered at her frequent exclamations of delight.

"You think every thing's beautiful, seems to me," said 'Ria, as her teacher got down upon her knees to examine a bit of green moss peeping out from among the brown leaves; "every little thing that grows."

"Yes," said Fanny, with a smile, "my Father made them all."

Five minutes' walk through the woods brought them to the spring, a little stream that bubbled out of the hill-side and trickled down into a basin it had worn for itself in the clayey soil below. The hill was covered with trees; the yellow-leafed maple, the crimson ash, and the amber oak, were all bright with the slanting rays of the sun; while about their tops, and far down the glen, where the stream went stealing along, there hung a purple haze, a dim misty light, that softened the landscape, and filled the air with a dream-like repose.

While the children ran a little way down the stream, to search for the fern leaves, Fanny sat down on an old stump to rest. Their voices died away in the distance, and she was enjoying the beauties of the scene alone, when a rustling among the trees caused her to look up, and a moment after Maud appeared coming down the hill.

" You here, Maud ? I thought you went with the rest after the ferns," said Fanny.

" No," said Maud, leisurely chewing some winter-green leaves, " I 've been up yonder to Cherry's grave."

" Who was Cherry ?" inquired Fanny.

" Cherry was my bird. He died in the spring, and I buried him up under the maples," said Maud.

" Poor bird! What made him die ?" said Fanny.

" I don't know. I reckon it was to plague me," said Maud, swinging her sun-bonnet over her head. " I had him about six weeks, and just as I began to love him, one day he up and died. Every thing does just so."

" But you find plenty left to love, Maud ?"

" No, I don't ever mean to love any thing any more. Pa said he 'd catch me another bird, but I would n't have it. It would die jest like the other. Every thing does. I don't car'."

" O, Maud, don't talk so. It is n't right. God has given us so many beautiful things to love, that we have no right to complain, if now and then He takes something away. If your bird and your flowers died, Maud, He has left you all your dear friends; your father and mother and Aunt Phebe."

" Aunt Phebe will die, too, some day," said Maud " she 's always talkin' about it."

"We must *all* die some day, Maud. If we are ready, it does n't much matter when."

"You don't want to die, Miss Hunter?"

"No. I love to live in this beautiful world, and enjoy all the pleasant things God has placed here for us; but I *do* try to feel ready to die, whenever He thinks it best, and I pray to Him every day to prepare me for death."

"Aunt Phébe just wants to die," said Maud. "I wish she would n't, neither."

"If we ever get to Heaven, Maud, I expect we shall all wonder how we ever could love this poor world so well."

"Where every thing dies," said Maud.

"Yes, and where, by taking away those we love, God is trying to wean us from it, and draw our hearts up to Him."

"Yonder 's the girls," said Maud, hastily.

"O, such times!" cried Joy, running up with both hands full of fern leaves. "Such times! Johnny fell in the mud, and 'Ria lost her shoe haulin' him out, and Cal snagged her coat-tail, and I was so full of laugh, I laid right down and rolled."

"Snagged her coat-tail?" repeated Fanny, not understanding the nature of Cal's misfortune.

"Yes, jest see what a great slit," and Cal just then appearing, holding up the torn garment, Fanny understood that she had torn the skirt of her dress on the bushes.

"Now Cal will have something to fret about for a week," said 'Ria.

"O, no," said Fanny, examining the rent, "this can be easily mended, I think. And now, girls, straight for home. See, the sun is nearly down, and we have quite a walk before us. What a bunch we have got here. Who will help me carry them?"

"I, and I, and I," said three or four together, and sharing the bundle with all, that each might have the pleasure of obliging her, Fanny took up the line of march.

"What's that?" she asked suddenly, as a sound like distant thunder broke the stillness of the air.

"Nothin' but a flock of partridges," said Maud; "they always make that noise when they rise. Sometimes you can hear 'em half a mile off."

"Indeed! How do such little creatures contrive to make such a noise?"

"They make it with their wings," said Cal; "but they ain't so very little, after all. Dave shot one last week over nine inches long, and just as fat as it could be."

"They are pretty creatures," said Fanny, "with their tufted heads and spotted breasts. We call them quails in Connecticut, and in the fall of the year they perch upon a rail-fence or an old apple-tree, and call out 'Bob White! Bob White!' by the hour together."

"That ain't what they say here," said Maud. "When it's going to rain, they sing out, 'More wet! more wet!' and when it's going to be clear, then they say, 'No more wet.'"

"Perhaps the Missouri partridges speak a different language from the Connecticut quails," said Fanny, laughing, "or rather, as somebody's imagination supplied both phrases, it's just as easy to fancy it to be 'Bob White,' as 'more wet.'"

"I never heard 'em say any thing but 'More wet,'" said Maud, who never liked to give up a point; "and I'm sure it's a great deal better for 'em to tell us about the weather, than to be callin' out, 'Bob White' all the while."

"Very well, 'More wet,' be it, then," said Fanny. "Ah, here we are, most home again. Now where shall we press our leaves?"

A long consultation followed. There was no room in the house, *that* was certain, neither were there books to press them in. Fanny thought newspapers would do, if some heavy, even weight, could be found to cover them.

'Ria suggested the meal-box in the loft, over the school-room, and as no better place could be thought of, hither they all repaired. A quantity of old newspapers were procured, and at it they went, Fanny, upon her knees in the midst, superintending the operations.

The leaves were laid smoothly upon one page, and carefully covered with the opposite, then another layer of leaves and a layer of paper, and so on till all were nicely arranged.

"I declare I had n't the least idea they were so pretty," said 'Ria, as they arranged the last layer. "Now, however shall we lift this great, heavy box, half-full of meal, to get them under?"

"Lor, that 's nothin'," said Maud. "I could 'most do it myself. If Miss Hunter will just slip the papers under while we lift up this end, we 'll have it done in a jiffy. There, now, I reckon that 's heavy enough to smooth out the wrinkles."

"We 've had a grand time, have n't we?" said 'Ria, as they ran across the yard.

"Yes indeed," said little Joy, "I never see a grown lady act so much like a little girl as the new teacher does. She had jest as much fun as any of us."

CHAPTER IX.

DISTRESS IN DOMESTIC LIFE.

Two weeks passed, and Fanny became thoroughly domesticated in Mr. Catlett's family. She was often surprised herself at the readiness with which she fell into their peculiar way, for the change from her former mode of life, could scarcely have been greater had she been suddenly transported to some foreign land. With perfect good humor, she accommodated herself to the circumstances in which she was placed, making friends with all, and in the faithful performance of her daily duties, gradually finding that cheerfulness and contentment she had struggled so hard to attain.

Yes, Fanny was really happy, notwithstanding those doleful anticipations in which she indulged the first evening of her arrival. Her letters to the parsonage, which at first, it must be confessed, were rather sad in their tone, soon grew more cheerful, and the anxiety they had excited in the widow's heart, causing her to put some close questions as to the real nature of Fanny's feelings, was allayed by the frank and earnest assurances of her perfect content.

There were inconveniences and little discomforts, such as she had never known in New England, but they oftener afforded her amusement than any other feeling, and called into exercise all her Yankee ingenuity in getting up expedients.

For instance, when she found that there was neither closet, wardrobe, or bureau in the house, and her silk dresses were in a fair way to be injured by lying folded in her trunk, she set her wits to work to contrive some safe method of storing them away. It would never do to hang them about the room, for Viny raised a furious dust with her broom every morning, and after a rain the walls were streaked with wet. On applying to Mrs. Catlett, that lady informed her rather coldly that Nanny kept her dresses in a trunk, and on Fanny's explaining that her trunks were too closely packed to admit the addition, Mrs. Catlett showed so little disposition to help her that she soon changed the subject, and determined to contrive for herself. She wondered that Mrs. Catlett should trouble herself so little about the matter; but had she heard the lady's remark when she left the room, the mystery would have been explained.

"What business has she with her silk gowns, I should like to know?" said Mrs. Catlett. "A teacher come all this ways to work for pay, and more fixy than Nanny, or any of the girls."

In ignorance that she was committing any crime by possessing a respectable wardrobe, Fanny set herself to work to dispose of it. On climbing up into the loft, a bright thought suggested itself, and running down stairs she borrowed an old sheet, and tying the dresses therein, she suspended it by the united four corners from a peg in the center of the low roof. Here it hung in perfect security, Fanny surveying her contrivance with the greatest satisfaction.

The trouble of keeping every article of dress and the toilet continually locked in her trunk, was not slight, but this was a precaution that, in Mr. Catlett's establishment, was absolutely necessary.

" What! my comb, and brush, and work-box, and every thing, Nanny?" she inquired, when that young lady was impressing upon her the necessity of this course.

" Yes indeed, Miss Fanny; if you don't want 'em took, and used, and mebbe carried off, for good and all. There's no keepin' any thing here, unless it 's under lock and key. Servants are so thievish. Ours ain't a bit worse than other people's; they are all jest alike, takin' every thing they can lay their hands on, and you know they are always pryin' round."

Fanny accordingly locked up every thing, and after two or three losses occasioned by her own carelessness, she grew as careful as the rest. The children each had their own separate trunks, and even little Joy went about with a key dangling from her neck by a long string. As for Mrs. Catlett, she bore upon her arm a basket of keys, heavy enough to weigh her down, and never was it out of her sight three minutes at a time, unless, as occasionally happened, she went visiting, and left Miss Nanny in charge of the house.

Fanny found many things to excite her wonder in Mrs. Catlett's household arrangements, and though she did not undergo Miss Ophelia's trials, in rummaging Aunt Dinah's kitchen, she saw enough of the shiftless, slovenly manner in which things were done, to shock all her New England ideas of neatness and order. Then, too, their old-fashioned ways, clinging to the customs and habits of their Virginia ancestors, and rejecting all the laborsaving machines of the present day; not only doing every thing in the hardest possible manner, but persisting in calling it the best; all this excited her amusement and wonder. She was sometimes seized with the impression, that she was carried back fifty years, so greatly were they behind the age, and so nearly did some of their customs corre-

spond with what she had heard her grandmother relate
of her young days.

There was not a stove on the premises. A large open
fireplace extended half across the room, and scorched
one's face with the heat from burning logs, while the
breezes whistled round back and feet most merrily. A
decanter of whisky, and half a dozen glasses, stood always
upon the sideboard for the entertainment of visitors, and
the gentlemen, and frequently lady guests, were invited
to take a drink.

"Viny," said Fanny one day, as she was passing
through the yard, where the girl was washing, "why
don't you have a bench to set your tub on, and not wash
with it on the ground? I should think it would break
your back."

"I neber heered ob sich," said Viny, with a grin;
"what de use, anyhow? ground good nuff to wash on,
Miss Fanny."

"Yes, but it's so much harder. Then there's Aunt
Tibby, she hasn't a bit of a table in the kitchen, and
makes up all her bread and pies with the rolling-board
flat on the floor."

"Dat's de way, Miss Fanny; don't want no table lum-
berin' up de kitchen."

"And bakes every thing, bread and cake, and all, in
one little bake-kettle. I don't see how she ever gets
through."

"Lors, Miss Fanny, every body on de prairie does jest
so. You see we's allers used to it—dat's de reason."

Another cause of wonder to Fanny, was the strict attention paid by all the family to old Madam Hester. Kind,
respectful treatment, such as old age and infirmity always
demands, would not have surprised her; but Mrs. Catlett's
eager, almost servile attention to her slightest wants, and

A DECAYED SPECIMEN OF VIRGINIA ARISTOCRACY.

the reverence with which all appeared to regard her, excited her curiosity.

One evening after the children had gone to bed, and the old woman, in the midst of her rambling talk, was led up stairs, Fanny ventured to broach the subject.

" Mrs. Catlett," she said, " how long has Madam Hester been in your family ? "

" How long ? well, let me see. Aunt Mercy died two years before we moved to Carolville, and that was eleven, yes, twelve years next June. I remember, because Cal was a baby, born the very week Madam Hester came here to live. How I did fret, for fear she 'd go to Cousin Wortley's. They were n't so nigh of kin, neither ; but I reckon if Mr. Catlett rode over there once, he went twenty times to see about it."

" What relation is she to you, Mrs. Catlett ? "

" She was own aunt to my mother, Miss Fanny. You see my grandmother Wortley, was a Mason, and Abby Mason, that was her own sister, married Paytére Peters, son of Governor Peters. Madam Hester is own granddaughter to Governor Peters of Virginia."

" Indeed ! " said Fanny, seeing that she was expected to say something.

" Yes, and there is n't any better blood in Virginia than runs in her veins. I tell you, Governor Peters stood among the first. I 've heard my grandmother tell about his house down in Richmond county. She used to tell about his piles of silver plate, and the great dining-hall where they never set less than twenty at table, and the carriage he rode in, with silver mountings, and his blood-horses and all that. I 've sat and listened to her hours and hours."

" An old Virginia gentleman," said Fanny.

" Yes, and when the war came, then he lost it all. The British just went through that part of Virginia, and plundered every gentleman's house on the road. The old governor was gone, and the women folks and the servants were all there were in the house—and they had to run off in the woods, and hide to save their lives. Madam Hester and Mercy were little bits of things; but before she lost her mind, she used to tell how they stayed there in the woods all night, and how her mother and grandmother cried and sobbed, when they saw the sky red with the burning house. Well, they just lost every thing. When they crept back, it was nothing but a pile of smokin' ruins. The plate and the beautiful furniture, and every thing was all gone. They said the old governor never got over it. He let every thing run to waste, and, before he died, was a poor man."

"And Madam Hester?"

"O, her father owned a place down in lower Virginia, and they all went there to live. When he died, she and Aunt Mercy kept on with it as well as they could; but you see the land was mostly run out, and they had to sell a servant or two every year to make out a livin'. I don't know exactly how it came about, but when Aunt Mercy died, the place would n't hardly pay the debts, and Madam Hester was left without a penny in the world."

"Was she ever married?"

"No, she was going to be once, they said, but her lover died in the wars, and she never found another to suit her. They say she was one of the handsomest women in Virginia, as proud and stately as a king's daughter, and the best dancer in all the country."

Fauny recalled the image of the hideous, decrepit old creature who had just left them, and wondered if she ever could have been beautiful and graceful; if the face now yellow and wrinkled, could ever have called forth praises by its beauty and bloom, or if that form now bent and those limbs now tottering, carried off once the palm in the dance. She was going off in a reverie, when Mrs. Catlett's voice recalled her.

"My mother was always proud of her kin," she said; "but I believe the old lady would have been ready to jump out of her skin, if she had thought we should have a grand-daughter of Governor Peters of Virginia living with us in the house twelve years."

"It is very kind in you to take care of her in her old age," said Fanny.

"Very kind in us!" repeated Mrs. Catlett, in great surprise. "What do you mean? It's an honor, let me tell you, Miss Hunter, that don't happen to a family every day. Kind, indeed; any body might be proud of having a grand-daughter of Governor Peters, of Virginia, under their roof!"

Fanny was greatly abashed at her mistake, and with an apology for her stupidity, took up her candle, and bade Mrs. Catlett good-night.

So intently was she meditating upon the honor of entertaining a grand-daughter of Governor Peters, of Virginia, that she did not observe the obstacle in her way, and had nearly fallen over a little heap curled up at the head of the stairs. Quickly recovering herself, she stooped down to see what it was, and recognized black Tilla, her head resting upon the floor, and her little bare feet drawn up under her.

"Why, Tilla, is this you?" said Fanny. "What's the natter?"

"O! miz'ry!" said Tilla.

"What is it, Tilla? Are you sick?"

"Mighty poorly!" said the child, in a hopeless tone.

"Well, why don't you go to bed? Come, don't lie there," said Fanny, attempting to lift her.

"O! don't, Miss Fanny, please," said Tilla. "If you

jest would n't touch me. I 's got such a misery in my
side."

" Well, don't you know it will make it worse to lie out
here in the cold ? You must come in by the fire."

" I jest don't want to stir," said Tilla. " O ! mis'ry, I 's
so bad !"

" Tilla, get up this instant, and come in by the fire,"
said Fanny, in a tone of command.

The child obeyed, rising with difficulty, and once or
twice repeating the exclamation of suffering.

" Now, Tilla," said Fanny, after making her as comfortable as she could, with a piece of old carpet and a quilt
from her own bed, "now, Tilla, don't you lie out in the
cold again when you are sick."

" Miss Cal done kick me out !" said Tilla.

Fanny groaned in spirit. She had that morning given
her scholars a lecture upon cruelty to animals.

" I hate Miss Cal," said Tilla, an expression of malignity
crossing her features. " I hates 'em all, I do. Lors!
what if Miss Car'line hear me say dat ?"

" Hush, Tilla, you must n't talk so ; it 's wicked."

" I does, Miss Fanny. O ! mis'ry !"

" Do you feel so very bad, Tilla ?"

" Mighty poorly !" said Tilla, the same old, hopeless expression returning to her face.

" Why don't you tell Aunt Phebe, and let her give you
something to make you well ?"

" She can't, Miss Fanny. She says it 's in my bones."

" Does Mrs. Catlett know you are sick, Tilla ?"

" Who ? Miss Car'line. She don't car'. She won't
hear to me, when I telled her I 's sick. She say 't ain't
nothin' but lazy, and she cuff me roun', and call me names,
and Massa Dave he say, ' I wish she 's under ground.' I
wish I was dar, too," said Tilla.

" O ! Tilla !"

" I does, 'cause I's in ebery body's way, and thar don't nobody car' for me, not de fus one, only Marthy, and dey hates her too."

" There 's one that loves you, Tilla. Did you ever hear about Jesus Christ ?"

" I's heered Aunt Phebe tell."

" And how He left his beautiful home up in the sky, and came down and suffered, and died, for just such poor little ones as you. He loves you, Tilla. He says, 'Suffer little children to come unto Me, and forbid them not.' He wants you to be good, and He will be a kind friend to you, and by-and-by take you to a beautiful world, where you will never be sick any more, or feel pain and trouble again. You 've heard about heaven, Tilla ?"

" Aunt Phebe sings about a holy city, 'way up above the sky."

" Can you say the rest ?"

Tilla repeated a verse of a familiar camp-meeting hymn :

" 'There is a holy city
  'Way up above the sky,
A bright and shining temple,
  Where Jesus dwells on high ;
And all the saints are shouting,
  Arrayed in robes of white ;
With golden harps to praise Him,
  They dwell with Him in light.' "

" And don't you want to go there, and be one of those bright angels ?"

" O ! yes ! Miss Fanny," said Tilla, clasping her little thin hands, while the tears ran down her cheeks.

" Well, then, you must be one of God's own children ! You must try to be like this blessed Jesus, gentle, and kind, and loving, even to those who are unkind to you. This is the way Jesus did; and when wicked men beat Him and spit on Him, and nailed Him to the cross, till He died, He forgave them, and prayed for them. Will you try to be like Him, Tilla?"

"O! Miss Fanny, I can't," said Tilla. "I spec' I never get thar, anyhow. Thar can't nobody be good, when every body's a jawin' an' crackin' 'em, round all day. Dey all hates me. 'Pears like I must hate 'em back agin. 'T ain't no odds, anyhow. O! mis'ry!"

"Tilla, did you ever ask God to help you to be good?"

"Don' know how."

"Will you kneel right down now, and shut your eyes, and say a little prayer after me?"

"Yes, Miss Fanny."

She knelt upon the floor, and clasping her thin hands, solemnly repeated the few simple words Fanny uttered, then sinking down upon her bed, was fast asleep in a moment.

Fanny gazed upon the puny face, retaining even in sleep its sorrowful, care-worn expression, and then drawing the scanty covering over her bare feet, she left the child to her repose.

CHAPTER X.

ONE morning Mrs. Catlett rose in a particularly bad humor. It was a cold wet day, the fire was slow in burning, the baby cross, and Martha and Tilla half asleep. Fanny woke with a confused idea that something unpleasant was going on below, and the fretful tones of Mrs. Catlett's voice, mingling with the patter of the rain against the windows, suggested the idea of that "continual dropping that weareth away a stone." She opened her eyes, wide enough to see that it was barely light, and was sinking away into another doze, when a loud exclamation from Mrs. Catlett, followed by a rush of little feet in the direction of the passage, awakened all the sleepers, and the next moment Martha burst into the room, her face beaming with delight.

"O, Miss Nanny, you all get right up; Massa Jack done come!" she cried.

They needed not a second bidding. All were out of bed in an instant, hurrying on their clothes, and overpowering Martha with questions which they could not wait for her to answer. "When did he come?" "How long has he been here?" "What did ma say?" "O how glad I am!"

"Don' no nothin' 'bout it," said Martha, "only Miss Car'line she go inter de passage to undo de fron' door, an'

O my! what a screamin', an' de nex' minit Mass' Jack come walkin' in."

"O dear, where is that Viny," said Joy, nearly crying with vexation; "I never can fasten these hooks, and every body 'll be dressed first. Do somebody help me." Fanny fastened the troublesome dress, braided Maud's hair, and tied a hanging shoe-string, and then, after all had gone, proceeded more leisurely with her own toilet.

"I wonder if I shall like him," she thought, as she stood a moment at the window before going down. Women were hurrying to and from the kitchen, while in the doorway stood Tibby, stirring up the batter bread for breakfast, and two or three of the men, with axes on their shoulders, lingered about, waiting for a word from "Mass' Jack." All seemed full of joyful excitement. "They are glad to see him," thought Fanny, "that is a good sign;" and putting a few finishing touches to her dress, she hastened down stairs.

The room was looking very bright and cheerful, a good fire burning on the hearth, and the table spread for breakfast. With his back to the fire, his hands crossed behind him, stood the master of the house. He was a muscular, broad-shouldered man, full six feet high, dressed in clothes a good deal the worse for wear, and a hat slouched over his eyes. His face was rough with a week's growth of beard, and a large quid of tobacco disfigured one cheek, but his features were not unpleasing, and there was a good-humored twinkle in his gray eye, as he looked down upon the new teacher.

"Well, come on," he said, after staring at her a moment as she stood timidly upon the lower stair. "What are you afraid of?"

Fanny advanced, and gave him her hand.

"Why you are a young thing, ain't you?" said Mr.

Catlett, looking down upon her as a bear might eye a mouse. " Well, what are you doing out here, hey ?"

" Trying to drive a little knowledge into your children's heads," said Fanny with spirit, for she was not pleased with her reception.

" Whew !" said Mr. Catlett, starting back in mock alarm. " Sharp, now, ain't you ? A Yankee girl, cut and dried, from Connecticut, hey ?"

" Now, Mr. Catlett, do be quiet," said his wife. " Miss Fanny don't know how to take your jokes. Just let her alone, and tell us when you got here. The children have kept up such a clatter I hav'n't found a chance to put in a word."

" Well, marm," said Mr. Catlett, " as nigh as I can *guess*—ain't that what you Yankees say, Miss—what's your name?—I got here between twelve and one o'clock last night."

" But why in the world could n't you let us know you was here ?" said Mrs. Catlett, " and not lie out in the porch all night. How do you reckon I found him, Miss Fanny, when I went to undo the door ? There he lay, curled up on the floor, as fast as a log. I reckon he 'll be down sick with a chill to-morrow."

" Miss Calacanthus don't you fret," said ·her husband. " Do you s'pose I wanted such a screechin' and screamin' in the middle of the night, as you women always get up at such times, with every chick and child on the place raisin' hob generally. I just lopped down there to have a quiet nap before morning. Come, ma, tell some of them women to toat in breakfast. I want to eat. O, Madam Hester, how do you find yourself?" he continued, advancing to shake hands with the old creature.

She looked up at the sound of his voice, and a gleam of something like intelligence passed over her face.

"O ho, you have come," she said. "You have been gone a long time, a mighty long time, and there's them that's been a watchin' and a waitin', but they are in their graves—O ho." She shook her head feebly, and tottered to her seat.

"She gets more wanderin' every day, Mr. Catlett. It seems like she was failing fast."

"No good will come on 't," said the old woman suddenly. "I always telled them no good would come on 't. Always a goin', never contented to stop in any place. I telled them they 'd rue the day they sent the boy off to seek his fortin."

"There, Mr. Catlett, that 's just the way she puts in lately, 'specially when we say any thing about Dave 's going away. I declare, she scares me sometimes—"

"You are easily scared, then," said her husband. "Can't you see it 's old times she 's talkin' about?"

"It ain't no use," said Madam Hester, "I tell yer I 've warned 'em ag'in and ag'in, but it runs in the family, and them that 's fated is fated. There 's trouble ahead, O ho—"

"There, now I hope she 's done," said Mrs. Catlett. "I 'm sure I think heaps of Madam Hester, but I can't help thinkin' times, that she 's like a black raven sittin' there in the chimney corner, croakin' out evil. She 's always sayin' something gloomy."

"Fiddlesticks! women are always pickin' up something to fret about. Come, now, let 's have breakfast, and let Madam Hester alone."

"O, pa, did you know what a great hole you have got in your hat? Two of 'em, right opposite each other," said Cal, holding up the unfortunate beaver.

"Gracious! Mr. Catlett, it 's a bullet-hole," said his wife; "where *have* you been? Did you get into a fight?"

"Hold your tongue," said her husband; "it's none of your business where I've been; and put down that hat, child, this minute, and come to breakfast."

"Pa puts *his* elbows on the table," whispered little Johnny.

"What's that you say, jackanapes?"

Johnny hung his head.

"Speak up, can't you," said his father.

"Miss Fanny says we ought n't to put our elbows on the table, and *you* do," said Johnny, timidly.

"So that's it, is it?" said Mr. Catlett, his good humor apparently restored; "our Connecticut school-marm teaches the young ones better manners than their daddy's. Well, so it goes. By the way, wife, have you had any pumpkin-bread yet?"

"Why, no," said Mrs. Catlett, "they have n't toated up the pumpkins. I reckon it's time, though."

"Nor any onions?" said Mr. Catlett.

"Lors no! what are you drivin' at, Mr. Catlett?"

"No wonder Miss What's-her-name's a trifle home-sick. Bless you, wife, we must have pumpkin-bread for a week to come. You see Miss Fandango," said Mr. Catlett, gravely, "we've got half an acre of pumpkins, and a powerful big bed of onions, so you need n't go to sighin' for the leeks and garlics of Weathersfield. Ain't that where they go it so strong in the onion line?"

"Mr. Catlett, ain't you ashamed," said his wife; "you fairly make Miss Fanny blush."

"So much the better," said Mr. Catlett, "I want to see a little Yankee bloom now and then. The chills don't leave much on the Missouri girls' cheeks."

"Pa, you don't call her right," said Johnny; "her name is Miss Fanny."

"Well, that ain't much of a name, Johnny. I want to improve it."

"It 's a right pretty name, I think," said Johnny.

"What in patience have you been doin' to that nigger?" said Mr. Catlett, as Tilla brought round her young mistress's plate; "she looks as ashy as Tib's lye-kettle, and as doleful as a tomb-stone."

"She always looks that way," said his wife. "She 's the ugliest brat on the place. I believe she tries to look just as bad as she can to pester me. See her now, with her forehead puckered up and her mouth drawn down like an old woman. I can't bear the sight of her."

"Well, what 's the matter, anyhow?"

"Nothing at all," said Mrs. Catlett, sharply. "She puts on, and makes believe she 's sick, to get shet of work, I reckon; though, goodness knows, she has little enough to do."

"O, Mass' Jack," said Martha, stopping suddenly with a plate of batter-cakes in her hand, "she *is* sick. She 's right sick. Dat's what makes her look so."

"Hold your tongue, you jade," said her mistress; "how dare you contradict me?"

"Please, Miss Car'line, I did n't mean no harm. I reckoned you did n't see how bad she was gettin'."

"I see how saucy *you* are gettin', and I 'll take you down a peg, too, if you don't mind yourself."

"Come, come, ma, let a fellow have one quiet day, can't you, before you let off steam," said Mr. Catlett; "and try to put a little grease on to that young one, for the credit of the place. The crows would n't pick her as she is now."

"Mass' Jack," said Martha, following him as he sauntered out into the back porch, "if you only would tell

Miss Car'line, Tilla's sure enough sick. She won't hear to me, nor Miss Fanny."

"It's none of my business, Marthy," said Mr. Catlett; "I never interfere with the house-servants."

"Jest this once, Mass' Jack."

"Marthy, what are you foolin' about out there?" said Mrs. Catlett's angry voice.

Martha looked wistfully in her master's face, but its careless good-humored expression, gave her no encouragement to brave her mistress's wrath, and slowly and sadly she returned to her presence.

"Dave, where's them crack dogs you was tellin' about?" said Mr. Catlett, lounging in the doorway where Dave was feeding the hounds.

Dave gave a low whistle. "Here, Othor," he said, as a large tan-colored dog bounded toward them.

"There's a hound!" said Dave, admiringly. "Look at that head, will you? and his chest. There's some breadth there."

"They ain't bad," said Mr. Catlett, examining the dog critically.

"No," said Dave. "You ought to see that dog run. The way he clears the ground is n't slow. The first time I took him out was the day after you left. There was I, and Mack, and the Turner boys along. We took their two dogs and this fellow. Bob Turner's always crackin' up his dogs, you know, and they are prime to run. Well, sir, we started a deer. I had the stand down by the hollow, at the edge of the oak thicket. I waited about half an hour, when I heard a crashing in the under-brush, and next minute a full-grown buck came out of the thicket within three rods of me. I fired and missed. I tell you I felt streaked. I reckoned, of course, I'd seen the last of him, and was cussin' my bad luck, when Othor dashed by me on the full run. I knew he was n't far behind, for I heard his voice in the woods. But what do you think? Just as he was goin' it full split one way, here comes the deer back the other. Something had turned him, you see; he doubled, and wanted to take to the thicket again. Othor met him about half way down the hollow. I tell you 't was a picture. The buck stood with his head down and his feet close together, and the hair on the ridge of his back bristling like a wild cat's; and Othor squatted flat on the ground, and cocked his head one side, kinder knowin' like, but his eyes watchin' the other like a rattlesnake's just afore it springs. Well, sir, they looked at each other about a minute, and the deer made his first bound. Just then my ball hit him. He staggered a little, and Othor had him by the neck directly, and held him down till I cut his throat. I never felt afraid for that dog's spunk afterward."

Mr. Catlett heard the story with deep attention.

"Well, here 's another," he said. "What kind of a crittur is this?"

"O! that dog is prime! Here, Uno, you must have a word, must you?" A beautiful black hound, spotted with white, trotted up with a low whine, and thrust his cold nose in his master's hand.

"There, sir, that dog and his mate—they are just alike, you see—I reckon will beat any thing on the prairie. They are young yet, and I hav n't tried 'em at runnin', but if they turn out as well as they promise, they 'll go a leetle ahead of any thing we 've seen yet. You see they are lighter built than Othor, but just look at their muscles, you won't find much fat there."

"No," said Mr. Catlett, "you 've kept 'em as thin as rails."

"That 's the nature of 'em, you see. They are just cut

out for runnin'. Such knowin' fellows, too. That dog,
Uno, all but talks."

"What do you call 'em?" said Mr. Catlett.

"Uno and Ino," said Dave—"right *knowin'* names,
ain't they?"

"Who named 'em?"

"Well, I was tryin' to think of some good names for
'em, and Miss Fanny she thought of these—I called 'em
so right off."

"Pretty good."

Just then Fanny appeared on her way to the school-
house, followed by all the children. The dog no sooner
perceived her, than he left Dave, and bounded to her side.
Fanny laid down her book, and stooped to caress him. It
was a pretty sight to see them together, the slender girl,
and the great gaunt hound fondling her little hand, and
yielding his noble head to her caresses.

Dave hastened forward to pick up her book, and taking
an autumn blossom which he had found somewhere in the
woods, from his button-hole, he gave it to her. She
thanked him by an exclamation of delight, and a look from
her brown eyes that Dave remembered all day.

"It's mighty queer," he said, after she had disappeared
in the school-house, "that dog took to her from the very
first, and he never seemed to notice any other woman."

"Dogs and boys sometimes do mighty foolish things,"
said Mr. Catlett, dryly, "but how does she work it, sure
enough? Keep any thing of a school?"

"Well, you'd think so. I never see any thing like it.
When she first came here, I reckoned she would n't make
it go at all. She looked so young, and had such childish
ways with her, I reckoned our young ones would get the
upper hand the first thing, but it's right the other way.
I never could see how she manages it, for out of school

she carries on with 'em like she was as young as any ; but you can't hire 'em to do any thing she don't like. I don't see how she 's got round 'em so, I 'm sure."

"The same way she 's made over a tolerably sensible boy into a lady's man, with posies stickin' in his button-holes," said Mr. Catlett.

Most of the morning was spent by "Massa Jack" in going about the place, visiting the wood-lot, the stable, the tobacco-house, and the corn-crib, holding good-natured talk with the servants, and taking a general oversight of matters and things about the farm. Notwithstanding Mrs. Catlett's doleful anticipations of the state in which Mr. Catlett would find every thing on his return, that gentleman appeared to be very well satisfied with the progress of events during his absence.

"That 's pretty well, Uncle Jake," he said to an old gray-headed negro, who, in his knit woolen cap, red shirt, and homespun trousers, was chopping away at a little distance from the other hands.

"Bress yer soul, Mass' Jack," said the old man, wiping the perspiration from his face, "dis yer ain't nothin', it don't begin ; I 'se seen de time when I could cut six hundred feet of timber a day easy. Ole bones ! Mass' Jack, ole bones ! dey wants *greazing* up once in a while."

"Well, come up to the house, after night, Uncle Jake, and we 'll grease 'em up with a dram."

"Hi ! dat 's de sort !" said the old man.

Passing on to the tobacco-house, and from there to the corn-crib, they were returning by the quarters, when Aunt Patsey stepped out of her cabin, with a little black image in her arms.

"Mass' Jack, don' forget de baby !" she said.

"Bless me ! so I did !" said Mr. Catlett. "A new one, ain't it ? Well, to be sure, it 's quite peart. What do you call it, Pats' ?"

"Polly Ebenezer," said Patsey, with a grin.

"Ebenezer!" said her master. "Why, that's a boy's name."

"So dey all telled me, but la sakes, it don't made no odds. It's a good name, anyhow; Aunt Phebe she sings,

"'Here I raise my Ebenezer,'

dar's whar I got it, you see."

"Yes, yes," said Mr. Catlett, "I did n't see the gist of it before. I've no objection to your raisin' as many Ebenezers as you 've a mind to."

Aunt Patsey grinned again, and retreated into her cabin.

From Mrs. Catlett's frequent declarations that her trouble and anxiety arose from her husband's absence, Fanny concluded that on that gentleman's return, all would flow on smoothly as a summer stream, but she soon found that the troubled waters were not thus easily stilled. Mrs. Catlett was one of those unfortunate persons who must worry about something all the time, whose happiness consists in being *un*happy, and who, if no real cause for fretfulness exists, will, by some means, invent one.

When relieved from the care of the field hands, she had all the more leisure to scold the house servants, to pick flaws in the children, and to fret generally over her misfortune in being at the head of such an establishment. Her husband listened to all her complaints with the most perfect nonchalance, sometimes falling in with what she said, and declaring that she *was* the most miserable woman in the world, and that he always knew it, and at other times making no reply at all. Occasionally, however, he became angry, and bade her be quiet, a course that stilled her instantly, for she stood in great fear of her husband's wrath.

CHAPTER XI.

OUR three discomfited worthies, as they rode along by moonlight, to go back in the line of our history somewhat, were busy planning their revenge upon the impudent and unreasonable squatter, who was strangely unwilling to give up his claim and cabin, food and shelter, just as winter approached, after the labor of a whole season, to their imperious mandate. They would rouse the whole prairie, liquor 'em up well, surround the claim, search for the cabin, burn it to the ground, and scatter its inmates. It would never do to allow a free soil settlement to grow up within thirty miles of La Belle Prairie. It would work the worst kind of mischief among the niggers. They could n't stand it nohow. But why such an army to put down one Yankee and his son? This question they did not raise in words, but much of their talk was intended to answer it. It was n't any use to spill the blood of gentlemen born. Where there were so many lazy devils round, they might as well have enough to make sure and safe work. "Wife and children," said Catlett, who was really quite a domestic man, as has already appeared. "They are plaguy close shooters," said Turner, "as that hole in your hat testifies, neighbor, and there 'll be hot work before we are done with 'em. They 'll fight like devils, see if they don't." Tom said nothing, but sur

veyed his begrimed person and grated his teeth. They
talked over, also, what sort of story they should tell to
excite the neighbors. They did not say it, but what they
said meant that it would never do to let it be known that
three of the chivalry ran from a Yankee and a half. "Shall
we say a dozen?" said Catlett. "Twenty," said Tom.
"Fifty," said Turner. "It won't do to be too steep,
though," said the squire, "a dozen is enough." So it
stood at a dozen. It may surprise our readers, but neither of these capitalists of the prairie ever read Shak-
speare, or had heard of such a personage as Jack Falstaff.
After this they discussed whether they should have a
meeting at Belcher's store, who should be spokesman,
whether they should be mum to their families till the
gathering, and who should ride round and drum up all
hands. At last, as they neared Catlett's house, they concluded that they would have a meeting at the store, that
they would keep perfectly quiet until then, that Catlett
should be spokesman, and Turner and Tom drum up all
hands. And if they did n't make the rascally Yankee rue
the day he laid his hand on a Missouri gentleman, it would
be because there was n't any spunk left on the border.
So they bade Catlett good-night, who arrived as afore-
said.

"Dave," said that gentleman at dinner, "I want you to
go to Belcher's with me this evening. Tell Jerry to gear
the horses right away."

"You ain't going to send him off, are you? said Mrs.
Catlett timidly; for her husband looked somewhat awry,
and met her looks of suspicion and anxiety in a way that
convinced the lady that he was not to be questioned too
closely.

"Don't you fret," returned her lord and master, and
there was acquiescence.

"There's something on Mr. Catlett's mind," she said, as soon as he was gone; "a fight or a drinking row, I'll warrant. That man is always getting into some scrape, and now poor Dave must be dragged into it. Viny, hand me my pipe on the sideboard, and a shovel of coals. Dear me, what a world of trouble this is."

"Well, ma, I don't reckon there's any thing very bad going on this time. I'm sure pa has been pleasant enough all the morning."

"Nanny, you don't know your father as well as I do. He's very peculiar about such things. If he's fretted about any thing, and don't want me to see it, he always puts on just that way. I see through it, though. I have n't lived nigh twenty-five years with him for nothing. I tell you he's got into a muss somehow. I should n't be in the least surprised to see him brought home a bloody corpse some day. 'T would be just my luck."

"Sorrow and trouble! sorrow and trouble!" mumbled the old woman from the corner. "I telled 'em 't was a comin'."

In a brief time the subject of these doleful forebodings arrived with his son at Tom Belcher's store. The number of horses tied to the fence in front, gave token of quite an assemblage within, and they found, on entering, that the room was full; full not only of men, but of smoke and the fumes of whisky, for Belcher had orders to put a barrel on tap. Such an event was never known to fail to fill his store, with a crowd in the interest of the man who paid the bill, from time immemorial. It is even rumored that Catlett once advised a Methodist preacher, who came to hold a series of meetings in the neighborhood, which were thinly attended, just to take one of his barrels of whisky to the ground, and tap it, and if it would n't draw him a crowd, he might set him (Catlett) down for a fool.

"And," says he, " as I'm favorable to religion, I don't care
if I throw in the liquor to help on the good cause."

There was an immense stamping, and clapping of hands,
and hurraing, when Catlett and Dave entered.

"Halloa, squire! you're the man appointed to address
this meeting, Turner says. Go it, old hoss! we are
ready," says Belcher.

"Had n't we better organize?" said a voice in the corner. "I likes to see things done constitutional. I nomi-
nates T. Belcher, Esq., as chairman of this meetin'. Gentlemen, as many as in favor, say Ay." All sang out
"Ay!" "Contrary minds the same sign." "Ay!"
they roared again. "It's a unanimous vote." Mr. T.
Belcher took the chair amid thunders of applause, placing
a box on the counter, and squatting on it. "Now we are
ready for your speech, Catlett," says the chairman. "A
secretary first," bawled the constitutional man. "I nom-
inates Tom Walton." "Have him?" The store roared
with the yells—"Tom! you're it! You'll find pen and
paper out there by the desk."

"Now, Mack, confound you! if you've any thing else
constitutional, out with it, for we want to do all that up
now and hear the squire."

"All right now! let him fire!"

"Hold on a bit, squire," said the chairman, "I m as
thirsty as the devil! Hand up the mug there."

"Had n't we all better liquor round, to kinder get into
a glow first?" said one.

"Second the motion!" said a man, out at the elbows,
who was already holding on to the counter for support.

"Hain't you got another mug, Tom? We are consuming time this way."

"It's whisky we are consuming!" said the out-of-elbow
man, "or you need n't trust my gullet any more."

"Come, come, gentlemen!" said constitutional Mack, "I call you to order!"

"Order! order! order!" roared the crowd. Tom Belcher here resumed the reins.

"Now, gentlemen, we are all ready, let's hear the squire clear through, and drink no more whisky till he's done, if we die for 't."

"Agreed! agreed!" cried the crowd.

Here Catlett arose amid deafening shouts.

"Fellow-citizens, and neighbors—I appear before you as the representative of three honored gentlemen of La Belle Prairie, Joe Turner, Tom Walton, and my humble self, to present a cause which I know will stir the inmost recesses of your souls, and rouse you up to deeds of glory. 1 will be short, and tell the plain facts, which, if I mistake not, will thrill your spirits, animate your hearts, and—and make your hair stand on eend!

. "You know, fellow-citizens, that Turner, Tom, and I have been over in Kanzas (great sensation), looking out peaceful homes for our children. Fellow-citizens, I selected a spot, and Tom, as he will testify, nailed my claim to a tree. We traveled all over Kanzas for weeks, and on returning found that some daring rapscallion of an abolitionist had torn down the writing and scattered it in pieces to the winds of heaven. Friends and neighbors, imagine the feelings of grief and indignation that swelled our hearts as we surveyed the relics of this damning deed (immense sensation). As we stood in wonder hoping to light upon the scalawag, behold, there rushed forth upon us, a dozen stout abolition devils, armed to the teeth, and with hellish shouts, pitched into us pell-mell. Fellow-citizens, it were vain to attempt a description of the scene which followed. I upset two, Turner knocked down several, and Tom drove his charger over a gang, but they were too many

for us, and had they been good shots, your friends and
neighbors would not be here to-day to recite the story of
their wrongs. Behold this hat! see where the villains'
bullet went through! (yells and groans mingled with cries
of shoot the devils! hang 'em! roast 'em alive! etc., etc.)
And now, my friends, we appeal to you. Will you rest
content while such murderous villains are threatening the
lives and insulting the rights of your fellow-citizens?
Will you stand tamely by and see our claims destroyed,
our sacred rights invaded, and—and our hats punched with
bullet holes? Will you, I say? (Tremendous sensation.)
Come, then, return with us in a body, break up their settlement, burn their cabins, and drive them, at least, a hundred miles into the wilderness. I appeal to you, noble
sons of Missouri, and will only add, that Turner, Tom, and
I will pay the liquor."

"We'll go!" "Hang the devils!" "Set me down for
one!" "Oaths!" "Big words!" "A little more liquor!" "Open the enlistment books!" "Shoot 'em!"
"Hurrah for Catlett!" "We'll fight for you, old hoss!"
"No shirking!" "Stand fast!"—and general noise and
excitement followed this speech.

When at last order was restored, the constitutional Mr.
Mack rose to offer the following resolutions:

"A drink round first! The squire's speech was dry—
no, I was dry!" "Yes, a drink round, that's the talk."

So round went the mug. When all was done, "Now,"
says Belcher, "speak up, Mack."

"You ain't quite constitutional in your way, Belcher.
However, never mind. I move the following resolutions:

"*Resolved*, That the outrageous attack by' abolition
meddlers upon our fellow-citizens, peaceably exploring
Kanzas, rouses our highest indignation, and regard for
our own safety, and the safety of our wives and children,

impel us to unite our hearts and hands for the common safety, and that we pledge ourselves to expel these invaders from our borders.

"*Resolved,* That Tom Belcher's be the rendezvous for all our citizens on the morning of the fifteenth, who shall then and there appear, armed and equipped for service, and that Col. Joe Turner be appointed commander to the expedition.

"*Resolved,* That a call to arms and a notice of this gathering shall be nailed up in Belcher's store."

"Them's um." "Mack knows." "Put 'em, Belcher!" "Ay! we are ready." "Go it." "Them in favor, say Ay!"

"Ay!" roared the gang with an unearthly sound.

"Now let's liquor round and adjourn," said the out-of-elbow man. "Agreed," cried the lot; and the door opened and Catlett and his son emerged into the open air. Neither of them had drank too much.

CHAPTER XII.

AT length the sun of the fifteenth of October, which was to become as famous to the people of La Belle Prairie as the sun of Austerlitz, dawned upon that quiet settlement. Early in the morning, a barrel of whisky had been rolled out by Belcher, and placed in a convenient spot, with the mug under it for general use. Scarcely had this task been accomplished, when a customer for the first dram, in the shape of a man, with an old knapsack and battered drum, came swaggering up to the spot.

"Ho! Jenkins, it's you, is it; first on the ground? Well, you'll do for the music, to say nothing about such chaps as you being good food for powder."

"I say, Belcher, you'd best let a feller alone, when he's come to do you a good turn. I vow, if it ain't mean the worst way, to begin in that style," said the man, growling out his words with catched breath, as though restraining his passion through fear.

"Never mind, Jenks, don't get touchy now, there's no harm done. Just take another drink, and come into the porch. It's prime whisky, real first brand. Tell you what, Jenks, the gentlemen of La Belle Prairie don't do things by halves."

"Humph!" said the man.

Scarcely were they seated, ere another and another

came straggling along, and soon a little crowd gathered around the center of attraction, the whisky-barrel, shouting, gesticulating, and preparing themselves, after the most approved fashion in those parts, for the day's work. At length, when about thirty had appeared on parade, Dave and Catlett came galloping down the road, upon their best horses, and a moment after, Col. Joe Turner, mounted in like manner, made his appearance.

After some general talk and bluster, which occupied at least half an hour, the colonel tapped Catlett on the shoulder.

"Come, squire, we ought to be on the move," he said. "We've got a long day's work before us at the shortest, and if that sprig of a Tom would only come on, I'd just form a line and commence the march. Loitering ain't going to be the thing to-day."

"Are the wagons ready for the poor devils on foot, Jenkins the drummer, and the whisky?"

"All here, and the barrels in," sung out Belcher.

"Let's be off, then," said Catlett, "Tom can chase us with his Arabian high-flyer. I wouldn't wait another minute."

"Beat the muster-call, Tim," said the colonel, and drawing his rusty sword, a relic of the Revolution in old Virginy, which had descended as an heir-loom in the family, and was said to have been the one that Cornwallis surrendered at Yorktown; drawing this famous sword, as he gave orders to the music, he rode off in fine style, in his old regimentals, and the plume of his chapeau, dilapidated by the ravages of time, waved, that is what was left of it, in the wind.

"Bravo!" cried the squire, and there was a universal shout. After forming the line and taking the roll, the colonel made preparations for starting. Filling two wagons with four or five of the poor devils on foot, as he significantly called them, with a barrel of whisky in each wagon, he placed them behind to take the dust. The gents on horseback were marshaled in front, and all being ready, our colonel commanded Jenkins to strike up "Yankee Doodle," and off moved the cavalcade to the scene of conflict. Never was there a more determined set of men. Col. Joe did not inventory himself a penny below Cæsar or Napoleon, as he played his military antics on his charger, with drawn sword, while his noble band, stimulated by the whisky and their own passions, stood ready to back him in any exploit of valor.

Thus, in military glory, rode on this great expedition of all the prairie, with a white skin, including "tag-rag and bob-tail," to attack, as they supposed, a dozen Yankees, but as we, and the valiant leaders know, a Yankee and a half.

Let not the reader suppose that, ludicrous as the whole project thus far appears, there may not be some sad work before it is completed. This reckless, half tipsy gang will hardly return to their homes until mischief is accomplished; and if among them all there be found a heart with some kindly sympathies remaining, it may find cause before night to beat with sorrow and shame, for the cowardly deeds that are done. Methinks I see grinning devils hovering over those whisky barrels, giving each other, now and then, a chuck in the ribs, and writhing and twisting about with suppressed laughter, while the image of a death's head seems to play along the line of the cavalcade.

Crossing the ferry, a few miles from Belcher's, on they moved with bluster, and fume, and swell, and oaths, and whisky, through the quiet and peaceful fields of Kanzas, toward Catlett's claim. Tom Walton came galloping up to them in an hour's time, crying out—

"No you don't; I would n't miss being in this fray for any money whatever." Tom knew the strength of the foe.

What this party said during the hours which elapsed till they arrived within half a mile of the claim, is of no kind of consequence to any mortal man, nor is it in any degree essential to our history. Indeed, one good at guessing could not get far out of the way, were he to trust to his guess. We hasten on our narrative, then, to this very spot.

Excited by drinking, and frantic with the rage of their fierce words, up rode the party to their work, which neither Catlett, Dave, Turner, nor Tom had expected to be such as it proved to be. They hoped to frighten the Yankee off the premises, and take quiet possession without violence.

"Attention the whole!" cried the colonel; "halt! Yonder comes somebody quite a distance off. We must surround him, and take him prisoner. Understand? Don't a man of you fire. Surround him. That's it, ain't it, Catlett."

"To be sure. Perhaps it's one of the gang, and we can get something out of him. Move ahead, Turner. Do you hear?"

"Forward," said the colonel. "Jenkins, no music."

They moved on in silence.

The individual whom the colonel's sharp eyes had first descried, was walking leisurely along, and for some time did not appear to notice them. The place of meeting was an open prairie, with a little slope of woods on one side, and there seemed no retreat except by clear swiftness of foot against twenty good horses. The man, however, apparently meditated nothing of the sort, but closing his jack-knife, and throwing down a bit of wood he was whittling, he arranged his gun a little more firmly upon his shoulder, and marched boldly forward to meet them.

"Ho, there you are! The very chap we are after. You abolition Yankee, what are you about here?"

"Going on my own business, with no desire to interfere with yours. So let me pass."

"No you don't. Come, just take down your weapon. It's no use, you see. There's thirty of us at least. We've got a little matter to settle with you this fine morning, and if you give us any of your impudence, we'll make mince-meat of you. Boys, here's the very fellow that tore down the claim. Surround your prisoner."

The drunken squad, with oaths and curses aimed at the luckless man, obeyed orders.

"Now, give me that gun."

He allowed himself to be disarmed, for resistance with the present odds against him, would have been sheer madness.

"Now," said Catlett, stepping forward, "you are on my claim. You remember the squabble we had here, about a week ago. I told you then I'd bring you to terms. Now jest look here. I want you to promise to leave these parts, bag and baggage, before sundown to-night. Do you hear? I ain't jokin, neither. If you can do it quiet, why well and good. I don't want a row about it. If you can't, there are them to back me who would n't mind beating you to a jelly, and stringing you up like an acorn on yonder tree. Will you go?"

"My family are here for the winter, and I can not go," said the man, firmly.

"But don't you see that we can *make* you go, you infernal, obstinate Yankee?"

"You can murder me in cold blood," was the reply— and it was given in as steady a voice as though the speaker had twenty stout men, instead of his single arm, to back it—"but I will never consent to be driven off my own land by a set of lawless drunken ruffians."

"Do you hear that?" "Have at the rascal!" "Stop his impudence!" "Pitch into him, boys!" "We'll teach him!" These exclamations, mingled with oaths and curses, were heard on every side, and the crowd pushing forward, pressed close upon the prisoner.

"Hold on, boys! Keep off, can't you?" cried Catlett. "Stop 'em, Turner, they'll finish the fellow!"

It was too late. On some fancied provocation, Tim Jenkins, the drummer, hit the man with his drum-stick, and received a blow in return that leveled him to the earth. This was the signal for a general *mêlée*. They sprang upon him, striking him with the butt ends of their guns and pistols, pounding, kicking, and battering him in the most brutal manner. Blood flowed freely, and the sight of it seemed only to rouse them to fresh fury. "Make a clean job of it!" cried one in the crowd. "Put him through! Stop the devil's mouth!" At length some one plunged a bowie-knife in the victim's side, and the job seeming to be finished, the rest desisted from their labor. Both Catlett and Turner failed in all efforts to control the mob. Drunk and furious, they disobeyed orders; and then rushed to the whisky barrels, and betook themselves to the liquor.

"That's carrying it a little too far, Catlett," said Turner. "The poor fellow's done for, sure."

"No, no, there's life in him yet. Don't you see he breathes. What in thunder shall we do with him? Does any body know where his cabin is?"

"It's right down yonder slope," said one. "Don't you see the smoke above the trees?"

"Take hold, then, some of you," and two or three of the

men taking up the senseless body of their victim, bore him down the slope to his cabin, Catlett and Turner leading the way.

. His wife met them at the door. She held an infant in her arms, while two or three rosy children clung to her skirts, and peered shyly out at the strangers. The poor woman uttered a single exclamation of grief and horror, as the body of her husband was thrown down at her feet, and then kneeling beside him, she laid his head tenderly in her lap, wiping the blood from his face, and striving with her apron to stanch his bleeding wounds. As her hot .tears rained upon his face, the dying man opened his eyes.

"O, John, speak to me!" she cried. "Who has used you so? Can nothing be done?"

He shook his head feebly, and then raising himself for a last effort, exclaimed, "They murdered me like cowards!" and sinking back in her arms, immediately expired.

For a moment there was perfect stillness in the room. Even the hardened ruffians, who with oaths, and laughter, and drunken jests, had borne the murdered man to his own hearth-stone, were suddenly sobered, and with half-ashamed faces, peered in at the doorway, while Catlett and Turner in the foreground, surveyed with looks of real compassion the widow of their victim. Save the first glance of eager inquiry on their entrance, she had taken no notice of them, bestowing her whole attention upon her dying husband. Now, however, laying his head gently upon the floor, she rose and stood before them. She was a little woman, pale and meek-eyed, but there . was something almost majestic in her manner, as she faced them at this moment.

."What are you waiting for?" she exclaimed fiercely. "Do you want to feast your eyes over the misery you have caused? Well, take your fill, and then go back and tell yonder gang how the widow raved and groaned, and the little children cried over their dead father. It's a noble thing you men have been doing to-day, is n't it? Go back to your homes to-night, and when your wife sits by your fireside, and your children clamber on your knees, tell them how you have made one hearth desolate, a wife a widow, and four little ones fatherless. Look at him! You 've nothing to fear from him now. Come and take possession of his lands, nobody will hinder you—but mark me, they 'll never bring you any good, for the curse of the widow and the orphan will rest on them. Yes, I call God to witness, that I would rather be he that lies there stark and dead, than the man, whoever he is, that has bought this land at the price of his blood! You do well to cry, poor brat, the Lord only knows what will become of us."

"For heaven's sake come away, Turner, I can't stand this nohow," said Catlett.

"Now then, where 's the rest of 'em? Show us the Yankees. It takes us to do the business!" cried the crowd, as their leaders returned. "What 's the next word of command, captain?"

"Home!" said Catlett, gruffly. "You 've done full enough work for one day. Hang it, Turner, that woman's curses ring in my ears yet."

With shouts, and roars, and ribald jokes, the drunken mob returned to La Belle Prairie, but the instigators of the invasion were not quite so exultant over the victory as they had anticipated.

The still hours of the morning of the holy Sabbath had come, before Colonel Turner disbanded his troop.

CHAPTER XIII.

SUNDAY was a great day at La Belle Prairie. Mrs. Catlett liked it, because the house servants did their work better and quicker on that day than any other, in order to be released the sooner, and in consequence there was less scolding and fretting to be done. Nanny and 'Ria liked it, because pa and Dave were most sure to bring some gentlemen home to dine, and Mr. Turner or Mr. Mack occasionally rode home from church with the young ladies themselves. The children liked it, because on that day there was no school; they were dressed in their best frocks, and had cake or pie at dinner—an unusual thing during the week.

But better than all the rest, the servants liked this day of rest, for, with the exception of the house servants, they were entirely released from work, and had the whole day at their own disposal. Three or four of the women had husbands belonging on neighboring farms, and these came regularly on Saturday night to spend Sunday with their wives and children, often bringing with them some article of furniture they had fashioned with their own hands, after work hours, for the adornment of the cabin, or a bright ribbon or a new turban, bought with money earned after their regular day's work was over. These last were displayed with great pride the next day at meetin', for with one or two exceptions, they all attended a religious service held in a neighboring grove, where Uncle Cæsar, a venerable old negro on Massa Turner's place, officiated as preacher.

This once over, however, all religious observance of the day was at an end, and while the men with all the loose change in their pockets that they could muster, went over the prairie to the store, or down the creek to Cartersville, at both which places whisky could be procured, the women spent the afternoon in visiting, or in sunning themselves at the door of their cabins.

Occasionally a little group gathered round Aunt Phebe's chair to hear her earnest exhortations, for she was always ready to talk if any would listen, and even sometimes had been known to preach a sermon to an imaginary audience of her own. Many a good discourse had she given her fellow-servants, sitting in her arm-chair at the cabin door; "Uncle Cæsar himself could n't lay it off better," they declared; but notwithstanding the love and respect they all bore to Aunt Phebe, one meeting a day was quite as much as they could bear, and they generally preferred to stroll off to some neighboring farm, to talk over the news, and display some new article of finery, or rest themselves at home.

So Aunt Phebe was usually left alone in her arm-chair, and with her eyes half closed and an expression of perfect content resting upon her shining black face, she would spend the day in the happiest manner. Occasionally she would break forth into one of the camp-meeting hymns she so delighted to sing, and pause between the verses, to meditate upon the glories therein described, often sinking back in a kind of silent ecstasy, when, as she declared, it was all glory! glory! One hymn in particular, commencing, "Is there any body here agoin' my way," that in fif

teen or twenty-stanzas, follows the Christian pilgrim
through all the difficulties and dangers of his path, and
finally lands him safe on Canaan's shore, was her favorite
Sunday hymn.   She would sing it to its close, and by the
time she reached the last stanza, where, after struggling
long in the "dark river," he is led up the bank by "spirits robed in white," her soul would be filled with rapture,
and with her hands clasped and the tears streaming down
her cheeks, she would sing:

> "O bless de Lord, I 's got my crown,
> > Sing, Glory, Halleluyah!
> I 'll shout among de angels, Halleluyah!
> I 'll shout among de angels, Halleluyah!"

Such seasons Aunt Phebe dwelt upon afterward, with
great pleasure.   "I 's had a meetin' all to myse'f, chil'en,"
she would say, "me and de Lord.   O it 's jest a little taste
ob what 's to come!"

When the shadows lay long on the grass, in little com-
panies of twos and threes, the men came straggling home.
Their uncertain gait, their loud voices, and rude laughter,
their whole demeanor, so different from their usual quiet
submissive bearing, all told of the day's carousal.   With
empty pockets, and full heads, most of them returned to
the scene of their weekly toil.   Sunday was emphatically
their day.   Mr. Catlett had nothing to do with his hands
on the Sabbath, and whether they spent it in beastly intoxi-
cation, or in order to earn a few bits for themselves, hired
out to some neighboring farmer—for there are men wicked
enough to tempt the poor slave to labor on the Lord's
day—it was no concern of his.   Only in one particular did
he exercise his authority.   It was frequently the case that
under the influence of the whisky they drank, the men
became exceedingly quarrelsome, and a fight in the yard

was not an unusual event on a Sunday night. This would not answer, for their fighting, unlike their work, was not done by halves, and Mr. Catlett would find, perhaps, on Monday morning, one or two of his best hands missing, and on inquiry would ascertain that they were laid up in consequence of last night's pummeling. All fighting was accordingly forbidden on the place, and when the order was disobeyed, Mr. Catlett or Dave would step out, and mark the offenders, who received their punishment the next morning.

Mr. Catlett prided himself on being a very lenient master. His men had full liberty to drink whisky to any extent, provided they could find the wherewith to obtain it. They might curse and blaspheme in his presence without reproof, or indulge in any kind of wickedness that did not interfere with his profit; but when any indulgence unfitted them for his service, this was quite another thing, and must be attended to at once.

So passed Sunday at the quarters.

"Ebery one ob yer get up," was Viny's usual salutation to the sleepers up stairs, on a Sunday morning. "Dar's heaps to do afore meetin' time. Better be 'bout it, I reckon."

"O Viny, is it Sunday sure enough?" says one. "Does the sun shine, and can we go to church?" says another; while even little Johnny rejoiced in its being "preaching day," because he could "ride along with pa on Prince."

If Viny ever fretted, or lost her temper at any thing, Sunday morning would be the time; for what with running hither and thither, curling Nanny's hair, hooking 'Ria's tight gowns, and tying the children's shoe-strings, no chambermaid in a steamboat, in a storm, ever had a harder time to wait on her charge. But Viny's patience was inexhaustible. She took her own time for every thing, and while half a dozen voices were calling her in as many different directions, she kept coolly on with what she was about, laughed, till her gums were visible, at Miss Nanny's scoldings, pinched 'Ria's fat neck as she fastened her dress, and good naturedly received all the kicks Johnny chose to bestow, because his new boots happened to pinch his toes.

Below, Mr. Catlett got out the six-inch mirror, the largest the house contained, and commenced taking off his week's growth of beard, this being a lengthy operation, for which he could better spare the time on Sunday morning than any other, while Mrs. Catlett lounged about, superintending the arrangements for an early breakfast.

This over, the horses are geared, and preparations made for starting for church. First, the big wagon, drawn' by two of the steadiest farm-horses, drives up to the door, and into this the children clamber, a black boy, with his hat set jauntily on one side of his head, and rejoicing in numberless little tails of braided wool, acting as driver. This once off, at a good steady jog, the horses, one by one, are led up to the horse-block, Dave assisting Nanny, 'Ria, and Joy to mount; and springing upon his own beautiful gray, they all canter slowly down the lane.

Down the lane, and across the prairie, with its long grass waving in the wind, into the still woods, under the shade of the maples and oaks, past one or two clearings, where the monarchs of the wood have been lately laid low, and the ground is yet black and dry from the effects of the fire, along a path that leads up the side of Oak hill, and finally brings them to its summit, where stands La Belle Church. A space had been cleared to make room for the little unobtrusive building that bears this high sounding name. About the door, and under the shade of the trees, stand groups of children and young people, for many a pleasant meeting have they Sunday mornings here; and it is a common saying on the prairie, that more matches are made at La Belle Church than anywhere else. Dismounting at the horse-block, the ladies divest themselves of their long riding skirts, and thick gloves, and join the group under the trees, while up the hill side come the little children on foot, the path being too steep for wagons to ascend.

It was fashionable to attend church at La Belle Prairie. A colony of families, who twelve years before moved from a town near Richmond, Virginia, brought with them their church-going habits, and in the course of a year or two, organized a church, and built a place of worship. Though not as wealthy as many of the old settlers, they were influential people in their way, and before long it became quite the custom to attend church on the Sabbath. This practice did not in the least interfere with the dinner parties which were given on that day, for as but one service was held, and this in the morning, it was very convenient to ride immediately home from church with a few friends to dinner, and to spend the afternoon in chatting with the young gentlemen, in talking politics, or in rambling over each other's farms, to witness the progress of the crops.

There was no bell upon the church, and indeed none was necessary, for the people well understood that when the preacher came it was time to commence, and no sooner did his shaggy sorrel colt appear ascending the hill, than there was a general rush for the door, and by the time he entered, the people were mostly in their seats.

"John Carlton the preacher," as he was usually called, was born and brought up on the prairie. His father died while he was yet a boy, leaving him possessed of a large property, and a spirit as wild and untamable as ever brought grief to a parent's heart. For many years he

was known as the worst young fellow in a very bad neighborhood, a sort of ring-leader in every drinking frolic,
gambling scrape, and horse-race. His way of life broke
his mother's heart, and her last breath was spent in entreating him to repent, and become a better man. Though
for a time her death appeared to produce no effect, except
to make him if possible more wild and reckless than before ;
yet her earnest prayers were answered at last. Singularly
enough, he received his first religious impressions at the
theater, passed through days and weeks of agonizing conviction, and finally found peace in believing. He had received a college education, and instantly resolved to de-
vote himself to the work of the ministry, and return and
labor among his old companions.

So here in the little church on the hill he ministered
from Sabbath to Sabbath, and during the week traveled
miles and miles into the country, preaching in groves, and
log-houses, and wherever he could find people to hear.
And those who heard John Carlton once, were very apt
to come again. There was an earnestness and power
about his preaching, rude and uncultivated though it was,
that found its way to the heart. Nor was it strange, for
with his whole soul in the work, he preached what he
believed, and preached it so earnestly, that his hearers
for the time being were constrained to believe it too.
He seemed like one who, just escaped from some imminent
peril, endeavors by warnings and entreaties, to save his
friends and neighbors from a like danger. "He has a
way of pilin' up the horrors," said Catlett, "that makes a
feller crawl all over." The earnestness of his gestures
went far toward fixing the attention of his hearers. Tall
and sallow, his black hair already tinged with gray, and
his eye so sharp and piercing that you involuntarily
dropped your own before it; he was a striking figure in

the pulpit, and when roused with his subject, his words came thick and fast, and he threw his arms wildly about; there were times when women fainted and strong men sobbed aloud.

To-day his subject was "Remorse," and as he thus described its workings in the sinner's soul, it was observed that Jack Catlett gave more than ordinary attention:

"Look at the last hours of such a man. Health, reputation, character, all buried in a grave of his own digging, an old man before his prime, with a worn-out body and a ruined soul, wearied and disgusted with the world, and having drained the cup of sin to its very dregs, he has filled up the full measure of his iniquities, and lays himself down to die. Then Remorse seizes its victim. Not for the first time. No sinner, I care not how reckless he may be, or how seared as with a red-hot iron his conscience has become, but feels at times the gnawings of that worm that shall torment him through all eternity. There are moments when he *must* think, when the tormentor within will not remain torpid, and when in the midst of his revelry and drunkenness, he shudders and turns pale, as he feels it struggling and writhing in his bosom.

"He may plunge deeper into dissipation. He may pour down draught after draught of liquid fire, he may smother it in worldliness, or stupefy it by drunkenness, but it will not die. It lies there coiled up in his very heart, growing stronger every day, while he piles up sin upon sin, sin upon sin, for it to feed upon through endless ages. There was a way by which it might have been destroyed. The blood of Christ alone could take away its sting; but this he has trampled under foot; he has crucified his Saviour, he has blasphemed his God, and hell has already commenced in his wretched soul.

"His bosom-fiend rouses itself to full activity. He feels

its slimy folds, drawing closer and closer round his heart; and its sharp fangs quickly eating through the crust of pride and self-confidence with which he has enfolded it, are now tearing away at the very vitals. His body is all weakness and pain, but his soul is strong to suffer, mighty to endure. His neglected powers of mind, all aid in his torture. Memory recalls the days of his childhood; his first open sin, his neglect of his pious mother's prayers and entreaties, his misspent hours, his broken Sabbaths, his oaths and blasphemies against his God, all rise up in judgment against him. The still small voice of Conscience, long silenced but not dead, whispers its reproaches, reminds him of its faithful warnings, its unheeded pricks, and when in his agony he cries out that his punishment is greater than he can bear, Reason tells him that it is *just*. If Hope dare to whisper of pardoning mercy, it is silenced by the groanings of Despair. Too late! too late! He believes nothing, he hopes nothing. It is all horror and blackness to look back, and he dare not look forward. He loathes his own being, longs for death and fears to die.

"And he feels the worm tugging at his heart. There is a burning within, like a slow consuming fire, a sudden darting anguish as some hidden spot is laid bleeding and bare, and a continual tearing, grinding pain, as it eats its way deeper into his-being. No rest night or day. In weary tossings from side to side, his hours are passed, or if he falls into a troubled sleep, he wakes with the drops of anguish on his brow, and cries out, 'It gnaws me! It gnaws me!'

"O! is there no respite for the racked and tortured soul? Will the worm never cease to writhe, and twist, and gnaw within? A voice replies to his agonized cry— Never! Nature may sink under the torture. The body may perish, but that which suffers most is immortal, and

can not die. The wretch in the last extremity of guilt
and despair, may seek the suicide's grave! he may blow
himself to atoms, or bury his carcase in the depths of the
sea, he can not escape the fiend in his bosom, or the anger
of an insulted God. No need of sulphurous lake, or pit
of flaming fire; let but the sinner feel through the ages of
eternity, the burning, cankering, gnawing horrors of remorse, and it will be hell enough for the devil himself—
' For their worm dieth not, and their fire is not quenched.'

"Do you say that I have overdrawn the picture; that
God is too merciful ever to let a sinner perish so miserably.
I tell you that unless ye repent, ye shall all likewise perish.
You, young man—and *you*—and *you*. Let us pray."

The various postures assumed by the congregation at
La Belle church, would shock the nerves of a city audience.
Every man chose the free and easy posture that pleased
him best, stretching himself out at full length; elevating
his heels to the back of the next seat, or sitting upon the
back itself, and resting his lower extremities in his neighbor's lap. Here and there sat an attentive listener, but as
a general thing the air of listlessness and indifference upon
most of their faces, presented a strange contrast to the
earnestness of the preacher. Now and then a baby
squalled, or an urchin " talked out in meetin'," but such
occurrences attract little attention in a church " out west,"
where all the women bring their little ones, whose ac-
knowledged right it is to make as much noise as they
please.

At last the service is over, and the minister passing
slowly down the aisle, shakes hands with the old people;
speaks a pleasant word to the young girls, and pats the
little children on the head; then finding his sorrel colt
ready for him at the door—for John Carlton is a great
favorite with the young men, and there are plenty to do

this little service for him—he mounts and picks his way down the hill.

Now comes the most exciting moment to the young ladies, for while the old folks are exchanging scraps of gossip and invitations to dinner, the young men select the ladies of their choice, and request permission to escort them home. There are the same heart flutterings, and petty triumphs, and jealousies here in this wild spot, as in the busy walks of city life, only conducted upon a smaller scale, and concealed with less art. At length the decisions are all made, group after group depart, their voices grow fainter as they descend the slope, and presently the little church on Oak Hill is silent and deserted.

"There, Mr. Catlett, see that, will you?" said his wife, turning half round in her saddle to get a better view herself.

"See what? Mr. Tom Walton ridin' home with the teacher, and our Nanny taggin' on behind?" said her husband.

"No, no. Don't you see Dave waitin' on Boss Gamby? I always *did* think Dave was smart."

"Well, I don't see how he shows his smartness by pick in' out the ugliest-lookin' girl on the prairie."

"How stupid you are, Mr. Catlett. I'm sure she looks well enough. A little 'dutchy,' mebbe, but that's nothing. I tell you what, it would be the luckiest thing we ever did do, takin' those girls into school, if *something should happen.*"

"The Lord preserve us! if the women ain't hatchin' up a plot. You and Madam Gamby have been puttin' your wise heads together, I reckon, and have got it all cut and dried."

"Well, you may laugh, Mr. Catlett, but I tell you Dave could n't do a better thing for himself, and it's my opinion he sees it too."

"She's as ugly as thunder," said Mr. Catlett, "and as dull as my old jack-knife."

"She'll own as pretty a piece of land as there is on the prairie, and a dozen good hands to work it," said his wife.

"Hang the land!" rejoined Mr. Catlett. "A man may have too much of that for his peace of mind."

CHAPTER XIV.

AN INTERLUDE.

ONE evening, a few weeks after Fanny's introduction to Mr. Catlett's family, three persons were seated in the back parlor of an elegant mansion on ———— street, St. Louis, occupied by Judge Stanton of that city.

One of these persons was the judge himself, a middle-aged gentleman of commanding appearance, who, seated at the table with pencil in hand, and a small outline map before him, was pointing out various localities with great minuteness to a gentleman looking over his shoulder.

A young lady, dressed in the height of the fashion, was seated opposite, engaged in some fancy work, that displayed the whiteness of her hands to great advantage. She was a showy genteel-looking girl, with dark eyes, and a quantity of luxuriant hair, arranged in heavy braids about her well-formed head.

"And so you are really going to that barbarous place, Mr. Chester," she said, as soon as a pause occurred in the conversation between the two gentlemen. "It's too bad of you, to run off in the height of the season, when our circle is so small, and we can not afford to lose one."

The young man looked up.

"You flatter me," he said with a smile. "I fancy the vacancy I shall leave will be easily filled. Besides, I don't

intend to exile myself for any length of time. Two or
three weeks at furthest will finish up this complicated business, and that ended, I shall turn my face homeward with
a right good will."

"Ah, but two or, three weeks 'up the country' Mr.
Chester! You have n't the least idea how wearily they
will 'drag their slow length along.' I forewarn you that
you will nearly perish with the cold, besides half dying
with *ennui*. O, I don't know what would tempt me to
spend two or three weeks at cousin Jack's in the month
of November."

"Nonsense, Julia," said the judge, "you talk as though
we were sending Mr. Chester among barbarians, and not
to our own kith and kin. Cousin Caroline will give him
a good Virginia welcome, and make him as comfortable
as she can, and if his quarters are not quite as snug as his
bachelor establishment in town, it won't hurt him. When
I was in my prime as you are, Harry Chester, I spent
many a night on the open prairies of Missouri, and felt
the better for it, too."

The young man smiled.

"I have been tossed about enough for the last ten or
fifteen years, sir," he said, "to know a little of the rough-
and-tumble of life, but I anticipate nothing unpleasant in
your cousin's family, except my own reluctance as a
stranger to trespass so long upon their hospitality."

"Pooh! pooh! Have n't you seen enough of a Virginia gentleman to know that you can not do him a
greater kindness than by becoming his guest? Why, you
might stay a year at Cousin Jack's, and not wear out
your welcome. There's always room in that house for
one more, and when they ask you to come again, they
mean it. It will be a work of charity to go."

"Papa is right, there," said the young lady. "Any

thing to break up the dreadful monotony of such a life as, they lead, must indeed be a blessing. Your visit will give cousin Nanny something to talk about for an indefinite period of time to come. A real live beau from town will be quite an event on the prairie. By-the-way, Mr. Chester, I beg you won't be led captive by the charms of my sweet unsophisticated country cousin." This was said with the least bit of irony in the tone.

"Never fear, Julia," said the judge, "Mr. Chester is too great a favorite with you city tulips, to waste his ammunition on a simple prairie flower—hey, Harry?"

"Well, sir, I shall endeavor to withstand the temptation in either case, provided there is any occasion. The law is my only mistress at present, and demands such devoted attention as to leave me little time, even if I had the disposition, to seek another."

"Just hear him, papa. Was ever any thing so coolly spoken. To tell a lady to her face that he prefers those dry, stupid law books to the delights of female society. He deserves just what he is going to get, complete banishment."

"Spare me, I beg," said Mr. Chester, with uplifted hands. "I intended no such dreadful inference, or if my unfortunate remark must be so construed, I appeal to the judge to say whether my frequent visits here do not prove that my practice does not agree with my profession."

The judge laughingly assented, and the young lady blushed.

"Now, then, let us have some music, and send this gentleman home," said the judge. "You have a long ride before you reach La Belle Prairie, Harry."

"Papa," inquired Miss Julia, throwing herself upon the sofa after the visitor had departed, "do you know anything about Harry Chester's early history? He spoke to-night as though he had seen hard times."

"Well, I suppose he has," said the judge. "Any man who makes himself, has a hard time of it, but all the more credit to him if he gets to the top of the ladder. Harry Chester began at the first round, and if he goes on as he has commenced, there 's no telling where he will stop."

"He seems to be a great favorite of yours, papa. Did he tell you all this himself?"

"Not he. He has too much good sense to intrude his private concerns upon other people. Squire Patsley, of Philadelphia, told me about the young man when he first came to St. Louis three years ago. It seems he was brought up to expect a fortune from an old gentleman, who adopted him when he was quite a boy, but just after he entered college the old fellow died without a will, and the whole of it went to half a dozen nieces or some other relations. How he managed to get through college, or study his profession, I don't know, but he did do it, and has as fair a practice now as any young lawyer in the city. These are the kind of men who make something."

"Well, I don't see why you must send him 'way up the country, papa, to collect. debts and what not. If he is such a nice young man we want to keep him here."

"Because he can attend to the business just as well as I can, and see to that case in court at —— at the same time. A good clear head for business he has too," said the judge. "I liked the way he took hold of that case. A promising young man! a very promising young man!"

CHAPTER XV.

CROSSING THE RUBICON.

LA BELLE CREEK, was the name of a small stream, which winding through the patch of low marshy ground skirting the prairie, finally emptied itself into the muddy waters of the Missouri. Its banks were thickly covered with a growth of underbrush, and shaded by trees, that even in winter shut out the full rays of the sun, and when in foliage, cast a dense shadow upon the water beneath. A rude bridge, constructed of logs, crossed the stream at a point where the road led down to its banks, but the frequent freshets had long since carried off its main supports, leaving it impassable except to foot passengers. A tree had also contributed to its destruction, falling directly across it, and crushing one end nearly down to the water's edge.

Upon the seat thus formed, Fanny Hunter reclined one mild day in November, gazing listlessly into the dark water beneath, and now and then lifting her eyes with an expectant glance, to a narrow footpath leading into the thicket on the other side. In her hand she held a bunch of myrtle leaves; their glossy greenness contrasting beautifully with the bright scarlet of a few berries clinging to a withered stem. It was in search of more that Fanny's companion had just left her, pleased with the admiration her teacher expressed at the few, and saying that she knew of " a heap yonder in the thicket. If Miss Fanny would wait a minute on the old bridge she would fetch them directly."

They had taken a long ramble since four o'clock, and Fanny was but too glad to rest a few moments before starting for home. But moment after moment passed, and Maud did not return. The sun had set, and the shadows between the trees grew blacker and blacker. The solitude of the place was oppressive. Fanny began to grow nervous, and called aloud to her companion. There was no answer. She heard "big William" on the prairie, calling home the cattle to the milking, and the distant whirring of a flock of partridges, but this was all.

To add to her alarm, the sound of a horse's hoofs a moment after struck her ear, apparently coming down the road leading to the creek. Fanny knew that this road had fallen entirely into disuse, the bridge being broken, and the stream impassable at this point. A moment's reflection dispersed her fears. "It's only big William hunting up the cattle," she thought to herself. "He will take the path to the thicket, and not see me at all if I sit still." The horseman, however, seemed to have no such intention, for he appeared a moment after at the summit of the hill, and began slowly to descend. Checking his horse on observing the ruined condition of the bridge, he gazed round him with an air of doubt and perplexity.

By the dim light now fading fast away Fanny could not distinguish the stranger's features, but his form was erect, and youthful, and his general appearance that of a gentleman. Wondering whether she was observed, she sat perfectly quiet, until after a moment's hesitation, he resumed the descent, having apparently made up his mind to ford the stream at all hazards, though its angry appearance, and the swiftness of the current, ought to have convinced him that it was impracticable.

His reluctant steed had taken the first step into the water, and his master was endeavoring to urge him forward, when a voice close by exclaimed,

"You can't cross here, sir. The ford is further up the stream."

The stranger looked up with a start, and beheld a slight, childish figure, wrapped in a dark hood and mantle, perched upon the old bridge, nearly above his head.

"You must turn back," said the soft voice again, "the current here is too rapid."

"And who are you, little one," said the stranger, "set here to warn belated travelers of the dangers of the way?"

"No matter who I am," said Fanny, "it's your business to take my advice and turn back."

"But where am I to go?" said the young man, in a perplexed tone. "I must cross the creek somewhere to-night, and one place is as bad as another, I suppose."

"O, no, there is a crossing a little way up the stream, where the water is quite shallow," said Fanny.

"Ah, well, that will do; but how shall I find it, my good girl?"

"Good girl, indeed!" thought Fanny. "What does the man take me to be?"

"I don't know that I can tell you exactly," she said, after a moment's hesitation. "It's a little below the bend, I think—no, I'm wrong, it's above."

"Do you know the place?"

"Perfectly well."

"Come, then, you have proved too good a friend thus far, to leave me in the lurch now. If it isn't too far, suppose you guide me to the crossing, unless your friends will feel anxious about you," he added. "It is late for little ones like you to be out."

"I must be remarkably youthful in my appearance to-night," thought Fanny, greatly amused at her adventure. "Well, shall I go with him? One thing is certain, I'm safe enough while I keep the creek between us."

"Ah, well, never mind," said the stranger, construing her silence into reluctance. "I presume I can find it myself. Many thanks for your timely warning."

"I will show you the way, sir," said Fanny. "Keep close to the bank, and I will walk along on this side of the creek, till we come to the crossing."

"You are shy," said the young man; "well, have it your own way." So saying he turned his horse's head, and Fanny descending from her elevated seat, they commenced their walk.

It was a short one, but she had ample time to plan her escape, for she had no desire to encounter the stranger's closer observation. Accordingly, after indicating the precise spot where he was to cross, she turned and fled with such rapid steps, as to be entirely hidden in the darkness, before the young man discovered her absence.

She found Maud waiting for her at the bridge, and only pausing a moment to relate their adventures, they hurried toward home, Fanny requesting her companion not to speak of this meeting unless questioned respecting it. She thought it probable that the stranger she had just aided, was the same Mr. Chester who was expected from St. Louis, and whose visit Nanny had talked about every day for a week.

"We won't let him know, Maud, if we can help it, that it was I who assisted him on his journey; and if we can only get there first, and be sitting by the fire with our bonnets and shawls off, he will never suspect us."

So saying, Fanny hastened on, and taking a short cut across the plowed ground, they reached the house just as Martha was bringing in the first plate of batter-cakes from tho kitchen. Throwing off her bonnet and shawl, Fanny seated herself at the table, and was quietly sipping her coffee, when a loud barking of the dogs, followed by a knock at the door, announced an arrival.

"It's Bob Turner," said Nanny, smoothing her collar, and arranging her hair.

"No it ain't; he's gone to Cartersville," said Dave.

"Well, run to the door, David," said Mrs. Catlett, "and Marthy, wipe the 'lasses off of Johnny's face. Goodness! what a looking table."

In the midst of the confusion that followed, the visitor entered, and Fanny recognized at a glance the hero of her adventure. Advancing with a free and gentlemanly air, he introduced himself as Mr. Chester, of St. Louis, and receiving a cordial welcome from the family, in five minutes was seated with them at the table. He made himself at home directly, adopting, as Fanny thought with great tact, the frank, jovial manner most pleasing to western people, and well calculated to remove any restraint his presence might have inspired.

In the course of the evening, he related his adventure at the bridge, laughingly describing Fanny as some wood-nymph, or spirit, who, after guiding him through the danger, sank into the ground, or suddenly disappeared in some equally mysterious way.

"She did you a good service, whoever she was," said Dave. "There's a mighty deep hole just under the bridge, and the current sweeps round it like a whirlpool. It's a plaguy dangerous place, anyhow."

"I can't think who it could be," said Miss Nanny. "There's Milly Turner; she lives just over the creek; but they are mighty choice of her, and wouldn't let her be out after night for any thing. Besides, she's a dread ful timid child herself. Do you remember what she looked like, or how she was dressed, Mr. Chester?"

"Not in the least. I only know a little thing hailed me from the top of the bridge, in a voice as low and soft as a silver bell, guided me safe to the landing, flitting through the woods among the trees like a fairy as she was, and when I looked to behold her, lo! she had vanished into thin air."

"Mebbe 't was a spirit," said Maud, with wide open eyes. "There was a man drowned in the creek once, and Aunt Tibby says his ghost comes and walks there nights."

"Nonsense, Maud," said Nanny.

"Well, I don't car', Aunt Tibby and Uncle Jake saw him one night, when they was comin' home from corn-shuckin'. He had a great club in his hand, and something white over his head."

"Yes," said Dave, "a great ghost that. Some thievish nigger comin' home from corn-stealin'."

"Mine was no bad spirit," said Mr. Chester; "of that I am convinced. Its mission was to warn me of hidden dangers, and guide me into safe paths. I should like just such a guardian angel all my life."

"Well, it's a wonder to me who it could be," said Mrs. Catlett.

"So let it remain," said the young man; "I hardly want the mystery explained. I am going to amuse myself by thinking that a new era has dawned upon me, and that henceforth I am to be attended in all my wanderings by the little fairy sprite, who is only to make herself visible in times of great peril and distress."

"Now, Miss Fanny," said Nanny, after the visitor had retired for the night, "we shall have somebody to wait on us to church besides Dave. A town gentleman, too, fixed up in his kid gloves and gold chain. Sha'n't we feel crank?

Somehow town gentlemen appear so different from any body round here. What's the reason, ma?"

"It's 'cause they are so fixy, Nan," said Maria, "that's all. You and Belle Boynton now will be pullin' caps for the city beau; but I don't see why he's any better than Tom Walton or Bob Turner."

"They are all a set of monkeys," said "Massa Dave," scornfully, "jingling their watch-chains and talking nonsense to the girls. It's about all they're good for, in the long run."

"Dave is put out 'cause the town gentleman is so much better lookin' than he is," said Cal. "He's afraid Miss Fanny will like him best."

"Shut up," said her brother, in no very gentle tone. "You children talk too much."

"He *is* mighty good-looking," said Nanny, "and not a bit stuck up for all he was dressed so fine. I felt kinder afraid of him at first; but, lor, he was just as easy as any of us, and hitched his chair up to the fire like he was at home. I reckon we shall have grand times Christmas."

CHAPTER XVI.

"Do you ride to-day, Mr. Chester?" inquired Dave the next morning at breakfast.

"Yes, the court meets at ——. I must be off directly, for it's quite a ride. Some ten or fifteen miles, I believe."

"Well, I'll go along as far as the store, I reckon; Marthy, go tell Jake to gear the horses."

It was a bright, clear morning, and Fanny stood in the open doorway after the gentlemen had gone, admiring the winter landscape spread out before her. Directly in front, lay the open prairie, its brown surface spotted here and there with groups of cattle turned out every day to pick up what nourishment they could from its dry and scanty grass. On one side, the windings of the creek could be traced, by the row of tall trees that skirted its banks, and on the other, a picturesque-looking log-house, the blue smoke curling from its chimney, relieved the monotony of the scene, and gave token of life and activity in this wild spot.

From the wood-lot near the creek, was borne on the still air, each stroke of the hewer's ax; and the bleating of the sheep, and the lowing of the cattle on the prairie, could be distinctly heard. The turkeys, geese, ducks, and guinea-fowls in the yard, kept up a continual clatter, while two or three gaunt hounds lay sunning themselves in the porch and under the eaves of the house. There was something cheerful and invigorating in the scene, and Fanny stood in the doorway till a touch on the arm drew her attention, and, turning round, she perceived black Martha waiting to speak with her.

She was a stout, full-grown mulatto girl, on whose good-looking face a smile was generally to be found, and whose musical voice, singing some camp-meeting hymn, or wild negro melody, Fanny had often heard as she sat in school. Like most of the women, she was indolent and careless, but so perfectly good-humored, that all Mrs. Catlett's scolding failed to disturb her equanimity, and her mistress was often more provoked at the stupid unconcern with which she received her severest reprimands, than she would have been had she given a saucy reply. "Yes, Miss Car'line," Martha would say, submissively, and perhaps repeat the offense five minutes after.

"Well, Martha," said Fanny encouragingly, "what do you want?"

"Tilla done tell me how Miss Fanny pick her up off de star' t' other night. So good an' kind now, won't think no harm if I ask somfin?" said Martha.

"O, no, Martha. What is it?"

"Miss Fanny, it 's Tilla," said Martha with sudden energy. "'Pears like I can't live no ways and see de way dey goes on wid dat child. Miss Car'line say she ain't no 'count; but, Miss Fanny, she 's all I 's got, and to see her jest pinin' away to skin and bone, with nobody to see to her but me, and now they 's goin' to send me off, and she 'll be left all alone. O lors what shall I do?" and Martha covered her face with her apron.

"Going to send you off, Martha? Where?"

"Why, long Mass' Dave, Miss Fanny, over to Kanzas

Aunt Tibby, she hearn 'em talkin' about. it last night, and Uncle Tim, and Jerry, and Aunt Adeline, and me, we's all goin' to be sent. Aunt Adeline, she's glad, 'cause she's Massa Dave's nurse, you know; but how can I leave my poor child, my Tilla."

"Is Tilla your sister, Martha?" said Fanny.

"Yes, Miss Fanny, dar's only us two left. Daddy died wid de fever, and dey sold mammy down river, when Tilla was a little suckin' baby. She put her into my arms, she did, and told me to take car' ob her, and be a mammy to her, and now—"

Martha's voice was broken by her sobs, and the old ragged apron was thrown over her face.

"You see, Miss Fanny," she said at length, "she was allers a little sickly thing—'pears like she neber got over bein' tuck from her mammy; she jest pined and pined; and Miss Car'line she got sot agin her den, and said dar wa'n't no use in tryin' to raise de brat. O, Miss Fanny, I thought heaps of her; an' I neber lef off watchin' and tendin' her, and I prayed de good Lord jest to leave me *her*, and he did; and now dey keeps her workin', and strainin', and toatin' Miss Hetty round, and no rest day nor night; and O Lors how ken I bar' it?"

"Have you told your mistress how sick she is, Martha."

"Have I! Miss Fanny? I's been down on my knees, and jest begged her for de dear Lord's sake, to be good to Tilla. She won't hear to me, 'cause she say Tilla's contrary, and it's all crossness; but O! Miss Fanny, when de body's ailin', 'tain't nat'ral to be allers jest so. Miss Hetty, she's curus times, and Tilla bein' weakly, can't bar' so much as some. She's a growin' weaker all de while, and some day she'll jest lie down an' die, she will!"

"What can I do to help you, Martha?" said Fanny, gently.

"I don'no, Miss Fanny, 'less you could speak to Miss Car'line 'bout it. Mebbe she'd hear to you. You see you might tell her how you see Tilla was weakly like, and not let on dat I'd been jawin' 'bout it. If Miss Fanny *would* speak to ole Missus now?"

She seized Fanny's arm in her eagerness, and awaited her answer, as though her life depended upon it.

"I will, Martha," said Fanny; "I will do the best I can for you."

"O, bless you, Miss Fanny, I knew you would, and—and you'll ask her not to send me to Kanzas with Mass' Dave, and leave my poor child all alone, won't you? Yes, Miss Car'line, I's comin," she called out cheerfully, as her mistress's fretful tones were heard at the door of the breakfast room.

Martha's anxious face haunted Fanny all that day, and she watched for an early opportunity to speak to Mrs. Catlett alone. It was not long before one presented itself. That very evening, as Tilla was tottering across the room under the weight of her young mistress, she was so unfortunate as to encounter Master Johnny under full headway, and not being strong enough to resist the shock, the two fell backward, Miss Hetty bumping her head severely upon the hard floor. Mrs. Catlett was excessively angry, and seizing the trembling culprit, she bestowed upon her what Fanny thought a very heavy punishment for the offense. The child's piteous cries as the blows fell thick and fast upon her bare neck and shoulders, of "O Miss Car'line! O please, Miss Car'line! I did n't go to do it! O, I will be good! O dear! dear!" went to Fanny's heart, and she lingered a moment after the rest retired for the night, to intercede for the poor child.

"Mrs. Catlett," she said, "I want to say a word to you about Tilla. I think the child is sick."

"Do you?" said Mrs. Catlett, laughing. "Well, when you've seen as much of lazy niggers as I have, you'll change your mind."

"But she shows it in her looks," said Fanny. "There's an expression of pain on her face all the time. I am sure she is sick."

"She's no more sick than you are," said Mrs. Catlett. "She's growin' up rather spindlin' to be sure, and those yellow niggers always look ashy."

"But she seems to have no strength," said Fanny.

"No, I reckon not. I never saw any of 'em that did, when there was any work to be done. She had strength enough to fight me awhile ago, when I was whipping her. The good-for-nothing thing! She'll beat the baby's brains out with her carelessness one of these days—mother's precious little darling!" said Mrs. Catlett, with a loving glance toward the cradle.

"It was an accident, Mrs. Catlett," said Fanny, gently. "I saw her when she fell. I believe she would no more harm little Hetty than you would. She seems very fond of her. But I really think she is not strong enough to do much at present."

"Well, I should like to know what she has to do, Miss Fanny, except to mind the baby?"

"Hetty is getting quite large and strong, you know, especially for a sickly child to carry about. I am sure it is hurting her very much."

"I declare, Miss Fanny, one would think we were working the child to death to hear you run on. I 'spose she's been takin' on to you about it, sniveling and frettin'."

"No, Mrs. Catlett, I found her on the stairs the other night, and she seemed so sick and appeared to be in such pain, that it excited my sympathy. I thought, perhaps, with all your cares, you might not have observed her."

"Well, now, Miss Fanny, you see you don't know the first thing about it. It is n't at all with our servants here, as it is with yours in New England. I 'spose there they 'll work as long as they can stand, because they get pay for it, but here its jest drive, drive all the while, to get any thing out of 'em. I 've known 'em to lie by for weeks and weeks, to get rid of work, and they 'd be so cunning and put on so, any body that was n't used to 'em, would think they were ready to step off. Now that Tilla, she 's peart enough when she chooses, but I 'spose she saw you look soft and pitying-like, and so she went to playing off her tantrums. She don't come to *me* with her complaints, she knows better."

"Well, Mrs. Catlett, it does seem to me that there 's no deception in the case. Would n't it be possible to give Tilla a chance to get well, and let one of the other children take her place a little while. Aunt Phebe would nurse her up, and make another child of her."

"Indeed!" said Mrs. Catlett, with sudden energy, "she shall do no such thing. We should have half the servants on the place settin' up to be sick. You had better let these things alone, Miss Fanny. Mr. Catlett never had the name of being hard on his hands, and the great trouble with me is they run right over my head. If you begin to listen to all their complaints, you 'll soon have your hands full, I tell you. Let 'em all alone, that 's my advice."

Fanny turned away with a sigh. It was hard to reply to Martha's anxious inquiring look, the next morning, by a silent shake of the head, and to see poor Tilla day after day plodding wearily under her burden, but there was no help for it, and Fanny by this time knew Mrs. Catlett too well ever to renew the discussion.

CHAPTER XVII.

"MA," said Maria one day, "there's going to be a big meetin' up the creek next Tuesday. Can't we go?"

"Where, child?" said Mrs. Catlett.

"Up the creek, in Mount Zion Church, you know. It's only a little ways, and we want to go."

"Well, you can't. Nobody but poor white folks go to big meetins. There'll be a perfect tribe of 'em there, and I don't want you mixed in with 'em."

"Why, ma, the Turners are all going, and Mr. Boynton's people, and most every body on the prairie. It's right respectable."

"Who told you the Turners are all going, 'Ria?"

"Jinny Turner her ownself, at church to-day. O, ma, do let us go!"

"What! and give up school a whole day, child?"

"O! Miss Fanny won't mind jest for one day. We haven't had a holiday this long time back."

"Well, how are you going to get there, and who'll take care of you all day. Dave can't go; he's got to pack up that tobacco."

"Nanny says she'll go, and I reckon Miss Fanny will too. Mr. Chester, the town gentleman, would, only he's so busy with his law business. But, ma, if you will let big William drive us over the creek in the farm wagon, we can walk the rest of the way jest as easy as not, and then he can come after us at night, you know."

" Well, there.'s your dinner."

" We can take a snack, ma. Every body does to big meetin'."

" We might go to Madam Gamby's for dinner," suggested Cal. " It 's only a little ways from Mount Zion Church, and she 's been here a dozen times to eat since we 've been there."

" Yes, you might do that," said Mrs. Catlett. " Well, I don't know as I care; if Miss Fanny's a mind to give up school, and will go and take care of you, I reckon you can go."

" I too ?" said Johnny.

" O, no, Johnny, you are too little. You stay at home and keep ma company—there 's a good boy."

" Miss Fanny 'll go, I know she will," said Maria, "'cause she never went to a big meetin', and I mean to tell her what fun it is."

" Well, don't you say a word to your father when he comes home," said Mrs. Catlett. " He 'd take my head off if he knew I let you go, he 's so choice of having his children mix up with the common folks."

It was not difficult to obtain Fanny's consent to the plan, and the morning proving bright and clear, every thing was arranged to the children's satisfaction. Leaving the farm wagon the other side of the old bridge, just where the horse path led up from the creek, they pursued their way slowly on foot. Their path for some distance wound along the bank, and then, striking into the woods, led them through bush, and briar, and tangled under-brush, into the very depths of the forest. While they were yet struggling with its difficulties, tripping over leaf-covered roots, and catching their dresses in the clinging briars, a confused sound of voices broke upon their ears, and the children came running back to tell them "that meetin' had begun, for they heard 'em singin'." They stopped a moment to listen, and the children's merry voices were hushed, as the solemn cadence rose and fell upon the morning air, now swelling full and clear, as the breeze bore the sounds toward them, and now sinking to a low murmur, which died among the trees.

With slower steps, and serious faces, they pursued their way, and, in a few moments, emerged from the woods upon a gentle slope of ground, where, surrounded by beech and maple-trees, stood the little log church. Horses were tied to the trees in great numbers, while the wagons from which they had been detached, stood near at hand. Not a soul was to be seen outside the building, and flushed and wearied with their walk, they sat down under an old tree to rest.

The congregation were still singing, but what the music had gained in power, it had lost in solemnity. Its harmony and softness were all gone, and the low murmur was exchanged for a deafening chorus, in which voices of every conceivable variety—base, tenor, and treble—vied with each other to make the most noise.

At the top of their lungs they were singing,

> "I want to go!
> I want to go!
> I want to go there too!
> I want to go where Moses is!
> I want to go there too!"

their voices growing more and more vigorous with every line, until at the last they reached the very climax of vio lence, and shouted

> "I want—to—go—there—*too!*"

as though they would bring the roof down.

THE BORDER PREACHER.

"Come, let's go in," said 'Ria, after they had listened
to a couple of stanzas.

"Wait till they get through singing, 'Ria."

"Lors, Miss Fanny, 't will take 'em an hour. When
they sing 'I want to go!' they just begin at Adam, and
go clean through the Bible. They've only got to Moses
you see, yet."

The door was wide open, and struggling through the
crowd they entered the low building. It was literally
jammed with people, in all sorts of positions, sitting,
kneeling, standing, and a few lying flat upon the floor.
Even a rough plank overhead, which in some way helped
to support the roof, was thickly crowded with men and
boys, who sat dangling their limbs above the crowd.

Fanny gazed with astonishment at the strange assembly
in the log church. There were young men and maidens,
old men and children, but of a description that she had
never seen before.

It was not their poverty of dress that surprised her,
though she had seldom seen so ragged and forlorn a set,
but a certain look upon their unhealthy countenances, a
sullen, cowed expression, that told volumes of abject suffering, and humiliation. Middle-aged men were there,
upon whose unshaven faces there was none of that look
of manly self-reliance that characterizes the same class of
laboring men in New England; and women, in old straw
bonnets, and rusty black shawls, whose sallow, care-worn
countenances, and wrinkled brows, bore the same hopeless expression; — untidy girls, and great, shambling,
stupid-faced boys, and little puny children, with un-
combed hair, and frocks sewed together at the back, to
keep them from falling to pieces. A few there were of a
different stamp, neighboring families, who, like Mr. Catlett's children were well dressed, and in every respect

superior, but the body of the assembly was made up of that miserable and despised class, to be found in every slave State—"poor white folks."

The singing ceased, and a tall, bony man, near the altar, commenced a long exhortation, cheered on by groans and ejaculations. Then some one struck up,

> "I'm bound for the kingdom,
>   Will you go to glory with me?"

It was sung amid shouts, and groans, and clapping of hands, and, before it was finished, a young man upon the seat overhead, who for some moments had exhibited signs of great excitement, suddenly "lost his strength," and fell upon the crowd below. This was the signal for a general tumult. In a moment half a dozen were on their knees, praying over him, others were shouting, and calling on the saints to praise the Lord. There were sobs, and groans, and shrieks. A woman started up in the corner, clapping her hands, and in a shrill voice cried, "Glory! glory!" then falling from her place, some one loosened her bonnet strings, and her long black hair swept the floor, while with her pale lips she still continued to whisper "Glory!"

Suddenly a man rose from his knees, and turning with flushed face to the people, himself trembling in every limb, he cried out, "I do confess my sin this day. May the Lord have mercy upon me. I am defiled with blood! I have slain a man to my wounding, and a young man to my hurt.' Pray for me, ye children of the Lord."

"Why it's Colonel Turner," said 'Ria. "What's come over him, to talk Methodist this way?"

The people were greatly affected by the appearance of such a man of mark under conviction. The shouting and singing recommenced with vigor, while the ministers near the altar, pressed forward to speak with him.

Up to this moment Fanny had thought of nothing but the scene before her, but a suppressed sob drawing her attention to Maud, who was seated at her side, she was startled at the expression of her face. The child had risen from her seat, and with her hands clasped, and her really beautiful eyes full of tears, was gazing intently before her.

" O !" she said with a long sigh, as Fanny took her hand, " I wish I could die here !"

Her lip quivered, and she burst into tears. Fanny bent down, and strove to soothe her excited feelings, but she was trembling all over, and her agitation seemed to increase every moment. Whispering to Nanny that she would wait for her in the grove, she took Maud's hand, and they crowded their way out of the house. They walked a little way, and sitting down on a log with her arm about the child's waist, Fanny waited till she was quite calm, and then inquired into the cause of her agitation.

" What was it, Maud ?" she said.

" I don't know, Miss Fanny, I never felt so before."

" How did you feel, Maud ?"

"O, so queer. Like I wanted to laugh and cry all at once. And O ! Miss Fanny, when that pale woman whispered glory, glory, it almost killed me. I wanted to do jest so, and scream, and cry as the rest did. Why did you make me come away ?"

" Because you were so excited, Maud. The noise and confusion had almost taken away your senses."

" But it was real good, Miss Fanny. Mebbe if I had stayed there I should have got religion too."

" What do you mean by getting religion, Maud ?"

8

" O, prayin', and shoutin', and all that, jest as these people in the big meetin' are doin'."

" Is that all ?"

" Well, I s'pose afterward they read the Bible, and go to meetin'."

" Is *that* all ?"

" I reckon so, Miss Fanny."

" Ought they not to be sorry for their sins, and lead different lives ?"

" Yes," said the child, carelessly.

" And how did you feel in the big meeting; like giving up your sins, and praying God to forgive you, and beginning a new life ?"

" Lors, Miss Fanny, I did n't think any thing about that. I jest thought how happy I was, and that I should love to get right up, and shout and sing as the rest did, and then—and then you made me come away."

" Well, suppose I had let you stay there, and you had got religion, as you call it, how would you know that you had really found Jesus Christ ?"

" Why I should jest *know I had*, Miss Fanny."

" Because you shouted and sang with the rest of them, Maud ?"

" Yes, I reckon," said the child, looking puzzled.

" And then if you should go home, and keep on living just as you had before, and doing things that you knew were wicked, and that God had told you not to, would that be living a Christian, Maud ?"

" No, Miss Fanny. I ought to mind Him too."

" Just so, Maud. So you see it is n't by singing and shouting that we can tell whether people are really good and love God, but by the lives they live, and whether they always are ready to serve Him."

" Aunt Phebe is," said Maud.

"Yes, I believe she is," said Fanny. "We can all learn something from Aunt Phebe's earnest piety."

"Look! Miss Fanny, meetin's broke up," said Maud. "They all come pourin' out like a flock of sheep. Now they'll eat their bacon and corn-bread under the trees. I reckon they'll be cold enough, though. O! there's Nanny and the girls. I wonder if they see us. Yes, they are coming this way."

"Hurry, children," said Nanny, "for if we are ever so little behind the time, Madam Gamby will have dinner all cleared away. She's just stingy enough to be glad of the excuse."

"Well, we might have taken a snack like the rest of the people," said Cal. "Who wants to trudge way over here for a bit of bacon and corn-bread. It's all Madam Gamby gives you, anyhow. The last time she had a dinin'-day, there fairly was n't enough for second table, and she cut the cake in slices about as thick as a piece of thread paper."

"She's a regular screwer, but I'd rather take my chance with her, than to sit down under the trees with all them poor white folks," said Maria. "Nanny don't let's tell ma how many they was there. I was right shamed myself to be seen."

"Pooh! I was n't," said Cal. "They won't hurt us if we keep our distance."

"Look yonder, Nanny!" said Maud. "There's old Aunt Fatty toatin' a great apron full of light wood up the hill. It's a shame to make such an old woman work any how."

"Hush, Maud! she'll hear you."

"No she won't, she's as deaf as a post. How'dy Aunt Fatty," screamed Maud at the top of her voice. The person addressed, a crooked old woman, did not raise her head, but slowly toiled up the hill under her load.

"There! I told you so. Madam Gamby has owned that woman ever since she was married, and she's 'most as old as Aunt Phebe, pa says. I think she might give her her bread and bacon the rest of her life."

"I too, Maud; and then there's poor old blind Uncle Ben, that she keeps grindin' corn at a hand-mill all day."

"I thought you sent your corn down the creek to be ground," said Fanny.

"So we do, all but Madam Gamby, and she don't believe in havin' any thing done off the place, specially as Uncle Ben is blind and can't do any thing else."

"Well! here we are at last," said Nanny. "I declare I have n't a breath left."

They had reached the top of a steep hill, and clambering over a stile placed across a stump-fence, in a ruinous condition, the house stood directly before them. It was a log building, one story high, with a wide door and two windows in front. These last had no glass, but were protected by wooden shutters, which could be opened or closed at pleasure. The ground before the house—there was no fence—was smooth and hard—but though there were plenty of pigs about, no children were to be seen—a circumstance that Fanny could not but remark, accustomed as she was, on Mr. Catlett's place, to see the two in equal numbers, playing harmoniously together at all hours of the day.

Madam Gamby was waiting at the door of the house to receive her guests, bidding them welcome in a voice that could be heard half across the yard. The room into which they were ushered, extended the length of the house, but was separated into two parts, by a curtain of dingy cloth hanging from the center rafter. This was drawn, and the further part of the room presented a busy scene. A woman was weaving at the hand-loom in one corner, assisted by an active little fellow, eight or ten years old, and five or six girls were spinning with silent industry. Round a huge pile of wool in the middle, was seated a group of children, picking and packing as fast as their little fingers could fly. The place was in as perfect order as an apartment could be, which contained nearly all its mistress's household possessions, from her best gown and petticoat, down to a skillet and a dishcloth. Through the backdoor, which was wide open, could be seen the cook, busy over the kitchen fire, and the noise of Uncle Ben's handmill reached their ears. Not an idler was to be seen. It seemed strange to see the woman who was setting the table—an operation generally occupying from half to three quarters of an hour at Mrs. Catlett's—proceeding steadily with her business, going to and from the kitchen, without once stopping to chat with the cook, or hang five minutes at a time over the well-curb, as was Martha's invariable custom—to hear the constant whirring of the spinning-wheels, and the regular strokes of the weavers' lay. Over all these operations Mrs. Gamby presided with lynx-eyed vigilance, her sharp voice and quick energetic tread, being heard in all parts of the establishment in a moment's time.

"Hard at it, Madam Gamby, as usual," said Nanny, as the lady, having placed seats for her guests, and called Boss to take their things, sat down again to her work.

"Yes, yes, Miss Nanny. We don't have no lazy minutes here. A minute's a minute, I tell 'em, and there's nothin' like keepin' 'em at it. Lina, here's this seam to stitch. Come, don't be foolin'."

A sprightly yellow girl, with large eyes and soft wavy hair, seated on a low stool at her mistress's feet, was stealing a curious glance at the strangers from under her long lashes, but started when Madam Gamby spoke, and quickly resumed her work.

"Are you cutting out the servants' clothes so early, Madam Gamby?" said Nanny; "why ma won't begin this month yet. 'Pears like we had n't but just got their winter suits made up."

"Fore-handed! Miss Nanny, fore-handed!" said Madam Gamby, plying her shears, which snapped off the cloth very much as their owner did her words. "I never was one of your after-dinner folks. This kind of work has got to be all done up before plantin' time. You Tom," to a little urchin on the wool-pile, "mind yourself. I'll be in there directly."

Just then the old woman, whom they had seen coming up the hill, appeared at the door. She was a full-blooded African in form and feature, bowed and wrinkled by old age and hard work.

"Here, you!" said Mrs. Gamby; "who told you to leave your spinnin'?"

"Please, Miss Betty, I wants a holiday," said the old creature. "Reaumatiz mighty bad now-a-days. I's right sick, Miss Betty, I is."

"Go back to your work," said her mistress. "You'll have that stint done by night, too, mind yer. I'll be down there in the course of the day."

The old woman still lingered.

"Go," said her mistress, decidedly.

"You see she's foolish," said Madam Gamby, as the old creature hobbled slowly away; "you've got to be right up and down with such. I reckon she see there was company, and thought 't would be a good time to try one of her tantrums."

"Do you get much out of such a broken down old creature?" said Nanny.

"Well, now, there's more wear in such than you'd think for to look at 'em," said Madam Gamby. "The old thing grunts and grumbles a heap, but I should n't wonder if she held out to work a couple of years yet. She's mighty tough, you see."

"She ain't a bit fit to work," said Maud.

"Hush, Maud," said Nanny.

"What does the child say?" said Madam Gamby.

"I say she ain't fit," said Maud, with a crimson face. "She's old, and crooked, and most blind, and you had n't ought to make her work—so there!"

"Maud Catlett," said her sister, "ain't you ashamed of yourself?"

"No, I ain't," said Maud.

"Lor', Biny," said Madam Gamby, "get the little girl your old rag baby to play with. We must give her something to amuse herself with."

Maud darted a look of rage and indignation at the speaker, and rushed out of the house.

"O, let her go," said Nanny to Boss and Biny, who had followed her to the door. "I'm sure she's as well out there, if she has n't any better manners than that."

"Never mind the child," said Mrs. Gamby, "I see Suke's a bringin' in dinner, and you must n't eat without tasting my cherry bounce. They do say it's prime. Miss Hunter, if you'll hitch your chair along, I'll haul up a jug."

Fanny did as she was requested, and raising one of the boards that composed the floor, Madam Gamby stretched her long arm down the cavity, and brought up a large stone jug, containing this favorite western beverage. A portion of it was poured into a tumbler, from which all took a sip, somewhat after the manner of the morning dram at Mrs. Catlett's. "Now, then," said Madam Gamby, as they gathered round the table, "eat!" an in junction they all followed, for their long tramp had made them very hungry. Fanny thought of poor Maud, bonnetless and dinnerless, and would fain have followed and hunted her up, but she knew not where to find her.

After dinner, it being too late to return to the meeting, they made the tour of the premises, Madam Gamby really sparing time to act the part of guide. She took them to the smoke-house, the stable, and the sheep-pen, descanting at length on her method of managing these several departments. They listened to an accurate statement of the amount of hog's flesh she had salted and prepared for smoking, with her own hands. "There's only a few things," she said, "that I don't let my niggers do, and one is to pickle the bacon. They have enough to do, tho', about hog-killin' time, *that* you'd better believe. Last January we killed forty head in one day, and I tell you I kept every man, woman, and child down here, at the hog-pen, three days hand runnin'. Them girls did n't keep out of it, neither. My daughters are goin' to be brought up for farmer's wives. None of your lily fingers for me," with a glance at Fanny's hands. "They was right here, in the midst of it."

"We had the pig tails to roast, any how, Miss Fanny," said Biny. "Did you ever eat a pig tail roasted in the ashes ? It 's mighty sweet."

"No," said Fanny, laughing. "The children all came into school one day, brandishing their pig tails, but they did n't look very inviting to me, I must confess."

"Lor', Miss Hunter," said Madam Gamby, "you must n't be so delicate. You won't catch any of our young farmers if you are too nice to eat pig tails."

"When I am in a strait for a husband, I 'll try to learn, Mrs. Gamby," said Fanny, demurely.

From the smoke-house, and hog-pen, they visited the

hennery, and their attention was directed to the rich store of corn in the loft above.

"You are such a good manager," said Nanny, with a sigh; and Madam Gamby confessed that she did understand a thing or two about carrying on a place.

"Come here in plantin' time, Miss Nanny," she said, "if you want to see things fly. I don't keep no lazy bones about me then. If you must have a tribe around, make 'em do enough to pay for their bread and hominy, that's my way. Some folks say that niggers can't be smart, that they are naturally slow. I don't believe it. I've tried 'em these twelve years, and I don't reckon you get any more out of your white servants there in Connecticut, than I do out of my niggers. It depends altogether on how you manage 'em whether you make 'em profitable or not."

It was a favorite topic with Madam Gamby, and while she entertained them for an hour, with her method of managing the hands, Fanny watched the women as they pursued their daily tasks.

Their work was done quicker, and more thoroughly than that performed by Mrs. Catlett's house servants, but there was a dull, hopeless expression on their faces, that told of overwork, and little recreation. Fanny did not sympathize with Nanny's admiration of their hostess's management, and anxious about Maud, and weary with exertion, she was glad when the day drew to a close, and Nanny declared that "they must go that instant, for big William would certainly be waiting for them at the creek."

"Where can Maud be?" she said, anxiously, as they descended the hill. "I have been so worried about her."

"I was mortified to death," said Nanny. "I'm sure I don't care what became of the child. Madam Gamby will owe her a grudge as long as she lives."

"Ma can't blame us," said Cal. "Nobody can stop Maud when she gets in one of her tantrums."

"There she is now," exclaimed Fanny. "O Maud, I am so glad!   Where have you been?"

The child bounded toward them, her dress pinned over her head instead of a bonnet, and her cheeks glowing with exercise.

"Lor, Miss Fanny, you need n't have felt worried," she said, as she allowed her teacher to pin her shawl which she had brought upon her arm down the hill, "I 've had a grand run, and I ain't cold a bit."

"You lost your dinner, though, miss," said Nanny. "Just right for you, too, talkin' so saucy to your betters."

"No, I did n't lose my dinner, Miss Nanny," said Maud. "Lina gave me some of her hominy in the kitchen, but did n't I have to scrabble under the bed, when old Madam Gamby was comin'."

"I wish she had caught you," said Nanny, "and given you a real smackin'."

"Miss Fanny, do *you* think they should make that poor old woman work so hard?" said Maud, appealing to her teacher.

"No, Maud," said Fanny, "I think not, but it was not right for you to tell Madam Gamby so, especially in the way you did."

"I could n't help it. I was jest as mad as I could be. I went right down to old Fatty's cabin, and told her to run away."

"I should like to see her," said Nanny, laughing, "she 's too foolish to know her way off the place."

"Well, Miss Fanny, she *is* real hard on her servants," said Cal. "You see how ashy they all look. It 's 'cause she half starves 'em, and makes 'em work so hard."

"And O! Miss Fanny, she did jest the funniest thing

once," said 'Ria. "You see there was company comin', and she wanted the little niggers to look fat and greasy, and so she made 'em rub their faces with old bacon rinds, and one of 'em, black Tom, I reckon it was, told of it afterward. I was fit to kill myself laughing when I heard of it."

"I don't think it's any thing to laugh at," said Maud. "I think it's real mean to treat 'em so."

"Well, you may all talk," said Nanny, "but I tell you what, Madam Gamby's a real manager, and she's layin' up money hand over fist. Those girls of hers, will be better off than any of *you* one of these days."

"I'd rather be poor all my days, Nan," said Maud, "than get money out of such old women as Aunt Fatty, Had n't you, Miss Fanny?"

CHAPTER XVIII.

DAVE TAKES POSSESSION.

THE time had now arrived when, if Mr. Catlett would secure his claim, he must send Dave and a gang to take possession of the cabin, vacated by the widow and family of the dispossessed Yankee, and settle on the premises. The boy was full of young blood, and eagerly embraced the opportunity of setting up for himself in the world, but Mr. Catlett seemed to have lost much of his enthusiasm, proceeding in the necessary arrangements with a reluctance that was observed and remarked upon by the family.

"What's come over you, Mr. Catlett?" his wife said one day, when he had replied with more than usual impatience to Dave's eager inquiries. "It seems like you was all out of the notion of the thing. I'm sure awhile back you was fierce enough about it. I shall begin to think that you are as chicken-hearted as neighbor Turner, who, they say, made a kind of confession in Mount Zion meetin'. What did you do over there in Kanzas the other day, anyhow, squire?"

"It's none of your business what I did. You, women, are always for knowin' too much," was the reply in any thing but a gracious tone.

Col. Joe Turner and Madam Gamby had already established settlements within a few miles of the claim, and here Dave would find neighbors. Young Turner could hunt and fish, and ride about with him, and they would have great times together. Dave was very sanguine and self-confident. "Give me my dogs, and Uncle Tim," he said, "and you may keep every other blasted nigger on the place. They 'd only be in the way, anyhow, and Tim and I are prime to manage."

"Tim, indeed!" said his mother, "and how do you reckon we can get along without him here? You must think you are of great consequence, Master Dave, to take off the very best hand on the place. He knows more than half the white men on the prairie, and we can't give him up nohow, so you may just make up your mind to take Jerry, or little Charles, and leave Uncle Tim where he belongs."

"I sha'n't, though, please you, Mrs. Catlett. I reckon I know what I 'm about, and if I can't take the nigger I want, I'll stay at home, that 's all."

"It 's jest as I told you. They are a quarreling and snapping over it a'ready," said Madam Hester. "This move won't bring no good to nobody."

"Pa, did n't you say Uncle Tim was to go?" said Dave, as Catlett appeared in the doorway.

"Yes, and I 've just been over to see that old skinflint, Madam Gamby, about takin' the feller's wife along. Uncle Tim took on so about leavin' her behind, I thought I 'd fix up that all straight."

"Now did you ever see such a man? As though it made any odds whether his wife was along or not. I would n't humor my niggers so much, if I was you, Mr. Catlett. What did the old woman say?"

"O, she was on hand, 'cause it happened to fall in with her plans. If it had n't, there would have been another tune played. However, it 's all fixed, and Uncle Tim will nigh about jump out of his skin for joy, I suppose."

Tim had married about a year before, one of Madam Gamby's house-servants, a smart, good-looking mulatto girl, a dozen years younger than himself, whom he was as proud of introducing on Sundays and holidays as his "woman," as any young husband of a fairer race, is to display the beauty of his blushing bride. There never was a kinder or better husband. Many a long evening did he spend in putting together, after his blundering fashion, some convenience for Lina's cabin; a chair for herself, perhaps, or a cradle for the baby, to be carried home Saturday night as a surprise; and when the evening brought them together, the baby dressed in its gayest frock, and Tim following with a proud, happy look, Lina's movements as she bustled about to get her "ole man's supper," they presented as pretty a picture of domestic happiness as one might wish to see.

"There, ma, what did I tell you?" said Dave triumphantly. "I'm glad there's somebody to fix things beside you on the place. I dare say you'd put me off with old lame Uncle Jerry, and mebbe Aunt Phebe to match, if you had the fixin' off to do."

"You can talk as you please, David, my son, but you'll never find a better friend than your despised mother. It's a great trial to have such ungrateful children. Viny, hand me my pipe and a shovel of coals."

"It runs in the blood," said Madam Hester. "No good, no good!" and she shook her palsied head, and raised a skinny finger quite significantly.

Finally, after a great deal of talking, it was settled that Tim and Jerry, Aunt Adeline and Jinny, should be handed over to Dave; and if, by and by, he required more, more should be given him. All the arrangements were made long before the eventful morning, and great was the hurly-burly when the cavalcade moved from the door. It consisted of the squire, Dave and the servants, Othor, Uno, and Ino, a wagon-load of domestic utensils, with a stock of meal for hoe-cakes, and bacon for more substantial food.

Madam Gamby, who was going over to visit her place and see how things came on, rode up the lane just as they were starting; and Uncle Tim's heart beat quicker, and his broad face broke into a smile, when looking back, he espied the white horse, and the pretty face of his young wife, peeping out from behind the old lady's ample form. Madam Gamby always "rode double," if there were two to go. "There was no sort of use in sparing another horse," she said, and therefore, though a ride of thirty miles might not prove the most comfortable thing in the world, in the crowded position both parties occupied, thus, and thus only, was it to be taken.

"There they go," said Nanny, as the whole party started down the lane, on a slow trot. "If Dave only had a wife now, he would be fixed off nicely. It's a pity little Rosa Turner wasn't out of school, ain't it ma?"

"Rosa Turner, indeed!" said Mrs. Catlett. "I promise you, Nan, our Dave looks higher than that."

"Why, how you talk, ma! The Turners are right respectable. Mrs. Turner is always telling about their aristocratic blood."

"O, yes! I know they come of a good family; but when a young man is looking out for a wife, Nanny, family is n't every thing. Between you and I, the Turners are pretty well run out, and have to sell a nigger or two every year to keep up the place. When the old colonel dies, those girls won't be worth a sixpence."

"Dave likes her, ma. He always waits on her at all the dining days and night parties."

"He's young, Nanny, yet; but he's coming to his senses for all that, as you'll see one of these days."

It would be hardly worth our while to trace the steps of our party, as they proceeded to David's new home. It was a gloomy day in November, and as, after a tedious ride of several hours, they descended the slope, at the foot. of which stood the cabin, the wind moaned dismally through the naked branches of the trees, and rattled the door and windows of the deserted house.

"Take hold here, Uncle Tim, and help shove this plaguy door open," said Dave. "I should think there were seven devils holding it to, on the other side, by the way it sticks."

Tim's strength quickly overcame the resistance, whatever it was, and the door flying open with a crash, precipitated that worthy individual across the sill, and permitted the exit of a large bat, which dashed its wings in Mr. Catlett's face.

"Lors-a-massy!" said Uncle Tim, raising himself on his hands, and knees, and gazing after the creature of ill omen. "Lors-a-massy, Mass' Jack, but dat's a mighty bad sign, any how."

"Get up, you fool, and don't lie staring there as if you had seen a ghost," returned Mr. Catlett, "and be off all of you, and pick up some light wood, and we'll have a fire. Pah! the place smells like a cellar."

The room into which they entered did not, in fact, present a very cheerful appearance. There were a few dead embers upon the hearth, and a tea-kettle, and one or two other articles of household use, as though the former residents had left the premises in haste. Cobwebs hung thick upon the walls, and the floor was covered with dust and rubbish, but through it all Mr. Catlett discerned a few dark stains, the meaning of which he well understood, and from which he turned away his eyes with something like a shudder, but quickly sought again as though irresistibly attracted by the dismal tokens.

"As snug as any thing can be," said Madam Gamby, taking a survey of the premises. "I wish some Yankee had left the like on my land. Our folks have to live in a deal poorer place than this. Howsomever they are used to it. Well, it's time I was off. Good luck to you, Dave. I shall look for you to-morrow, over to my diggins. Set your niggers at work first, though, fellin' some of that fine timber, yonder. It's prime for buildin', and you must begin as you can hold out, my boy. Work 'em well, or it won't pay. That's my advice."

"Hang the woman," said Dave. "Who cares for her advice? I reckon I can manage without any help from her."

Mr. Catlett spent several days with his son, directing Uncle Tim and Jerry how to build their cabin, initiating the boy into his new business, reconnoitering the country, trying the game, and setting the wheels of house-keeping in motion. Nothing occurred worthy of notice during this time, excepting the death of Othor, killed by a shot from an unknown hand—a dog Dave declared that he would n't have taken fifty dollars for—and a bullet-hole made in the squire's new hat, in an equally mysterious way.

At length, Colonel Turner coming over to visit his claim, it was decided that Mr. Catlett should return to the prairie with him, leaving Dave and his household to shift for themselves.

The evening before his departure, he was accosted by Jinny, one of the female servants.

"Mass' Jack," she said timidly, "please can't I go back to de prairie wid you, to-morrow?"

"Go back to the prairie, Jinny? What for? You ain't getting home-sick, be you?"

"Why no, not 'zackly, but—well, you see, Mass' Jack, it's kinder curis here, any how. 'Pears like, I'd rather be in de old place."

"What's curis? What do you mean, girl?"

"Lors, mebbe 't aint nothin', Mass' Jack, only Adeline and me, we get talkin', and we say it must be sperits. Dar ain't no flesh and blood round here to be cuttin' up such shines, and—and—"

"What shines? Hang it, girl, if you don't tell me what you mean, I'll teach you how. Come, out with it."

"Why, lors, Mass' Jack knows. Dat ar hole through Mass' Jack's hat, now, can massa tell how it come dar? and de shot dat killed Othor?—was any body round to shoot de bullet?—and de buck-shot dat come whizzin' in at de open door toder day, and hit de kettle on de fire. O Mass' Jack, it's sperits, and no mistake, and me and Adeline, we tinks it ain't no good sperits, neither. It's a dreadful lonesome place, Mass' Jack."

"Shut up your head, Jinny, and don't let me hear another word of your nonsense. No, I sha'n't take you back to the prairie with me, spirits or no spirits. So there you are."

The next day Mr. Catlett and Colonel Turner returned to their respective homes, and reported progress.

CHAPTER XIX.

CHRISTMAS.

THE business which had brought Mr. Chester to La Belle Prairie, detained him longer than he had anticipated. Three weeks passed away, ere it was completed, and then the Christmas holidays were so near at hand, that the family would not hear of his going.

"The town gentleman" had established himself as a universal favorite among the household. Even Dave, thawed out of his sulky ill nature by the other's jovial frankness and good-humor, had declared before he left for Kanzas that he was n't "a bad fellow after all, though he did wear a gold chain to his watch, and cover his hands with kid gloves." The house servants soon learned to call him "Mass' Henry," and to watch to bring him his coat and hat, or for a nod or a pleasant word from him as he crossed the yard, while Miss Nanny declared "there was n't such another polite, pretty-behaved gentleman in all St. Louis." She was particularly anxious that he should remain over Christmas.

"There'll be sure to be two or three night parties on the prairie, Miss Fanny, and it will be so nice to come walkin' in with the town gentleman, and all the other girls lookin' at us. O! I hope he'll stay."

The visitor appeared quite ready to remain. The wild life he was leading on the prairie, pleased him well, and he entered with great zest into all the plans for hunting parties and other amusements.

Though a resident for the last few years, of the city, Harry Chester was not unaccustomed to country life at the west, and he fell at once into the ways of the family, experiencing none of the shock at the sudden change from his city home, which had so tried the courage of our New England girl. Indeed, the same low room that had filled Fanny with such horror, had a peculiar charm for him, and returning at night from his long rides over the prairie, he watched for the first glimmer of light from its uncurtained windows, and welcomed it with real pleasure.

He thought of the blazing fire on the wide hearth, lighting up the faces of the children, and making them look ruddy in its cheerful glow, of the well-spread table, where the corn-bread and coffee tasted better than anywhere else, of the boisterous welcome that awaited him, and of a young girl, in a dark merino dress, and black silk apron, who was sitting quietly knitting by the fire.

The evening was the pleasantest part of the day, and after the table was cleared, the cups washed, and the younger children safely stowed away in the trundle for the night, a comparative state of quiet prevailed. It was then, while Mrs. Catlett and Nanny, with a candle upon a chair, between them, worked away upon the servants' clothes; and Fanny, with Yankee industry, plied her knitting-needles, that Mr. Chester entertained them with the news from the St. Louis paper, or read a few pages from some favorite book, brought forth from the recesses of his portmanteau. There were long talks, too, which made the evening pass so swiftly that Mrs. Catlett declared, "she had to hint, and hint, before ever she could get them off to bed." There were walks now and then on a pleasant Saturday afternoon, through the leafless woods, or across the prairie, when the children running on before, left Miss Nanny and the teacher to entertain the stranger. There were many gallops across the prairie, and more quiet rides to church on Sunday, so that the young people were much together.

Christmas week there was no school, but such a succession of dining days, and visiting days, and day parties, and night parties, that Fanny, who looked forward to the week as a season of rest, thought that the regular routine of school duties would be less fatiguing.

Christmas at La Belle Prairie was the one jubilee of the year, something to be talked about for six months beforehand, and to be remembered as long after. It was a time of feasting and recreation for both master and servant. Days before, preparations commenced in the kitchen. Various smells issued from thence—savory smells of boiled, baked, and roasted meats; and sweet, delicious smells of warm pastry, and steaming cakes. Aunt Tibby was rolling pie-crust, or stirring cake all day long, and the chopping of sausage-meat, the pounding of spices, and the beating of eggs, was constantly heard. Every thing was carried on with the greatest secrecy. The children were all kept out of the kitchen, and when "somfin' good" was to be transferred therefrom to Miss Car'line's storeroom, Aunt Tibby came sailing in, holding it high above the reach of the curious little heads.

"I don't care," said Cal. . "There's six pound-cakes all in a row on the store-room shelf. I see 'em when ma opened the door; and Marthy says one of 'em's got currants in it, and there's a little shoat thar roasted whole. O! how I wish Christmas was come."

Coming suddenly upon Maud one day, Fanny found her with her apron half-full of bran, while her fingers were busily at work upon a few pieces of faded silk. Maud tried to hide them at first, but finding by Fanny's question of " What is it, Maud ?" that it was too late, she looked up with a tired, flushed face, and said,

" Miss Fanny, don't you tell now! will you? I'm makin' a pin-cushion for Aunt Phebe, but it won't come square, all I can do. It acts awfully."

" Let me see what the trouble is," said Fanny, and sitting down, she examined the poor cushion ; which, indeed, under Maud's hands, was not soon likely to come into shape.

" You see," said Maud, " I want to give aunty a Christmas gift, and I thought a cushion would be so nice, 'cause her old one that she wears pinned to her waist, you know, has burst a great hole, and the bran keeps tumbling out. I'm going to make her a right nice one, only I wish 't was brighter, 'cause aunty likes red, and yellow, and all them, so bad."

Fanny searched her piece-bag, and brought forth bits of gay ribbon, the sight of which threw Maud into ecstasies of delight, then giving up the morning to the job, she cut and planned, and fitted and basted together, getting all in order, so that Maud could do the sewing herself.

" Aunty would n't think half so much of it if I did n't," said the child.

Well and faithfully Maud performed her labor of love, giving up her much-prized runs on the prairie, and resisting all the children's entreaties to play with them, till the Christmas gift was finished. It was no small task, for Maud most heartily hated to sew, and her fingers were any thing but nimble in the operation. "I always did despise to sew, Miss Fanny," she said, " but I'm going to make this cushion for aunty anyhow."

It was finished at last, and, as Maud expressed it, " was just as beautiful as it could be." There never was a prouder, happier child. She did not thank Fanny in words for her assistance, but that night she came softly behind her, and putting her arms about her neck, gave her an earnest kiss, a proceeding which called forth an exclamation of surprise from Mrs. Catlett, for Maud was very chary of her caresses.

Christmas morning came, and, long before daylight, every child upon the place, both black and white, was up ready to "march in Christmas." There had been mysterious preparations the night before, such as the hiding of tin pans and glass bottles under the bed, and the faint tooting of an old horn, heard down at the quarters, as though some one was rehearsing a part. Fanny was also astonished by an application from little "darky Tom" for permission to use her school-bell, the said cow tinkler not being remarkable for sweetness of sound.

"O, yes, Tom, you may take it; but what can you want of it?"

"Could n't tell no ways, Miss Fanny," said Tom, with a grin. "Mebbe Miss Fanny know in de mornin'."

Morning did indeed bring an explanation of the mystery. Assembling in the yard, the children marshaled themselves into marching order; Maud, of course, being captain, and taking the lead, bearing an old tin horn, while little black Tom brought up the rear with Fanny's unfortunate cowbell.

In this order they commenced "marching in Christmas" to the music of the horn, the beating of tin pans, the rattling of bits of iron and pieces of wood, the jingling of bells, and the clapping of hands. Into the house, and up stairs to the very doors of the sleeping-rooms, they all marched with their horrid din. It was received with tolerable good-humor by all but Nanny, who, deprived of her morning nap by the tumult, raved at the juvenile dis turbers of the peace, and finally threw her shoes at them as they stood on the stairway. These were directly seized upon as trophies, and carried off in triumph to the quarters, where the young performers went through with the same operations.

"Christmas gift! Christmas gift!" was the first salutation from the servants this morning, and it was well worth while to give them some trifling present, were it only to hear their extravagant expressions of gratitude and delight. It was impossible to forget for a moment that it was Christmas. One could see it in the faces of the servants, released for a whole week from their daily tasks, and rejoicing in the prospect of dances, and parties, and visits to friends and kindred on distant plantations. The children, too, with their boisterous merriment and constant talk about the holidays, seemed determined to bear it in mind, and the great dinner—the one dinner of the year—in the preparation of which Aunt Tibby had exercised all her skill; this, in itself, seemed to proclaim that it was Christmas.

"O, Miss Fanny," said little Joy, "don't you wish Christmas lasted the whole year round?"

The short December day was fast drawing to a close, as a party of four rode leisurely along the road crossing La Belle Prairie. The ladies, though scarcely recognizable in their close hoods, long blue cotton riding skirts, and thick gloves, were none other than Miss Nanny Catlett and our friend Fanny, while their attendants were Mr. Chester, the town gentleman, and Massa Dave Catlett, who had come over from his new home in Kanzas, on purpose to enjoy the Christmas festivities on the prairie. One of those night-parties, of which Nanny had talked so much, was to come off at Col. Turner's, and this was the place of their destination. In accordance with the customs of society in these parts, they were to remain until the next day, and, accordingly, black Viny rode a little in the rear, mounted upon old "Poke Neck," and bearing sundry carpet-bags and valises, containing the ladies' party-dresses.

As they rode slowly along, chatting gayly and enjoying the still bright day, a young man, mounted upon a beautiful gray horse dashed by them on the full gallop, slightly touching his hat as he passed.

"There goes Tom Walton," said Nanny. "How saucy in him to gallop by in that style. He thinks because he is rich, that he can do any thing."

"Isn't that the young fellow that spends so much of his time at the store?" inquired Mr. Chester. "He looks very like one I see there every time I stop for letters."

"That's him," said Dave. "It's Tom Walton, the richest young fellow anywhere about. He's only twenty-two or three, and owns one of the tallest farms in Missouri, and twenty good hands to work it. I tell you he's one of the lucky ones."

"Such possessions bring plenty of care and responsibility with them," said Mr. Chester.

"To some, mebbe, not to him. He takes it easy. He keeps an overseer, and does nothing all day but hunt or lounge in the store. He hasn't half the care that I have."

"Nor half the enjoyment, Dave, if I read his face right. He has a very restless, discontented look, to me."

"Well, he's been a pretty hard boy, you see, for all he's so young. One while, before the old man died, he was so bad it seemed like he'd drink himself to death. He's steadied down now, though, and does pretty well."

Just at dusk our party reached their journey's end, and dismounting one by one from the horse-block in front of the house, they walked up the yard, and were met in the porch by Miss Belle Turner, Nanny's particular friend. This young lady, with long curls, and a very slender waist, performed the duties of hostess in a free and easy manner, ushering the gentlemen into the parlor, where a fire was blazing on the hearth, while the ladies, with their attendant, were conducted up stairs to the dressing-room.

Here a dozen or more were engaged in the mysteries of the toilet, braiding, twisting, and curling, while as many servants were flying about, stumbling over each other, and creating the most dire confusion in their efforts to supply the wants of their respective mistresses. The beds and chairs were covered with dresses, capes, ribbons, curling-irons, flowers, combs, and brushes, and all the paraphernalia of the toilet, while the ladies themselves kept up a continual stream of conversation, with each other and their attendants.

Into this scene Nanny entered with great spirit. Shaking hands all round, and introducing Fanny, she hastily threw off her bonnet and shawl, and bidding Viny unpack the things, she set about dressing in good earnest.

"How nice to get here so early," she said. "Now we can have a chance at the glass, and plenty of room to move about in."

Fanny wondered what she called plenty of room, but had yet to learn the signification of the term when applied to the dressing-room of a western party. Thicker and faster came the arrivals, and it being necessary that each lady should undergo a thorough transformation in dress, before making her appearance down stairs, the labor and confusion necessary to bring this about can be imagined. Such hurryings to and fro, such knockings down and pickings up, such scolding and laughing, in short, such a

Babel of sounds as filled the room for an hour or two, Fanny had never heard before. Completing her own toilet as soon as possible, she seated herself upon one of the beds, and watched the proceedings with great interest.

"You Suke, bring me some more pins, directly" "O please, Miss Ellen, mind my wreath!" "Jule, how much longer are you goin' to keep the wash-bowl." "Dar now, Miss Eveline, done get her coat all wet." "Did you know Tom Walton was here? I see him in the passage." "Miss Belle, that's *my* starch-bag." "There, now! don't them slippers fit beautiful." "Why don't that girl come back." "O, 'Liza, just fasten up my dress, that's a dear girl!" "Come, girls, do hurry, we sha'n't be dressed to-night."

How it was all brought about, Fanny could not tell, but at last the ladies were dressed, the last sash pinned, and the last curl adjusted. Dresses of thin material, cut low in the neck, with short sleeves, seemed to be the order of the night, which with wreaths, and bunches of artificial flowers in the hair, gave the ladies a ball-like appearance. With Miss Belle at the head, they all descended to the parlor, and found the gentlemen strolling about, employing themselves as they could, till the night's amusement commenced; and, indeed, both ladies and gentlemen manifested such eagerness to adjourn to the dancing-room, that the signal was soon given, and they proceeded forthwith to a log building in the yard, formerly used as a school-room.

"Will you walk with me?" said a young man, who happened to be standing near Fanny in the passage.

Fanny looked about for an acquaintance, but there was none in sight, and perceiving that all were on the move, she accepted the stranger's proffered arm.

"You may not know me," said the young man. "My

name is Walton—Tom Walton. It ain't best to be set about introductions here in the country."

"No," said Fanny, smiling.

"And now, as I know you, and you me, would it be out of the way to ask you to be my partner in the first cotillion?"

"Thank you," said Fanny, "I don't dance."

"Don't dance!" exclaimed Mr. Walton, in extreme surprise. "What upon earth will you do with yourself all night, at a Christmas party, without dancing?"

"Look on and see the rest," said Fanny, "and study human nature."

"It will be mighty tiresome business, I reckon," said the young man. "Well, here we are."

As he spoke they entered the dancing-saloon, and a rude one it was, lighted by a great fire in the chimney, and by tallow candles stuck between the logs. Benches were placed here and there about the room, and leading Fanny to a seat, Mr. Tom Walton placed himself beside her, with the evident intention of pursuing the acquaintance.

Belle Turner had taken good care to secure the services of the town gentleman as an escort, and Nanny was made happy by the attentions of young Mr. Turner, who was generally looked upon as her beau; while Dave stalked about with a modest, blushing, little girl, hanging upon his arm, his perfect opposite in appearance and manners.

Dancing soon commenced, and was carried on with great vigor, the young people making up in activity, what was lacking in gracefulness of motion. Set after set was made out, the ladies vieing with each other to see who should dance the most, while those who were left, chatted gayly together in groups, or tried their powers of fascination upon some long-limbed specimen of humanity.

"Nanny," whispered Belle Turner, as she stood near

that young lady in the dance, "do you see Mr. Tom Walton talking away to your new teacher? Who introduced him, I wonder?"

"Dave, I reckon," said Nanny. "Tom Walton was mightily taken with her the first time he saw her. He told Dave to-night she was the prettiest-looking girl on the ground."

"Of all things," said Belle, with a toss of her curls, "I think she looks right old maidish, with that high-necked gown on, and she has n't so much as a rose in her hair."

Miss Belle's own head was ornamented with a staring wreath of flowers, and she was shivering in her thin dress; the present cold made endurable only by the prospect of future warmth.

Fanny was growing very weary of Mr. Tom Walton's society, when he suddenly started up, exclaiming, that "Miss Belle would never forgive him, if he did n't dance at her party. If Miss Hunter would keep her seat, he would see her again in the course of half an hour."

"How very kind," thought Fanny; but Mr. Chester just then appearing, and taking the vacant seat, she was soon engaged in a pleasant talk with him.

"What calls the gentlemen up stairs so frequently?" inquired Fanny, innocently, as groups of two and three disappeared up the steps leading to the room above.

"You are not aware, then, what a formidable rival the ladies have up in the loft?" said Mr. Chester, gravely, though there was a comical expression about the corners of his mouth.

"No, indeed."

"Well, I only hope you may not witness the overpowering influence sometimes exerted by this same rival," said Mr. Chester; "but, honestly, Miss Hunter, there is serious danger that some of these light-footed young gentlemen may, ere long, be obliged to relinquish their places in the dance, all through the attractions presented to them up yonder."

"I don't in the least know what you mean."

"In plain words, then, there is a barrel of whisky up there, and various bottles and glasses, from which the gentlemen slake their thirst."

"Are you in earnest, Mr. Chester?"

"Certainly I am. It would not answer, I suppose, for ladies to intrude upon their modest retirement, or I could convince you in a moment."

"How can you joke about it, Mr. Chester? I think it is perfectly scandalous."

"Well, it is bad enough," said her companion, more gravely. "One living at the west becomes accustomed to such things."

"*I* never will," said Fanny. "If I had known these Christmas parties countenanced intemperance, I would have stayed at home."

"And yet we hear a great deal about your wine-drinking parties there in New England," said Mr. Chester. "Is it so much worse for the gentlemen to do their drinking out of sight, than to pour down glass after glass unblushingly in the presence of ladies?"

"I know," said Fanny, "there are such things even now in Connecticut as wine-drinking parties, and I blush to own it; but public opinion is fast frowning them down, and our glorious Maine law is putting a stop to every thing of the sort."

"Are all the New England ladies so strongly opposed to this evil practice? If their united influence were brought to bear against intemperance, would it not almost supersede the necessity of a Maine law? I *have* heard of such a thing as ladies *preferring* the society of a gentleman, whose conversation was enlivened by a glass or two of something stimulating. Very few are as frank in acknowledging it, as one young girl here to-night, who I heard remarking to a lady friend, that 'Mr. Mack had taken just enough to make him witty and smart.' It is true, Miss Hunter, though you look so incredulous."

"It is very humiliating," said Fanny, "but I can not let any insinuations against the New England ladies, go undisputed. I *do* know, and will stoutly maintain, that the ladies there almost with one voice, have chosen the right side, and have given all their influence to bring about the desired end."

"One could not well doubt it," said Mr. Chester, "if you are to be taken as a sample. But see, the dancing has ceased, and the crowd appear to be moving, shall we follow them?"

"A set supper," Nanny had several times expressed a hope that Mrs. Turner would provide, and she was not disappointed. The long table was bountifully spread with the substantials of this life, and though not in the style of an entertainment in Fifth Avenue, it was admirably suited to the guests, who partook of it. A roasted "shoat" graced each end of the board, a side of bacon the center, while salted beef, cut in thin slices, with pickles and cheese, constituted the side-dishes. Hot coffee, corn bread, and biscuit, were passed to each guest, and a piece of pound-cake, and a little preserved fruit, for dessert.

There was plenty of laughter, and coarse joking at the table, and the flushed faces, and increased volubility of the gentlemen, gave too certain evidence of the truth of Mr. Chester's assertions. Mr. Tom Walton stood between Miss Belle and another young lady, who appeared greatly amused at his sallies of wit, and his swaggering, self-sufficient air. Fanny was mortified and distressed at the scene before her, and mentally determined that this

should be her last party while she remained at La Belle
Prairie.

Perhaps Mr. Chester divined her thoughts, for he soon
proposed leaving the table, and she gratefully accepted
Dancing recommenced immediately after supper, and was
kept up till a late hour of the night, few exhibiting any
symptoms of fatigue. Fanny felt grateful to Mr. Chester
for remaining by her side the rest of the evening; dread
ing to be left alone a moment, lest she should be exposed
to the rude attentions of some of the young gentlemen
present. Tom Walton, she knew, was only prevented
from joining her by the presence of her companion; and
by this time she had conceived for him the most thorough
contempt. An hour or so after supper, this young gentleman, with two or three boon companions, was slaking his
thirst in the loft above.

"I tell you, boys," says one, "was n't them great times
over to the election, hey? The twenty-ninth now was a
great day and no mistake. Did n't we make the Yankees
stand round? They say there was n't a dozen free State
votes cast in the Territory, and I believe it, if they all
made as clean work as we."

"The squire did the matter up brown," said Tom,
"when we put him in, scaring off the rascally abolition
chairman. He 's got pluck."

"But the greatest sight to be seen, was old Marm
Gamby, in men's clothes, puttin' in a vote for every one
of her scrawny niggers, men, women, and children. I
thought I should die a laughin'. She swore she 'd do it
beforehand, but I did n't believe the crittur had brass
enough. By jing! she gave twenty votes if she gave
one."

"Yes, and she swigged down the whisky with the best
of 'em, and rode round on that old white horse, cursin'

and swearin' at the abolitioners. I never saw such a specimen."

"Tom, they say Dave Catlett is shinin' up to one of them great Dutch gals of hers. Is that so? Thunder, if it is, Dave's a greater fool than I thought him. Why, she's a regular chip off the old block. Dave will be black and blue before they've been tied a month. What do you say, Tom?"

"I say I don't know any thing about it, anyhow. The girl has got a pretty piece of property to back her, and as for the grit, Dave's got enough of that himself. Did you see him order off that spunky abolition boy and his mother. Blast me! if I didn't think the boy was going to fight, but his mother whispered to him, and he gave in."

"What right had he there, anyhow, tryin' to vote? He's nothin' but a boy."

"No more Marm Gamby ain't a man, Turner, and you see she come it nicely."

"He said he wanted to vote for his dead father, who had been a resident six months, when somebody murdered him."

"Yes, and did you see the squire about that time. He turned as pale as a cloth, and stuttered and stammered like he didn't know what he was about. If Dave hadn't spunked up so, I believe the old man would have let him vote, and owned up to killin' the man, too."

"I reckon Catlett thinks he bought that claim rather high."

"Hush, boys," said Tom, "I was in that fray. The fellow brought it all on himself. He just got his deserts for a blasted, obstinate, impudent Yankee. That's so. And you'd better behave, and not talk that way about gentlemen before their friends, or there'll be a muss."

"O, Tom, don't get riled, now. We didn't mean the

9*

first thing. Of course it was all right. We always sup-
posed so. 'T was a fine job. He! he! he! Holloa
Dave, gettin' dry, are you? Well, you've come home to
Christmas? How do you like it over there?"

"First rate! high times huntin' and goin' it. Turner
and I are right jolly. Plenty of fun, and more flyin' bullets than you can shake a stick at. George! they come
whizzin' in at the windows every day, and they don't seem
to come from nowhere, neither. Aunt Adeline—that's
my woman—says it's the old boy himself, and I reckon
she ain't far out of the way."

"Ain't you lonesome?"

"Pooh, no! not a bit of it. Would n't come back to
the prairie for nothin'. It's all so wild and independent
like. Tom, you would n't find it any object to be prinkin'
over there all day."

"The reason you don't prink, is 'cause you can't look
anyhow if you do," said Tom.

"O, shut up, Tom, and what's your hurry. Come sit
down and let me tell you how I shot a deer the other
day. It was just the neatest piece of work. You see—"

"Hang your stories, Dave. I can't stop now. There's
lots of pretty girls down stairs waitin' to dance with me.
It's really too bad to keep them in such suspense."

"Well, be off, then, and look out sharp, Tom, or the
town feller will cut you out with Catlett's pretty little school-marm. He 's been shinin' up to her all the
evening."

"The langest day maun hae an end," says the old Scotch
proverb, and it was with a sigh of relief that Fanny at last
saw Uncle Jake lay down the tortured fiddle, and the
dancers with lingering steps and wishful eyes retire to
seek the few hours of repose that were left of the night.
"Confusion worse confounded" reigned for a time in the

apartment appropriated to the ladies' use, and the numer-
ous-couches spread upon the floor increased the difficulty
of navigation. At last, when quiet seemed restored, and
Fanny was sinking into a peaceful sleep, she was aroused
by her neighbors in an adjoining bed, three young ladies,
who declared that they were "all but starved, and must
have something to eat before they could go to sleep."
One of the black women was dispatched to the store-room
for some slices of cold bacon, and sitting up in bed, with
the candle before them, they made a hearty repast.

"Of course you can't eat half as much as you want at
table," said one of the young ladies, apologetically; "one
always wants to appear delicate-like before the gentlemen."

"What in goodness' name, Nan, made breakfast so
late," said Dave the next morning, or rather noon, as
they were returning home; "I thought one while we
was n't goin' to get any."

"Why, you see, they had n't any wheat flour in the
house for the biscuit," said Nanny, "and they had to send
three miles over the prairie to Mr. John Turner's, to borrow some."

"Twenty people invited to stay over night, and no flour
in the house?" said Fanny, in amazement.

"It rather shocks your Yankee ideas of looking out
ahead, Miss Hunter," said Mr. Chester, laughing. "We
are used to such things out this way."

"Lor, Miss Fanny, people can't remember every thing,
you know," said Nanny; "Belle says they never thought
a word about it till this morning."

CHAPTER XX.

ONE day, while Aunt Phebe was dozing in her arm-chair, and the little black babies under her charge had taken the opportunity to crawl into the ashes, her nap was interrupted by the sudden entrance of Maud. Without speaking, the child took her usual seat on the low stool close to the old woman's chair, and fixing her eyes on the floor, continued for a few moments in moody silence.

"Now what ails de child?" said Aunt Phebe at length, who was pretty well used to such exhibitions of ill-humor, though they had been less frequent of late. "Come, tell old aunty all about it. Any bad lessons to-day?"

"I hate lessons," said Maud, "and I hate the old school. I wish pa would n't make us learn any more. I do so."

"Lors, now, what's come over de chil'?" said Aunt Phebe, in astonishment. "Gettin' on so fast wid her lessons, and sich a pretty lady for teacher, too."

"I don't car'!" said Maud, sullenly, "I wish she'd go away."

"Dat ain't Miss Maud speakin' dat ar way," said the old woman, sorrowfully; "dat ar ain't my chil', no how; 'bout Miss Fanny, too, so good an' gentle. Here she come las' night, tellin' ober what good lessons her scholars gets, and dem soft eyes o' hern, shining all de while for joy. 'Why, Aunt Phebe,' says she, 'I'm real proud of 'em;' bless her heart, she said dem bery words, she did, ouly las' night."

"I reckon she ain't very proud of me," said Maud.

"You don'no 'bout dat, honey. Sha'n't let on, no how, but I knows what she said, to make ole aunty's heart glad, I does. What's put it inter Miss Maud's head to shift 'bout so?"

"Well, aunty, she's so strict with us. She won't let us whisper, nor play, nor do the first thing in school, and this evening she took away all Johnny's marbles; and I would n't learn any lesson, and she made me stay in all play-time, and I was real mad then; just as mad as I could be."

"Well, tain't no way for my chil' to act; gettin' mad at nothin an' losin' her lesson. Do a heap more harm to her own sef, dan odder folks. What keeps her here now, when Miss 'Ria, and Cal, an' all ob 'em gone off walkin' wid de teacher?"

"'Cause I would n't go, aunty," said Maud; "they all asked me to, but I would n't."

"Why not, honey?"

"'Cause I was mad, aunty."

"Well, now, what de use gettin' mad, anyhow. Miss Fanny she don't want yer foolin' in school; she wants yer to learn heaps, 'cause she says so; and old aunty, she wants to see her chil' head ob 'em all. But lors! 't ain't no use talkin'. Miss Maud knows book-larnin's ob great 'count now-a-days; 'spec' she 'll know heaps, and be a real lady, one ob dese years, when ole aunty gone up to glory."

"What makes *you* want me to know heaps, aunty?" said Maud, in a softer tone.

"Caus' I lubs my chil'," said the old woman, laying her

withered hand upon Maud's head. "If ole Phebe could see her chil' a growin' up good, and kind, and lubly, she'd be all ready to go right up. Dat ar's what lays on her heart times."

"Aunty," said Maud, looking up lovingly into the old woman's face, "I *will* learn my lessons to please *you*, and I will try to be good, but oh, it's so hard, times. Ain't it mighty hard work to be good, aunty?"

"'Deed 'tis," said Aunt Phebe. "Dar ain't nothin' so hard in dis yer world. Satan allers standin' round, puttin' snags in de way. You got to fight him chil'en, fight him mighty hard, too. Miss Fanny she say las' night dar's nothin' like prayin'. I b'lieves it too."

"Miss Fanny prays every morning in school, aunty, and last Sunday evening, you know, when it was so warm, we all went down to the creek, and sat on the old bridge, and she talked real pious to us, like you do times, aunty, and we sung hymns, and she told us stories out of the Bible. She tells pretty stories, and she plays with us, and shows us new games, and never gets mad when we don't understand, like Nanny does. Does prayin' keep her from gettin' mad?"

"I 'spec' so, honey. Dis prayin''s a won'erful ting. But, lors! if I didn't come nigh to forgettin' dem ar gauba peas I baked dis yer mornin', a purpose for Miss Fanny. Jest fetch 'em out ob de bake-kettle, honey an' I'll take de shucks off."

"I'll shuck 'em for her, aunty," said Maud, eagerly. "Let me. Miss Fanny likes gauba peas, 'caus' I heard her say so the other day," and Maud was soon busily occupied in preparing Aunt Phebe's gift for the teacher whose absence she had so lately wished, talking cheerfully all the while about school to Aunt Phebe, who occasionally put in a question or remark.

Conversations of this kind often passed between the old
woman and the child, commencing in an angry discontented mood by Maud, but invariably ending in smiles
and good humor. Once put upon the right track, no one
understood better how to manage Maud than Aunt
Phebe; and as no one else possessed half the influence
over her, Fanny found that she had enlisted on her side
an invaluable assistant. Maud could be led much easier
than driven, and when Fanny failed, as with all her skill
she sometimes did, in exacting obedience, Aunt Phebe
would take up the matter, and contrive to bring her into
a state of perfect submission.

To Aunt Phebe's cabin Fanny often resorted, to tell
over her little joys and sorrows, and to listen to the words
of cheerful hope and courage, that fell from the old woman's lips. She took great comfort in her society, while
next to Maud, there was no person Aunt Phebe appeared
to love so well as "Miss Fanny."

"Aunty," said Maud, as she was shucking the pea-nuts,
" do you think pa will be vexed, 'caus' Miss Fanny teaches
us so much religion?"

" 'Deed I don't, Miss Maud. Mass' Jack got eyes in
his head well as odder folks. Can't help seein' de good
Miss Fanny doin' us all. Who put dat ar notion in de
chil's head?"

" Nanny said she reckoned he 'd think it took too much
time," said Maud.

"Lors, Miss Nanny don't know. It don't neber hender
nobody to stop an' pray on de road. Don't you b'lieve dat."

" O, there they come," said Maud, as she ran to the
door to empty her shucks. "There they come, Cal, and
'Ria, and Joy, and there's Miss Fanny, and—why, aunty,
she 's got Mr. Chester, the town gentleman, with her, and
I declare they are comin' right this way."

"Lors, be they? Dinah, fetch up de stools, and take de baby out ob de ashes. Here, Jake, you can toat I'olly down to de spring awhile. Dar, now, we's ready," said Aunt Phebe, looking complacently round her domain.

"Howd'y, Aunt Phebe?" cried a chorus of young voices, and she was soon surrounded by a group of children, all talking at once, while the elder portion of the company followed more leisurely.

"Behave, chil'en, can't ye?" said Aunt Phebe. "Hush a minute. Don't s'pose want to speak to Miss Fanny, dar, an' young massa? Lors, Miss Fanny's cheeks look jes like my June roses when de dew's off. 'Pears like libin on de prairie 'grees wid her de bes' kind. Mass' Harry come in to see ole Phebe, too! Great honor dese days. Hope you are well, massa?"

"Very well, Aunt Phebe," said the young man, advancing to shake hands. "I stopped a moment to say good-by. I leave early to-morrow morning."

"Dar, now, dat ain't de best news in the world. What goin' off for jes' get a little 'quainted? S'pose got tired ob de country. Mighty dull up here for town folks, dey say, any how; but 'pears like Mass' Harry got along mighty pleasant wid us all."

"I am very sorry to go," said the young man. "I have found it any thing but dull up here." He spoke in a tone, the sincerity of which it was impossible to doubt.

"You like it den? Dat curis, now. Miss Fanny she like it, too. Come here todder night, tellin' how happy she were, but, lors! Mass' Harry, it don't take much to make Miss Fanny pleased. She carry a little heaben ob her own wid her, whareber she go. Dere now, Miss Fanny, need n't shake yer head 'bout it. Must tell de truth, leastways."

"Go on, Aunt Phebe," said Mr. Chester, laughing.

"Miss Fanny's testimony can't be received in the present case. It has no weight."

"Dar's odders 'sides ole Phebe tinks dat way," said the old woman, slyly. "Mr. Tom Walton mighty fond o' huntin' dese times, and dem Turner boys gets heaps ob holidays."

"Come, children, we must go directly," said Fanny, "or we shall lose our supper. Mr. Chester, you and Aunt Phebe can enjoy a conversation together, only I advise you to choose a more interesting subject. Thank you, dear," to Maud, who just then was slipping her present into Fanny's pocket.

"Dar, now, nebber did see what a hurry Miss Fanny in. Won't hardly get a chance to say good-by. Likely I goin' to keep Mass' Henry here arter *she's* gone. Hi! no doin' dat. Well! well! far-well, Massa Henry. De good Lord go wid ye, and gib yer good luck in dis world, and de world to come. It's like you'll nebber see ole Phebe's face agin on dis sid' Jordan—but I hopes I'll see yer up yonder. I wishes yer heaps o' good, massa, and ole Phebe's blessin' won't do you no harm leastways —."

CHAPTER XXI.

POOR WHITE FOLKS

THE winter passed rapidly on the prairie, and Fanny's first vacation was approaching. The children were anticipating a great many delightful rambles with their teacher, whose company now seemed as desirable as it had once been unwished. Mr. Catlett, too, had planned a ride to Cartersville some pleasant day with Miss Fanny and his daughter Nanny, for companions; and Mr. Tom Walton had been over twice within a week, to arrange a pic-nic excursion, to take place during the holidays. All these plans were scattered to the winds, by a letter which arrived from St. Louis the day before school closed. This important missive was from Cousin Julia Stanton, and contained a cordial invitation to Cousin Nanny, and Miss Fanny Hunter, to spend a couple of weeks in the city. Nanny had been talking all winter about a visit to St. Louis, and was only too delighted to receive the summons; but how Miss Fanny came to be invited, was a question that puzzled her not a little.

"I did n't reckon they knew we had a teacher," she said, in talking the matter over with her mother. "I don't see how they found it out."

"I do, then," said 'Ria. "It was that young sprig of a lawyer, that was here last winter. I always knew he took a notion to Miss Fanny."

"Why, 'Ria Catlett, did n't you know he was engaged to Cousin Julia? Take a notion to Miss Fanny, indeed! Why she 's only the teacher."

"She 's a smart lady, anyhow," said 'Ria, "and a pretty one, too. But who told you that young Chester is engaged to Cousin Julia? I never heard it."

"Bob Turner told us. He 's in Uncle Edward's family a good deal, you know, when he 's in town, and he says Mr. Chester is there most every day, and it 's town talk that they are engaged. But about Miss Fanny, I reckon that was the way, ma, sure enough; and I 'll be right glad to have her go with me, too. I sha'n't feel the least bit ashamed of her. She sets up in company as pretty as any body."

"Ashamed of her!" said 'Ria. "Well, that 's a good one! She 'll have a heap more occasion to feel ashamed of you, Nanny."

"'Ria," said Mrs. Catlett, "I can 't allow you to talk that way to your sister. Miss Fanny is very well. We are all pleased with her, but when you get to making comparisons between her and Nanny —"

"You are right, ma," said 'Ria, gravely. "It is a little too ridiculous to be sure."

"Of course you 'll go," said Nanny, who announced the news the moment Fanny came in from school. "We 'll have just the nicest times."

"I should love to go dearly," said Fanny, "but—"

"No buts, Miss Fandango," said Mr. Catlett. "If you want to go, that 's enough. The thing 's settled."

"Not exactly," said Fanny. "You know I 'm a stranger to Judge Stanton's family."

"Granny fiddlestring! Can't you remember that you are out of Yankee land, where they count the cost of every meal of victuals! You'll be welcome there as long as you 'choose to stay."

"You did n't hear me out, Mr. Catlett," said Fanny; "that is not what I intended to say, but allow me to tell you, that if ever you should sojourn in that same Yankee land, you would find they could teach you, Missourians, something about hospitality."

"Now we 've raised her spunk," said Mr. Catlett, who was always delighted if he could draw Fanny into a defense of the Yankees. "You'd teach us hospitality, would you? Come, tell us how, I want to begin to learn."

"No, Mr. Catlett," said Fanny, pleasantly, "I 'm not going to say another word on the subject. You see I'm what you call 'touchy,' in all that pertains to my old home, and so I must bite my lips and be silent."

"Besides," said Nanny, "that is n't the question. I want to know whether Miss Fanny goes to town or not? Don't you think she ought to, ma ?"

"Miss Fanny must do as she pleases about it," said Mrs. Catlett; "but she need n't stop for fear of not being welcome. Your Aunt Susan likes mighty well to have young people about her, and I reckon you would have fine times together."

"Times! times!" said Madam Hester, catching the last words. "There ain't been sich since the old gineral died. Dances, and parties, and weddin's. And they do say the gal caught a husband at one of 'em." She nodded her head knowingly, and sank back again.

"There, girls, you see what Madam Hester thinks about it," said Mrs. Catlett. "Who knows what may happen."

"I would n't go, Miss Fanny," whispered Cal; "we want you here so bad."

"I would then," said Maud.

"What do you talk that way for, Maud? Do you want to get rid of Miss Fanny?"

"No, indeed, Cal. I'd want her here as bad as any of you; but I hope I would n't be mean enough to keep her, when she could go to town and see all the sights."

"You *will* go," said Nanny, beckoning Fanny into the passage.

"Yes, Nanny, I will go."

"My sakes, now, how we shall have to scratch round to get ready. She says we must be sure to get there the first of the week, and here 'tis Thursday now. You can't think, Miss Fanny, how funny I feel about going. One time I want to go so bad, and then again I feel kinder 'fraid."

"Afraid, Nanny?"

"Yes. You don't know what smart folks they are. Uncle Edward is just the politest gentleman you ever see, and Aunt Susan so lady-like and soft spoken, and then Cousin Julia; I never see any body put on as she can; and she's so fixy we sha'n't look like any thing by the side of her."

"In dress, do you mean?"

"Yes, you see there's only her left. The other girls are all married off, and she just has every thing she wants. I s'pose she'll step off pretty soon, and then the old folks will be all alone."

"Is she engaged?"

"So they say. Bob Turner was down last week, and he says 't will be a be."

"Who is the happy man? Do you know?"

"Lors, yes, it's Mr. Chester, that was up here Christmas. I think it's a grand match. He's so handsome and smart, and she'll have plenty of money. They say Uncle Edward is mightily pleased about it. But, there, I must go this minute and get ma to stop Patsey weavin', and let me have her the balance of the day. If you 'll believe it, Miss Fanny, there 's only one woman on this place that 's any thing of a seamstress; that 's Patsey, and she 's the weaver; so it 's mighty hard to get any thing done. But I don't care if ma does scold. I 'm going to have that blue worsted frock of mine taken in, in the body. It don't fit half tight enough—town ladies are always so little round the waist. Then there 's my black silk. That fits beautiful, if it only had some new trimming; and we must be sure and take our lawn frocks, 'cause we shall be asked out to night parties. If I had known certainly that we was going, I 'd have sent down by Dave, when he took down the beeves, and got me a new frock."

"O we shall do very well, Nanny. Of course they won't expect us country girls to be in the fashion exactly. We will try not to disgrace them, by dressing shabbily, and they will make all due allowance for deficiencies."

"*You* always look trim in a bit calico, Miss Fanny. I never see any body keep their things so nice as you do."

"Any thing but nice, Nanny; but there! if my head is n't too much turned by the prospect of this town visit. I think I will go into school. Come, scholars, mine; 'Ria, Cal, and Maud, it 's past one o'clock."

The day before, Fanny had supposed herself perfectly contented to spend her vacation on the prairie; but when the invitation arrived, the prospect of a change seemed so refreshing, that she wondered how she could ever have gone through the year without it. "Our little Connecticut school-marm," as Mr. Catlett loved to call her, was not indifferent to dress. She was too much of a woman not to possess the feminine trait of liking to appear well in the eyes of others, and she accordingly set about her preparations for the visit, with a great deal of zeal and pleasure. The old sheet was brought down from the loft, and the silk dresses released from their long confinement, every wrinkle smoothed and every fold adjusted; and when this was done, packed carefully in the black trunk, with others for more common use. Next the traveling-hat, with its green ribbons, underwent a careful inspection, and with a little pressing and the insertion of a fresh lining, was made to look, as the children said, "jest as good as new."

The doing up of the collars and under-sleeves belonged to Viny's department, and proud and consequential she felt when she brought them up stairs where the young ladies were packing their trunks.

"They look beautifully, Viny," said Fanny; "so sheer and white. We must give you the prize for doing up muslins. Look, Nanny."

"Yes, yes," said Nanny, who was very busy at her trunk; "just put them on the bed, Viny, and hand me them shoes, and then go and tell ma to send up my black spencer, if it 's mended. Come, be off."

Still Viny lingered.

"What is it, Viny?" said Fanny. .

Viny opened her hand slyly, and displayed a piece of silver.

"Would dat ar buy one ob dem little straw hats, like Patsey's baby got, Miss Fanny?"

"Yes," said Fanny, "do you want me to get one for you."

"If Miss Fanny would now," said Viny, "tied with a little red ribbin. Mighty fixy, you know."

"Well, I will get you one," said Fanny. "Never mind about the money. You keep it safe till I come back, and then we 'll see about it."

"Mebbe Miss Fanny won't have 'nuff to last," said Viny, still proffering the coin.

"O yes, never fear for that."

And Viny went down stairs rubbing her hands, and talking softly to herself, "Dat ar Patsey braggin' 'bout her baby; nothin' but a blue skinned nigger, anyhow. Don't begin wid mine."

This was the commencement of a long list of commissions to be executed in town. Not alone for those upon the place, though every servant had some little trifle for Miss Nanny or Fanny to get, but every body in the neighborhood seemed in want of something, and no sooner was it known that Nanny Catlett and the new teacher were going to town, than the requests came pouring in. Mrs. Turner sent for some children's dresses, Mrs. Baldridge for a dozen yards of sheeting, and Madam Gamby for three yards of cap bordering, of a certain width, to cost not over a bit a yard, and as much below that price as it was possible to obtain it.

The young ladies undertook all the charges, promising to do the best they could, Nanny remembering that they should have cousin Julia to shop with them, and show them all the best stores.

"Your father is going to the store with you, Nanny, to see you off," said Mrs. Catlett, as they were taking an early supper before starting. "He don't like to have you go alone, especially as you've got to wait at Belcher's."

"Must we take the stage at the store?" said Fanny, in surprise. "I thought you always staid at Mr. Baldridge's."

"So we do, but they're all gone down to Cartersville, and there's no private house on the road except Tim Jenkins's."

"Tim Jenkins's!" said Nanny, in great disgust. "I think I see myself stopping there! You see it will be

pleasant enough at the store, Miss Fanny. There's two
rooms, you know, and they'll give us one all to ourselves.
We can't reckon on gettin' much sleep any how, for the
stage starts at two."

Just then Mr. Catlett appeared, and big William soon
after, driving the wagon to the door, the good-byes were
said, and the party drove merrily off.

At the store Mr. Catlett jumped out to see what
accommodations he could procure for the ladies, but soon
returned with a long face.

"Now we are in a hobble," he said. "There isn't an
inch of room here. There's three men from Cartersville,
waitin' to take the stage, and a couple of drovers from up
the country. They are a rowdy, drunken set, any how,
and besides they'll have to use both rooms."

"What in the world shall we do?" said Nanny.

"Well, I don't see but one way, and that is to drive on
half a mile further, and stop at Tim Jenkins's. They'll
find a room for you in their old shell, and it won't do you
any hurt for one night."

"Mercy on us!" screamed Nanny, "stop with them
'poor white folks!' Why, pa, you are crazy! I'd rather
wait in the road."

"Well, you'll have to, if you are so set about it, or else
turn about and go home, for it's the only way I know of,"
said Mr. Catlett.

"Why can't you let big William drive us on to Hull's?"

"That would be smart! Five miles and back after
night, over such a road as this. No, we'll go home, and
wait another day."

"O dear! Miss Fanny, what would you do?" said
Nanny.

"I think we had better stop at this Mr. Jenkins's. If
we waited another day we might not be any better off.

I suppose they are liable to be full any night at the store."

"Yes, indeed," said Mr. Catlett. "There's a deal of travel just now from up the country. Come, Nanny, do show a little common sense for once in your life."

"But they are such low people," said his daughter. " wouldn't have it known we stopped there for all the world."

"Well, nobody will know it, and you needn't have the first thing to do with 'em, only to stay there in the room they give you, till the stage comes along."

"I shouldn't wonder if they wouldn't let us stay," said Nanny. "Such people are always spiteful to their betters."

"Pshaw! they'll be proud of the chance to keep you. Drive on, William."

"Well," said Nanny, "I never thought I should come down to askin' a lodgin' of 'poor white folks.' If I didn't want to go so bad, I'd turn right round and go home now."

A ride of half a mile over the prairie, brought them to their stopping-place. Fanny could just see in the thickening darkness, that it was a small log house, a little back from the road. At the noise they made in stopping, a wooden shutter was pushed open, and the figure of a child, with long hair, and a dirty, haggard face, appeared a moment, holding a lighted candle in her hand.

"Oh, dear," said Nanny, "that's the young one, I reckon. How I hate to go in."

"Hush up!" said Mr. Catlett, "they are comin' to the door."

It was opened by the man who had paid Mrs. Catlett a visit the day after Fanny's arrival. His face expressed a kind of angry surprise on seeing who it was, and he made a movement as though he would have shut the door in their faces, but restrained himself.

"How are you, Jenkins?" said the squire. "These women want to stop here till the stage comes along. Baldridge's gone, and the store's full. Can you give 'em a room?"

"I'll see," said the man, coldly. And setting down his candle, which was stuck into an old bottle, upon the floor, he left them together.

"I told you how 't would be, pa. You've come on a fool's errand after all. He looked like he'd bite a door nail in two," said Nanny.

Just then a woman came courtesying forward. She had a lean, sallow face, with gray locks hanging over it, and was dressed in a ragged black petticoat, and a short gown, while her feet were slip-shod and stockingless.

"Walk right in, ladies; walk right in to the fire. I'm sure you are quite welcome," she said, courtesying between each sentence, and smoothing down her rags.

Her servile politeness seemed more offensive to Nanny than the man's sulky ill-humor.

"We are plenty warm," she said, hastily drawing back as the woman approached. "Could you let us stay in this room till the stage comes along?"

She looked round the forlorn apartment as she spoke, which occupying half the house, opened directly upon the front door.

"La, yes;" said the woman. "Pa, you step right out, and toat in an armful of that light wood, and scare up a fire. You'd better come in where it's warm, ladies. This room ain't used much, and it feels mighty agueish to me." She shook as she spoke till her rags fluttered.

It was not an inviting place. The close cellarish air was reeking with the smell of boiled cabbage, and long cobwebs were flaunting from the bare rafters overhead. The floor was partly broken up, and some of it appeared to have been used for fuel, an ax still lying by a half-split plank. Two or three barrels and boxes, some old shoes, a few carpenter's tools on a shelf, and a bunch of dried herbs hanging in the chimney-corner, was all the room contained, and nothing could exceed its desolate appearance.

But Nanny refused to go into the apartment where the family lived. She appeared to think that this would place her too much upon an equality with her entertainers, and begged Fanny so earnestly not to go, that she prevailed, and they both sat shivering on an old box till a fire was kindled, and began to diffuse a little warmth through the room. The man performed this task in sulky silence, and after bringing in an armful of wood from the other room, he left them to themselves.

"Now, then," said Mr. Catlett, "I 'm going back to Belcher's, and when the stage takes us up there, I 'll give you a signal. You must be sure to wake up and be ready."

"Wake up!" said Nanny. "I 'm sure I don't reckon on sleepin' one single wink. That man has a dreadful, dangerous look to me. What an ugly scowl he put on."

"Poor creatures!" said Fanny. "They look as though they had seen hard times."

"I reckon them sort of people always do," said Nanny, in an indifferent tone. "Poor, miserable, shiftless, no account things! Well, now, this is a little more like. Come, Miss Fanny, you help me toat this old box nigher the fire, and we 'll really be tolerably comfortable."

"Nanny," said Fanny, after a pause. "We are treating these people very rudely."

"How?" said Nanny. "We have n't had any thing to do with 'em that I know of."

"Well, that's the very thing. Here we are under their roof, and warming ourselves by their fire, and yet treating them with cold contempt. I don't think it is right."

"Why not, pray? Do you think we are going to keep company with 'em out there in their hog-pen?"

"I think we ought to go and sit with them a while," said Fanny. "It seems so proud, and hard-hearted, to be away here by ourselves, as though they were not good enough to speak to."

"Well, they ain't," said Nanny, bluntly.

"Besides," said Fanny, thoughtfully, "they seem very poor, and wretched, perhaps we might say something to comfort them and do them good."

"Fanny Hunter, you are wild," said Nanny. "Go and sit with those low folks, and hear over their grievances? No, indeed; you won't catch me at it. Ma never allowed us to speak to 'em, if we could help it, and the very niggers turn up their noses at 'em."

"I can't help it," said Fanny. "I feel sorry for them, and if you would n't mind staying alone awhile, I should like to go in and talk with them."

"Now, Miss Fanny, you ain't goin' in there sure enough? If you knew what a disgrace it is to be seen speaking to such people, you would n't stir a step. I'm sure you ought to be ashamed for our sakes, if you don't care yourself."

"If it's a disgrace to have any thing to do with them, Nanny, you and I have disgraced ourselves pretty thoroughly by asking a night's lodging. I don't think tha treating them kindly now that we are here, can make the matter any worse. Besides you are not in the least responsible for what I do; I will take all the blame, if there is any. But if you feel afraid to stay alone —"

"O! go, if you choose," said Nanny, a little testily.

"If you can find any comfort in keeping company with such folks, I'm sure you are welcome to go."

Fanny hesitated a moment, and then knocked softly at the door of the next room.

"May I come in?" she said, opening it a little way.

The woman tipped the contents of a chair upon the floor, and hastened to set it near the fire, inviting the young lady to be seated, but the master of the house, who was idly whittling a bit of wood, did not raise his eyes.

It was a wretched place, as filthy and comfortless a den as was ever claimed by a poor creature for his home. From the rotting timbers overhead, with their broad cracks, through which the wind whistled, down to the dirty floor and the unswept hearth, all told a tale of thriftless, abject misery.

They had just finished eating, and the woman was shuffling backward and forward, between the table and a shelf in the corner, where she stowed away the unwashed dishes and the remnants of a corn-cake, from which they appeared to have made their meal. A little girl, ragged and dirty, was squatted flat upon the floor, munching a bit of the crust.

To her, Fanny first addressed herself, but her attempts at commencing an acquaintance were met only by a broad vacant stare, and a continued munching at the crust.

"Can't you speak to the lady, Jane?" said her mother. "You need n't mind her, miss, she don't see much company, and feels kind of strange, you see."

"How old is she?" inquired Fanny, pleasantly.

"She'll be ten next September; but she's small of her age. The chills seemed to have stinted her growth. I'm in hopes she'll take a start by-and-by."

"Have you found a school for her yet?" said Fanny.

It was an unfortunate question.

" No," said the man, gruffly, " thanks to such as you, the brat's left to grow up a heathen. You can think of that for your comfort, when you are teachin' the rich man's children."

" O, pa, don't," said the woman.

" I was a fool for goin'," he continued, without heeding the interruption. " I might have known the kind of answer they'd give me. Their very niggers, curse 'em! hooted me out of the yard. I might have known it. What do you care what becomes of the poor man's young 'uns, so you get another sort to work on?"

" Mr. Jenkins," said Fanny, gently, " you forget that it was not I who refused to teach your little girl. I can't choose my own scholars."

" O, eh, you are like all the rest of 'em. You like the rich man's money the best. You'd trample us down to the very ground you tread on. That's what you'd do. And put the miserable nigger-drivers over our heads."

" Why, pa, I'm sure you said the young lady was a mind to take her, if the mistress was willin'," said the woman. " Don't talk that way now, don't!"

" Well, mebbe she was," said the man, drawing his hand over his forehead, as if to clear his thoughts. " I get confused times, and can't remember. These troubles are drivin' me crazy, I reckon. You see I *did* want that gal to know something," he continued, pointing to the forlorn child. " She's the last of five as likely children as any of your nigger owners' brats. The fever carried off four of 'em, one after the other, and when the last two lay dead in the house, and she goin' the same way, I prayed the Lord to spare us just this one; but there! she'd be better off, lyin' alongside the other four."

" O, pa!" said the woman again.

"And why not?" he said sharply, "You know what she's growin' up to, and how the very nigger wenches will look down on her. You know the life we've led in this cursed country, where it's a disgrace to a man to work for his living, and any lazy fool that can keep a few niggers to wait on him, turns up his nose at an honest mechanic. There's republicanism for you! We are all free and equal here, young woman, ain't we? When I came to this country, I had a wife and four children as likely as any body's, a good trade, and a pair of stout arms to work it, and one hundred dollars in cash that I laid out on this place, 'rot it! We've been here just ten years, and you see what we are."

He rose to his feet as he spoke, lean and gaunt as the very image of famine, and as Fanny gazed from him to his wretched companion, who in her filth and rags stood listlessly leaning against the chimney, and upon the pallid, half idiot face of their child, his words came home to her with terrible reality.

"Yes, you see what we are," he repeated bitterly; "'poor, no account, white folks,' they call us; hardly good enough for their niggers to speak to. And what's made us so. Tell me that, will you? Did n't I come here, ready to dig and work, week in and week out, to keep my family respectable. We were poor, to be sure, but my house was as clean and my children as well dressed as any body's. How did I come to be a shiftless, lazy, good-for-nothing fellow, and my wife what she is, hey?"

He turned fiercely to Fanny for an answer, but she only shook her head.

"I'll tell you," he said, hissing the words out between his clenched teeth, "it's this cursed *slavery* that's done it. It's robbed us of our honest livin', it's cheated us and starved us, and dragged us down lower than the ly-

ing, thievish, black-faced rascals they call slaves. Slaves!
They are all slaves in this confounded hole. The masters
are slaves to their servants, and the servants to the masters, and we—we are the lowest slaves of any. Did n't I
slave it for 'em when I joined that rascally expedition over
the border, to rout a man off his own land? Did they
tell you it was Tim Jenkins, 'poor white folks,' that struck
the first blow, and led on the cowardly slave-holding devils to do the rest. Hey? What did I do it for? Because they paid me for it, girl. It's only for such kind
of work they pay white folks in Missouri. I 've seen the
time when I 'd have gone on my knees to 'em for a job of
honest work, to keep my wife and children from starving."

"Is there no way of getting employment?" said Fanny.
"Can't you find some kind of work?"

"Can I? Have n't you been long enough in this vile
country to find out that there 's no such thing as free labor
here? Would any body pay out money to a white man,
do you think, when they could get a nigger for nothin'?
I tell you, girl, the richest slave-holder in Missouri will go
with his roof unshingled and his chimneys tumbling down,
before he 'll pay an honest white man a sixpence. The
abolitionists talk about the wrongs slavery brings on the
niggers; let 'em tell what it does to the white man. I
could tell how it's ruined one family." He leaned his
head on his hand and groaned aloud.

"Why don't you move to a free State?" said Fanny.
"It 's but a little way into Illinois."

"Who is going to buy my place?" said the man.
"There are plaguy few as big fools as we were, when we
had the whole west to choose from, and settled down in a
slave State. Nobody ever comes from the free States
here to live. There 's hundreds to Illinois where there 's
one to Missouri. They can't but see what a curse there

10*

is on the land, how the very air is tainted, and stinks of slavery. Good Lord! it chokes me now. I have n't drawn a free breath since we crossed the river. No, no, gal, the devil sent us here, and stay here we must till we rot."

He flung himself out of the room, slamming the door ehind him.

"Deary me!" said the woman, wiping her eyes with ner ragged petticoat, "to see him now, and to think what he was when we come here. As good a workman at his trade as there was anywhere about, and so cheerful and happy, whistling at his work, and kind to his children. Well, well!"

"Where did you live before you came to Missouri?" said Fanny.

"We lived in York State. My four children was all born there. We had a snug little place to live in, that we calculated to own before we died, but my man he took a notion to come west, and there could n't nothin' stop him. Well, we pulled up stakes, and come out here, and the first year we was all of us pretty much taken down with the chills. There was n't a neighbor within a mile, only Mr. Baldridge's folks, and they never would have any thing to do with us from the first. Well, you see, I had every thing to do, to wait on the rest, and I 've kept round when my head felt like a bushel-measure, and my hands would have sizzed if you 'd put 'em in water. We had a long spell of 'em, and the two girls never got up; they kinder pined away, and in the hot weather the fever took 'em, and we buried 'em both out yonder in the woods."

She stopped a moment to wipe her eyes, and went on.

"About that time this child was born. I 'd been kinder ailin' all summer. There did n't seem to be no strength

nor courage in me, work was dredful scarce, and then the
ague top of it all, made us all feel pretty low. The poor
little thing came into the world, right in the midst of all
our trouble, and it seemed as if it was stamped into her
from the very first. I never said any thing to my man
about it, but she ain't like the other children. She began
to shake the first hour she was born, and she's kept it up
by spells ever since. I can't help thinkin' I gave her so
much of the sorrow and trouble that was on us all, that
she'll never get over it. She'll sit there, cowerin' over
the fire, hours and hours, just as I used to. My man he
thinks if we got a little learning into her, 't would make
her more like other children, but I've an idea she's got
to carry that load through life. Poor thing! I don't know
but we'd all be better off in our graves."

"All this trouble and sorrow must lead you to think
sometimes of that world where none can ever come," said
Fanny, gently.

"It's precious little time such as we get to think about
another world. It's all we can do to keep soul and body
together in this," said the woman.

"But a world so full of pain, and distress, is hardly
worth one's whole life time of care. In the midst of want
and trouble, it is a blessed thought that God has a home
for those who are prepared to spend an eternity of bliss
with Him."

"I'm sure I don't want to live any more, if I once get
through here," said the woman. "One life is quite
enough for me."

"But you *must* live," said Fanny, earnestly. "Don't
you know that your soul can never die?"

"Yes, I know," said the woman, in a careless tone.
"I've no time to attend to such things."

Words were thrown away, so utterly careless and indif

ferent did she appear, and bidding her good-night, Fanny
returned to the other room.

She found the fire reduced to a bed of coals, and Nanny
with her shawl wrapped about her, stretched upon the
old box, fast asleep. She threw on a fresh log, and sitting
down, watched it crackle and blaze, while she thought
over the events of the evening. There was but a thin
partition between the rooms, and for an hour or two
she could hear the movements of her neighbors, the gruff
voice of the man now and then breaking the silence, but
the greater part of the conversation being carried on by
the woman. At length all became quiet, and leaning her
head on her hands, Fanny fell into a dreamy, half dozing
state, in which she could see nothing but the face of Tim
Jenkins peering out upon her from the decaying fire, in
grotesque shapes. It started up suddenly from a blackened ember, or grinned horribly from a bed of ashes,
dancing and flickering about a moment, and disappearing
only to spring up again in some doubly hideous form.

How long this continued she could not tell, but she was
suddenly roused from a deep slumber by a shrill whistle,
which broke the stillness of the air, and waking Nanny, they
hurried on their bonnets and shawls, and the next moment,
the rumbling of the stage was heard coming up the road.

Is was a clear, moonlight night, and as Nanny stepped
out of doors, she uttered an exclamation of surprise and
dismay.

"Mercy on us, Miss Fanny, it's a mud wagon!"

The vehicle thus denominated was a long, awkward
concern, set upon heavy wheels, and with a white cloth
top, being similar in appearance to a peddler's cart, or a
Shaker farm wagon.

"Come, are you ready?" said Mr. Catlett, jumping
down from his seat by the driver.

"O, pa, why did n't they come with the stage?" said Nanny, disconsolately.

"Because the road is so bad. They got mired last night the other side of Hull's."

"It seems as if every thing went against us," said Nanny. "The idea of drivin' into town in a mud-wagon. It 's too provoking! Just see what seats, and not a bit of straw in the bottom for our feet."

Long after the rude vehicle was plodding over the road, Nanny continued her complaints, and only ceased when sinking back in the corner, she fell into an uneasy slumber. The ride was in the highest degree uncomfortable; the wagon without springs, and the roads in the worst possible condition; and when about day-light they entered the narrow street of what had formerly been a thriving French trading village, but was now so small as scarcely to deserve the name, our travelers were too thoroughly chilled with the cold to think of any thing but the comforts of a fire and a warm breakfast.

At the only public house the village contained, with its projecting roof and long porch in front, they alighted, and quickly found comfort in its ample fireplace, where the great logs were burning as cheerily as at La Belle Prairie. A good breakfast and a little "fixin' up," made different beings of them, and when, on starting, the hateful mud-wagon was found to have been exchanged for the regular stage, Nanny's spirits all returned, and the rest of the journey was performed as prosperously as even that difficult young lady could have wished.

CHAPTER XXII.

CITY LIFE.

In Aunt Susan's pleasant breakfast-room, behold our country guests assembled one morning, as cozily settled as though they had been members of the family circle for weeks, instead of having spent the three previous days in staging it over a rough road.

Mrs. Stanton had a cordial, motherly way with her, and a habit of addressing all young persons as "my dear," that caused a stranger at once to feel at home in her society, and there was a tone in her voice that reminded Fanny so strongly of her mother, as once or twice to bring the tears into her eyes. "Cousin Julia" was all smiles and politeness, a very fine-looking girl, Fanny thought, with her dark eyes, graceful form, and proud bearing. The judge was just what she had imagined him to be, a gray-headed, gentlemanly man, somewhere between fifty and sixty years of age, a little stately in his carriage, but kind and affable in manners. He appeared late, and bowing slightly as he entered the room, walked straight to his wife's seat, and with a grave "good-morning, Mrs. Stanton," he gave her a hearty kiss, after which he shook hands with his guests. This happened every morning, the judge never omitting the ceremony, it being one of his old Virginia customs that must always be observed.

"We must have out the carriage, Julia, this fine morn-

ing," said the judge, "and show our young ladies a little
of the city.   Miss Hunter tells me it is all new to her, and
as for Miss Nanny, they have kept her up on the prairie
so long, that she must have forgotten all she knew about
us here."

"Harry Chester spoke of calling this morning, papa.
Our visitors are old acquaintances, you know, of his,"
said Julia.

"Yes, yes, I remember how they kept him up there
last winter, gallanting them about, till our young ladies
thought they had lost him for good and all.   Well, if
there's a younger beau in the question, of course I shall
stand no chance, though I *have* seen the time when young
ladies thought twice before they refused my invitations.
Hey, wife?"

"I can hardly tax my memory so far back, judge," said
Mrs. Stanton; "but Julia, my dear, you need not give up
your ride.   Mr. Chester can go with you; the carriage is
roomy."

"Yes, mamma," said Julia, "and then we can visit the
picture-gallery, you know.   It is so much pleasanter to go
with a gentleman."

"With a *young* gentleman, you mean," said her father.

"Now, papa, you know you never have time to go to
such places.   Of course we should n't think of asking
you."

"O, no, you are very considerate.   The young gentleman's time is of not the least consequence, I suppose."

"That's his look-out, papa.   He never seems in a grea
hurry at such times."

"Well, young ladies," said the judge, "I find that I
must now tear myself away from your charming society.
Julia, if I find you teaching these country lasses any of
your citified tricks, for instance how to lay snares for un

wary birds, I shall send them back to their prairie home forthwith, as the only way to keep them uncontaminated. So now be cautious. And give me a cup of Virginia water, and then I'm off."

They were standing in the hall, and stepping to the further end, where, upon a stand, stood a bucket of water, with a battered old gourd-shell hanging above it, Julia filled it, and brought it to her father. "There, young ladies," said the judge, with a flourish of his strange drinking-cup; "there's the gourd-shell that hung in my father's log-cabin in Virginia. I've drank out of silver cups since, but water never tastes half so sweet."

In the course of the morning Mr. Chester made his appearance. He seemed delighted to see the new-comers, and sitting down between them on the sofa, entered into an animated conversation about the prairie-people. Fanny, on her part, met him again with sincere pleasure, and either the cordial frankness of their greeting, or their freedom of conversation, excited Cousin Julia's notice.

"You became very well acquainted with Harry Chester last winter, did you not, Miss Hunter?" she remarked, as they were tying on their bonnets, preparatory to the ride. "You met quite like old friends."

"Did we?" said Fanny. "Well, I suppose, in a certain sense, we are. Friendships formed in the country, where we are dependent upon the home-circle for nearly all our society, ripen very fast, especially if the parties are gathered under the same roof. Nanny and I feel as if we had known Mr. Chester for years, instead of weeks."

"Yes, indeed," said Nanny. "He came right in, and made himself as much at home as if he had always lived there. He seemed kinder like one of the family. I tell you, Cousin Julia, it's a grand thing to have any one come so."

"Especially if that one is n't a disagreeable person in himself. Harry Chester must have been good company for you those long winter evenings."

"I reckon he was," said Nanny. "We missed him dreadfully when he went away. Did n't we, Miss Fanny?"

The ride was very pleasant. The country visitors were too busy in "seeing the sights" to attend to any thing else, and Julia and Mr. Chester kept up an animated conversation on the front seat, only stopping now and then to point out places of note. At the gallery of paintings, Fanny found occupation for a day, and her companions becoming a little out of patience at her slow progress, finally left her to take her own time in following them through the room.

When at length she looked about for them, Nanny was sitting upon one of the benches near-by, and Julia and Mr. Chester standing at the other end of the room. Their side-faces were turned toward her, and Julia, who was just then talking earnestly, had laid her gloved hand upon his arm, while he, Fanny thought, was gazing admiringly at her upturned face.

"How well she looks!" thought Fanny, "and what a handsome couple they make! We have come at a wrong time, I am afraid, to interrupt their pleasant little *tête-à-têtes*."

Returning again to her picture, she forgot every thing else, till Cousin Julia touched her on the arm, and asked, playfully, whether "she would stay there all day or go home and get some dinner?"

"One could afford well to lose a dinner, with such a rich treat before them," said Fanny, in the same tone; "but excuse me I have really kept you all waiting. Let us go at once."

"You are not half satisfied," said Mr. Chester, noticing her regretful glance as they left the room.

"No," said Fanny, laughing. "I'm leaving the feast very hungry."

"So am I," said Julia, "though in a different sense. My ride has made me very sharp for dinner. Come, or the soup will be off the table before we get there."

"Will you spend some long morning here with me?" said Mr. Chester, as they were going down stairs. "I should like to examine some of these pictures with you."

"I should like nothing better," said Fanny, frankly.

"Well, then, we will consider it settled," said the young gentleman.

"What is that you will consider settled, Mr. Chester?" said Cousin Julia, looking back.

"Only that Miss Hunter and I are coming here again, leaving all you young ladies, who are in such a hurry for your dinner, behind," said Mr. Chester, laughing.

"Treason! Nanny. Do you hear that?" said Cousin Julia, gayly; but she waited until the loiterers came up, and gave the conversation a general turn till they reached home.

The days passed swiftly away to our country friends. There was so much to do, so many things to see, and such a variety of occupations to fill up every moment, that time fled away like a dream. To Fanny, it was next to returning to her old home. This sudden change from her prairie life, with all its discomforts and inconveniences, to the comforts and even luxuries of a city residence, from the society of the uneducated and coarse, to a circle of refined and cultivated people, was almost too delightful to be true. She woke every morning with the vague expectation of finding her pleasant chamber, with its snowy bed, and graceful curtains, exchanged for the low, comfortless room, with its dozen occupants, on the prairie, and of hearing, instead of the chiming of the city clocks, the horn blown under her window, or big William's voice calling the cattle. Cheerful and happy she had been in the country, but this return to her old way of life, was so delightful, that her spirits seemed almost uncontrollable, and insensibly her enlivening influence spread itself through the house.

"I like that little New England girl," said the judge one day. "There's something very fresh and sparkling about her. She seems like a bird just uncaged, that flutters and sings, to try its very freedom. And, after all, she is so graceful and lady-like in her buoyancy, that one never thinks of calling her rude."

"Oh, no," said Mrs. Stanton, "she is far from that. I have learned to love her very much. With all her gayety, I am sure she has deep feeling, for when she spoke of her mother did n't you see how the tears came into her eyes. Poor child, I'm afraid she has had hard times this winter, at cousin Jack's."

The love and pity that Mrs. Stanton felt for the solitary girl, showed itself in her gentle words, and kind motherly ways. She invited Fanny's confidence, advised her in little matters about her dress, doctored her for a slight cold, and by a hundred little deeds of kindness, won her way into Fanny's heart. Poor child! she had scarcely known before how much she had missed a mother's tenderness, or how large the vacant place in her heart had been, till it was in some measure filled by this unexpected kindness. She gave her whole heart to this kind friend, and could scarcely have felt more grateful had she saved her life.

There was but one member of the family whose affections Fanny had failed to engage, and this was Cousin Julia. From the first, she had regarded her visitor with coldness and suspicion, and though perfectly lady-like and courteous in her conduct, omitting none of those polite attentions due to a guest, Fanny could not but feel at times that there was no heart in them. It was the only drawback to her happiness, and she troubled herself not a little to divine the cause. She admired cousin Julia exceedingly, often thinking, as she witnessed the grace and dignity with which she performed the honors of her father's house, how well fitted she was to adorn the high station which providence had assigned her.

And, indeed, there was much in Julia Stanton to call forth admiration. The pride and darling of her parents, she had received every advantage that money could obtain, and possessing naturally an attractive person and a quick, though somewhat superficial mind, she had grown up a decidedly brilliant girl. Such an one is not apt to lack admirers, epecially, if in addition to her other attractions, she is heiress to quite a fortune. Cousin Julia was toasted and flattered to her heart's content, and could at any moment have taken her pick from half a dozen suitors dangling in her train. But, though she dispensed her favors to all, dancing with one, riding with another, and flirting generally with the third, Fanny's quick eye singled out the favored one, and she felt more and more convinced, that the report which had reached La Belle Prairie, of cousin Julia's engagement, must be true. Indeed the young lady did not deny it herself, but when joked upon the subject by Nanny, put on that conscious modest air, that girls in such cases know very well how to assume, and which implies much more than they are willing openly to confess.

The color would sometimes flush into her cheek at the sudden mention of Harry Chester, and her wonted calmness of manner change to restless excitement, when his name was announced at the door. Her dress, too, received more than usual attention, if she were going with him to a lecture, or a concert; and she often watched his every look, and listened to the accents of his voice as though her very existence depended upon them. It was curious to mark the change that love had produced in the proud, self-respecting girl, and it seemed strange that she could not rest calmly in the consciousness of his love.

And he, the favored one, who among so many competitors had secured the prize, how did he bear this victory? He certainly manifested none of that restless excitement so observable in his fair lady-love; indeed he seemed almost too calm and self-possessed for a newly-accepted lover, nor did he single her out in the presence of other ladies by any exclusive attentions—he is too gentlemanly for that, Fanny thought—but he certainly did appear to enjoy her society exceedingly, and found some excuse for calling at the house every day. Then, too, he was always contriving long walks or rides into the country, on purpose, as Fanny thought, to secure her company a little while to himself. If this was his object, he had great reason to be grateful to Fanny for her exertions in his behalf. She puzzled her brains to find ways and means by which they might now and then be left together. If they were walking she always contrived to draw Nanny a little in front, or at home, found some urgent excuse for leaving the parlor. She often thought he gazed proudly at Julia, as she crossed the room; and once when they were going to a party, and Fanny was arranging some white rose-buds in her hair, she looked up suddenly, and caught such a look of tenderness and admiration in his eyes, that though she knew it was intended for another, its very warmth brought the color to her own check.

She often wished that Julia would permit her to love her, for she longed to congratulate her upon her choice, to whisper that she could not fail to be a happy woman with such a life companion, and this without an idea that such praises could be misunderstood or interpreted to express any thing but a disinterested regard for the person to whom they related. Fanny was very simple-hearted, and in her humility feeling herself far removed from cousin Julia's sphere, it never occurred to her that her evident appreciation of Mr. Chester's merits could excite any thing like jealousy in her fair hostess's breast. But cousin Julia gave her no opportunity to express any of these feelings, avoiding all intimacy, and giving her clearly to understand that she was her guest, and nothing more.

"She thinks I am 'only the teacher,' I suppose," thought Fanny. "O dear!" and she strove to bear the slight as well as she could.

With Mr. Chester, on the contrary, she was upon the best of terms. He had always treated her with consideration and kindness, not less now, when surrounded by beauty and fashion she made but one of a brilliant circle, than when, thrown together in the solitude of her prairie home, they held long talks together by the Christmas fire. He seemed to take a pleasure in drawing out her ideas upon various subjects, treating the opinions she advanced with respect, and explaining his own in return. Their long talks were resumed, and many a pleasant hour was spent—Fanny seated upon the corner of the sofa, working upon some crotchet-mats, to be carried home to Mrs. Catlett as a present, and Harry Chester beside her, engaged in some animated discussion.

Any body but our simple, unsuspecting little Fanny, could have seen that these talks were not pleasing to Julia, who occasionally tried to break them up, and transfer the gentleman's services to herself for the rest of the evening. It happened frequently, however, that some other admirer claimed her exclusive attention, and Fanny and Mr. Chester found themselves in some quiet corner for the hour together. Fanny made no attempt to conceal the pleasure she felt in these interviews. She had been so long deprived of intelligent society, that she prized it exceedingly, and felt very grateful to Mr. Chester for taking so much pains to amuse her, even giving up the pleasure of cousin Julia's society at times, to sit by poor little *her* on the sofa, and talk.

Harry Chester was a very self-sacrificing young man !

CHAPTER XXIII.

THE PATRIARCHAL INSTITUTION IN KANZAS.

"MISS FANNY, what do you suppose Dave is about to-day?" said Nanny, as the two young ladies sat together at work. "I wonder how he likes his new farm. Planting time is most over, and if it's as pretty a place as he says, it must be right pleasant there. How mighty smart he feels to be a man, all set up for life at eighteen. Only think of it! Our Dave!"

"I wish we could peep in upon them some day, and see the young massa, with Uncle Tim, and Aunt Adeline, and Jinny. Quite a snug little establishment they must have over in the wilds of Kanzas," said Fanny.

"Well, Miss Fanny, who knows but that we may. Pa said he thought it would be a grand idea to go over there after harvestin', and make Dave a visit. You know after the hot weather, it's right unhealthy on the prairie, and we might scare off the chills and fever, by goin' to a new place for a while."

"What! all of us, Nanny? Your mother and the children and all."

"Well, not the youngest, mebbe, but ma, and you and I, and one or two of the others. Ma says 'Ria could keep house for two or three weeks. She wants her to learn how."

"Well, that is an idea! Where could Dave put us all? There can't be room in his little cabin."

"Pa said there might be one built hard by, on purpose for us. You know it need n't be put up very tight, for it will be warm weather anyhow. They want another, too; for pa says the place is n't half worked, with only two men; and just as quick as he can spare another hand, he means to send Uncle Charles over. I expect Dave will have all the best hands before he gets through. He always was put above the other children, anyhow. But should n't you like to go, Miss Fanny? I think it would be real fun."

"Yes, I should like a taste of the wild life one must lead over there. But, Nanny, how shall we get along with the mysterious proceedings—the whizzing bullets, the strange noises, and all the other disturbances. Your mother is terribly afraid of ghosts."

"O, Miss Fanny, you don't think it's ghosts, do you really, now?"

"Not I. It may be the spirits, though, that tip tables, and pinch fingers, and carry on generally in these days. Hey, Nanny?"

"You are joking, Miss Fanny, ain't you, now?"

"Yes, Nanny, depend upon it, it's folks in the flesh, good, solid, substantial spirits, like ourselves. I should n't wonder—"

"Wonder what?"

"Well, never mind, I guess I won't say what I was going to."

"O, yes."

"Not now, Nanny, not now."

Possibly the reader is as curious to know about Dave in his border life in Kanzas, as Nanny and Fanny. We have left him there ever since the Christmas holidays, and the

11

spring has come, and planting time most over. So let us
trip it from St. Louis over, and while the girls are still
talking about him, we will see what he is about.

"Tim, you 'll have to plant that corn over again. The
rascals have pulled up every blade as sure as the world.
What a torment to live in this cursed hole. I swear
there 's no use in tryin' to do any thing."

Dave was leaning on his gun, under the big oak to
which the claim had first been nailed, while Uncle Tim
was squatted upon the grass near by, mending a harness.

"Lors a' massy! Mass' Dave, you don't mean to say
dat ar corn all pulled up, arter we 's waited so long to hab
him sprout. Well, if dese carryin's on don't beat dis nigger anyhow."

"And, Tim, I 'm goin' off to the woods; sha'n't be home
much before night, I reckon. You and Jerry better go
right at that patch of corn. Let old Poke Neck's harness
alone. The old man will be hoppin', if we don't have a
good crop of corn."

"Well, Massa Dave, jest keep out of dem traps, dat's
all. Golly! I reckon massa did n't find it de nicest ting
to get cotched and held fast by de leg all day. Might
hab been dar yet, if Uncle Tim had n't come along."

"Confound it!" says Dave, soliloquizing; "if I could
catch the scoundrels, would n't I whiz a little cold lead
through 'em. I wish, if the old man thinks it 's such a
prime place, he 'd come over and try it himself. Hang
me! if I don't think the devil 's here in bodily shape.
Adeline, she says she 's seen a woman skulkin' round;
but blast me! it ain't no woman."

To complete the series of Dave's misfortunes, Uncle
Tim the next day came home from the field sick, and before night was in a raging fever. There was no doctor
for twenty miles about, and Dave, who had never been

sick in his life, was not competent to nurse an ailing cat. The women, too, were but indifferent nurses, and poor Tim might have suffered for want of proper attention, had not his faithful wife been near at hand. When his young master stepped into the cabin where Uncle Tim lay, the poor fellow opened his eyes and begged so piteously for his wife, that Dave dispatched a messenger at once to Madam Gamby's claim, to fetch her over.

Madam Gamby, who all through planting, had divided her time between her farms in Missouri and Kanzas, happened just now to be spending a few days in the latter place. Lina was allowed to come, and with an anxious heart hastened to her sick husband, and after watching by him all night, returned early in the morning to her daily toil. This went on for two or three days, Tim continuing very sick, until one evening Lina presented herself at the door of the house, with her apron at her eyes.

"I wants to see de young massa," she said to one of the servants.

"Mass' Dave's out yonder in de hen-house. Sit down a crack, can't ye?" said Adeline, kindly. "You look clear tuckered out. Is Uncle Tim worse to-night?"

"I don'no," said Lina, "I hain't seen him. Miss Betsy say she can't spare me no more nights, 'cause I ain't fit for nothin' days. How ken I be, and he lyin' so bad sick?"

"She!" said Adeline, indignantly, "so mighty stingy. I reckon you've arnt her enough to make it all up if she give yer a week to wait on yer ole man."

"She never gives nothin' to nobody, Adeline," said Lina. "She says Massa Dave here ken hire me if he will. She's sent me over with a billet to him."

"O, lors! I don't reckon he will!" said Adeline, thoughtlessly, and then seeing the grief her words had given the poor girl, she tried to take them back.

"Well, mebbe he will," she said. "He's mighty good-natured times."

"O! what shall I do if he won't?" said Lina. Adeline could think of nothing comforting to say, and they sat in sorrowful silence till the young man came in, when Lina timidly presented her note.

"What's this?" said Dave, when he had finished it. "Hire another hand, when we've got more than we know what to do with now! Nonsense! What is the woman thinkin' of? No, no, she can't make a clean penny out of us that way. Tell your mistress, I'm obliged to her, Lina, but I could n't think of hirin' any more just now."

"Massa, you sha'n't lose nothin' by it if you only will," said Lina, in a trembling voice. "I's a beautiful sewer, I is; every body says so, and I'll make it up to you, sure. I'll work nights after my ole man gets better; O he wants me so bad! Do, Mass' Dave."

"If Mass' Dave would now," said Adeline, "Uncle Tim calls for her all day long."

"Madam Gamby is a heap better able to spare you two or three days for nothin', than I am to hire you. You must go to her, girl. I can't do any thing for you, except to see that Uncle Tim has good care, and that I look out for. I give up all Jinny's time to him, and she makes quite a decent nurse, besides goin' in myself two or three times a day. You ought to be satisfied with that."

"But Miss Betty say I must n't come no more nights, 'cause I can't work de next day so fast. O, dear, I sha'n't see him at all!"

"You must go to your mistress, girl. I know of no other way," said Dave, coldly.

Lina turned away sobbing, as though her heart would break.

"Lina," said Adeline, kindly, and a detaining hand was laid upon her arm, "don't feel so bad about it. We'll

take good care ob Uncle Tim.   He sha'n't want for nothin', and Jinny or me 'll come over ebery night and let you
know how he comes on."

"Lord bless you, Ad.," said Lina, "but dar can't
nobody do for him like me.   It don't make no odds how
much he 's out; he always knows when Lina 's round.   O,
dear! it ain't right, no ways, to keep husband and wife
apart dis way.   Is it?"

"Well, dar's one ting, Lina; Tim 's in de good Lord's
hands, and I reckon he 'll take care ob him.   Can't you
make dat ar a comfort, girl?"

" De good Lord helpin' me, I will;" and Adeline heard
her ejaculating as she crossed the yard, "O, Lord, take
care of him!   Do, Lord! do!"

" That 's just like old Madam Gamby," said Dave, when
Lina was out of hearing.   "She 's always in a strain to get
somethin' extra out of her gang.   She could spare Lina
as well as not, before the busy season began, and she
reckoned I 'd do it, 'cause Tim is such a good servant."

" Well, Mass' Dave, I could n't keep from feelin' sorry
for Liny, noways," said Adeline, who having nursed Dave
when a baby, was allowed some liberty of speech.   "She
wants to see Uncle Tim so bad; and she takes such
mighty good care ob him, too.   'Pears like she 'd mos' go
'stracted over it."

" She 'll see him fast enough, Ad., don't you fret.   Marm
Gamby can't keep that girl home nights, I 'll be bound."

" Don't you b'lieve dat, massa.   Madam Gamby, she 's
gotten a way with her, of pryin' round, and keepin' track
of 'em all, dat makes 'em as 'fraid ob her as def.   O!
Mass' Dave, dar don't nothin' go right on dis yer place.
De pot biles over ebery day, and Othor, he died, and den
dem little shoats, and now Uncle Tim, he's got de fever.
Lors, Mass' Dave, dar won't nothin' come straight, till we
make tracks for de prairie."

CHAPTER XXIV

THE GERM OF DISASTER IN THE FAMILY.

BEFORE we return to St. Louis, let us look in upon them at La Belle Prairie. All day Mr. Catlett was off with the men, superintending the sowing of great fields of corn, plowing up the new ground, and setting out the young tobacco-plants. In the garden, Mrs. Catlett was equally busy, and with skirts tucked up to her knees, and a large sun-bonnet shading her features, she traversed the walks, keeping a sharp look-out upon the groups of women under her charge.

All the house servants who could be spared, were kept for several days hard at work, hoeing, raking, and preparing the beds for seed, while the younger portion of the household were employed in running hither and thither as general waiters to all.

"Miss Car'line kinder curis, any how," said Viny one day when her mistress was at a safe distance; "but lors! if you want to see de wool fly, come here 'bout plantin' time, dat's all. Dar can't nobody do nothin' right den."

Viny was not far out of the way. The lady's additional cares brought with them an increase of fretfulness and ill-humor, that made her more unreasonable than ever. One day every thing had gone wrong. The turkeys scratched up her young lettuce-plants, the bag of cymbling-seeds could not be found, and finally, by an unlucky push, she sent black Jake sprawling at full length over a newly-planted bed of cucumbers, where the urchin lay for a moment in speechless amazement, his legs and arms extended like a frog, and his open mouth full of sand. This last disaster capped the climax, and throwing down her box of seeds, Mrs. Catlett gave vent to her excited feelings in a torrent of angry complaints against black servants in general, and her own tribe in particular. In the midst of her tirade, little Dinah came running up the garden walk, shouting as she approached,

"O, Miss Car'line! Miss Car'line! Come up yonder quick. Dat ar' Tilla done got a fit, fall clar 'way down de new room stars."

"Who? What?" said Mrs. Catlett, but half understanding the sudden announcement; but before it could be repeated, the girl Martha, who was working near, sprang past her with one bound, and was hastening toward the house, when her mistress's voice called her back.

"Here, you! Come back this instant. Who told *you* to quit work?"

"O, Miss Car'line! Let me. It's Tilla! She's done hurt herse'f! 'Deed I mus' go!" said the girl, turning again toward the house.

It was a step toward rebellion that Mrs. Catlett would not suffer.

"Don't tell me you must," she said, angrily. "Stay where you are and mind your work till I come back."

Martha looked after her a moment, as she hastened up the walk. There was a rebellious fire in her eyes, and she took a step or two forward, but the habit of submissive obedience was too powerful to be resisted, and with a deep sigh she resumed her work.

"Never mind, Marthy," said Aunt Patsey, leaving her

own work a moment to say a comforting word, "mebbe she ain't bad hurt. Dat ar Dinah allers tells big stories."

"O, Patsey, I trembles all ober," said Marthy, "I so afeard for her. If Miss Car'line *would* let me go thar."

"Well, mebbe she will, when she comes back. Leastways 't ain't far to night, you know."

Poor Martha watched for her mistress's return with trembling eagerness, and when at last she appeared, inquired so anxiously after her sister, and begged so humbly to go to her, were it only for five minutes, that had Mrs. Catlett been in any other mood, she must have consented.

But she was irritated at the girl for attempting to go without her consent, vexed at the interruption, and mentally determined to punish her for her rebellion.

"No, you can't go," she said sharply, "so you may just keep on with your work. The brat's well enough. She tumbled down stairs, and hurt herself a trifle, that's all. Aunt Phebe 's got her down there docterin' her up.' She'll be well enough in an hour or two."

And so the poor soul, with dizzy head and aching heart, went on with her toil. She scarcely heard the reproofs she brought upon herself, by the careless manner in which her task was performed. She thought only of poor Tilla lying sick and suffering so near her, and she strained her ears to catch the first blast of the horn that called the men from their work, and put an end to the day's labor. At last, when the sun appeared to touch the edge of the prairie, and the fragrance of the blossoms on the trees grew sweeter, as the night-dew kissed their petals, when the frogs began their evening song, and big William's voice was heard on the prairie, calling home the cattle, then the welcome sound was heard, and shouldering their rakes and hoes, the women walked slowly to the house.

Would Miss Car'line release her now, or must she work on another long hour, in dizzy, sickening dread? Martha looked anxiously in her mistress's face, but saw nothing there to lead her to hope that she would be excused from her usual round of house-duties. She dared not make the request, but hastened to draw out the long table and prepare it for the evening meal. To her whispered inquiries about the accident, the little ones told her all that they knew. "Tilla was toatin' Miss Hetty up de new room stais. Miss Hetty she got mad 'cause Tilla set her down to rest, and she crack her so hard, she tumble ober and ober clar way down to de bottom. She lay dar in a fit till Miss 'Ria pick her up, an' now she down to Aunt Phebe's. Aunt Phebe say she ain't nigh so bad as she was."

And so the poor soul worked on, a little more hopefully, beguiling the time by picturing to herself the pleasant evening they would spend together, by Aunt Phebe's fire; Tilla released for one night from her duty of rocking Miss Hetty to sleep, and the babies all packed off to their mother's cabins. She had almost forgotten her fears in these delightful anticipations, but only to have them come back to her heart with a quick, sudden pang, as Aunt Patsey entered the room. Patsey had her own particular duties to attend to out of doors, and never appeared in the house at this hour. What brought her here now, and why did she steal so softly behind her mistress's chair, with such a sad mysterious face?"

Two little words explained it all. Words whispered so low, as scarcely to be heard by the person addressed, but falling with fearful distinctness upon another's ear. With one agonized cry they were echoed—

"Tilla dead!"

A moment after, the door of Aunt Phebe's cabin was

11*

flung violently open, and Martha sprang in. The fire flashed with sudden brightness as she entered, lighting up a group of children huddled together in the chimney-corner, and the figure of the old woman busily employed about something at the bed-side. The girl pushed her rudely aside, and taking her place, stood gazing silently at the dead child. There was no room for doubt. Death was stamped upon every feature. The face wore the same look of suffering it had borne in life, but the teeth were set, and the hands clenched as in the last struggle.

The little worn-out frame was at rest, "earth was past," and it was "well with the child," but woe to that heart, whether it beat in the breast of a monarch, or slave, which having but one object in the wide world to lose, wakes some day to find its idol cold and motionless in death.

There was perfect stillness in the low cabin. The mourner's grief seemed too intense for any outward expression of feeling. The poor stricken heart could find neither tear, nor cry to show its agony. As in nature, the calm that sometimes precedes a tempest, is more frightful and oppressive than the storm itself, so was it with that silent anguish. To Aunt Phebe, who watched the poor girl, as she stood motionless and stupefied beside her dead sister, it was a relief when the flood-gates of sorrow were opened, and her grief found vent in tears, and sobs, and broken ejaculations.

"Let me! let me!" she said to Aunt Phebe's attempts at consolation, "'t ain't for long. O, Tilla! Tilla! Don't you hear me callin' to you? wake up, and speak to me just dis once! O, lors, she's dead! she is! and I'll neber see her again!"

"Dar, now, honey, you hush up," said Aunt Phebe. "De good Lord he want Tilla up yonder. He'll make her a bright angel in glory! tink ob dat, honey!"

"I knows it, Aunty—I knows she's heaps better off! She's got shet ob all her misery now; but O lors, dar ain't nothin' lef' for me! nothin'! nothin'! O, Tilla! I wish I's dead too! I do! I do!"

"No, no, honey, don't you talk dat way. We's all got mighty little time to lib anyhow. You must n't hurry de Lord Almighty. Dar's a work for ye here, Marthy. Your poor chil' dat was sick, and achin', she got through. De Lord tuck her up to glory, whar she'll neber feel no more pain, nor sick, and de bressed Jesus, He'll wipe all de tears away. O! when de time comes we'll all be mighty glad to get dar. 'Pears like I could n't wait, times, but Marthy, dars somefin to do to get ready. Do you tink of dat, when yer talks dat way?"

The girl had sunk upon her knees by the bed-side and buried her face in her hands.

"Marthy," said Aunt Phebe, solemnly, "long time back, when ole missus, down dar in Virginny, sold away my two babies, I felt like you do. Dar did n't 'pear to be nothin' lef'; 'pears like I went crazy times, and did n't b'lieve in no God, nor no heaben, nor nuffin. O, Marthy, den dar come a voice to me sayin' Phebe! Phebe! call on de Lord! And I did, Marthy, and dat ar brought in de light. I giv' my precious babies right up to Him, and He showed me 't was all a comin' out right, for yer see if dem babies had been lef' to me, ole Phebe would lub dis poor sinful world a heap too well. Now dar aint nuffin left but de Lord; and O, Marthy, He's ebery ting! ebery ting! De Lord He gibs, and He takes away; can't yer say Praise His name?"

"Aunt Phebe," said the girl suddenly, raising her head, "it don't 'pear like God Almighty wanted Tilla to die. I don't b'lieve He had de fus ting to do wid it! not de fus ting! Dar's odder folks got to 'count for it! and O, aunty, I spec' I 's dreadful wicked, but I does wish dey could go to torment for it."

"When we's got our own badness clean wiped away, Marthy," said the old woman, solemnly, "dar 'll be time nuff to tink 'bout odder people's. Torment's a drefful place, chil'en! a drefful place! You all keep out ob it."

"Yon 's Miss Car'line," said little Dinah, as the lady entered through the open door.

Mrs. Catlett's face wore a softer expression, and she spoke in a kind tone.

"Marthy," she said, as she approached the bed, "I 'm mighty sorry. I had n't the least idea the child was so bad, or I 'd have let you seen her."

"It don't make no odds now," said the girl, in a cold, dry tone.

"I never once thought of her dyin'," said Mrs. Catlett, speaking to Aunt Phebe. "She dropped off wonderful sudden, though she was always an ailin', weakly kind of a child. There! there! Marthy, don't take on so. We all feel sorry for you, but it ain't no use frettin'. You must try to be resigned."

"How ken I? O Tilla, Tilla!" said the girl, sobbing passionately.

"Well, I 'm sure I 'm sorry for you, Marthy, but it won't do no good to fret so about it. Come, don't cry any more."

"Oh, Miss Car'line," said Martha, turning full upon her mistress, "I 'm thinkin' how one ob dem kind words would hab warmed *her* poor heart, dat was froze up for want ob lub and kindness. Oh, Miss Car'line, you need n't a be good to me. It only jest breaks my heart; when I 'd hab gone down on my knees to bless yer for one little smile for poor Tilla, dat was pinin' away for de lack. Oh, lors! it ain't no use now. She'll neber hear no hard words agin."

"*I* never was hard on the child," said Mrs. Catlett, in a more natural, because a sharper tone. "She never got any hard words from me, if that's what you mean; and Marthy, I hope you won't forget who you are speaking to if you do feel bad."

"I's done, Miss Carline," said Martha, in a calmer tone; and wiping her eyes with her apron, she sat down quietly by the bed-side.

When Mrs. Catlett had given the necessary directions about the child's burial, she left the cabin, and black Viny and another sympathizing servant crept silently away.

All this while the children, unnoticed and uncared for, sat huddled together in the warm chimney corner. The fire had burned down to a huge bed of glowing embers, which cast a ruddy glow upon their dark faces and shining eyes, but threw the further part of the room into deep shadow. Two little urchins had fallen asleep, drowsiness overcoming their curiosity, and their regular breathing mingled with the sighing of the wind in the chimney.

"Jake, oh, Jake," said Dinah, almost below her breath, and casting a frightened look at the dark shadows in the corners of the room. "Does yer hear de wind blow?"

Jake nodded assent.

"What make him howl roun' dis yer house so to-night, hey?" said Dinah.

"Don no," said Jake, shaking his head, and rolling up his eyes.

"I does," said Dinah. "I heerd Mr. Turner's Chloe tellin' all about it. Yer see when good folks die, reel pious folks, yer know, like Aunt Phebe, den you hear de south wind blow soft. Dat's de good angels come to toat de soul, clar away up to glory, *way up* inter de high blue ; and de wind is de music dar wings make when dey fly."

"Lors, now is it ?"

"Yes,.but when de wind howl roun' de house like he do now, dat de ' big black man' chasin' de bad soul roun' an' roun', and by-'n-by he cotch it, and toat it clar down ter torment. Does yer hear him now ?"

"Oh, Dinah," said Jake, his teeth chattering with fear, "does yer reckon he'll done cotch Tilla's soul dis yer night ?"

"Well, nig, I spec' he will," said Dinah solemnly. "Dar was allers heaps o' badness in dat ar Tilla. And dey do say, Jake, he likes little niggers' souls de best. Mass' Jack he tell Uncle Joe one day, dat niggers was all ready for de debble de fus' minit dey was born."

"Oh, Dinah, ain't you scar't ?"

"Hush up, now, dar's Aunt Phebe."

"Come, come," said the old woman, as she approached, "what yer doin' here, chil'en, dis time o' night ? Yer oughter been in bed tree hours ago. Come, scatter all ob yer," and administering two or three pokes with her cane, she quickly had them all out of the house.

"Now, den, nigs *run*," said Dinah, "he's close en to yer, sure," and, taking to their heels, they were soon lost in the darkness.

We return now to our young ladies in St. Louis.

CHAPTER XXV

JEALOUSY.

AFTER one of the evenings when Julia had been engaged with a gentleman visitor, and Fanny and Mr. Chester had enjoyed a long talk on the sofa, the young ladies were seated in Fanny's sleeping apartment, toasting their feet before the fire, and unbraiding their tresses, preparatory to retiring to rest.

"What a tiresome evening," said Cousin Julia, with a yawn. "I have been bored to death."

"Have you?" said Fanny, in surprise. "I have enjoyed it exceedingly."

"No doubt, Miss Hunter. We were not all favored with such agreeable company. Harry Chester can be very pleasant when he chooses."

"And did you ever see him when he did n't choose?" said Fanny, with a smile.

"I 'm sure I can't tell. I see so little of him of late, that I scarcely know whether he is agreeable or otherwise," said Julia.

Fanny looked up in surprise. "Did I monopolize his society this evening?" she said, innocently. "I 'm sure I did n't mean to be so selfish."

Julia burst into a laugh.

"Don't be alarmed, Miss Hunter," she said, with the least bit of sarcasm in her tone; "you are quite welcome to monopolize his, or any other gentleman's society, that you happen to fancy."

"Not if by so doing I deprive some one else who has a far better right," said Fanny, quite seriously.

"Nonsense, what a solemn matter you make of it. Nobody insists on their rights here, that I know of. Come, Nanny, you promised to sleep with me to-night, you know. Good-night, Miss Hunter, pleasant dreams to you."

"That girl is a strange compound of artfulness and simplicity," said Julia, when they were alone.

"Who! Miss Fanny?" said Nanny, in a tone of surprise.

"Yes, this same Miss Fanny, who you all appear to think such a paragon of excellence. Do I astonish you, Nanny?"

"Yes, indeed. What *does* make you think so?"

"Because I happen to be a little more observing than the rest of you, Nanny. It is perfectly astonishing to me that you should all be so deceived in that girl. I have seen through her from the very first."

"Why, Cousin Julia, I think she's just the frankest creature I ever saw. I'm sure Uncle Edward thinks so too, for he said something the other day about her being so transparent."

"O, yes, I know. Papa thinks she's the sweetest little innocent in the world. She makes him believe black is white, with that honest face of hers; but I tell you, Nanny, it's just because she has the art to conceal art. Well, never mind, you'll find her out one of these days.'

"I'm sure I don't know what you mean, Cousin Julia, or what has set you against Miss Fanny so. She likes you mightily, because she said so the other night."

Julia laughed. "That's another piece of art, Nanny. I happen to know that she doesn't like me, because I

stand sadly in her way. I only asked her here out of
pity. Harry Chester said she was a little young thing,
away from all her friends, a poor minister's daughter, or
something of the sort; is n't she?"

"Yes," said Nanny. "I don't believe Mr. Chester
thinks there 's any thing out of the way in her, for he paid
her a great deal of respect last winter. They used to have
nice times together."

"Yes, I presume so," said Julia, the color flashing into
her face. "She understands perfectly well how to worm
herself into any body's favor, with her innocent, babyish
ways. Gentlemen are very apt to be taken with that af-
fectation of simplicity." .

"I don't think she tried one bit, Cousin Julia. It all
seemed to come natural enough. She was the only one
that cared much for the books he read, and so of course
he used to bring 'em to her."

"Books?" said Julia. "So he used to read to her,
did he?"

"Lor, yes, whole long evenings. Ma and I used to get
so sleepy, but he never seemed to get tired of it, and had
to be hinted off to bed 'most every night. He 's sent her
up books since by the stage. I tell you, they were real
good friends. I don't reckon he would agree with you.
Of course I don't think she 's perfection, and I should n't
think of making an intimate friend of her, you know, because she 's only the teacher; but then I like Miss Fanny
very well, and so does every body on the prairie."

"You are generous, Nanny. I don't believe she deserves this warm defense from you. Now tell me truly,
has n't she tried her arts on some of your beaux up there?
How is it with that Mr. Turner, that used to think so much
of you, and Mr. Mack, and all the rest? Has n't she
tried to cut you out with some of them."

"Lor, Cousin Julia, Bob Turner don't think much of *me*, I reckon," said Nanny, her blushes telling another story; "and the gentlemen all seemed to like Miss Fanny upon the prairie, but nobody in particular, unless it is Mr. Tom Walton, and of course he would n't think of her a minute, because he 's so rich and every thing. He could take his pick of all the girls on the prairie."

"She might think of *him*, though, Nanny, and I have a great opinion of Miss Fanny's patience and perseverance, with such an end in view. You would feel vexed enough to see the greatest prize upon the prairie carried off by a poor Connecticut school-mistress."

"Cousin Julia," said Nanny, suddenly struck by a bright idea, "you are jealous of Miss Fanny. That 's what makes you talk so."

"Jealous of her!" said Cousin Julia, her face flushing crimson. "You compliment me very much, Nanny, by imagining that there is any occasion."

"I dou't think there is any occasion," said Nanny. "I think you might let Mr. Chester look at her once in a while, if he *is* engaged to you. I 'm sure any body can see that he don't care for the first person but you."

Cousin Julia looked very angry at the first part of this speech, but seemed a little mollified at its close.

"You are too ridiculous, Nanny," she said; "you ought to know me too well to think for a moment that I should be influenced by any such low motives. No, indeed, what I have said about her is out of kindness to you, lest she should entrap you in some of her arts before you were aware of it. I don't wish to be too hard on her. I presume it 's a good deal the fault of her education. You see she has probably been brought up in a dependant situation, where she has been obliged to act a servile part, and cringe and fawn round people, while at the same time she was looking out for her own interests. A girl very soon learns to be cunning and deceitful in this way."

"I should think her kin were very respectable," said Nanny, "from what I 've heard her say."

"What sent her way out here to teach school for a living, then?" said Julia.

"O, I don't know, Cousin Julia. I don't love to talk about it with you, you are so hard on Miss Fanny."

"I see you are as completely taken in as the rest, but at least, Nanny, you will promise not to betray my confidence, and repeat this conversation to her. It could do no good, and of course I intend to treat her with strict politeness while she is my guest. You won't tell her, will you?"

"I would n't tell her for all the world, Cousin Julia; she would feel dreadfully about it, and go home this very day, too. I tell you she is as independent about some things as you are, if she is only a poor teacher from Connecticut."

"You are very sparing of her feelings, Nanny. I doubt whether she would stop for yours, if they came in her way."

"She _is_ jealous," thought Nanny, "for all she's so stout about it, and I 'm glad I teased her a little, too, about his reading to the teacher. I think it 's too bad, and I mean to give Miss Fanny a little hint about it, so that she need n't go on provoking her to it. I know she does n't once think of such a thing."

"Miss Fanny," she said, the first time they were alone together, "did you notice how funny Cousin Julia acted last night?"

"Yes," said Fanny; "she surprised me very much. What did it mean?"

"I 'll tell you, Miss Fanny, she 's just as jealous of you as she can be."

"Why, Nanny, it is n't possible. The same idea came into my mind last night, for the first time, but I dismissed it at once, as being too ridiculous to be true."

"It 's so, though," said Nanny, very confidently, "you may take my word for it."

"O! I hope not, Nanny. What makes you think so ?"

"Well, last night's actions is one thing, and then I 've seen her watch you on the sofa together, when you was talking, and she looked mighty riled, and—well, there's a good many reasons."

"Why, Nanny, I have felt so free and unrestrained with him, just because I knew him to be engaged, and I think the same thing has influenced his treatment of me. Then the idea of Cousin Julia, with all her grace and beauty, with the full assurance of his love, having any thing to fear from *me*. O, Nanny, it is too ridiculous."

"I know it 's mighty foolish; but don't you see, Miss Fanny, she thinks so much of him, she can't bear to have him speak to any one else. How silly people act when they are engaged, anyhow. I 'm sure I would n't let every body see how much I thought of a man, if I *was* going to marry him."

"Wait and see," said Fanny, smiling, but the smile soon disappeared.

"Nanny," she said seriously, "Cousin Julia surely can not think that I have been to blame in this matter, that *I* have tried to engross his society."

"Well, I can't say, Miss Fanny; but I reckon if you could contrive to keep out of his way a little more, it would please her better."

"Nanny, I have never sought his society," said Fanny, her color rising.

"I know it, Miss Fanny, but mebbe she thinks you have. Engaged people are so touchy."

"I am very, very sorry; I did not dream of such a thing."

"There, now, I 've fixed it beautifully," thought Nanny, "and without giving her the least idea that Cousin Julia has been runnin' on so to me. I 'm sure I don't see how any body can think bad of her, after looking in her face."

Meanwhile Fanny was thinking the matter over. Had she really given Julia occasion for jealousy, or in any way drawn from Mr. Chester the delicate attentions he had bestowed. No, her conscience acquitted her of all intentional wrong. She had enjoyed his society exceedingly, and she had taken no pains to conceal it from Julia herself. Perhaps *he* had seen it, too, and it had led him to give her more; but what, then, must a gentleman be deprived of all other ladies' society because he happened to be engaged? What right had Julia to grudge her a little of his pleasant conversation, when she would enjoy it all her life? Fanny was feeling quite justified, and was working herself up into a pitch of indignation against the young lady, when she suddenly stopped. Was this kind? Was it right? She commenced again, and thought of the subject from the other side.

Mr. Chester. had been very kind and attentive to her. She certainly had occupied a large portion of his time the last week, which otherwise he would have devoted to Julia. He had taken pity on her as a stranger, and he liked her too, she believed, in a brotherly way, and so he had denied himself the pleasure of Julia's society, sometimes, just to gratify and amuse her. With his man's eyes, he did not see how this would affect a sensitive girl in the first flush of an engagement, when she would naturally expect him to be engrossed by her. But she (Fanny) ought to have seen it, and however much she liked his society, have put a stop to those long talks at once. She

had been very much to blame. No wonder Julia had
treated her coldly. Unconsciously she had caused her
much unhappiness. And now how could she remedy the
mischief? Should she go to Julia, have a plain talk, and
explain every thing ? - What was there to explain, though ?
It would only occasion embarrassment if she mentioned
the subject· at all. No, she would say nothing about it;
but she would at once commence a different course. She
would avoid Mr. Chester's society whenever she civilly
could; all those long talks on the sofa must be given up
at once; and she would let Julia see very soon that she
had no occasion to cherish a suspicious thought concerning
her.

"Yes, Nanny," she said at last, "I am very glad you
have spoken about this, though it distresses me not a little. I see plainly that I have been blind, and now that
my eyes are opened, we will soon put things to rights."

"And, Miss Fanny, we are going back to the prairie
in a little more than a week. I sha'n't be so mighty sorry
to leave town after all. I feel so kinder lost in the crowd
times, that it makes my head ache. Don't you, Miss
Fanny?"

"I have enjoyed it very much, Nanny;" said Fanny,
rather sadly.

"Well, so have I; but after all, La Belle Prai ie is the
best."

CHAPTER XXVI.

"A SOUTH-SIDE VIEW."

"WELL," said Judge Stanton, throwing down his paper, "there's not much news. Miss Fanny, how do you like Missouri?"

"I know very little of Missouri," said Fanny, "having lived only at La Belle Prairie."

"But you have seen enough to compare it with the country towns of the land of steady habits and wooden nutmegs."

"Now, Judge Stanton," said Fanny, "have you, too, taken up that foolish prejudice against Connecticut, so common here at the west? Do you not know that wooden nutmegs are myths, the truth lying at bottom being, that settlers from Yankee-land, by their general education and good business habits, are superior to their neighbors."

"Tut! tut! Miss Fanny, don't become excited now. I respect Connecticut as truly as you, and was only afraid that you saw the disease of Missouri as plainly as I. Would we had the hardy energy and cultivated character of the freemen of your native hills, to infuse the life-blood into the State of my adoption, dying of consumption even in its infancy."

"And what think you is the cause?" asked Fanny.

"Clearly enough, Slavery. I am an out-spoken man, and you need not keep your lips so close, Miss Fanny, for

the power of the system is not half so great in this State
as it looks to be, nor is it anywhere. Slaveholding politicians are good generals, and like Washington at Valley
Forge, keep up a good show of strength, on a very small
capital, cheating their northern allies into support of the
system. There is no real strength in it, and it would fall
of itself if party maneuvering would let it alone."

"This from a southern man!—When, and how?" said
Fanny. "Oh, would that it might."

"Now, there you are," said the judge, laughing. "You
see it has come out in spite of you. You have seen enough
of the system at La Belle Prairie, to loathe it with disgust.
No wonder! I loathe it too, and have got quite clear of
it, and I would all Missouri was clear of it. You ask
how it is to fall? I will tell you. By forcing it out of
its supports from political power. It is that which keeps
it alive. If it could be driven out of Washington, it would
die by its own diseases. It all rests with Connecticut,
and its kindred Free States. If these would only firmly
withstand the slave power, so that we could rely upon the
northern forces as allies, we, who hate slavery, in the
Slave States—and there are more of us than you imagine—
would join our forces, and take the political, and social
prestige away from the little oligarchy, which wield it
now. But we can not do any thing alone."

"Your senators say they will destroy the Union," said
Fanny.

"The Union is indestructible," replied the judge, rising
from his chair. "It is no dissoluble contract, as Webster
has established it for all time. North and South, there
will always be enough to rally round the Union, with its
glorious memories, to put down all traitors. A few senators and representatives in Congress, under the pressure
of our present social and political ideas, may talk large

and loudly, but it is folly to be alarmed. Did you ever read Burke, Miss Fanny? There is great wisdom in a single figure of his, which I would commend to all northern politicians: 'Because a few grasshoppers under a fern make the field ring with their importunate chink, while a thousand oxen, under the shade of the British oak, chew the cud and are silent, do not think that they who make the noise are the only tenants of the field, or that they are any thing more than the insignificant, noisy, hopping insects of the hour.' "

"It is a very vigorous figure," said Fanny. "No, I never read Burke. But, after all, is there not some danger of a civil war. Though the Union will finally stand, may it not be at the price of blood. So the southern people tell us, you know, and my good father in his parsonage always feared it."

"Civil fiddlesticks, Miss Fanny. Do you think our States are inhabited by fools. War is a serious matter, and can not be forced upon a people as easy as mere blustering for slavery. Those who do not hold slaves at the South, will let the cavaliers talk blood and thunder, so long as it frightens the Yankees, and will not try to stem the popular current, which runs in favor of slavery, so long as they are left to grow rich out of the prodigal slaveholders, who, making their money easy, are good customers. But when these same cavaliers pitch their tune upon the key of war, and taxation, and ruin of business, this same non-slaveholding majority of the Southern States, will make a rare discord, and declare that it takes two to make such a bargain."

"You speak very confidently," said Fanny. "I wish my father could have taken your view of the matter. It would have saved him many an anxious hour, and set his heart completely at rest."

"Why, my dear girl, it is perfectly clear! What have the people who hold no slaves to fight for? They bluster, indeed, to get the slaveholder's custom, but it would be ruin to rush into a war; and so, in the days of nullification, all the States skulked away from fighting, showing the white feather to the great Old Hickory. You see the majority of the white people at the South care not a fig for slavery, excepting as they get rich out of the prodigal planters."

"Go on, please," said Fanny, as the judge paused. "Is that all, as the children say, when I pause in a story?"

"Well, now," continued the judge, pleased with his listener's attention, "if our free States would stand upon the dignity of right, and expect no longer to save the Union by wire-pullers, but only by manly and upright policy, there would be no danger. If in the next presidential canvass, the people of the North show an undivided front, and a determination to drive slavery from the White House, the work is done. Our Toombs's and Atchisons go to the tomb of the Capulets, and the Southern States will show that there is a deep conviction within them against slavery, which is now restrained only by the pressure of power, and that comes from Northern intrigue and want of integrity."

"I believe you are right," said Fanny.

"Certainly I am. There is a deep under-current working against this institution, in all the slave States. There is a wide-spread moral sentiment against it. But it can not express itself. Why not? Because a Southern oligarchy, with wealth and training, and political education, have allied themselves with two elements at the North, the one that of greediness for office among the bad, and the other that of conscientious cowardice, lest the Union should fall, on the part of the good. With these allies,

they have developed such a social power, that we at the
South who hate slavery, being without the supports and
coherences of our opponents, can do nothing, and it would
be worse than useless to show ourselves."

"Yet people say the North has nothing to do with
slavery."

"It has every thing to do with it. It could not exist
without the North. All that is necessary is to crush the
social and political prestige, which binds it upon the necks
of the South. It would then unquestionably die out. The
North can and must do that. What do you think we
want of slavery in Missouri?"

"It effectually cuts off free labor," said Fanny, "and
makes poor white folks the very dregs of society."

"Precisely," said the judge. "It completely destroys
industry; and this is the foundation of true prosperity.
Labor is dishonored, and when that is so, the curse of God
inevitably results. Why should Missouri be behind Illinois, but because of slavery? Would a Connecticut
farmer want to work by the side of Cousin Catlett's niggers?"

"Not he!"

"There is precisely the philosophy of the subject. And
yet the power which rules us, is about to force it upon
Kanzas, perhaps Nebraska, and only God knows where
its boundaries shall be."

"That repeal of the compromise seemed to me a breach
of faith."

"It was a breach of faith! shameful beyond measure
but after all, that is not the worst symptom in the case.
It is only a symptom of a deep-seated disease at the
North, which must be cured before there is any hope of
success. The North has the 'Western shake.' It wants
large doses of quinine. If there was only firm principle

at the North, which would offer itself as a basis for the now unseen moral sentiment of the South, and would stand by it, we might in our age see the death-blow given to slavery."

"Do you mean slavery in the States. I suppose that is entirely under State control."

"Certainly it is, and States are under popular control. Just so soon as a firm public sentiment, unyielding and unbending, is found at the North, which shall destroy the slave power in the general government, then the slave power in the States will also be destroyed, and we shall be left to reason out the question with all its difficulties among ourselves. It will become a moral question and not a political one. There will be no disturbing influences, and therefore we may be sure of the result."

"But they say slavery is so interwoven with society as to make it next to impossible to get rid of it."

"All humbug, Fanny. The trouble is not in the complication of the subject, but in the refusal to try to unravel it. I do not suppose we can crush it at once. Was not Connecticut a slave State?"

"Certainly, a long time ago."

"But there were slaves in Connecticut only a few years ago, Fanny; how did this happen?"

"They were the remains of the ancient slavery. The old people, who were not freed by the act of emancipation. These, too, you know, have been set at liberty."

"Ah, yes, I see you are pretty well posted up. I did not know but I might catch you tripping. Well, now, was not Connecticut a free State before that last act was passed?"

"To all intents and purposes, as you lawyers would say, it was."

"I go further than that, and maintain that just so soon

as the spirit of slavery is changed, and the States begin to legislate for the good of the slave, instead of as now the good of the master, then the institution has received its death-blow. Just so soon as the great northern public sentiment is formed, we shall begin to make laws to preserve the family relation, secure education, unlock the Bible, give opportunities for rising in worldly goods, present inducements to the purchase of freedom; every one of which laws, just to the extent of each, abolishes slavery. Then just as the British serf passed into the free citizen, so will the American slave, till at last a universal decree of emancipation shall complete the work."

"O let us pray that such a time may come," said Fanny, earnestly.

"Not now, Fanny," said the judge, gravely; "I am opposed to the praying of women in public. Wait till you are alone, if you please."

"Why, Judge Stanton, if—"

Here a servant entered, informing the judge that a gentleman was waiting for him at his office, who quickly obeyed the summons, leaving Fanny to *pray alone.*

CHAPTER XXVII.

FANNY's resolution was faithfully kept. No sooner was she convinced by Cousin Julia's hasty words, and Nanny's assertion, that she was the cause of any unpleasant feeling, than her whole course of conduct was changed. She was not one to do any thing by halves, and in her anxiety to convince Julia that there were no grounds for her suspicions, she suddenly began to treat Mr. Chester with such coldness and formality, as greatly to astonish and perplex him. From a frank, open-hearted girl, in whose eyes he always read a welcome, and whose thoughts he could almost interpret in the expressive changes of her features, she all at once became, in his presence, distant and constrained, avoiding his society whenever she decently could, and when, as frequently happened, he would not be put off, but forced her to remain, she seemed to endure, and not as formerly enjoy, his conversation. Once or twice, indeed, she relapsed into her old manner, lifting her eyes frankly to his face, and speaking in her free, open way, but just as he would begin to rejoice in the change, she would seem suddenly to recollect herself, and make up for the relapse, by treating him ten times more stiffly than before.

This conduct was so unlike Fanny, that Mr. Chester knew not what to make of it, and though grieved exceedingly, it was some time before he became seriously offended. But when it had continued nearly a week, and he could obtain no explanation, though he sought it earnestly, his spirit was roused, and he determined to make no more efforts to conciliate one who so uniformly treated him with neglect. Fanny had no idea that she was overdoing the matter, or manifesting real unkindness to one who had shown himself so warm a friend as Harry Chester. She thought only of her own privation when she avoided him, it was so hard to check the kind words she wanted to say, the frank manner she had always used toward him, and to deprive herself of the pleasure of his society. When she had treated him with unusual coldness, and continued in it a whole evening, she considered that she had done an excellent thing, and thought it all over with great satisfaction, while he, vexed and grieved, knew not what to make of her, and sighed for the days that were past.

By-and-by Mr. Chester made no more efforts to bring about those long talks on the sofa, but left Fanny entirely to herself, or to some other gentleman, while Cousin Julia was engaged at the piano. He took less and less notice of her, and avoided her society. Fanny fancied that this was just what she wanted, and tried to convince herself that she was quite as happy as before; but it would not do, and the evenings were long and dull. She missed, she knew not what, and began to sympathize fully with Nanny, in her wish to return to the prairie.

"You and Harry Chester have had a falling out," said Julia one day.

"O, no;" said Fanny, quietly.

"Indeed! I thought it must be. He treats you so distantly, and expresses such an opinion of you. You must have offended him in some way."

"No," said Fanny, again.

"You treat him very coldly."

"I think very highly of him, nevertheless. So highly, that I consider him worthy even of you, Julia;" said Fanny, with a smile.

"Nonsense! He was speaking to me about it last night. He says he has not given you the least occasion for such a sudden change; that when you first came, he took some little pains to entertain you, thinking you might be lonely among strangers."

"It was pity, then," thought Fanny.

"He laughed about it, and was so rude as to say that if you had no further use for *him*, he thought he could manage to get along without *you*. He is very plain-spoken, I think."

"He thinks me fickle in my friendships, I suppose," said Fanny, with a faint attempt at a smile.

"He did insinuate something of the sort," said Julia, carelessly. "It is the crying sin of our sex, you know;" and she went off humming a tune.

Poor Fanny crushed back a tear or two, and went on with her work.

It was while matters were in this state, that Mr. Tom Walton came to town. The young ladies met him one evening at a concert, after which he became a constant visitor at Judge Stanton's house. As he appeared to have no business in the city, it seemed very probable that his visit was in some way connected with the young ladies' stay there. He dressed in the height of fashion, and driving a dashing span of grays, seemed determined to impress people generally with a sense of his importance. He singled out Fanny as the favored object of his attentions, and annoyed her exceedingly by his close attendance, and his pressing invitations to ride, which, with a single exception, she invariably declined, for he was in every way disagreeable to her, and she felt humbled rather than flat-

tered by his evident admiration. His dress, his swaggering manner, and his blunt, braggart style of conversation,
proclaimed him to be no gentleman, and it was only good
nature and consideration for his feelings, that induced
Fanny to treat him with common civility.

But he was the "rich Tom Walton, the greatest catch
on the prairie;" and even Nanny, with all her good-
nature, could hardly forgive our little Connecticut girl for
being the favored one.

"I declare," she said one day, when Fanny had been
almost forced into the only ride she took with him, as the
grays dashed away from the door, "I declare, Julia, she
is the least bit of a flirt after all."

Julia laughed. "I thought you would come to your
senses, Nanny. You will find her to be just the design-
ing creature I told you."

"And yet she says she does n't like him. She made
believe that she would much rather stay at home, than to
ride with him."

"Probably," said Julia.

As they dashed down the street, as ill luck would have
it, they met Mr. Chester. He touched his hat to Fanny,
and glanced, as she fancied, curiously and disdainfully at
her companion.

"He thinks I have given up his friendship for such society as this," she thought, bitterly. "I would have been
glad to keep his respect, if nothing more."

The next evening they were going to a concert, Julia
with Mr. Chester, Nanny with Tom Walton, and Fanny
with the judge, whose escort she had secured to save herself from the company of her prairie beau, whom Nanny
was but too proud to accompany. It happened, however,
that in running down stairs Julia sprained her ankle, and
though she thought little of the accident at the moment,

yet by evening she was obliged in consequence to remain at home.

The two young gentlemen made their appearance at the appointed hour, but the judge did not come, and after waiting some time, Mrs. Stanton proposed that they should go at once, leaving him to join them in the hall. Fanny playfully protested that she must wait for her escort, but her objections were all overruled, principally by the tone and look with which Mr. Chester said to her, when no one was listening, "Are you so unwilling to go with me?" Fanny shook her head, and with something of her old frankness of manner, put her arm in his.

She scarcely knew what was said during the walk. She only remembered that he was kind again, that she was thinking to herself all the while that she had not quite lost him for a friend, and that he said something to her as they entered the hall, about "being Fanny Hunter again to-night." And why should she not? Julia Stanton was not there, to be vexed by his kindness to her. Surely she might throw aside the vail for one evening.

The judge did not come, but nobody missed him. The concert was second or third rate, but neither of them thought so, and though it continued two mortal hours, they considered it very short. When Fanny ran up to her own room, her cheeks were still glowing with pleasurable excitement, and the tones of her companion's voice were ringing in her ears, and yet there was a guilty, self-accusing feeling within that caused her, after a little, to sit down and think it all over.

The result was not satisfactory. In vain she tried to reason away the suspicion that troubled her; and convince herself that it was because she had broken her resolution, and given Julia more occasion for jealousy, that she was feeling so guilty. But it would not do. She felt that there was still another cause, and she finally put the question frankly to herself, whether for her own sake, as well as Julia Stanton's, it would not be best to avoid Mr. Chester's society. However much she might shrink from the humiliating thought, that the companionship of one who was solemnly pledged to another, was becoming dangerous to her peace of mind, the conclusion forced itself upon her, that in some measure this was beginning to be true.

Poor Fanny! She thought she could have borne any thing better than this humiliating acknowledgment, and she paced her little room with rapid steps, bitterly upbraiding her own weakness. "It was time," she thought, "high time that I avoided him, before I come to be one of those silly, love-sick girls, whom I have always despised."

If, in the midst of all this self-upbraiding, it once or twice occurred to her that Mr. Chester himself had been somewhat to blame, and that there had been looks and tones that evening that the lady of his choice would not be pleased to see addressed to another, if this thought arose in her mind, she instantly dismissed it, and concluded that her own weakness had misinterpreted what he intended as mere brotherly kindness.

"O dear, dear," said Fanny to herself, at the conclusion of her cogitations, "I wish I were out of all this, and back again on the prairie."

Meanwhile a scene of quite another character was transpiring in cousin Julia's room. Mr. Tom Walton not proving very talkative or agreeable at the concert, Nanny found ample time to observe Fanny and Mr. Chester, and she amused herself by thinking how she could excite cousin Julia's jealousy, by her remarks upon their evident enjoyment of each other's society. She was not an ill-natured girl, and had no intention of doing Fanny an injury, but the prospect of rou ing her cousin a little, and getting up a scene, was quite irresistible. She accordingly repaired at once to the young lady's chamber, hoping to find her still up. She was not disappointed. Cousin Julia, with her graceful form wrapped in a loose morning-robe, was stretched upon a lounge in the middle of the room. She held a book in her hand, but threw it down with a yawn as her cousin entered, and with a " Well, Nanny," sank back languidly upon her pillows.

" Well, cousin Julia, you ought to have been there," said Nanny.

" Have you enjoyed the evening, Nanny ?"

" Yes; not so well as some other folks, though."

She waited for an answer, but the young lady appeared too sleepy to give one.

" I declare," she said at last, getting out of patience, " you would n't be lying there half asleep, if you had seen the carryings on that I have to-night."

" What carryings on ?" said cousin Julia.

" Well, mebbe you would n't think of it as any thing out of the way here, but up the country it would make a talk, to have such actions going on."

" What in the world are you driving at ?" said Julia, impatiently. " Can't you speak out, Nanny ?"

" I s'pose you felt mighty safe and easy here at home, and your beau off waitin' on another lady," said Nanny, significantly.

" Of course I did," returned her cousin, haughtily. " I 'll thank you to tell me why I should not !"

Nanny, who at all times stood a little in awe of her beautiful cousin, was quite taken aback by this manner of receiving her hints, and would gladly have left the communication just where it was; but Julia had raised herself

on her elbow, and with her eyes fixed upon her, was waiting for a reply.

"I'm sure I don't know, Cousin Julia," she said at
length; "for pity's sake don't look so solemn about it. I
was only in fun."

"And when you are ready to explain, I should like to
know what all the fun is about," said Julia in the same
tone.

"I declare, Julia, you frighten me. It was just nothing
at all, only Fanny Hunter flirted all the while at the concert with Mr. Chester, and I thought I'd tease you a little
about it."

"Where was my father?" said Julia, calmly. "I thought
he was going with Fanny Hunter."

"He didn't come, though; they had it all to themselves."

"I hope they enjoyed it," said Cousin Julia, indiffer-
ently.

"They acted like they did," said Nanny, a little provoked with her cousin for not exhibiting more feeling.
"They appeared to be making the most of it."

"And what do you know about it?" said Julia, her usually soft voice raised to rather an unlady-like pitch. "How
could you tell whether they were flirting or not?"

"Well, of course I didn't hear what they said; but we
sat a little way behind 'em, and I could see how thick they
were, and how he leaned over once in a while and looked
into her eyes; and she—"

"And she," said Cousin Julia, impatiently, interrupting
her; "how did the unsophisticated little innocent take it
all?"

"O, she sat there smiling away, with such a pretty
color in her cheeks, as happy as you please. It seemed
'most a pity when the concert was over, to break it all up."

278 WESTERN BORDER LIFE.

"It *was* a great pity," said Julia, bitterly. "And now, my dear coz, is this all the pleasant information you have to give me?"

"Yes," said Nanny, "we all came home together, and she went straight up to her own room, and I came in here to tell you about it."

"It was very kind of you," said Julia, dryly; "and now as I am an invalid, and very sleepy and tired beside, I hope you will excuse me and let me go to bed."

She looked any thing but sleepy, with her curled lip and flashing eye; but Nanny took up her lamp and bade her good-night. "Well," she thought, as she closed the door, "Cousin Julia is the strangest girl! Who would ever have thought of her taking it so cool?"

Julia's troublesome foot obliged her to keep her room for several days, and the irksomeness of the confinement, together with the pain it caused her, kept her in a state of nervous irritability, that tried the patience of all about her, and even called forth a rebuke from her gentle mother.

"Julia, my dear, what ails you?" she said. "I never saw you so impatient before. You have borne longer confinements than this, with only one for company, and here are your two friends ready to sit with you and amuse you in any way you fancy. Let Miss Hunter read to you awhile this morning. It will divert your attention from yourself, and do you good. Shall I send for her?"

"O, no, mamma. I only want to be let alone. I am tired to death of company. I wish you would contrive to get rid of them."

"You will feel differently, Julia, when your foot is better," said her mother, quietly.

That same evening, however, the invalid accepted Fanny's offer to read aloud, and when in an hour or so the

girl came up to tell Miss Hunter that Mr. Chester was in
the parlor, Julia appeared so unwilling to lose her society,
that she very gladly remained, sending word that she was
engaged with the sick one. This happened twice or three
times, and then Mrs. Stanton insisted upon Fanny's going
down, though Julia would gladly have detained her.
Fanny, in her simplicity, thought that she was making
some progress in the young lady's regard, and was only
too delighted at the change; the sarcastic remarks that
invalid now and then dropped, falling harmlessly to the
ground, because she did not in the least understand
them.

"Go down, my dear," said Mrs. Stanton, as Fanny still
lingered, "Julia will not be so selfish as to detain you.
Nanny is there, and I will soon follow you."

As she entered the parlor, Mr. Chester rose to meet
her. He was alone, and Fanny, who had expected to
find Nanny in the room, was a little embarrassed by the
warmth of his reception. It was their first meeting since
the night of the concert, and there was something in his
manner which, in despite of all her brave resolutions, prevented her from being so calm and self-possessed as she
had intended. Half unconsciously she took her old place
on the sofa, and Mr. Chester sat down beside her.

"You have come at last, Miss Hunter," he said, re-
proachfully. "I began to fear that those dismal excuses
were to continue forever."

"And if they continued ever so long, you ought to be
the last person to complain, considering in whose service
I have been detained. You should be in a grateful rather
than a complaining mood."

"Yes, certainly," said Mr. Chester, apparently a little
rebuked. "We all feel a deep interest in Miss Julia's
recovery. Is she better to-night?"

"Much better, and will join us below in a day or two.
Is n't this good news ?"

"It is, indeed. We shall all be together once more, in
bodily presence at least," he added. "I would we could
as readily be united in spirit again."

"Has there then been a division ?" inquired Fanny.

"You know that there has, Miss Fanny;" said Mr.
Chester. "Every thing is changed. Why, to me the
house itself bears a different aspect; and whereas I once
entered it, in all boldness, confident of a kind reception
and beaming smiles, I now come with fear and trembling,
doubtful whether I am welcome or no. The gate used to
give a little welcome squeak when I pushed it open ; the
lilacs nodded their heads encouragingly to me as I passed,
and the door-bell jingled out, 'Come in! come in!' But
now the very gate sighs dismally, the lilacs shake their
heads, and the bell—well I think every time that it may be
sounding the knell of my departed hopes."

"Doleful!" said Fanny, with mock solemnity. "Now
for the cause of this distressing change. Where rests
the blame? How shall we exorcise this evil spirit?
this household sprite, that has been enticed under our
roof?"

"The fault, if there is any," he replied, looking her full
in the face, "rests with one person, and she—" he hesitated a moment—"she is too good and lovely ever to do
any thing wrong."

"Ah, now I understand," thought Fanny. "There has
been a lover's quarrel, and I am to be made the mediator.
Well! well! Cousin Julia shall see that I am truly her
friend after all." Then turning to her companion, with a
beaming smile, she said,

"And if it turn out to be the fault of neither, but only
a trifling misunderstanding, what then ?"

"Then," said Mr. Chester, eagerly, "we might be friends again."

"And this would raise you again to the comfortable state of mind you described just now?" said Fanny.

"No—it would be happiness compared with the coldness that has existed of late, and I have looked back with inexpressible regret to those days of confidence and friendship, but even those would not satisfy me now. I shall never rest in perfect content till all uncertainties are done away, and that day may never come, or if it come, may plunge me into utter despair."

"I do not understand you, Mr. Chester," said Fanny. He had spoken so seriously that she gave up her jesting tone.

"May I explain my meaning?" he said, and then without waiting for her reply, continued, "I am so happy, I would have said a week ago, so *unhappy* now, as to be deeply and irrecoverably *in love.* I fancied, nay, in my presumption, I felt almost certain, that the feeling was returned, but in those happy days I delayed to bring matters to a crisis, and now I dare not, for my certainty has changed into the most distressing doubts."

"Are they not engaged then, after all?" thought Fanny. "How wrong in Cousin Julia not to have denied it, and we all thinking it a settled thing."

His anxious face recalled her, and she blushed under his gaze, to think that she had cast reproach upon her, whom he considered perfection itself.

"Do you not see why every thing here is changed to me, why I dread to come, and yet can not stay away?"

"Has she been unkind, then?" said Fanny.

"Is not indifference and neglect sometimes worse than actual unkindness, Miss Fanny?"

She remembered how his own coldness had grieved her

awhile ago, and answered faintly enough in the affirma-
tive.

"You are sorry for me," he continued, "I see it in
your face. O, Fanny! Miss Hunter! can you give me
any hope?"

His tone so tender, so passionate, thrilled her to the
heart, and struggling to retain her self-possession, she
turned her face from him. "O, dear! why of all others
must he choose *her* for his confidante, and pour into *her*
ears the story of his love for another—and that other!
Well, any one with half an eye could see that she was dying to hear the words he felt so afraid to speak. Afraid!
She would say yes, and thank you too in a minute.
Should she tell him so at once, and end this ridiculous
scene. No, that would be unkind to Julia, but she would
give him to understand as delicately as possible, that he
had no occasion to despair, encourage him to make the de-
cisive declaration, and thus speedily settle matters between
them."

"I see," he said sadly, as she turned toward him again,
"that you have nothing to say."

"You see no such thing," said Fanny, smiling; "I have
something to say, and if I seem trifling and unsympa-
thizing now, it is because I view this whole matter in a
hopeful light. I am weary of these doubts and fears, and
tell you in all confidence, that if you will follow my advice,
they shall disappear directly. Can you trust me?"

"With my whole heart," said the young man.

"Then," said Fanny, raising her eyes calmly to his face,
"cast all these fears of yours to the winds, and in hope
and confidence, put the question that shall decide your
fate at once."

"Do *you* advise me to this step?" said Harry Chester,
his face flushing with sudden surprise and pleasure.

"I do," said Fanny. It was hard, after all, to meet that beaming look.

"And it shall not end in disappointment?"

"In a blissful certainty," said Fanny, smiling.

"Heaven bless you for those words! Fanny, dear Fanny!" he caught her hand, and pressed it passionately to his lips.

Had he fallen dead at her feet, her face could scarce have undergone a more sudden change. She snatched away her hand and sprang to her feet, her eyes flashing with anger, and the red blood crimsoning her fair face into a deep blush.

"What do you mean? How dare you insult me thus?" she said rapidly.

In the extremity of surprise, he too had risen, and they stood confronting each other, she in insulted dignity, and he in perfect bewilderment, as to what it all meant.

"How dare you treat me so?" she repeated, tears of pride and mortification filling her eyes.

"What have I done?" he asked. "I would cut off my right hand rather than give you pain. Do you not believe me?"

She could not well disbelieve it, with that anxious face before her, and the angry flush gradually left her own.

"Then," he said, interpreting the change in her countenance as if she had spoken, "if in the first flush of delight your own words gave me, I frightened you by my vehemence, forgive me; and O! Fanny, repeat them. Tell me once more that I have not loved you so long in vain."

"Me!" said Fanny, losing every other feeling in that of intense surprise. "What do you mean? Of whom have you been speaking?"

"Of you, Fanny. I have never loved any one else."

She gave him a look full of surprise and eager inquiry.

"I thought—they told me—Cousin Julia," she stam·
mered.

"Who told you, and what, Fanny?" he said, gently.
"What strange mistake is this that perplexes you?"

"I always supposed you engaged to her, Mr. Chester,"
said Fanny, frankly.

It was his turn to look surprised now.

"Engaged!" he said. "Engaged to Julia Stanton! Is
it possible, Fanny? Could you imagine such a thing for
a moment, when you must have seen that I was striving
in every way to win your love;" and then, as overcome by
the strange developments of this interview, Fanny sank
down upon the sofa, he continued earnestly, "will you
believe me when I solemnly declare to you again, that I
have never loved any one but you, and that in you lies
the power to make me happy or miserable."

He waited for her reply, while trembling and astonished
she could hardly keep back her tears. At this moment
Mrs. Stanton entered, and Fanny, a poor dissembler at
best, finding it impossible to control her agitation, hastily
left the room.

As she passed the door of Julia's chamber, the young
lady called her in; and striving to hide her agitation,
Fanny paused at the threshold to see what was wanted.

"O, come in," said Cousin Julia, in a fretful tone;
"don't be in such a hurry to get away from me. I want
to hear about your pleasant interview;" and then, with a
searching look at Fanny's flushed cheeks and tearful eyes,
she continued tauntingly, "ah! something exciting, I see.
Come, tell us all about it!"

"Excuse me, Julia," said Fanny, "some other time."
and she turned toward the door, near which she was
standing.

"No, no, you shall stay now," said Julia; and then seeing that Fanny was still intent upon leaving the room, she sprang forward in spite of her lame foot, and standing in the doorway, prevented her from going.

"You shall stay *now*," she repeated, with sudden violence. "This has been going on long enough, and now I will know what it all means."

Her listener was so astonished at the angry vehemence with which she spoke, that she knew not how to reply.

"You may look as innocent as you please," she continued, "but you know perfectly well what I mean. You dare not deny that you have been working in an underhand way ever since you came into this house."

"Julia," said Fanny, calmly, "I don't in the least understand what you mean; but it is unworthy of you to talk in this way, and I can not listen to you. Will you let me pass?"

"You *do* know. You *do* understand," said the young lady, with increasing warmth. "Don't you think that I have seen through your soft ways and pretended friendships? I tell you, Fanny Hunter, you have kept one object in view ever since you came here, and if you go away without its accomplishment, it will not be for want of perseverance and labor. I have borne it in silence long enough, and now I will speak. I tell you again, that you know perfectly well what I mean."

There was nothing like guilty consciousness in Fanny's eyes, as she gazed earnestly at the angry girl, but a look of grieved surprise, as though shocked and hurt, rather than angered at the charge.

"Julia," she said, "what I have done to vex you I do not know; but this I can say: if I know my own heart, it contains none but the kindest feelings toward you; nor would I knowingly injure you in the slightest way."

"O, no, you have manifested the most disinterested regard for me," said Julia, bitterly.

"What have I done?" said Fanny. "What is it that has vexed you so?"

"What have you done!" said the young lady, her pale face flushing crimson. "You have been trying to steal away the heart of the only man I ever loved, when it was all mine, till you came between us with your baby face. *That* you would call an act of friendship, perhaps."

"Julia," said Fanny, all her womanly pride aroused by this cruel charge. "You know that it is false. Your own heart must tell you, that you are wronging me. When I avoided his society, and ran the risk of losing his friendship entirely, by my coldness and indifference, did this look like working in an underhand way to gain his affections? I have given all my influence in your favor, and oh, Julia! how could you think so meanly of me as to imagine that I would cherish such a design for one moment, supposing as I did, until this evening, that you were solemnly engaged to Mr. Chester."

"And who told you I was *not?*" said Julia, turning pale again.

"He told me himself," said Fanny.

Julia gazed at her a moment. "He told you himself," she repeated bitterly, an expression of rage and scorn crossing her beautiful features. "*You?* and what more he told you I can see, in your tell-tale face. Go," she said, stepping aside, "go, I never want to see you again."

She leaned, pale and trembling, against the door-way.

"Julia," said Fanny, her eyes filling with tears, "forgive me if I have spoken harshly. O do not let us part in anger."

Julia again motioned her toward the door, and slowly and sadly she left the room. Seeking the quiet of her own chamber, Fanny sat down in such a whirl of excitement, that she could hardly think at all. With a feeling of sincere sorrow and pity for Julia's unhappiness, there was mingled a confused sense of joy, of a consciousness of some great happiness that had suddenly come upon her, and which, though clouded by the remembrance of those cruel reproaches, was still spreading a sunny influence over her heart. *He* was free, and had spoken words, the import of which could not be mistaken. She thought no further than this; the present joy was all that she could bear; and when, at last, Nanny came in to talk awhile before going to bed, she was met by such a beaming smile, as she had not seen on Fanny's face for many days.

"Only one day more, Miss Fanny," she said, as she rose to retire, " only one more day, and we shall start for the prairie again. The corn must be a foot high by this time, and plenty of lettuce and asparagus in the garden. Oh, what would keep me in this hot city all summer, I wonder!"

CHAPTER XXVIII.

"UP THE COUNTRY."

THE next day was spent in preparations for their departure, and though Fanny sought eagerly for an opportunity to speak with Julia alone, it grieving her much to part with her in her present state of feeling, the young lady took particular pains to avoid an interview. Fanny thought she appeared a little ashamed of last night's violence, and once or twice her eyes fell before Fanny's anxious look; certain it was, she treated her with strict politeness, and in no outward manner exhibited a trace of the feeling she had so lately manifested.

The day seemed very long to Fanny, and when, in the evening, two or three visitors dropped in, each jingle of the door-bell made her start. It was unusual for Fanny to be nervous. Was it for Mr. Tom Walton that she was looking? That personage made his appearance in the course of the evening, and invited the young ladies to ride up to the prairie in his new buggy, informing them with considerable pride, that he had purchased the span of grays, and intended to take them up the next day.

To Nanny's great surprise, Fanny gently but decidedly declined his invitation for herself, referring him to Miss Nanny to answer on her account. He seemed greatly astonished, and a little offended, but did not condescend to urge the matter, or even to give Nanny the opportunity to decline also.

'Why, Miss Fanny, how could you?" said Nanny, after he had gone. "Only think of riding up in his beautiful buggy, instead of that old lumbering stage. Why, all the girls on the prairie would know it, and be just as jealous of us as could be. How came you to do it, Miss Fanny?"

"Because I did n't like to be under obligations to Mr. Walton for such a long ride, Nanny, and besides, I really prefer going in the stage."

"Well, that's funny, when we could go in half the time, and in such crank style, too. I reckon you never will get the chance again, for he seemed real put out about it. But there! do you reckon Harry Chester is going to let us go off without so much as bidding us good-by. He knows we start early in the morning, for I told him so myself."

Fanny was revolving the same question in her own mind, and could find no satisfactory reason why the young gentleman did not come. The evening passed, however, and early in the morning our country guests took their departure. Fanny receiving a warm embrace from Mrs. Stanton, and a cordial shake of the hand, and a "God bless you, Fanny!" from the judge.

A couple of hours after they had gone, Mr. Chester called. He found Julia alone in the parlor, and learned to his great astonishment that the ladies had departed.

"Gone!" he repeated. "The judge told me they would remain another day. I inquired particularly, for though I was called out of town upon urgent business, I would have put it into other hands, and remained, had I supposed it was my last opportunity of seeing them. How could the judge have made such a mistake?"

"I believe I told papa yesterday, that they were to remain another day; but they afterward changed their minds," said Julia.

13

He seemed greatly disappointed, and sustained his part of the conversation in an awkward, absent-minded manner, until Julia turned it upon their late visitors, and more particularly upon Fanny. She spoke of her intelligence and pleasing manners, etc., etc., till his listlessness was all gone, and he responded eagerly to all that she said.

"Yes, she is a sweet girl," said Julia, " what a pity it is that she is engaged."

"Engaged!" said Harry Chester, with a start.

"Yes, certainly. Did n't you know it? To a young theological student, or a minister, back there in Connecticut. It seems a pity. She might do so much better here. There's young Strong, I think appeared to admire her very much ; and, indeed, she is a favorite with most gentlemen."

"Miss Julia, are you sure that this is so?" said Mr. Chester. "Such reports are so unreliable."

"This about her engagement? O, yes! there is n't a shadow of a doubt. She has received letters regularly from him all winter, Nanny says, and indeed she makes no secret of it herself."

"Why did n't you tell me this before?" he said, almost angrily.

"Why, really, Mr. Chester, I did n't imagine the intelligence would have affected you so deeply. I would have spared your feelings still," said Julia, with a wicked smile.

The raillery seemed more than he could bear. He paced the room a moment with rapid steps, and then bidding her a good-morning, left the house.

She watched him down the steps, and turned away from the window, with the same wicked smile upon her lips.

The farm-wagon that bore our travelers from Belcher's store to their home on La Belle Prairie, wound its way

along the smooth road, and down the little hill leading to
the creek. It was after sunset, and the soft air was full
of the fragrance of the prairie flowers, while the trees by
the creek, hung heavy with their rich foliage. Nature
had clothed the prairie in its summer attire; and the
change from the nakedness of winter, and the scanty ver-
dure of spring, to the full luxuriance of summer, was very
great; and Fanny, gazing around her, and drawing in
great draughts of country air, thought that La Belle
Prairie had never so well deserved its name.

They had crossed the creek, and were just entering
upon the little patch of woods this side, when a child's
voice called them to stop, and a moment after little Maud,
with her hands full of flowers, suddenly appeared in the
path before them. They waited for her to scramble into
the wagon, which she had no sooner done, than dropping
her flowers, she threw both arms round Fanny's neck,
and kissing and hugging her, burst into tears.

" O, Miss Fanny, I'm so glad !" she sobbed.

Fanny pressed the affectionate child to her heart, and
almost cried with her, while Mr. Catlett and Nanny
seemed quite at a loss to understand the scene.

" Well, I declare," said the squire, " to see that, now,
when the young one has been counting the days and hours
till Miss Fanny came back; to meet her in that way crying away as if she was sorry."

" It's just because I'm so glad, Miss Fanny, ain't it ?"
said Maud, with another hug.

" Have you been waiting for us here all alone, Maud ?"
said Fanny.

" Yes. You see the girls would have come with me if
I had told 'em, but somehow I wanted to see you first
myself. Was that selfish, Miss Fanny ?"

There was no selfishness in the little, beaming, upturned

face, and Fanny only pressed the child closer to her heart.

"O, there's my flowers, Miss Fanny! I forgot all about them. See, I made a wreath for you to wear, you know,-'cause we must crown you when you first come home. O, we have wanted you back so bad."

"And Aunt Phebe?" whispered Fanny, as she allowed the child to arrange the wreath of wild flowers on her bonnet, "is she well?"

Maud shook her head. "Miss Fanny, aunty's gettin' too good to stay here. O, I wish she did n't *want* to go, and then mebbe we could keep her."

There was abundance of shouting and rejoicing when the farm-wagon drove up the lane, and in the joyous welcome they received from all, and in the abundance of good cheer brought forth for the occasion, our wanderers were pretty well convinced, that after all there was no such place as "La Belle Prairie."

CHAPTER XXIX.

THE GERM SPROUTS.

"What in the world has come over that girl?" said Mrs. Catlett one day, as Martha left the room, slamming the door behind her; "I declare I'm completely worn out by her tantrums; and if I so much as speak to her, she glares at me with those great ugly eyes of hers, till I'm actually afraid of her. And Mr. Catlett, he won't do the first thing to help me, 'cause he says I must see to the house-servants myself. O, dear! I reckon you've found out by this time, Miss Fanny, that I'm more of a slave than any body on the place, niggers not excepted."

"Ma, it's your own fault," said Nanny; "you give 'em such a free run, that they jaw at you to your face, and make faces behind your back. If you only kept as snug a rope now as Madam Gamby, you'd get along easy with 'em all. That girl did n't used to be hard to manage. I've seen a great many worse."

"Well, she's powerful ugly now, Nanny," said Cal; "you don't know how she's carried on since you've been gone. You ought to have seen her shake the baby the other day, when she thought nobody was nigh. O, my! She looked like she could tear her eyes out and feel the better for it. Ma, you don't know how her eyes did glare."

"I know," said Mrs. Catlett; "it's really dangerous to have the girl round. I believe she'd do the baby a mischief any time she could get a good chance. Sweet little innocent! Mamma's bunch of love!"

"You see, Nanny, if you'll believe it, she hasn't got over moping for that Tilla's dyin' yet," said Cal; "and somehow, she feels a kind of spite against us all, as if we were to blame for it, and the baby more than any body else."

"For my part," said Nanny, "I wasn't so dreadful sorry when that young one died. She never was of much account, and I don't reckon ever would be; and, as pa said, it was kind of a disgrace to have such an ashy nigger round."

"O, Nanny!" said Fanny, "don't talk so. She was every thing to Martha; and I think we ought to make some allowance for her just now. She really seems to be beside herself since Tilla died. I'm sure, Mrs. Catlett, she used to be one of the best-natured, obedient house-servants that you had."

"Well, I don't know but she did do as well as any of 'em," said Mrs. Catlett; "they are all bad enough, and now she's worse than all the rest put together."

"O, Miss Fanny!" said Maria, at this moment bursting into the room, "just see your beautiful new lawn frock. It's all tore to slits."

There was a general exclamation of surprise as 'Ria held up the tattered garment, a pretty spotted muslin, which Fanny had finished the day before, and laid away up the new room stairs for safe keeping.

"Where did you find it? How did it happen? Who could be so mean?" were the questions eagerly put, while Fanny stood silently gazing upon her ruined property.

"It's that awful Marthy, I know it is," said Cal.

"Why you see, ma," said 'Ria, "a little while back I see Marthy come out of here, slammin' the door shut like she

was mad, and then go creepin' up the new room stairs,
where you told her never to go, and so I thought I'd follow her, and see what she was up to. Well, when I got
to the door, there she stood in the middle of the room,
with Miss Fanny's beautiful new frock in her hands, tearin' a great slit in it, and when I called out to her to stop,
she just looked at me like she'd take my head off, and she
put it between her teeth, and tore at it with her claws,
and stamped on it with her great feet like a wild cat, as
she is. I never should have got her off, if Maud had n't
helped me. Lors! I thought I should have died laughin',
for all I was so mad, to see Maud fly at her. She made
the wool fly, I tell you."

" You think we had better make allowance for her, don't
you, Miss Fanny?" said Nanny. " A pretty subject for
pity, ain't she ?"

" O dear, dear ! Miss Fanny's beautiful new gown; it
ain't good for nothin'," said little Joy. " Now you can't
wear it to meetin' next Sunday, can you, Miss Fanny ?"

" There! Come in here, you mean, hateful, horrid,
spiteful creature, you," cried a voice in the passage, and
presently Maud appeared with a flushed face and flashing
eyes, pushing Martha before her; " I hope they 'll whip
you awfully, I do. If I was a grown woman, I 'd whip
you almost to death."

" Maud, behave yourself," said her mother, " and leave
the girl alone."

" I won't then, ma !" said the child; " you don't know
half her badness, to spite Miss Fanny so; the very best
friend she's got in the world; always takin' her part, and
makin' excuses for her, when we told over her pranks. O,
you feel crank now, don't you, when you 've spoiled her
prettiest gown, and made her feel so bad ? You—you—
O how I hate you."

"Maud! Maud! for pity's sake stop!" said Fanny.
"I would rather lose a dozen gowns than have you say
such dreadful things."

"I can't help it, Miss Fanny. It's in me, and I must
talk it out. O, I do hate her, and I know it ain't wicked
to hate such. Well, Miss Fanny, I will try to quit, if you
look at me that way, only it's true, every word of it, just
as true as the Bible."

Meanwhile, the object of this indignation, still grasping
a fragment of the torn dress in her hand, stood gazing
from one to another of the speakers, with a look of sullen
malignity upon her face, that gave little token of repent-
ance for what she had done. There had, indeed, been a
remarkable change in the girl. At Tilla's death, every
good and hopeful feeling of her nature seemed to have
taken its departure. Her step lost its elasticity, her voice
its cheerful tone, and from a careless, good-natured creature, who went singing about her work, and brought upon
herself many a scolding by her boisterous light-heartedness,
she suddenly became gloomy, silent, and morose, going
about her daily tasks with a heavy step and downcast
look; or if at some sharp rebuke she was roused a moment from this apathy, there was a flash in her eyes, and
an expression on her face, that her mistress had never seen
there before.

"I'm not at all surprised," said Mrs. Catlett, "there's
nothing too bad for such creatures. But look here,
Marthy, I want to just say to you, that this ain't a goin'
to do. You haven't gone this while without a trimmin'
for nothin'. I sha'n't touch you. You've got beyond
me, but perhaps you don't remember that you've got a
master, and a set one too, when he undertakes a thing.
I shall hand you over to him, and we'll see what you'll
catch to-morrow morning. The teacher is not to be in-

sulted, and have her gowns tore off her back under this
roof for nothin', I can tell you."

"Never mind about the dress, Mrs. Catlett," said
Fanny. "Indeed I don't want her punished on my account."

"Are you wild, Fanny Hunter?" said Nanny. "If
you can sit still, and see your best gowns tore to slits, I
can't and won't. Them sort of actions must be stopped
in a hurry. I hope pa will take her in hand."

"I'm sure she is sorry," said Fanny, anxiously, "I
can't bear to have her whipped, for any thing she has done
to me. Let her off this once, Mrs. Catlett, do."

"Well, if you ain't the strangest girl," said Nanny.
"If any body had worked me the mischief that wench has
you, I reckon I would n't waste much breath on her.
You have such queer notions."

"I don't want her whipped," persisted Fanny. "Come,
Mrs. Catlett, the offense was committed against me. Do
let her off."

"Don't ask *me*," said the lady. "I'll have nothin' to
do with it. You must go to Mr. Catlett. If, after he
hears the story he's a mind to let her slip, he may. I
sha'n't try to whip her. But, as Nanny says, Miss Fanny,
you are very foolish to waste your breath on such creatures. I'll be bound, now, you can't get her to say she's
sorry for what she's done."

"Here, you Marthy," said Nanny, "tell Miss Fanny
you are sorry you tore her gown, quick now!"

The girl made no answer.

"Speak, you bad girl;" cried Maud, "don't you hear
Miss Fanny takin' your part. You ought to get right
down on your knees this minute, and ask her to forgive
you."

"I won't, den," said Martha.

13*

The silence that succeeded this bold answer, was broken by old Madam Hester in the corner:

"Well, of all things," she said, "jest to think of it. She pawned off all her mother's silver spoons to get up that party, and starved in a garret at last. Her mother was a Watkins."

"Marthy," said Mrs. Catlett, sternly, "how dare you talk so to Miss Maud?"

"Dare," said Nanny, "she dare do any thing. Miss Fanny, there's a sweet spirit for you! It looks like bein' sorry, don't it? Now, then, for my part, I'll be right glad to see her whipped, and pa's the man that'll do it, too."

That evening, when Mr. Catlett returned from the field, Fanny was waiting for him at the porch.

"Can I speak with you a moment, sir?" she said.

"Well, ma'am, I reckon," said Mr. Catlett, throwing himself lazily down upon the bench, "what's wantin' now?"

Fanny briefly related the morning's occurrence, and concluded by requesting that Martha should not be punished this once.

Mr. Catlett had taken a cake of tobacco from his pocket, and with a penknife was leisurely paring off the edges. "Well," he said, looking up when she had finished, "well?"

"That's all," said Fanny, "only I hope you will grant my request."

"You do? Well, now, why not?" said Mr. Catlett, "'specially seein' it's so reasonable. If she'd come to me, like the other girls, for money to buy new traps, or any thing of that sort, I might stop to think about it a little; but, Lord, jest look at it! Why, says she, all I want is for you to give your niggers full swing, let 'em do all the mischief the devil puts into their hearts, only

promise never to give 'em a whippin', that 's all she wants.
Look here, you little Connecticut school ma'am, brought
up on the Bible and Catechism, did you ever hear this
text, Spare the rod, and spoil the nigger ?"

"No, sir," said Fanny, laughing.

"Well, it 's there, anyhow, and you 're a pretty parson's
daughter to be preachin' up t' other doctrine. 'Oh,' says
you, 'bear patiently with 'em, scold a little *easy*, sometimes, when they cut up very bad; don't hurt their feelin's, though, 'cause they 've got hearts under their black
skins jest like white folks.' You 'd let em break your
dishes, and tear your nice traps, and raise hob generally
on the place, and when it came to whippin'—' Oh, Mr.
Catlett,' says you, 'don't! don't! it 's such .a dreadful
thing,' and off you go into hysterics, or a cat-fit, or something about as bad."

"Nonsense, Mr. Catlett ! you don't know me."

"Yes, I do; and if that little chicken heart of yours
was half as tough as a nigger's hide, you'd get through
the world easier. Bless you, child, a whippin' 's nothin'
to 'em, they are made to be whipped. They need it jest
as much as my sheep need shearin', only a mighty deal
oftener. There, don't look so solemn about it. Mass'
Jack ain't the worst master in the world, if he is 'trab-
blin' de broad road,' as Aunt Phebe says. Come on,
now, let 's have some supper."

"But you don't promise, Mr. Catlett," said Fanny.

"There, you are at it again. I never saw any thing
like it. There 's no use arguing with a woman. You may
give her a dozen reasons why you can't do a thing, and
nary one of 'em will she hear to, but fly right back to
where she started from. No, ma'am, I don't promise,
and I don't mean to, neither. There, now, is that
enough."

"It ought to be, perhaps," said Fanny, "but at the risk of making you angry, I must say a word more. I shall not sleep a wink to-night, if I think that girl is to be whipped in the morning, for tearing up one of *my* dresses. Mr. Catlett, if you should tell Martha distinctly that it was only as a favor to *me* that you forgave her, and that another such act would certainly be punished, would it do any harm or injure your discipline?"

"O no, not in the least," said Mr. Catlett. "Of course they would n't chuckle over it, and go on cuttin' up all the tantrums they please, knowin' that there's a little chicken-hearted abolitionist on the place, that could n't bear to hear a nigger squeal, and so kept hangin' round a feller till he promised what she wanted, jest to get rid of her little teazin' face. Come, come, Miss Fanny, you are prime in your line. Jest keep on with the white children, and let all these darkeys alone. I believe that's what I got you here for."

"One moment, Mr. Catlett," said Fanny, as he rose to go. "I don't think you ought to accuse me of interfering in what does not belong to me. You know the offense was committed against me, and it was my property that was injured. I thought I might properly have a voice in the matter. Besides, I preferred my request as a personal favor, with all due submission to you as master. I think it was quite enough to refuse me, without reproaching me with an an attempt to manage—"

"Now, there's dignity for you," said Mr. Catlett. "Who accused you of any thing, I should like to know? Well! well! that'll do now. I ain't a bad-natured feller, Miss Fandango, and I like you well enough to do most any thing you ask me, but you see yourself it would n't do to let such a thing go unpunished, or if you don't see it now," he added, looking back mischievously, "when you marry one of our rich young farmers, and settle down on the prairie, take my word for it, you'll make one of the best managers in Missouri. You, abolitionists, once converted, always make the tightest masters. You'll come to it."

"Heaven forbid!" said Fanny, fervently.

As she rose to follow him, she observed a dark figure start up from a clump of bushes near the porch, and steal round the corner of the house.

"Poor Martha," thought Fanny, "poor Martha."

The next morning when Viny came up stairs with her bucket of water, she brought the intelligence that Martha was not to be found.

"Where can she be?"

"Don'no, Miss Fanny. She done clar out some whar, I reckon; she got scart, 'cause she knew if Mass' Jack got hold ob her, she cotch it. Mass' Jack, he don't lub to whip, anyhow; but, Ki, when he does." Viny shrugged her shoulders significantly. "I hopes he will; good 'nuff for her."

"Why, Viny, I thought you and Marthy were good friends. You always used to take up for her, I'm sure. What's come over you?" said Nanny.

"Miss Nanny," said Viny, with a solemn shake of the head, "I's done wid dat ar Marthy. When she turn right round, and spite Miss Car'line, and all her best friends, den I say, dat ar ain't Marthy, it's de debble himself got into her, and de furder off I keep de better, 'cause mebbe he git inter me too. No, Miss Nanny, I's particular what company I keeps." Viny set down her bucket with great energy.

"Will pa get the men together, and go and hunt her up?" inquired 'Ria.

"No, I reckon not;" said Nanny. "They most always

get sick of it themselves, and come back in two or three days. It's likely she's not far off, down yonder in the woods somewhere."

"She asked me the way to the river the other day," said Maud.

"She?" said Viny, with uplifted hands.

"She did n't show her smartness there," said Nanny. "A heap you could tell her about it."

"Mebbe I know more than you think for, Miss Nanny," said her sister. "I did n't tell her, though, for aunty says it's wicked to run away. I told her *that*."

"You did? Well, you might have told her all you knew, for the hurt that would come of it. She could n't find her way to the river if 't was straight before her eyes. But, then, she'll be back fast enough, there's no danger. Our people all know they don't better themselves by startin' off so. Come, Viny, hook my frock, and don't be putterin' round all day about the chamber work. I want my pink lawn to wear to church to-morrow, and now Marthy's off, there'll be more for the rest of you to do."

CHAPTER XXX.

"Miss Fanny," said Maud, as she followed her teacher into the garden after tea, "was I so very bad yesterday when I scolded Marthy for tearin' your new gown ? What made you look so sorry at me ?"

"I was sorry to see you so angry, Maud. It is always wrong to give way to our passions."

"Well, must we always look pleased with folks when they do such spiteful things," said Maud. "I'm sure, Miss Fanny, you must have felt sorry yourself, to see your pretty new frock, that you 've worked at so long, all torn and spoiled."

"I did feel very sorry, Maud."

"But you did n't want her whipped, Miss Fanny ?"

"O, no; I felt more sorry for Martha than I did for myself, though, as you say, it was hard to see my new frock ruined; but only think what unhappy, wicked feelings must have been in her heart, Maud, to make her do such a thing. Would n't you rather lose a frock than to feel as Martha did, when 'Ria found her up the new room stairs."

Maud was silent.

"I know you had, Maud, ten thousand times. I would rather lose every thing I had in the world, than to lose the control over my bad passions, and sin against God "

"I s'pose you mean *me*, too," said Maud in a low voice, pushing the toe of her shoe deep into the sand. "I got mad and felt wicked like Marthy."

"My dear child, I was thinking of Martha entirely; but you don't need me to tell you, that such feelings as *you* showed yesterday were all wrong."

"Well, I was mad, Miss Fanny, and I did feel wicked and bad toward Marthy; but I'm sure I could n't help it. It was enough to make any body mad. It was so."

"You have gained the victory over such feelings before now, Maud."

"They are all in my heart, though, Miss Fanny; I don't think I ever shall get 'em out."

"You never will, unless you pray to God to help you, my dear child. O! how I want to see you one of those 'lambs of the flock,' that we sing about, Maud. A meek, lowly child of the blessed Jesus. Aunty and I are longing for the time when you will be a Christian."

Maud shifted from one foot to the other, dug her shoe deeper into the sand, picked a marigold to pieces, and then looking up shook her head.

"I can't never be that, Miss Fanny. There 's too much badness in me."

"There 's more goodness and forgiving mercy in your dear Saviour. What is that hymn we learned last Sunday about coming to Jesus, 'just as I am.'"

Maud repeated a verse.

"'Just as I am, without one plea,
  Save that my Saviour died for me,
  In all my sin and misery,
      O, Lamb of God! I come!'

And then there 's the big meetin' hymn, you know, Miss Fanny, that says,

" ' Come, ye sinners, poor and needy,
    Lost and ruined by the fall,
  If you wait till you are better,
    You will never come at all.
        Hallelujah !
    Sinners Jesus came to call.'

But, Miss Fanny, I don't want to talk pious any more to-
night; and there 's Daye now comin' from the office.   I
mean to go and see if he 's got any letters," and Maud ran
off as if only too glad of an excuse to get away.

Fanny walked slowly up and down the garden, a few
moments after the child left her.   She thought about
Maud with her impulsive spirit, and her warm, affectionate heart, and sent up a silent petition, that Aunt Phebe's
prayers and efforts might be crowned, by seeing the child
of her love a Christian before she died; about poor Martha and the punishment that probably awaited her; and
then her thoughts recurred to herself.   She felt strangely
at ease considering the uncertain position in which matters
stood between herself and Harry Chester, and smiled as
she thought of his ardent expression of feeling, followed
by this long interval, of what one would suppose would
be, to an earnest lover, a period of agonizing suspense.
He certainly had made no effort to ascertain whether the
happiness or misery which he had assured her it was in
her power to bestow, was to be his lot; and strange as it
may seem, Fanny experienced none of those heart-flutter-
ings, those alternations between hope and fear, so common
to young ladies in similar circumstances.   She felt a calm
consciousness of possessing Harry Chester's affection, and
she desired nothing more.

In pleasant, tranquil thought, she paced up and down
the walks, till it began to grow dark, then returned to
the house in time to hear Johnny repeat the little evening

prayer she had taught him, before he went to bed.   Then
Hetty held out her arms to be taken up, and by the time
she was sung to sleep with "Little Bo Peep" and "Billy
Boy," Dave was ready for a game at backgammon; so
that the short summer evening was soon spent, and Fanny thought no more of Maud until bedtime.

Meanwhile the child wandered off down the lane, ran
round the back way to give aunty a bunch of roses, and
while standing idly in the doorway of the cabin, thinking
that perhaps she had made Miss Fanny sorry again, she
was seized with a sudden idea.

"I know where she is," she said half aloud; "I'll bet
any thing she's down by the branch, and I mean to go
and find her, and fetch her back.   It won't be dark this
long time yet."

Stopping only to tie up her shoe, and throw on her
sun-bonnet, she started off for the woods.   The branch
was a little stream or tributary, as its name implied, of
La Belle Creek; and though on a bright summer day, the
walk would not seem long, yet before Maud was half
there, in the middle of the thick woods, into which she
had plunged, night had already descended.   Blacker and
blacker grew the shadows between the trees, and more
than once the child fancied she saw faces peering out at
her from behind their trunks, for she was well versed in
negro superstitions, and many a time had listened to ·
Viny's ghost stories with breathless eagerness.

It never once occurred to her to turn back.   It was not
in her nature to give up any project that she had under-
taken, and so though the rustling of the leaves overhead,
made her tremble, and once when a bird started up from
a bush in her path, and nearly flapped his wings in her
face, she screamed aloud, yet she still pressed forward.
Just where the noisy little stream emptied itself into the

muddy waters of the creek, a few of the tall trees had been cut down, and Maud was glad to perceive that there was still a little daylight overhead. She stopped long enough to take a refreshing draught of water, a broad, green leaf serving her for a cup, and to rest a moment, but it was very lonely. The cricket's chirp, and the mournful notes of a whip-poor-will in the thick woods, were all the sounds she could hear, and she soon hastened along the bank of the stream. A little way up, at the bend of a steep hill, that skirted it on one side, the force of the water during several successive freshets had worn away quite a hollow, and here, a year or two before, a runaway negro from Mr. Turner's place, had built himself a rude hut, and found a temporary retreat. It was almost in ruins, but still afforded a shelter from the heavy night dews, which in Missouri begin to fall at five o'clock. It was a wild, unfrequented spot, too, with water close at hand, and this was the place that Maud had fixed upon as the one to which Martha would be likely to resort. She was not disappointed. A pile of ashes and brands upon which the girl had baked her supper, was smoldering near the door of the hut, and upon some dried grass and leaves within, the runaway was stretched, fast asleep. This Maud saw, as soon as her eyes had become accustomed to the darkness of the place.

She lost not a moment, but called her aloud by her name. At the first sound the girl sprang to her feet, and catching up a large club lying close at her side, she looked wildly round.

"O Lord!—who's dat?" she exclaimed, as her eye fell upon Maud in the doorway.

"It's only me, Marthy! don't you know me?" said Maud.

The girl advanced a little way, and stirring up the fire

with her stick, a bright blaze sprang up, displaying the little shrinking figure in the doorway, with long, wet hair, and frightened eyes, and her own stout athletic form holding the heavy stick, and looking cautiously and fiercely round in search of hidden enemies.

"Yes, I know *you*," she said at last, "and now where's de rest?"

"There ain't any body else, Marthy; I'm come all this way alone to fetch you home."

"You come here alone! dat's a likely story," said the girl. "S'pose dey goin' to send a chick like you inter de woods dis time night. No, no, yer can't cheat me dat ar way. Dar's more yonder in de woods. Let 'em come, I don't car'."

"I declare, Marthy, there ain't the first person only me," said Maud, "and there did n't nobody send me neither, I come my own self."

"Well, if you did, it was n't the safest place to come arter night. S'pose yer mammy like ter hab yer here, honey? Mighty lonesome in dese woods. Hey, Miss Maud?"

"I ain't afraid," said Maud, though she moved a little nearer the door.

"Ho! ho! want to run, do ye? S'pose yer could get away if I wanted ter keep yer, hey?"

"You don't want to keep me!" said Maud, boldly.

"Don't I!" said the girl, with a wild laugh, and then suddenly grasping the child by one arm, and looking down into her face with such an expression of malignity and hatred, that Maud shrank and trembled before it. She continued in a half whisper, "Don't I? Ain't de debble standin' by dis minute and tellin' me what to do wid yer, yer little toad, yer little serpent's egg. I'll do it, too!" she said, setting her teeth and clenching the child closer.

"Was n't yer sent here a purpose?   O, Lord! how easy
I could hold yer dis way and smash in yer head, jest so,
d'ye see?   Would dey hear yer holler, tink?   Would yer
mammy hear yer, and feel like I did when dey made Tilla
cry?   Would any body know who did it, tink, or ebber
find ye 'mong de snags and slime in de bottom ob de
creek?   Ho! ho!"

As she stood brandishing the stick over the child's head,
her eyes flashing and her whole body quivering with passion, she looked equal to any deed of violence and blood,
while her little victim, pale, trembling, and speechless with
fright, was completely in her power.

"O would n't dar be a fuss," she continued, appearing
to gloat over the picture her imagination had formed.
"How dey would take on 'about yer; get out all de
neigbors, mebbe, hab a grand hunt, den by-an-by p'raps
find yer floatin' on de water, wid de mud in yer eyes and
har; toat yer up to de house.   O Lord, de fun!   Miss
Car'line, she come screechin' and screamin'! and I'd clap
both hands to hear her, so I would!"

"O, Marthy, what does make you hate us so?" said
Maud, "I'm sure we've been good to you."

"Good! what yer call good?" said the girl.   "Was dey
good to me when dey tuck Tilla, nothin' but a little suckin' baby, 'way from her mammy's arms, and sent her 'way
down riber, where she neber see her child again?   Was
dey good to me, when dey keep her grindin' and workin'
for 'em, week in and week out, and neber give her a kind
word, but plenty ob kicks, and cuffs, and whippin's!   Is
dat what yer call good?   O I *did* say dey was good
when dey lef' us two togedder.   I neber said one word
as long as dey let me keep my chil'.   I did de best I
could, and I kep on cheerful and happy till the last—
till--till—" she dropped the stick from her hand, **and**

covering her face with her ragged dress, cried out, "O Tilla! Tilla!"

Now was Maud's time 'to escape, for the grasp upon her arm was removed, and in the bitterness of her grief Martha seemed unconscious that any one else was present. She threw herself upon the ground, and sobbed and groaned like one in the extremity of mental anguish Something told Maud, however, that all danger was over and pity and surprise kept her chained to the spot.

"Marthy," she said, at last, "I don't *hate* you. I 'm, sorry Tilla 's dead, and I 'm sorry I got so mad with you yesterday. I came here to tell you so this very night."

"You are like all de rest," said Martha, suddenly, rising to her feet, her face wearing its same hard expression. "Dar ain't no odds. Dey larns you to beat us, and bang us, quick as yer old 'nuff to use yer fists. And we can't help it. Did n't I know dey was killin my chil'? Did n't I see her jest pinin' away and growin' weaker eb'ry day? An' did n't I beg Miss Car'line, for de Lord's sake, to save her. She! What she car' so dar was 'nuff left to do her biddin'. I said I 'd done," she continued, dashing the tears from her eyes; "I thought de softness was all driv' out ob my heart, and nothin' left but hate. I 's sure it feels hard enough, and heavy enough," and she laid both hands upon her bosom, and drew a long breath.

"Can't you pray?" said Maud, softly. "Aunty prays when she feels bad."

"Who to?" said Martha, sharply. "Not de Lord. He's done got through with me. He won't hear to nothin' I say. I prayed him not to let Tilla die, and he did. I don' no, I don't reckon dar is no Lord, but dar 's a debble, I knows dat, for he 's been a standin' by me dis bery night, a temptin' me on."

"Mebbe God was there too, holdin' you back," said

Maud. "Oh, Marthy!" she continued, tears of pity and kindness running down her cheeks, "you must pray and try to come good. I'm bad, too, and I hated you till I prayed, and now I don't hate you one bit, and I'm real sorry for you. I don't want you to stay in the dark woods all night; won't you come right home with me; O see how dark it is. I must go this minute."

"Is Mass' Jack, and Miss Car'line, and all ob 'em dar?" said the girl.

"Yes, but I don't reckon pa will whip you, Marthy. I'll beg him not to, 'cause you've had such a hard time without."

"Do you 'spose it 's a whippin' I'm 'fraid ob? Hav n't dey done worser tings to me dan hurtin' dis poor body. No, no. I's done bein' 'fraid. Dar ain't nothin' to be 'fraid ob, now Tilla's dead. I wants 'em all dar, I does. Yes, Miss Maud, I'll go," and, suiting the action to the word, she stalked out into the darkness, leaving Maud to follow as she could.

Follow she did, through bush, and briar, and brake, partly walking and partly running, to keep pace with Martha's hasty steps, and with all her efforts occasionally falling far behind, and losing sight of her in the darkness. Once pausing, lost and bewildered among the trees, she only traced the direction her companion had taken by the crackling of the underbrush, through which she passed, and exerting all her little strength, pushed on to overtake her. Any company seemed preferable to solitude in these dark woods. Her courage had been put to a severe test, and the little that remained, seemed scarcely sufficient to carry her through that dreary walk; but, when at length they reached the opening of the woods, the thought that she was so near home inspired her with fresh vigor, and bounding before her companion, she rushed through the yard, and into the midst of the anxious and astonished circle.

"Here she is," exclaimed half a dozen glad voices, and Maud saw the look of welcome light up those dear home faces, that half an hour before she thought she should never see again.

"Oh, Maud, where have you been? How could you stay away so late, and scare us all nigh to death? Why, child, you look as pale as a piece of bleached linen. Are you took sick? Has any—" Mrs. Catlett suddenly stopped, for close behind Maud, her glittering eyes fixed upon her mistress, stood Martha, the runaway.

"*You* back again!" she said, as soon as she regained her utterance.

Martha did not reply, but looked at Maud for an explanation.

"You see, ma, I found her down by the branch. I've been to fetch her home," said Maud.

"Oh, Maud, my child, how dared you?" said her mother, forgetting, in her appreciation of the danger, even to scold. "And you, Marthy, what have you got to say for yourself? Got tired of your quarters in the woods pretty quick, did n't you?"

"Miss Car'line, I 's come back," said the girl, "and I 's got jest one thing to say. I 's been on this place nigh about eighteen years, and now I 's done with it. I can't stay here no ways, and dat's what I come to tell yer."

She spoke rapidly, and with a kind of dogged determination, but without raising her eyes from the floor. It was hard, in the presence of her mistress, to overcome the old habit of submission, and openly rebel against the authority to which she had yielded so long.

"You can't stay here? You've done with it all!"

repeated Mrs. Catlett, bewildered by the sudden announcement. "What do you mean, you hussy?"

"Jest what I say, Miss Car'line. I's done your biddin' dese eighteen year, and now I must go somewhar else. Dat's all."

"That's all! Well, I must say, Mr. Catlett, that's laying it off cool. Did you ever hear the like of that? I always thought you was a saucy wench, but this goes a little beyond. You are gettin' tired, are you, and want to be your own mistress? Mighty independent, ain't you? Come, any thing more?"

"Miss Car'line, 't ain't no use talkin'. I sha'n't be any 'count on dis place. I'm clar set dar. If Mass' Jack would sell me now. Dar's a trader down yonder to de store makin' up a gang for Texas."

She turned to Mr. Catlett as she spoke, who, with his chair tilted back against the wall, sat smoking a cigar.

"And what in thunder do you want to go to Texas for?" he said, looking at her in astonishment. "This is the first time I ever heard any of you ask to be sent down river. Do you reckon you'd find it any easier there? They work 'em up pretty, well on them plantations, you'd better believe. What's come over you, gal?"

"I don'no, Mass' Jack; 'pears like dar could n't be nothin' worse dan livin' on dis place. But if massa don't want to sell me down river, mebbe he'd send me over to Massa Dave. I don't car' whar I go, so it's off ob dis place. Massa talked 'bout sendin' me dar once; but den I did n't want to go, cause—cause—now de Lord knows I can't get far enuff."

"Why, sakes alive! just to hear her run on," said Mrs. Catlett. "What makes you waste words on her, Mr. Catlett; don't you see she's got to have a regular breakin' in? Here, you Marthy, we'll show you there's some-

thing new to be learned on this place, before we send you
off to another. What have *you* got to say about where
you'll go and what you'll do? Do you know who you
belong to?"

"Yes, Miss Car'line," said Martha, looking her mistress
full in the face, "I knows. No danger ob forgettin' dat
on dis place. I b'longs to you, sure enough; but there's
one way of gettin' clar, and I'll do it, too. No use tryin'
to stop me, Mass' Jack, I will speak. Miss Car'line, you
has brought me down. You's been bringin' me down
dese eighteen years, and I's had all de bringin' down I
kin bar. Now jest hear to me. Sell me off down riber,
or somewhar. I don't car' how far off, so I get far enuff
off from dis place. I'll be a good servant. I'll do de
best I can for somebody else. I will *so*—but I call de
Lord to witness, dat if you won't do dis, I'll go drown
myself in de creek de fus chance I get. You know I'll
do it if I say so, and dar can't nobody stop me. If you
watch me day times, I'll steal off when you are asleep;
and if you tie me up, I'll starve myself till you let me
.oose. Leastways I won't be no more gain on dis yer
place. I don't want to live, anyhow. Satan tried to have
me do it when I was down in de woods. I'll do it, too."

Mr. Catlett rose while she was speaking, and whispered
a word or two to one of the servants, who immediately left
the room.

"Now, then," he said, placing himself directly in front,
and fixing his eyes sternly upon her. "Now, then, you've
had your say, I'll have mine. All this sounds mighty
grand, and you think it's smart to be threatenin' your
lawful owners to drown yourself, and all that; but just
let me tell you, such things ain't so easy done. Mebbe
we shall find a way to take you down a peg or two.
We've been a mighty sight too good to you, and there's

where the trouble lies. Here, Uncle Jim," he continued,
as a stout black man appeared at the door, " take this girl
and lock her up in the old smoke house till mornin'.
She 'll likely think better of her plans before we 've done
with her."

" Pa," said Maud, who, seated on a low stool, had listened to this conversation with breathless interest, " don't
whip her, please. I told her I reckoned you would n't if
she 'd come back and be good."

" She looks like it," said Nanny.

" Hush children, all of you," said their father, angrily.
" This is my business now."

Meanwhile Uncle Jim had laid hold of his prisoner, who
offered not the least resistance, and was leading her off.

" Lors, Uncle Jim," she said, " you need n't hold me
so tight. I sha'n't run away no more till I go for good
and all. Mass' Jack, I 've given you fa'r warnin'; Miss
Maud, don't you fret, I ain't afeard of a whippin';" and
she disappeared in the doorway.

" Mr. Catlett," said his wife, when the younger members of the family were off for the night, " it 's my opinion
you 'll have to sell that girl."

" Smart business that would be, to do just the thing
she wants."

" I know, but you 'll lose her if you don't. I 've seen
enough of her obstinacy to know that she 'll do as she said
the first minute she can get the chance. She 's got just
devil enough in her for that, and would as lief drown herself, if she took the notion, as to eat her dinner. If there
is a trader down to the store, it would n't do any harm to
see him, and find out if he 'd give a fair price for the
girl."

" I won't give in to her in that way. Do you reckon I
want her to think I 'm scared at her threats. You see it

would have the worst kind of effect on the other servants. Half a dozen of 'em heard her talkin' in that saucy way; and if you mean to keep any order in the house, you 'd better let me manage."

"Well, there 's another thing, Mr. Catlett. The children's lives ain't safe with that creature round. Here was Maud frightened all but to death, and says Marthy threatened to kill her. I reckon it was n't so bad as that; but then she is mighty dangerous. I can't bear the sight of her either. I 'd rather lose something on her, than have her round another year. But there 's no danger of losing. Niggers never were higher, and she always was a stout, healthy-lookin' girl. Come, Mr. Catlett, I reckon you 'd better ride down to the store in the morning, and see what kind of a bargain you can make."

"I tell you I won't do just the thing she wants," said Mr. Catlett.

"Well, if you don't want to do that, send her over to Dave awhile, till she gets cooled down a little. I 'm sure you said he needed another hand, and she 'll do very well in the field. The fact is, Mr. Catlett, I 'm afraid of the girl, and if you tried to whip her, you 'd have an awful time of it before you broke her spirit. Now you see she 'd do well enough for Dave, and you 'd get her off your hands as quiet as you please."

"Poor Dave seems to have trouble enough over there, without adding a she devil to his gang, but I don't know but you 've got the right of it, after all," said Mr. Catlett, with a yawn.

Perhaps he was convinced by the force of his wife's arguments, and perhaps he had been secretly of the opinion all along that this would be the easiest way to settle the matter, and only argued the case lest his firmness and resolution should be called in question. Certain it is that

he finally adopted her last plan, and it was settled that
Martha should be sent to Dave. To Dave she was accordingly sent the next day, Mr. Catlett driving her
over, with her bundle of clothes, in the farm-wagon. She
received the news of her disposal with a kind of sullen indifference, merely saying, that it "did n't make no odds
to her," but Mrs. Catlett declared when she was gone,
that a curse was taken off the place.

While the old folks were discussing the matter below
stairs, the children were not silent above. Maud was the
heroine of the evening, and descanted at length upon the
horrors of her situation, while her listeners plied her with
questions and exclamations.

"Maud," said Cal, after they had all gone to bed,
"did n't you feel awful when she stood there, with that
great stick over your head, looking so ugly, and you all
alone in the woods? Did you think she was goin' to kill
you, sure enough?"

"Well, I did for a minute, Cal, and at first I was so
scared, I could n't think of any thing, and at last I thought
about aunty, and pa, and ma, and Miss Fanny, and all of
you, and that I should n't ever see you again, and O, so
many things came into my thoughts all at once."

"What things, Maud?"

"O, I don't know—things that I 'd done, but the bad
ones most of all."

"That was funny."

"And then I remembered the story Miss Fanny told us
about Daniel in the lion's den, and how he prayed, and
God would n't let the old lions hurt him."

"Did you pray?"

"Not much. I tried to, but I could n't think of any
thing to say, only Johnny's prayer that he says nights. I
prayed that, and a little on to the end of it."

"What did you put on the end of it? That God would n't let Marthy kill you?"

"Yes, and that He'd take me up to heaven if she did, but it was n't any use, I know."

"Why not, Maud?"

"Because I have n't repented of my sins, and Miss Fanny says we must, or we can't go to heaven."

"O Maud, was n't you afraid to die? I think it's dreadful to be buried in the ground, like grandma, and little Neddy."

"I would n't be afraid," said Maud, "if I was like aunty and Miss Fanny, I tell you, Cal, when they die, they 'll go right up to God."

"I wish it was n't so hard to be good," said Cal, with a sigh. "I 'm sure I want to go to heaven when I die. Don't you, Maud?"

"Cal," said Maud, "if I had died down there in the woods to-night, I should n't have gone to heav'n. I know I should n't."

"Mebbe you would, Maud. Any way you did n't die, so I would n't feel bad about it."

"I can't help it, Cal. I keep thinkin' about it all the while, and O, dear, I wish I was a Christian."

"I reckon Miss Fanny would love to hear you say that, Maud."

"I ran away from her to-night," said the child, "'cause she talked pious to me. O, dear, how wicked I am."

"Well, never mind, Maud. I 'm sure it won't do any good to cry about it. Mebbe if you ask God He 'll give you a 'new heart.' Miss Fanny says that 's what we must pray for."

A new heart! Maud whispered the words over many times to herself, and with the simple prayer upon her lips she fell asleep.

CHAPTER XXXI.

ONE warm Sunday afternoon, Mr. Catlett, after accompanying some guests to the gate, sauntered down the lane and through the path in the woods, leading up the creek to the saw-mill. The day was very beautiful, and the sober stillness of nature contrasted with the boisterous merriment of his late companions, impressed itself even upon him, and he walked thoughtfully along. As he turned a bend in the creek, a strain of music was borne on the air to his ear, and as it was long past the time of the servants' meeting, the place besides being too distant for any sound from thence to reach him, he paused a moment to listen, wondering who it could be.

It sounded like the voices of children, and finding its way through the branches, seemed to come down to him from the very tree-tops—a low, pleasant murmur, now rising, now falling, now wandering all about in the sweet air, and then descending softly till it died away in silence, like the music of some distant waterfall, heard in the pauses of the wind. As he proceeded, the sounds grew louder and more distinct, and his rapid steps soon brought him to an opening among the trees, and looking a little way up the stream, he perceived at once where the music came from.

On fragments of the broken bridge, and on the mossy trunk of an old tree that lay across it, a group of children were seated, and in their midst, with the youngest in her lap, and the others close about her, sat the "little Connecticut school-marm." She was teaching them a hymn, reading a verse from the book in her hand, which the children repeated after her many times, until they could recite it alone, then singing it with them, and so on to the next verse. He knew that it was a hymn, for though too distant to distinguish the words, they sang them in an old psalm tune, that he remembered well, and that came back to him now like the murmur of home voices; for years and years ago, he had sung it when a boy, in the green woods near his father's door.

Again and again they repeated the strain, the teacher's voice in low, sweet tones, commencing the line, but soon lost in the chorus of young voices that took it up, till the old woods rang again with the melody. It was a pretty sight that group of little ones on the bridge, with the trees for a canopy overhead, and the water flowing beneath their feet, singing the praises of God among His most beautiful works. There was a chastened, subdued look upon their young faces, far from sad, but suggestive of the day and of the employment in which they were engaged, while in her simple white dress, her pale face lighted up with a smile of praise and calm happiness, she who sat with them as teacher, looked scarcely less youthful than they. The last verse was sung, and the book closed, before Mr. Catlett left the spot; and then turning back, after a few steps, he heard the murmur of a voice speaking in earnest tones, saw her pointing upward, and knew that she was telling his children about God and heaven.

He did not go up to the saw-mill, as he had intended; he had no wish to pass the group on the bridge; so stealing as a guilty person back into the woods, he walked hastily toward home, whistling a lively air as he went, and stopping in the lane for a frolic with the dogs. But as he passed the parlor window, and caught a glimpse within, of his daughter Nanny and Miss Belle Turner, in their Sunday finery, laughing and coquetting with two or three of the prairie beaux, he thought of the young girl with her pale face and simple white dress, whom he had just left singing hymns down at the old bridge. He wondered what made the difference.

"Mr. Catlett," said his wife that evening, ".what do you think about this teaching the children so much religion? Here's Johnny knows two or three hymns a'ready, and Maud has learned a whole chapter in the Bible by heart. Can't you stop it some way?"

"What for? Don't they learn any thing else?"

"Lors, yes, they are getting on right smart with their books; but if she goes on with 'em this way, I'm afraid they'll get to be Methodists one of these days. I reckon you'd better hint to her to hold up a trifle."

"Well, now, I thought you women believed in religion. What's come over you?"

"I have n't said any thing against religion. I think it's a good thing in its way. My grandfather was an elder in the Presbyterian church in Richmond, nigh about twenty years, and most all my kin are professors. Of course I've no objection to attending church, and all that; but you see she goes into it so strong, that she makes the children think they are just the wickedest creatures in the world; and here comes little Joy the other day, telling me it's wicked to get mad, that the Bible says so, and all that, the impudence! as though any body could help gettin' mad, with such a house full of servants as I have to manage."

"O, ho! there's where the shoe pinches, is it? The

religion that gives a good knock now and then at our own
sins, ain't the thing at all. Well, now, look here, wife,
we ought to think ourselves lucky to hire a chaplain and
a school-teacher all together. Mebbe she 'll sanctify us
all, if she only stays here long enough."

" Well, you may joke about it, but I tell you it will
likely work mischief one of these days. She 'll be teachin'
the servants next. We 've got one prayin' Methodist on
the place, and that 's enough, I should hope."

" You never had a better servant, let me tell you, than
this same prayin' Methodist you tell about."

" O, Aunt Phebe is well enough. It 's dreadful tiresome
to hear her run on sometimes. I 'm sure I don't know
what to do with two of 'em."

" Let 'em alone, wife, that 's the best thing you can do.
It won't hurt any of us to get a dab now and then."

CHAPTER XXXII.

The plan of a visit to Dave on his new farm, discussed by Miss Nanny and the teacher in St. Louis, had not been given up. "After harvesting," Mr. Catlett all along said, "they would certainly go," and accordingly no sooner was that busy season over, than the young people grew impatient for the fulfillment of his promise. "Every body was going," murmured Maud, "except we little folks, and 'Ria, who was going to keep house. Great times there would be with 'Ria for mistress.

The summer had been unusually warm. For weeks a hot dry wind blew from the south, a prickly, irritating wind, that heated, rather than cooled the air, and which Nanny thought so injurious to the complexion, that she sat all day in a huge sun-bonnet, a covering that exposed her to all sorts of attacks from the younger children, who could approach her on three sides without being discovered, and who delighted to tease her with their monkeyish tricks, just, as Johnny said, "to hear her fret." So oppressive was the weather that even the heavy dews that fell at night failed to cool the air, and the grass and the foliage looked parched and withered.

Accustomed to a cooler climate, Fanny suffered more through this season than any other member of the family. It was with no small effort that she overcame the languor and debility occasioned by the extreme heat, sufficiently to perform her daily duties. The sun poured its rays directly down upon the little school-house, and many a time by the middle of the day her head would throb so dizzily, that she could hardly read the book before her. The children, however, knew nothing of this. At such times her voice was more subdued, and her manner more gentle than usual, while with unwearied patience she explained the difficult passages in their lessons, drew pictures for Johnny on the slate, and set the copies for the closing exercise. If now and then she pressed her hand to her head with a look of pain, it was done so quietly that they did not observe it. "Miss Fanny never gets mad," said Cal. "If we act bad, she looks at us so sorry, it makes us feel a heap worse than if she scolded."

But after all were gone and the door closed behind them, the young teacher looked from the low window upon the wide waste of withered grass, and contrasted it with the green orchards of New England. The old parsonage, with its sloping yard in front, where the poplars cast their long shadows at this hour, the tidy flower-garden behind, and the blue mountain stretching away in the distance, came back to her view, until, sick and weary, the tears rose to her eyes, and she sank down upon her chair, to dream a little while about home.

"Our 'Connecticut school-marm' needs this trip as much as any body," Mr. Catlett remarked, "she's getting as pale as a lily, and I have n't heard her laugh right hearty for a week. Come cheer up, Miss Fandango. We'll take you over there where the breezes blow. The land's higher, they say, and it's all-fired hot on the prairie, and no mistake."

The day was set once and even twice for their departure, but several things had happened to postpone it. Mr. Catlett could hardly make up his mind that it was safe to

go. He knew all about the border troubles, and that an
expedition was now being planned to invade the country,
and force slavery upon the people. He well knew, for he
had been required to subscribe largely, how great this
preparation was. Nor did he deem it safe to traverse
the country with a party of ladies, at a time when he
would be liable to encounter an army of his fellow-mis-
sionaries, with plenty of whisky along. He, therefore,
waited, before starting, until he could receive certain news
of the intended invasion. This intelligence he at last obtained. Ascertaining that the army would not assemble
for at least six weeks, he determined to seize the opportunity, and make the long-wished-for visit.

So Mr. Catlett and his wife, Nanny and the teacher,
with Mr. Tom Walton for an escort, set off one fine morning upon horseback, while big William followed more
leisurely, in the farm-wagon full of household goods.
Dave was waiting to receive his guests, and after a right
cordial greeting, conducted them with no little pride and
satisfaction to the door of the cabin which had been built
especially for their accommodation. It stood close beside
his own, and was divided into two apartments, the one for
Mr. Catlett and his wife, the other for the young ladies.
It was a cozy little affair, and Jinny and Adeline had
taken a deal of trouble to prepare it for their arrival, arranging the few articles of furniture which had been sent
over from the prairie, to the best advantage. The little
mirror was trimmed round with wild flowers, and some
four-o'clocks, and morning-glories were growing under
the windows, while Uncle Tim had manufactured, after
his own fashion, a couple of wooden flower-pots to stand
on the table. That worthy individual also led them in the
course of the day along a shady path a little distance
from the house, and brought them suddenly upon a swing,

which he had suspended from one of the tall trees, placing
close by a rude bench, whereon they might repose when
weary. His delight at the young ladies' expressions of
pleasure, was good to behold, and even Mrs. Catlett remained cheerful and happy through the whole of the first day.

"Well, Tim, how are the crops?" inquired Mr. Catlett.
"Going to make a good year of it, boy?"

"Poorly! poorly! Mass' Jack. You see we got put
back heaps in de spring. Twice dat ar corn hab to be
planted, and de third crop got kinder wilted down, de
sun was so hot 'fore it started. Den t'ain't good land for
'backy, nohow, and taters, well dey's fa'r—yes, taters is
fa'r, but dat's all you ken say 'bout 'em. Mass' Dave
won't make his fortin off dis year's crop."

"Well, never mind, Tim. Better luck next year, mebbe. Now, old lady, are you going to make yourself comfortable here for a month or so, hey?"

"Well, yes, it looks real snug, Mr. Catlett. I s'pose,
though, we shall have some trouble. I sha'n't stay here to
have bullets whizzin' in at my windows. If there's any
such tantrums as that cut up, I shall leave, that's all."

"Nonsense, ma; who's afraid. I think it's *perfectly
charming;*" this was one of Nanny's city phrases. "And,
Miss Fanny, don't you remember how Cousin Julia was
always talking about her father's beautiful country residence? When we write, we can tell her that we have
got a country residence too."

Fanny did not hear, for Tom Walton was whispering
something in her ear at the moment—an occupation to
which he had devoted himself all along the ride from the
prairie. More than once the jealous Nan had nudged her
mother, and said softly, "Tom is making love." "Making
fiddlesticks," said Mrs. Catlett.

The day passed with the usual chat among families
when united, and all went merry as a marriage bell.

CHAPTER XXXIII.

THE SQUATTER'S REVENGE.

ONE night, not long after the arrival of Dave's visitors, the girl Martha was straggling about in the woods surrounding her young master's claim. Her restless, feverish spirit, seemed to find comfort in these expeditions, and no matter how hard the day's work, or how weary the body, night usually found her wandering about in the darkness, like some evil angel intent on mischief, and yet fearing to do any thing for the lack of helpers. To-night she had strayed further than was her wont, and having got some miles from home, how far she knew not, she found herself in the middle of a thick growth of trees, entangled with under-brush, where, after wandering awhile, she became completely bewildered, and knew not which way to go. In the midst of her perplexity, she came suddenly upon a rude sort of habitation, part wigwam, part log-cabin, built deep in the woods. A bright light streamed through the cracks, and guided her steps to the entrance, where, with torn feet and limbs she asked for admittance.

"Who's there?" cried a sharp female voice. "Zi, your gun! Quick, boy, we are tracked! we are discovered! Now stand by your mother. Shoot 'em if they are a dozen."

"No, don't shoot," said Martha, "it's only me, a poor lost nigger, no account, anyhow. Won't harm you. Hates nobody but Marm Catlett, that killed my Tilla."

"Did you say you hated Catlett?" said another voice; "Catlett of La Belle Prairie? Do you hear that mother? Good! You can't hate him worse than we do. Shall I undo the door?"

"I did n't say I hated Massa Jack. It 's Miss Car'line I hates de wust. She killed my child, but he let her—and, yes, I hates him, too. O, do let me in. 'Pears like I should die." They heard her sobbing without.

"Undo the door, Zi," said the woman's voice, "it can't do no harm, anyhow. If she 's an enemy, she 'll bring him here, and he 'll find a way to get in, without our leave; and if, as she says, she hates the man, why"—she whispered something to the boy, who immediately undid the door, and Martha entered.

"You are hurt and you are shivering," said the woman, surveying the forlorn object before her; "but before ever you warm yourself at our fire, swear that you hate that man, that devil in human shape, that you spoke of outside the door."

Her vehemence seemed to astonish even Martha.

"Why, lors, missus, what has he done to harm you?" she said.

"What has he done? Did n't he murder my man in cold blood! The best and the kindest husband, and the father of my children! Did n't he? And bring him in and throw him down at my feet like a dead dog! He stood by when I wiped off the death sweat, and says I, 'Speak one word more, John,' and says he, 'They murdered me like cowards!' I cursed him then, standing by the dead body of him that he killed, and I vowed to myself that I 'd be revenged. Did n't they drive the widow and the orphans from their home, with only this boy to pro-tect 'em? And does n't his own son warm himself at *my* hearth-stone, with *my* roof to cover him? A lazy, good-

for-nothing devil, that shoots in the woods all day! Good
Lord, girl, is n't that harm enough? Do you ask why I
hate 'em?"

"And have n't I reason to hate 'em, too? Did n't dey
kill my Tilla! my child! and bury her in de swamp?"

"Did they, did they kill your baby?"

"They made her work when she was sick and ailin',
till she died, and they would n't hear to me nor Miss
Fanny, when we begged 'em for de good Lord's sake not
to do it."

"Was she your child?"

"De same, missus, de very same. Mammy put her
inter my arms when she was a little baby, and says she,
'Take care ob her, Marthy. I gib her to you.' Dey sold
mammy down river, you see, and Tilla and me was left
alone. I always called her my child, and I could n't have
loved her better if she had been."

"Poor thing! they did you this great harm, then, and
you 'll hate them for it as long as you live. You need n't
swear. We are even, but, girl, do you know what *revenge*
is, and how sweet it is?"

"Don't I?" said Martha, grating her teeth. "Has n't
the debble stood by me times, drivin' me on, and oh, missus,
once he put de way straight afore me. One dark night
alone in de woods, dat child, *her* child, missus, dat killed
my Tilla, was sent to de bery place where I wus. Dar
was n't a livin' soul nigh, and de creek run a little way
iff. O, why did n't I do it?"

"Did you want to kill the child?"

"I did n't do it, missus. I said de debble told me to.
Mebbe I 'll do it yet, though, for all I let her go."

"Zi, she 'll do," said the woman. "We can trust her.
Will you join with us, and keep a secret, and help us to
do them a mighty mischief one of these days?"

"Won't I?" said Martha, a fiendish smile playing over her face.

"Sit nigher then, and speak low. The very wind may carry it to his ears."

"Not to-night, mother. Don't tell her to-night. The time has n't come yet," said Zi.

"Well, well boy, when then? You are always for putting it off, and I never shall sleep in peace, or the dead man rest in his grave, till the mischief is done."

"Come here again a week from to-night, girl, do you understand, and if every thing is right, we'll let you know what to do. And, mother, you forget that it 's after midnight, and I have n't had a mouthful of supper."

"True, true, boy, I forget every thing now-a-days but my wrongs. Those are fresh enough in my mind. Well, bring in the milk, Zi, while I take up the ash-cake. There, sit down on that stool, girl. Have you had any thing to eat?"

"Do you keep cows?"

"The nicest you ever see—gives plenty of milk."

"Mass' Dave keep three, and Adeline say dey all dryin' up. Can't squeeze over a quart out of nary one of 'em."

"Ha! ha! ha!" roared Zi. "Don't know how to take care of 'em, you see. Ours are first-rate, ain't they, mother?"

"It 's the curse, girl. Dave Catlett can't get any cows that will give him milk. Have you ever heard any bullets whizzing round them?"

"O, missus, it 's the dreadfullest place. Aunt Adeline she 'most goes crazy. She says it 's de debble. She want to get back to de prairie."

"Ha! ha! ha!" roared the boy again. "It 's haunted, sure enough."

"Zi, Zi, 't will be time enough to laugh when you win.

Come, boy, eat your supper. Sit up, girl, we are on equal terms in this matter. There's a close bond between us."

Zi, his mother, and Martha, made their meal over a board, with a pitch-pine knot burning for light, the same the slave had seen through the cracks of the hovel. It was near morning when Martha said she must hurry back before the sun rose, to her day's work. The boy accompanied her a little distance to point out the way, and just as they were about to separate seized her roughly by the arm, and cocking his pistol, held it within a few inches of her breast.

"Do you see this?" he said, sternly.

"Yes, massa," said the trembling girl.

"Now hear me, then. If you betray us, if you dare to tell those hell-hounds where we are, as sure as you stand here alive, one of these bullets shall go through your heart. I'll hunt you out if I search the world for you. Do you understand?"

"Yes, massa. O, please, massa, take it away. De Lord knows I hates 'em as bad as you do."

"Well, go then," he said, apparently satisfied.

Away sped Martha like a wild deer, leaping among the underbrush, and finally disappearing in the thick woods, while the boy took his way slowly back to the cabin.

"NANNY, who's that yonder riding down the hill at such a furious rate?"

"Goodness, ma, it's Tom Walton. I'think he'd better live over here and done with it. He's been to visit us three weeks hand runnin'."

"There goes Nan to prink, now," said Dave, as his sister ran into the other room; "just as if all the beaux came to see her."

"Well, who does Tom Walton come to see, if it is n't Nanny?" said her mother, with some spirit.

"Who did he bring that great nosegay to yesterday, ma, and run down in the woods after when he found she'd gone to walk?"

"Nonsense, Dave, he never would think of addressing a poor teacher like her. What are you talking about?"

"He might make a worse choice if he did," said the young gentleman.

"Well, you seem to find a great deal to admire in that little pale-faced girl. But as to Mr. Walton, I think he pays her very little respect. He always used to get Nanny down to the piano the very first thing when we were at home."

"Yes, and talk to Miss Fanny all the while. I've seen him," said Dave.

"Go way, Dave, you are too smart," said his mother.

"Well, there he comes up the walk," said Dave, "in his white pants and yellow vest. I reckon I must go and meet him. Tom Walton's a pretty clever fellow, and I don't think any the worse of him for likin' Miss Fanny."

An hour after, as Mrs. Catlett was in her part of the cabin arranging things for the night, Nanny entered, her carefully curled hair dangling about her ears, and her muslin dress lank and heavy with the dew.

"Why, child, where have you been?" said her mother.

"O, ma, such doin's! Tom Walton!—the teacher!" said Nanny, short for breath.

"What of them? Can't you speak? Why, child, how you act."

"I can't help it. I'm so flustered. Only think of it, ma; she's rejected him!"

"Rejected Tom Walton!" exclaimed Mrs. Catlett, astonished in her turn by the intelligence. "You are wild!"

"No, I'm not. I heard it with my own ears, or else I never would have believed it," said Nanny.

"What! reject Tom Walton, the handsomest young fellow on the prairie, and with his eighty thousand at least! Nanny, somebody's been telling you a story."

"Did n't I tell you I heard it with my own ears," said Nanny, half crying with impatience and vexation.

"Well, don't fret, Nanny; sit down and tell me all about it," said Mrs. Catlett. "How in the world did you hear it?"

"Why you see, ma, after sunset we went out to walk, Mr. Walton, and Miss Fanny and me; and he just talked to her all the time, and did n't pay me any respect; so by and by I got vexed, and said I'd stop at the swing. Miss Fanny she tried not to have me, but I would. Well, by-and-by I heard em coming back, and I hid in the bushes till they went by, and Miss Fanny she says, 'Where's Nanny? let me go and find her,' or something like that; and he caught hold of her and told her not to, for he had something particular to say to her. And then, ma, they sat down on the bench by the swing, and I right behind in the bushes, and I could hear every word he said. I declare I never was so surprised in all my life, and I could n't stir, you know, because they would find me out."

"Well, what did they say?" inquired Mrs. Catlett, eagerly.

" O, he came right out with it the first thing, and told her he never saw any body before that he liked half so well; that he had wanted to tell her so a long time back; and that if she would accept his heart and hand, he should be a very happy man. He said it just as if he had learned it all by heart, and in such a proud kind of a way, as if she would say yes in a minute."

"And why should n't she? Any girl 's a fool that would n't."

"But she did n't, though, ma. I could n't hear what she said very well, she spoke so low, but it was something about being very sorry, that she had felt afraid that it was coming to this, and that she would gladly have spared him the pain. Ma, you never heard any body break in as he did, right here. He asked her what she meant, and whether she understood what he said? in such an angry way, that it fairly frightened me."

"How dared she?" said Mrs. Catlett.

" She said yes, and ever so much more, but I could n't understand it. I only caught a word here and there, but it was plain enough to see that she refused him right out and out."

"And she nothing but a poor teacher, not worth a cent in the world! How *did* he take it?"

"He did n't say a word for about a minute. It seemed as though he did n't know what to make of it, and when he did speak, his voice sounded so strange, just as if he was angry, and was tryin' to keep it in. He said he hoped she would n't trifle with him; that she would think better of it he was sure; and O, ma, he began to plead so earnestly. I could n't tell you half he said; but she stopped him right in the middle of it, in her decided way, and then he rushed away from her as if he was mad, and she followed him, so that I could n't hear any more; but they made it up somehow, for he shook hands with her under the tree a moment after, and looked so sorry it went to my heart. Now, ma, did you ever see any thing like it?"

"She was a perfect goose!" said Mrs. Catlett. "No girl in her senses would refuse such an offer. She 'll never get such another chance as long as she lives. I 'm perfectly astonished that such a fellow as Tom Walton should want her."

"I know it, ma, and she took it as cool as if she was used to such things. She 's out there in the yard, now, talking with black Jinny, just as if nothing had happened."

*　　*　　*　　*　　*　　*　　*　　*

"Why, Tom, are you going to ride to-night?" said Dave, who was leaning against a tree, when Mr. Walton came by.

"Yes," said the young man, abruptly.

"Well, I 'll ride along with you a mile or two," said Dave. "It 's too dull staying here, and here 's pa's horse ready geared. Which way?" he continued, as Mr. Walton seemed undecided how to turn his horse's head.

"Any way, it don't make any odds," was the reply, and digging his heels into his horse's sides, the young man started off at such a pace, that Dave found some difficulty in keeping up with him.

"For goodness' sake, Tom, hold up, can't you?" said Dave, after they had ridden at this pace awhile. "You ain't on a wager, are you, that you need to ride so fast?"

Mr. Walton checked his horse, and waited till his companion came up.

"You would n't go ahead of me that way, Tom, if I had my own horse. Pa's old nag is slow-footed, anyhow."

"Dave," said Tom Walton, abruptly, "did you ever make a fool of yourself?"

"Well, I don't reckon I should want to own up if I had," said Dave.

"Such a *confounded* fool that you could n't help ownin' it?" said his companion.

"Why, Tom, what are you drivin' at?" said Dave.

"Because *I* have, and I should like to find company for my comfort," said the young man.

"Well, if Tom Walton, the smartest young man on the prairie, owns to playin' the fool, I don't know who may n't," said Dave. "When did it happen, Tom?"

"Just now, within the last hour, Dave. It's a pretty story to go round the neighborhood, ain't it, that the rich Tom Walton offered himself to Catlett's hired teacher, and got his walkin'-ticket?"

"Is that so, Tom?"

"Well, I reckon. And what do you s'pose the reason was, Dave?"

"Because she's a woman, I reckon, and likes to be contrary; though how any woman in her senses should make up her mouth to refuse you, is more than I can see."

"I believe it was just because I happen to be the *rich* Tom Walton, that she did it," said the young man, bitterly.

"No! You don't mean that, Tom?"

"I mean that when I would n't take no for an answer,

but must set before her a few of the advantages she would reap by being *my* wife, she stopped me short enough, by saying that if there was nothing else in the way, she never would marry a man with my possessions. I vow I know plenty of girls that would have me for that very reason."

"What did she mean?"

"Well, I suppose she meant because I owned niggers. I've known all along she was a bit of an abolitionist, but I did n't think she would have carried it so far. I did n't ask. I was flinging out of sight of the girl mad enough, when she called me back in her soft way, and when I would n't hear to her, she followed me, and laid her hand on my arm. I could n't have stirred then, any more than if there'd been a dozen stout men hold of me, instead of one puny girl."

"How you talk, Tom. I did n't think you were so deep in love. Did she make it up with you?"

"Did I make it up with *her*, you mean? There's no being mad with that girl. I could have gone down on my knees to her that minute if it would have done any good. Heigh, ho! Well, let it pass."

"Yes, I don't reckon you need to bother yourself over one girl, when there's twenty to be had for the askin'. And Tom, between you and I, I don't believe in marryin' for love, anyhow. It's a mighty unsubstantial thing to live on. I mean to look out for something more solid."

"That's your view of the matter, is it?"

"Yes *sir*. I s'pose I've had my fancies as well as other people, but I've got over 'em all. It's best to take a common sense view of the matter after all, and I tell you it's a mighty comfortable thing in the long run to have a snug little something to fall back on. It makes up for any lackings in the bride."

15

"What a venerable old philosopher."

"Well, the fact is, Tom, I'm lazy. There's no gettin rid of that. I never did love to work, and if I can find a way of getting shet of it all my life, who's a right to find any fault?"

"Nobody, to be sure. If a young girl that I know of, as poor as Job's turkey, and as proud as Lucifer, would look at things that way, the rich Tom Walton need n't have made a fool of himself to-night."

CHAPTER XXXV.

"Dave, my boy, how does that girl Marthy come on?"

"O, well enough, pa. She's a peeler to work, though it seems as if the devil was in her. She's out, Aunt Adeline says, about all night, and comes home with her clothes half in rags. But as long as she's bright and handy daytimes, I don't know as we need to fret about her. I reckon it's all straight."

"Keep a fast look out, young 'un. I've had more to do with niggers than you, and I tell you it won't do to give 'em too free a run. I've seen that girl myself skulkin' round after night, and hang me if I like the looks of it. I'm afraid she's up to some deviltry."

"Well, she or you have stopped the bullets, pa; that's one good thing. I ain't no coward, but it did make a fellow feel kinder crawley, to hear a ball whizzin' by every now and then, within an inch of his nose, and not know, for the life of him, where it come from."

"Well, well, boy, keep your eye peeled, that's all I've got to say, and you'll scare off the devils after a while."

This conversation occurred between father and son, after several weeks of the visit had passed. There seemed to be great quiet just now among the mysterious characters who haunted this region. A bullet had not whizzed by for a fortnight, nor any strange accident happened. The place was really getting quite comfortable and home-like; Aunt Adeline, indeed, insisted, with her superior knowledge of demonology, that the spirits were round just as ever, only *pretending* to keep still, so as to come down with a "mighty big crash by-and-by. They 'd cotch it pretty soon, she reckoned, and if old massa knew what was good for himself, he 'd get his traps together and go back to the prairie right off."

It was a singular coincidence, which afterwards came to their knowledge, that on these very days old Madam Hester, on the prairie, from her chair in the chimney-corner, muttered dolefully almost all the time, gesticulating with her skinny fingers, so that 'Ria declared she frightened her half to death, particularly when she caught such broken sentences as the following:

"They are all murdered! O trouble and sorrow! No good! No good! Why could n't they be content with what they had! Always gettin' more! runs in the blood! O me! O me!"

Aunt Adeline's predictions were in some measure true. The lull preceded a tempest. The plans of the conspirators, which had several times been thwarted when upon the verge of execution, neared their completion. With stealthy steps, night after night, Martha had found her way to the lone cabin in the woods, and held whispered conferences with the widow and her son, upon the safest and most certain way of revenging themselves. At these times, Martha herself was astonished at the bitterness and deep malignity the little meek-eyed woman manifested, when speaking of her wrongs and their perpetrators. At such times, there was a wild look in her eyes, and her hands trembled with convulsive energy, as she vowed that she would have her revenge.

At last, the eventful night arrived. It was well suited to their purpose, as black and starless as they whose deeds

being evil, "love darkness better than light," could desire.
It was early when the two commenced their work. Stealing to the enclosure where the cattle were kept, they
selected Dave's best cows, and drove them to their own
home in the woods. Dave afterward remembered that
waking from an uneasy slumber, he fancied he heard "old
Brindle" low close under his window, and wondered, half
dreaming, whether the cattle had broken their enclosure.
By the time this was accomplished, and the bars of the
cattle-yard and the stable let down, that the stock and
Mr. Catlett's fine horses might escape to the woods, it
was long past midnight. Martha, to avoid suspicion, had
remained at home, waiting for the signal which was to
call her forth to her part of the night's work. It came at
length, and stealing forth from her quarters, she joined
her companions at a safe distance from the house.

"Is all right, Martha?" whispered the widow, eagerly;
"the dogs tied and the light-wood ready?"

"All right, missus, and ebery soul as fast as a log."

"Come, then, make haste! we 've no time to lose, and
the hour for vengeance is come."

Hurrying before them with feverish impatience, she led
them to a pile of dry under-brush, which Martha had
carefully collected, and all three loading themselves with
the inflammable material, carried it to the cabins, against
which they carefully piled it. Again and again they returned with fresh loads, obeying the woman's directions
to make sure work of it.

"Mother," said Zi, stopping short when he had collected
his last bundle, "it goes against me to burn up the old
place, which father and I worked on so long. Can't we
burn t'other one, where the women sleep, and leave this."

"No, boy, no, we 'll burn 'em both to the ground!
Spare neither root nor branch, man nor woman, master

nor slave. Do you suppose I could live under the roof, that has harbored the murderer of my husband? No, no, Zi, let 'em all perish together!"

"O, lors, missus, you don't mean to burn up de folks, too," said Martha, opening her great eyes in horror. "You did n't say dat afore. I can't do no such thing. 'Pears as if I could n't, nohow. Missus, de debble's got you to think of doin' dat ar."

"No, no, you goose," said Zi. "We don't mean to hurt a hair of their heads. Only to drive 'em off the place and spoil all their goods. Mother don't know what she says. She 's wild to-night. You need n't look so at me, girl, I give you my word, we 'll give 'em time to escape. But, hark you! if you betray us, you are a dead nigger in the twinkling of an eye! Do you understand?"

"I ain't goin' to tell, massa. I wants to see Miss Car'line turned out of house and home dis cold night. She dat let Tilla shiver many a time with de cold. I does so! but O, lors, I is sorry for de teacher. I hopes dar won't no harm come to her."

"Stop fooling there, Zi. Hush all of you, what 's that?"

"It 's that pesky dog, mother; I was feared he 'd make us trouble. Crouch down here in the bushes awhile till he gets quiet."

"O! to be disappointed after all, when so near my revenge," muttered the woman.

"'T ain't nothin', missus," said Martha; "hold on a bit, and I 'll still de dog. He knows me."

She stole from her covert, and returned in a moment to say that all was quiet.

"Now, then, waste not a moment. Set fire to the cursed pile, and let me see it burn to the ground. Run, boy! This is the last bundle. Stay, give me your matches, and I 'll light the pile myself."

She seized the box, and hastening forward, set the piles in a blaze, her hand trembling, and her heart beating with excitement.

"Quite cheerful and warm, this cold night, mother," said the boy, with a chuckle.

"Warm to the heart that sees an enemy ruined."

"Lors, how it crackles. Now let's holler, or they'll all be burnt up," said Martha.

"Open your mouth if you dare, you cowardly nigger. Do you think we want it put out with a bucket of water? The thing must be done sure. Keep still, don't say a word. I'll give the alarm."

Fiercely glared the flame amid the darkness, lighting up the three faces which glowed in fiendish malice at the scene, and dancing, crackling, flashing, as though joining in their glee. Higher and higher it leaped, lapping the sides of the low cabins with its red tongues, now rising, now falling, and now rushing in wild eddies round the building. Still there was no stir within.

"O, lors, massa, I must holler. Dey'll be burnt up, sure. Why don't dey wake?"

"Come, mother, run now, while I give the alarm. It's time, as the girl says."

"And why should we wake them?" said the woman. "Hasn't the Lord put a deep sleep on them to their destruction. Go away, boy, go away, I'll stay and see the end. Martha—where has that girl gone?"

Martha had seized the moment, and quick as thought rushed into the cabin where Fanny slept.

"Quick, Miss Fanny! O, quick! De house is on fire! They sha'n't burn you to death! Get up! Get up! I say."

Roused from a deep slumber, Fanny sprang to her feet. The room was full of smoke, and the floor felt hot beneath her, while a bright light filled the building.   Before she could speak the girl was in the other cabin giving the alarm.   All was terror and confusion.   The fire was advancing so rapidly that but little could be done, and the men finding it impossible to save the cabin, soon gave up the attempt.   Mrs. Catlett, who had retained barely presence of mind sufficient to hurry on her clothes, ran from one room to the other, wringing her hands in impotent distress, while the two black women clung to her skirts, and screamed and howled in sympathy.   Fanny alone seemed capable of taking the lead, and with Nanny's assistance, succeeded in saving the greater part of their clothing, by far the most valuable articles in the house. The furniture and bedding were left to their fate.   By this time it was unsafe to remain longer in either cabin, and houseless and forlorn the family stood upon the open prairie, watching the destruction of their late habitation.

Mrs. Catlett and Nanny filled the air with their lamentations, but the squire, and Dave looked on in gloomy silence.

"Look yonder, Miss Car'line, dar 's two folks runnin'. Dar, jest by dat clump of trees.   See 'em."

Dave sent a shot in the direction pointed out, where, by the light of the fire, two figures could be distinctly seen, running as fast as their feet could carry them.   The noise of the report was followed by a shrill laugh behind, and turning, they perceived, by the gray light of the morning, the figure of a woman, standing with outstretched arms, half-way up the hill.

"There's one of the devils!   Shall I shoot, pa?" said Dave.

"Yes, do!" said the woman, laughing again, "murder the wife as you murdered her husband; it would make a pretty end to the night's adventures.   Does your mother like her quarters, boy? It's a comfortable night to be turned out of house and home! Ha! ha! ha! Fire away, boy. I can die in peace with such a pretty sight before me."

"Curse the she devil! Pa, just say the word."

"Put down your gun, boy! Would you fire on a woman?"

"Ha! ha! ha! Do you remember the widow's curse? Has your land yielded and your flocks increased? Have you grown fat on the widow's inheritance? Answer me that, Jack Catlett!"

"For heaven's sake, Mr. Catlett, send that horrid woman away," said Mrs. Catlett.

"He sent her away once with her fatherless children," said the woman, after a pause; for Mr. Catlett stood in moody silence. "He sent her away once, my dear, but she's come back to curse him. Let him try it again, if he will. Let him tempt the widow's curse. Ha! ha!"

With her wild laugh ringing in their ears, she disappeared among the trees. Mr. Catlett drew a long breath, and looked about him.

"Well, what's to be done now," said his wife, in a querulous tone; "are we to stand here shivering all day, with that horrid creature in the woods to fire on us. O dear! what did we ever come here for?"

"Jerry, bring some of those embers and a little light wood, and we'll have a fire. Are the horses all lost?"

"Please, massa," said Uncle Tim, coming forward, "I cotched old Poke Neck and one of de farm hosses jest back in de woods. I's tied 'em yonder to a tree."

"Well, hitch 'em to the farm wagon, and put in those trunks and other traps. Do you hear? We must get back to the prairie about the quickest."

"I'm as faint as death for the want of something to eat," murmured Mrs. Catlett.

"Is the smoke-house burnt up, too?" said her husband. "Jerry, go look in the ashes, and see if you can't find some bacon."

The man soon returned, bringing two or three blackened, half cooked pieces, from which the family breakfasted, after which they huddled into the farm wagon, servants and all, and in doleful plight started for the prairie.

"Where alive is that Martha?" said Mrs. Catlett, suddenly; "I have n't seen the girl since the fire."

"You are not like to, either," said Dave. "Curse the girl! I told you no good would come of sending her to me. She was head one in the devil's plot they 've hatched up against us."

"Jinny," whispered Adeline, as the two were squatted close together in the back of the wagon, "it 's a mighty bad ting to get turned out ob doors sich a cold night; but dar's good come out ob it, for it 's brought ole massa to his senses, and we 's goin' back to de prairie. For my part, I 's glad to say good-by to dis yer place"

CHAPTER XXXVI.

SIEGE OF LAWRENCE.

It was on the morning of the second of December that Mr. Catlett and his family responded to the writ of ejectment from the claim served on them by the widow of the murdered man and her son. It was a sad, chilled, irritated company, which old "Poke Neck" and his coadjutor drew along toward La Belle Prairie. The day was clear and cold, and the sun shone brightly on the scene. The ride was mostly taken in moody silence, interrupted now and then by the congratulatory chatting of Aunt Adeline, who regarded the whole affair with evident satisfaction.

About noon, Dave descried some large body, which seemed to be moving toward them, and called his father's attention to it. Mr. Catlett paid no heed to the boy for a long time; but as it approached nearer and nearer, his face assumed an anxious expression; and turning to his son he said:

"Dave, it's the army for Kanzas. I heard yesterday they were about marching to Lawrence, but I hoped we should get the start of 'em one day at least. What shall we do? There's no use trying to get away, for you couldn't worry Poke Neck off a walk. Meet 'em we must, for all that I can see."

"Well, pa, and what's the harm. We are friends, I s'pose. The ladies can cover up their faces if they don't

want to see so many men; and as for you and I, we'll
bear the laugh they raise against us, for being seen in this
plight, and get by as quick as we can."

"You don't know what you are talking about, boy.
Don't you know it's one of the rules of these fellows not
to let any body pass? Wife and girls, what do you think
of joining an army and besieging Lawrence?"

"O! Mr. Catlett, you are crazy. They wouldn't think
of making us turn about, would they? Mercy on us,
what shall we do?"

The young ladies said nothing, but their faces expressed
any thing but pleasure at the idea.

"Well, don't borrow trouble," said Mr. Catlett, carelessly; "I don't reckon you'll have to do it. They are
all people from about the prairie, and know Jack Catlett
well enough to trust him for a safe person. So don't
fret. And, Dave, see to the priming of the guns. Some
of these fellows may have too much whisky aboard."

The army, for such it turned out to be, of two or three
hundred, from the region about La Belle Prairie, had now
arrived within hailing distance, when up rode the officer
in command, with a rusty sword and dilapidated feather,
being no less a person than our gallant Colonel Joe Turner,
and not a whit better off for the liquor he had drank since
morning. Stopping short in mid career, as he caught his
neighbor in the farm-wagon, niggers and all, he burst into
a loud laugh.

"Ha! ha! ha! Catlett, where on airth did you come
from in such aristocratic shape? Got Dave and all his
tribe. Well, well, going to leave the claim, and show the
white feather to those devils that's playing antics on the
place, hey?"

"Just take your drunken squad along, colonel," said
Squire Catlett, and let me pass with my ladies. "When

you are yourself, sir, I will explain the particulars. So start up Poke Neck, William."

" Hold ! neighbor Catlett, not quite so fast, my fine fellow ! We don't let any body pass, friend or foe, that's one of our oaths. Besides, we want you and your son in the enterprise. Man of means, you know, squire. Foot the bills ! A pretty story it would be for you to stay at home with your wife and babies, when your countrymen are fighting for their rights. Why, neighbor Catlett, it's a glorious work we are engaged in. We are going to fight to the death, and exterminate every scoundrel from Kanzas, that's tainted with free-soilism or abolitionism. Is it a time for brave men to hold back ? Come, come, Catlett, face about. We'll give you better mounting, and as for the ladies, there sha'n't a hair of their heads be hurt."

"I tell you I sha'n't do it. You know well enough, colonel, there's no shirk-liver about me. I'm up to the scratch, and I'll pay my part, and do my part, too, but these ladies must be landed safe first ; I promised 'em, and my name ain't Catlett, if I don't fulfil. I tell you, Dave and I will be with you to-morrow, or next day. Come ! can't you trust an old neighbor ? I've said once, and I say again, my name ain't Catlett, if I don't see these ladies safe home to-night."

" Then it ain't Catlett, for go you shall," said another voice, and the squire recognized in the person approaching, a man great on the borders. " We'll let not a live soul, friend or foe, man or woman, go by us. That's a fixed thing with us. Ladies, your servant," he continued, touching his hat to the frightened females. " You need feel no alarm ; you shall receive the best of treatment. We already have one woman among the soldiers, shouldering her musket like the revolutionary dames."

"Is that Gamby along?" said Catlett. "Hang me! but you don't call her a woman? At any rate my women ain't of her build. So if you don't want a muss, just let us go on," and the squire began to flush, and bluster, and roll out big oaths, not proper to be uttered in the presence of ladies, or anywhere else.

"Let's let him go," said Colonel Turner to the men about him, who seemed to be chief. "It's plaguy hard!"

"No, no, not by a great sight, I tell you. What a pink-livered chap you are, Joe. Had n't you better make another confession at Mount Zion Church?"

The worthy colonel turned a look of fury on the speaker, and opened his mouth to reply, but changing his mind on the subject, remained silent.

"You understand, Mr. Catlett," said the great man of the border, "that this is a principle with us, and not in the least disrespectful to you or your ladies. We have made our plans, and if we give up one point, we may a dozen. We must stick to it to the letter."

"That's it! I likes that!" said a voice from the ranks, "it's constitutional."

"Let's give one shot apiece at the unmannerly scamps, and then rush by 'em, pa," said Dave.

"O! for heaven's sake, Mr. Catlett, give up to em," said his wife. "They'll murder us all if you don't. Dave, put down your gun this minute. Well, if this ain't trouble, I'd like to know what is."

No other course seemed to present itself to Mr. Catlett, for after a moment's hesitation, he took his wife's advice, and expressed his willingness to turn about.

"Now you talk like a sensible fellow," said Colonel Joe. "Bring those horses up from the rear, some of you, and we'll mount the squire and his son in good shape. And look here, neighbor, put your niggers back

BORDERERS ON THE MARCH.

in one of the baggage-wagons, and let the ladies have more room."

The arrangements were soon made ; the farm-wagon containing the ladies, placed in rear of the main body, while Mr. Catlett and his son, well mounted, kept close at its side, and after an hour's delay, the army thus reinforced, moved on.

As they passed the claim, the ruins still smoking, were visible, but Catlett turned away his head, and as the cabins stood a little under the swell of the hill, no one else noticed their destruction, unless it might have been Colonel Joe Turner, who also had his reasons for avoiding the topic.

Martha, from one of her skulking-places, observed the cavalcade, and soon discovering that her master and mistress with the young ladies, were of the number, she hovered about at a safe distance, like an evil angel, ready for mischief. So the army moved on toward Lawrence.

CHAPTER XXXVII.

BEFORE the army entered Kanzas, two of our *dramatis personæ* were traversing the Territory from a contrary direction. They were now approaching the road to Lawrence, along which these valiant soldiers will, almost at the same time, pass. They are engaged in earnest conversation. One is an old gentleman of fine open countenance, the other by far his junior, but resembling him in his genial nature. Let us draw near and listen to them.

"Harry Chester," said the elder of the two, suddenly checking his horse, and turning full upon his companion, "you are a fool."

The young man received this flattering announcement with a smile.

"Yes, sir," said the old gentleman, "I'm out of all patience with you. A young man that's got the start in life that you have, to throw up his profession for a foolish whim. I tell you it's downright folly."

"I think not, sir," said Harry Chester, respectfully; "I see it very clearly to be my duty."

"Fiddlestick's ends! What do you call duty? To give up a profession in which you are bound to rise, and that yields you now a couple of thousand a year, lose a year or two in getting a smattering of Greek and Hebrew, and for what? Why, to wear a long face and a black coat, and dwindle down into a country parson."

"And to accomplish more good, perhaps, in ten years as a minister of the Gospel, than I should in a whole life-time settling quibbles of law. No. no! judge, this is not a hasty resolution that I have taken up. Two years ago, when I first became a christian, it was my earnest desire to study for the ministry; but circumstances then seemed so peremptorily to forbid it, that I tried to give up the idea. Since then it has impressed itself more and more strongly upon my mind; and now that my aunt's death has opened the way by providing me the means, I dare not refuse to take up the work. My heart is in it too, and I know of no profession half as dignified and noble as that of a faithful minister of Jesus Christ."

"And I know of no common field laborer that works harder, or is half so much the public drudge. Our ministers, now-a-days, are over-worked and under-paid. I can see it all. You will be a worn-out, broken-down man before you are forty years old. Come! come! Harry, take an old man's advice. I have n't been a bad friend to you."

"You have been a father to me," said Harry Chester, warmly, "and I respect your opinions more than those of any other man living. It is only the strongest sense of duty that leads me to act contrary to your advice. I wish you could look at this matter as I see it. The wealth or the reputation that I might gain in my profession, seem of little weight compared with the happiness of spending a life in my Master's vineyard, in leading souls to Christ, if I may indeed be so blessed, and of meeting them at the last day as crowns of rejoicing. Who would exchange the bliss of that moment for all the wealth and honors that this world can bestow."

"Come! come!" said the judge, impatiently, "don't preach your first sermon before you are licensed. It is of no use talking with you. I see you are quite as head-strong as I thought you. ₄For my part, I don't put the good things of this life so low in the scale. I think a comfortable support against one's old age, is a grand good thing. But, there! we won't quarrel about it. If you will be blind to your own interests, I can't help it, that's all."

"And you will not entirely cast me off?" said Harry Chester, "even if you *do* think me a poor, blind, deluded fellow. I should, indeed, be making a sacrifice if I lost you for my friend."

"No, no, Harry," said the old gentleman. "No, no, there's a warm corner for you in my heart yet; and if you can bear with the old man's scoldings, he can bear with the young man's folly. And now, the next thing will be to talk it over with that little girl 'up the country,' I suppose. She's quite romantic enough to start off with you on a mission, or enter into any other project for the evangelization of the world. She knows all about it, perhaps already—hey?"

"She knows nothing, sir," said Harry Chester. He had suddenly grown very sober.

"It's time she did, then," said the judge. "Why, man do you think she will give you your walking-ticket, that you are afraid to tell her. She's got too little worldly wisdom for that. You'll be mated exactly, and starve together in perfect content, I doubt not."

"We shall never have the opportunity, judge."

"And why not? What makes you look so sober about it? has she said no, or have you changed your mind about her? I'm sure you told me once that you meant to win her if you could."

"I did," said the young man, with evident agitation. "She is every thing that is good and lovely. She was dearer to me than all the world beside; but that is passed, and it has been my constant effort for weeks to forget her."

"And why?"

"Because I have learned from a reliable source that she is engaged to another. O, it was a cruel blow," said the young man.

"It is not true, Harry. I know perfectly well to the contrary. Somebody has been deceiving you. Did it come from Fanny herself? Unless it did, don't you believe a word of it?"

"It did *not* come from her," said Harry Chester, "but from one who had every means of knowing."

"Nevertheless it is a mistake," said the Judge. "I know it to be so, from the girl herself; for once when I was joking with her, I forced her to confess that she was heart-free. Now, is she one to deceive me, even in jest? No, Harry, depend upon it, she is yours for the asking; and perhaps this very day is pining over your coldness and indifference."

"Your confidence gives me a faint ray of hope," said his companion. "There *may* be a mistake; I have despaired too soon, and I will know the truth from her own lips, at any rate; but look, Judge, just below the fork in the road, is n't that a body of men I see yonder?"

"It certainly looks very much like it," said the Judge. "I did n't know there were so many men in Kanzas. Harry, see to your pistols! I don't like their appearance."

Just as they were turning into the main road, they encountered a small party of a dozen or so from the army, who had advanced to arrest them.

"Stand! You are our prisoners!" said Colonel Joe Turner.

"By what right or authority? Show us your precept."

"By right of might. Do you want to dispute that?"

"But we are free citizens, traveling on business, which can not be delayed, and we warn you not to impede us."

"Nevertheless we despise your warning, and will force you to wait our leisure."

"But what does this mean? Who are you, that take upon yourselves to stop peaceable travelers, and compel them to obey? What is all this army gathered for, and where are you going?"

"To secure the rights of the South, and the triumph of slavery. Hey! young man, what means that curl of the lip? Are you an abolitionist?"

"No matter what I am," said Harry Chester, "I claim the protection of the law and my country."

Seeing resistance impossible, and relying upon their own uprightness, they yielded to their captors, and were immediately placed under guard.

In a few hours the army had joined the forces at Lawrence. The next day Tom Walton rode up on his prancing gray.

CHAPTER XXXVIII.

THE FLIGHT TO THE FREE-SOILERS.

THE weather was extremely unpropitious. The rain fell in torrents, and almost deluged the camp. A deserted house on the outskirts of Lawrence had been appropriated to the ladies, and every attention which was practicable was paid to them. Indeed, compared with those about them, their quarters were quite comfortable. Dave and Catlett chose to take soldiers' fare, camping out, near by the building.

It was an hour or so past mid-day when they arrived. A court-martial was immediately held, and both the prisoners were condemned to be hung on the morrow. The young man, in the excitement of the moment, when allowed to speak in his defense, had most unguardedly given free utterance to his sentiments, believing himself in a free country, and had even denounced slavery, and its extension into this new region, with great eloquence and power.

The whisky-drinking court, which sat in judgment, were excessively enraged at his abolition opinions, and at once passed sentence of death upon him. They deliberated longer over the judge, whose judicious reserve, and dignified bearing, seemed to put the cowardly ruffians in fear. At length they mustered courage to decree his execution also. So they were both remanded to their quarters, to be carefully guarded till the next day. The place of their confinement was to be the opposite room from that occupied by the ladies, in the same deserted house.

Fanny was looking out upon the drizzly day in a desponding mood, when the crowd ushered the prisoners along to their quarters. As they passed the window where she stood, the younger suddenly looked up, turning full upon her, a face, which though paler and sterner than she had ever seen it, she could by no possibility mistake. It was but for an instant, the crowd closed about him, and he was gone, yet in that instant the agony she experienced, as the whole extent of his danger flashed through her mind, convinced her how large a place he occupied in her heart.

With a faint expression of surprise, she started back from the window, and Nanny, who, in the further part of the room, was making her toilet to receive her beau, young Turner, asked, in amazement, "What was the matter?"

"O, Nanny, I have seen one of the prisoners."

"Well, what of it? You look more as though you had seen a ghost. Why, Miss Fanny, what ails you? How you tremble."

"Nanny, it is Harry Chester, of St. Louis," gasped Fanny.

"Harry Chester! O, Fanny, it can't be. Are you sure?"

"I saw him this moment pass the window; and, Nanny, he is locked up in this very house with us, and to-morrow morning he will be led out to die. I heard them say so. O, what shall we do?"

"And the other? who can the other be? If pa and Dave were only here."

"Where are they? Can't we find them? Something must be done without loss of time."

"I have n't the least idea, Miss Fanny. I have n't seen th m since noon, and it is n't safe to trust ourselves out of doors."

"Nevertheless, Nanny, we must help these men to escape—you and I."

"But how? They have put a guard of half a dozen men at least in the passage, and locked them in tight besides. We can't do the first thing."

"We can and we must. O! is there no one to help us?"

"Bob will be here directly, Miss Fanny. He will do what he can; but, lors, we can't save them, I know."

"So he will, but O, Nanny! there's no time to lose. 'To-morrow at dawn,' said that cruel man; 'to-morrow at dawn, you rebels, you die: So say your prayers faithfully, the young one is parson enough, and prepare for death.'"

"O, it's dreadful, Miss Fanny; such a pretty young man, too; but what can we do?"

Fanny was examining the walls. "Nanny," she said, "is the opposite room just like this?"

"Exactly, for I peeped in this morning. You see there's only these two rooms in the house, with that great wide passage between, and the loft overhead, and the guard are in the passage, and there's no possibility of getting to them to help them."

"Except from the outside, Nanny. And see, how this mud between the cracks in the logs crumbles away almost at a touch. Nanny, I have it! We must get them a saw, and let them cut their way through the logs. That will do. O, I do believe we can save them."

"But what will they do after they get out? The camp are all about us. They would be seen the very first thing. Then where can we get the saw, or get it to them? and do you reckon they would n't make some noise in sawing their way through these great thick logs? O, Fanny, I will help you all I can, but it does seem as if you was wild."

"No, no, Nanny, I never felt calmer or more self-possessed in my life. Uncle Tim has a hand-saw in the farm-wagon; I saw it this morning. After night we will steal out and get it to them through the cracks. Bob Turner must have some horses ready at a safe distance, and be on hand outside, to lead them out of the camp. Do you not see? and God will help us, and I feel that we shall succeed. And Nanny," she continued, glancing at the chair where Mrs. Catlett, worn out with fatigue and anxiety, had fallen fast asleep, " we will not vex your mother with this, if we can help it. Get ready as fast as you can to see Bob, while I look for Uncle Tim."

That worthy fellow was not far off, and when Fanny opened the window and beckoned him to approach, her summons was obeyed with the greatest alacrity.

"Well, now, what does Miss Fanny want ob a saw, anyhow?" he said in reply to her whispered request. "If dar's any little job she want done in dat line, Uncle Tim's de feller, anyhow."

"No, Tim, it is nothing that you can do. No matter what I want of it. You must keep perfectly still, and say not a word to any one. Hide it under your jacket—or stay—bring it in with an armful of light wood. Can you? If you bring it to me safely, it will be a great favor that I shall never forget as long as I live. Can I trust you, Tim?"

"To de ends ob de airth, Miss Fanny."

At this moment, Bob Turner, spruced up a little for his visit to his lady love, entered the house.

"O ho!" he said, as he walked into the passage where the guard were stationed; "you've got those abolition devils in charge, have you, against to-morrow?"

"Yes, hang it, if it ain't tough, too, after the march we've had to-day, to watch all night. Howsomever, they won't trouble any body a great while. They've got to swing to-morrow, sure. I say Bob, can't you get the ladies to hand over a little whisky. It's plaguy dry work."

"Bring your own whisky, blast it," returned Bob. "How do you reckon the ladies have got any?"

With trembling eagerness Nanny unbarred the door of their room, and let in the young man, who was quickly informed who one of the prisoners was, and the part he was expected to take in their deliverance.

Bob Turner shook his head gravely at Fanny's plan, bringing up objection after objection, all of which she foresaw and answered. Still he hesitated.

"O, for the sake of humanity, of justice, you will do this!" said Fanny, with clasped hands.

"For *my* sake," whispered Nanny.

The young man looked from one to the other of the pleading faces raised to his, and could resist no longer.

"It's as much as my neck is worth to do the thing," he said at last; "but, hang it, you are so set on it, I'll try."

"Heaven bless you!" said Fanny, fervently; while Nanny manifested her gratitude in a way that pleased him much better, for she threw her arms about his neck, and kissed him heartily on the spot.

Then in a whispered conversation they arranged all the particulars of their plan, Bob Turner expressing it as his opinion that the first and most important step to be taken, was to provide plenty of whisky for the guard, and in this manner put them off their guard as soon as possible. He was dispatched upon this errand, and by the time he returned night had fallen upon the camp.

Meanwhile Nanny had persuaded her mother to retire to rest, and had the satisfaction of seeing that lady snugly

16

ensconced in the little nook, partitioned by an old blanket
from the main room, where a couple of rude couches had
been spread upon the floor for their accommodation.

"Now, then," said Bob, "while I go and hunt up a
couple of fast horses, you, girls, had better set yonder
chaps at work. They'll have as much as they'll want to
do, to work their way out before midnight, and if those
fellows in the passage hear Uncle Tim's saw going, it's all
up with 'em, that's all I've got to say."

Stealing out at the back door, Bob started on his peril-
ous expedition, and the young ladies, after wrapping
themselves in their cloaks, Fanny hiding the saw beneath hers, silently followed him. The lights of the
camp were shining dimly through the rain and mist, and
as they crept softly along under the eaves of the house,
they could hear the voices of men in boisterous merriment,
in a tent close by.

"Keep close to me, Nanny. Poor girl, don't tremble
so! We have nothing to fear," whispered Fanny. "See,
this must be the place."

With a sharp stick she had brought, she worked away
the mud plastering between the logs, making an opening
through which she could easily thrust two or three fingers.

"They are here, Nanny. I see them," she said softly,
rising from the stooping posture she had assumed, "Harry
Chester and Judge Stanton."

The prisoners were conversing together in a low tone,
and as Fanny paused a moment before addressing them,
she caught a sentence or two of what they were saying.

"Will they *dare* to do it? Is there no chance of
escape?"

"I am afraid not, Harry. They dare to do any thing,
a gang of drunken ruffians are certainly not to be trusted."

"Oh! but to die in this way! To have my days cut

snort by this drunken crew! How can I bear it? And to think that by my imprudence and hot-headedness, I have shortened your days, too. God forgive me, I can not feel resigned!"

"Courage, Harry! Our trust must be in God."

"Judge Stanton! Harry Chester!"

"Hark! Judge. Did n't some one call our names?"

"I heard nothing, Harry. It must have been your imagination."

"Perhaps. My fancy plays me strange tricks to-day. Were it not for the utter absurdity of the thing, I could swear that not two hours ago I saw at one of the windows of this very house, the face of a young girl whom I shall never see again, unless, indeed, we meet in heaven."

"Harry! Harry Chester!"

"Who speaks?" said the young man, turning eagerly in the direction from whence the sound came.

"A friend! One who will help you to escape! Come closer. This way, both of you. Can you hear what I say?"

"Perfectly," said the young man. A thrill shot through his frame, and he felt sure that he had heard that very voice before from a little fairy perched up on an old bridge long ago. "Am I dreaming, or is' it Fanny Hunter's voice that I hear?"

"Hush! speak lower! Your enemies are all about us. I am here—Nanny Catlett and I—don't ask how. I have no time to tell you. Be content to know that we are here to save you! Can you trust us?"

"With my whole heart."

"Listen, then. With this saw which I have brought you, and your pocket-knives, you must work your way through the logs. There will be horses waiting for you outside the camp, and young Turner will be here at mid-night to guide you to the place."

"You are a dear, brave girl, Fanny!" said the Judge, "but I am afraid you are periling yourself for nothing. Do you know there is but a thin partition between us and our guard, and that even now we can hear their voices in drunken dispute. We thank you, Fanny, with our whole hearts, but the thing is impossible!"

"No! no!" the sweet voice trembled with earnestness, "it is *not* impossible! there are great risks, but I feel that they will be overcome. The men are very drunk, and they will be still more so by midnight. It is your only chance. Be prudent, and strong, and God will take care of the rest. O! promise me that you will make the attempt."

"She is heaven's own messenger, Judge. How can you hesitate a moment?"

"Come away! come away!" whispered Nanny. "I hear voices close by."

"I must go. Will you make the attempt, or be led out to a shameful death to-morrow?"

"O, come! Miss Fanny, we shall be discovered."

"Go, go!" said the Judge. "God helping us we will make the attempt."

Returning in safety to their room, the girls spent the remaining hours to midnight in watching with the most intense anxiety the progress of their plot. For a time they heard nothing but the patter of the rain against the windows, and the voices of the revelers in the passage; and rejoiced together as their drunken mirth grew more and more boisterous. At length Fanny's quick ear caught another noise, and, drawing her companion's attention to it, they listened with pale faces and shortened breaths to the distant, muffled sound of a saw.

"O, if they should hear it," said Nanny. "Can't we run round and tell them to be more quiet?"

"No, Nanny, depend upon it they will work as cautiously as they can. We have done our best; now let us trust them in God's hands."

The noise of the men was just now very loud, and they seemed to be in some dispute over the game of cards they were playing; but above it all, those long regular strokes continued; Fanny closed her eyes, and Nanny knew by the motion of her lips that she was in prayer. Slowly dragged the hours away, and with trembling voices the girls whispered each other, that every moment now, and every stroke of the saw, was bringing the prisoners nearer to liberty. Once, indeed, they thought that all was lost; for suddenly one of the men exclaimed with an oath, that he heard the sound of joiners' tools somewhere in the house. Hang him! but he'd know what it meant.

"Blast you, Tim Jenkins, go on with your play," said another voice, "you are always fancying something. It's only one of your plaguy tricks to throw up the game, when you are likely to lose your money."

"I don't hear any thing," said another voice. "Those poor devils in there have n't opened their heads for the last hour. Let's take a look in and see what they are up to."

"No, no, Dick, let 'em alone. They are safe enough. Come, take another swig, and go on with your game."

The sound to which Tim Jenkins alluded, had ceased the moment he commenced speaking, and was not heard again for some moments; but it did recommence at last, and though at times it seemed to the half distracted girls that it *must* be heard, so loud and distinct was it to their overstrained ears, no further notice was taken by the revelers, and near midnight it ceased entirely.

Bob was behind the time, and the poor watchers had every opportunity to indulge in doleful anticipations of evil, before he made his appearance. But come he did at last ; and stopping at the door to whisper the ladies that all was right, and the horses a quarter of a mile distant, waiting for them, he hastened to the prisoners. They heard nothing more, but when suspense becoming intolerable, they ventured out again to the place where Fanny had held her whispered conference with the prisoners, all was dark and still, and they thrust their arms into the space between the logs by which the captives had made their escape.

Wearied with watching, Nanny sought her bed, and Fanny was pacing the room back and forth in her anxiety, when a ponderous knock was heard at the door. Anticipating some evil, though she knew not why, with trembling hands she undid the fastenings, and in stalked Madam Gamby.

"Ah, here you are, you pale-faced abolition teacher! Where's the prisoners? There's a hole sawed through their room, and they are gone. And the saw's marked Catlett. Do you know any thing about it, hey? Now if you don't catch it here, I'm mistaken. You can't cheat me. I've seen you with that abolition rascal on the prairie before now. Why did n't you run off with him? You need n't try to look so innocent. You know you helped 'em off, and you'll be hung in their stead, too. I've complained of you to the governor, and they'll be here directly to arrest you."

"O, Madam Gamby! Would you have seen those innocent men murdered. Can a woman be so cruel?"

"Cruel! you fool, do you suppose such rascals were made to live? I'll show you what I'm made of. Ah, here they come! I told you they'd be after you."

There was a shuffling of feet and a sound of angry voices outside the door.

" O, Madam Gamby, save me! save me!" cried Fanny.
" Will you give me up to these ruffians?"

" Yes, I will.   There 's nothing too bad for you, you—"

Fanny stopped to hear nc more.   Almost deprived of
her senses by the woman's threats, and frantic at the
thought of falling into the hands of a set of drunken ruffians, she sprang past her persecutor like a frightened
fawn, and the next moment was rushing through the darkness and the storm.

On, on, she knew not whither.   Past the glimmering
camp-lights that seemed to glare at her with angry eyes,
through mist and blinding rain, over thorns and briars,
on, still on.   The rain beat down upon her uncovered
head, but she knew it not.   The thorns and briars cruelly
wounded her slender feet, but she felt no pain.   A hundred voices seemed calling her to stop, a hundred feet
hurrying in pursuit; and, with frantic haste, unheeding
darkness, wind and rain, the poor fugitive fled on.   On
and still on, till the glimmering camp-lights were but a
speck in the distance, and she felt that she was alone in
the solitude of the night.   Then faint and exhausted, she
pressed her hands to her poor fluttering heart, and sank
upon the damp ground.   She thought that her hour had
come, and that alone and friendless she must perish here
in the wilderness.   Raising herself upon her knees, she
prayed with clasped hands that God would take care of
her, and of those whom she had tried to succor, and then
kneeling upon the plains of Kanzas, she entreated the God
of freedom to save that noble Territory from the tyranny
of these minions of slavery.   At length her voice faltered
and ceased, a deadly faintness came over her, and she fell
exhausted upon the damp earth, while the rain beat down
upon her defenseless form.

CHAPTER XXXIX.

GREAT was the confusion and excitement in and about the house, when Catlett and Dave returned the next morning from their night-drinking and gaming in the camp. They had heard of the flight of the prisoners, and were as eager as any for their recapture, for the alarm had been given, and scouting parties sent out in every direction. Only by displaying the greatest presence of mind, had Bob Turner been able to escape capture with his charge, by several of these gangs. Once he with his party were entirely entrapped, and obtained release by his declaring that they were on the same business with themselves. Knowing Bob's voice, and supposing it all correct in the darkness, the party rode off in an opposite direction.

Bob took his prisoners, as he had promised, safe to the sentinels on guard about Lawrence, who admitted them, after suitable inquiry, within their ward. Immediately he wheeled about and returned without suspicion into the camp, making his appearance at the house about the same time with Dave and Catlett. Great was his indignation, when with them he learned how Fanny, the friend and confidant of his betrothed, being frightened by Gamby, had darted out into the darkness, and no trace of her could be found. As for Mr. Catlett, fire and fury prevailed in his words, when he heard these things, and **Dave** swore he would find Fanny if he went to the ends of the earth. Tom Walton, too, came in, with a pale, anxious face, and his collar quite awry; a sure sign that something had occurred to discompose him. But Tim's distress was the most affecting to behold. The poor fellow seemed to consider himself somehow to blame in the catastrophe, in that he had provided Fanny with the instrument by which the prisoners obtained their escape. "Lors! Miss Car'- line, if I had n't a gin her dat ar saw, she would n't a let de men out, and den dat ar Gamby woman would n't a come cussin' and swarin', to scare poor Miss Fanny out ob her seven senses. O lors! what did I do it for, any- how?" Tim blubbered about it all day, and Jinny and Adeline went round with their aprons to their eyes.

Upon Madam Gamby's head, Mr. Catlett heaped bush- els of wrath. If she was n't a woman he'd shoot her, sure, and if she would come to the wars, why should her being a woman defend her in such iniquity? Bob Turner was loud in his denunciations, but as yet kept his own secret.

Things were at this pass, when a gang of rowdies, with Gamby at their head, came to arrest Fanny, supposing her long ago returned from her flight. With oaths, and curses, they declared that she should be hung in place of the prisoners she had helped to escape. This was a little too much. No words can depict Jack Catlett's rage at this insult to his house. He raved with absolute madness, and swore if the lot did n't leave, he'd shoot 'em like dogs.

"So you uphold the gal in her treason and treachery to the camp?" said Madam Gamby, with a sneer. "Look out, neighbor Catlett, or you 'll get to be a suspicious character yourself."

"I uphold the girl! Of course I do. They should

16*

have shot me down before I would have seen two as true and noble-hearted men as ever lived, led to the gallows. I say she was a brave girl, with double the courage of some that talk big, and try to wear the breeches. I honor her for what she did."

The men, when they understood that they were sent out to arrest a young lady, who had been taken under their guard, vowed that they had been cheated by the rascally Gamby, and that they would have nothing to do with it. One of them said he knew the lady, and she was good and kind, and would have taught his child if she could, and he pitied her, driven out by that she-devil into the dark and cold, and hang him if he would n't be one to search for her, and bring her home dead or alive.

It was Tim Jenkins, the drummer. Gamby, left alone, blustered as loudly as any, and declared that it was the planters who introduced abolition gals on their places, who caused all the trouble. Finally she deemed it best to retreat before the squire's gun.

A search was immediately instituted for the lost girl. No sooner was all known, than hundreds volunteered to look for her in all directions. It was suggested in the camp that they 'd better hang Gamby in place of the escaped prisoners, and to insure good luck in their search, it being suggested that she was a kind of Jonah, anyhow; to which some one replied that the whale that swallowed her, would have the worst of it decidedly.

Mrs. Catlett and Nanny remained with the servants in great anxiety at home. One by one the parties returned from their fruitless search, with no news of the fugitive. One party alone who had ventured very near to Lawrence, brought with them a little torn gaiter, all drenched with rain and mud, which one of the men had found near the road-side, and which Nanny declared, with a flood of tears, to be one that Fanny had worn the day previous. It was reported that she was murdered, or had perished somewhere in the wild, or had lost her way, and was still wandering further and further into the wilderness. Catlett and Dave with a few determined spirits spent the whole day in scouring the country in all directions. At last, with great gloom, they concluded her forever lost, and returned down-hearted to the camp.

In the mean time the negotiations which begun between the leaders, almost on the arrival of the besiegers, were nearing their completion. They had been talked of in the camp, and discussed over whisky bottles and gaming-tables. But as all this has nothing to do with our history, we entirely pass it by. Suffice it to say that on the morning of the twelfth of December, Governor Shannon disbanded the troops, and they began to move away in straggling bands from the city. Catlett and his family went into Lawrence to tarry awhile in the hope that something might be heard from the lost Fanny. There was a possibility even that she might have strayed into the city. At all events every thing which could be done, should be done. The chivalric honor of a native Virginian, was aroused in Mr. Catlett's breast, and he resolved to spare neither time nor expense in the search. Determined as he felt, however, to leave no stone unturned, that might give any clew to the fugitive's whereabouts, he soon came across a helper, more earnest than himself. Almost the first persons he met in Lawrence, were his cousin, Judge Stanton, and Harry Chester, to whom he related the sad intelligence, before even congratulating them upon their own escape. Could it be possible that she was in Lawrence? They had seen nothing of her since their flight.

The judge was loud in his exclamations of alarm and

distress, and though the young man said less, he devoted his whole time to prosecuting the search, and mentally determined that he would never relinquish it, till she was found.

"We will advertise, and search the city thoroughly," he said.

"If money would be of any use, it is at your disposal," said Tom Walton.

"Every thing must be done to rescue so dear a girl, if she be yet alive!" said the judge.

"I have mighty little hope that she is," said Mr Catlett, with a sigh.

CHAPTER XL.

OUR story returns to Fanny, whom we left alone on the plains of Kanzas. Exhausted by fatigue, and the violence of the storm, faint and despairing, she sank upon the earth. But deliverance, even in her seemingly hopeless situation, was nigh. A quick step approached, a kind hand touched her, and a voice with which we are not unfamiliar, spoke to her.

"Miss Fanny! Miss Fanny! is dis you, sure enough?"
There was no reply.

"O, lors! she's dead I does believe! Poor lamb! What's sent her out in de cold and wet, dis yer night? Miss Fanny! I say! Lors, it's her, though, sure. Don't I know dat voice dat spoke so kind to Tilla. De Lord has sent me here just in time to hear her a prayin' all alone in de dark night; and I'll save her, too. Miss Fanny, can't you put your arms round my neck, and let me toat you a bit. I'm feared she's past speakin'. Well, I'll take her to dem dat will put life inter her if any body can."

Martha, for it was her, who returning from Lawrence to the camp, had thus been guided by Providence to the place where Fanny lay, raised the unconscious girl in her strong arms, and bore her safe to the city. There friendly hands were soon around her, and a motherly voice breathed words of love and pity in her ears.

It was long ere she opened her eyes or gave signs of returning life, and when at last she did so, reason had fled, and she only uttered incoherent expressions of alarm and distress, begging those about her " to save her! to let her go, or the prisoners would be murdered!" Her exposure had thrown her into a dangerous illness, and her new friends nursed her with the tenderest care, while Martha hovered about her, and with clumsy eagerness, assisted all that she was able.

The family, into whose bosom she was thus taken, was from old Connecticut, and being strongly anti-slavery in their feelings, had removed to Kanzas to do their part toward building up a free State. They had found Martha somewhere in the streets of Lawrence, and pitying her forlorn condition, had taken her under their protection, and were just now planning her escape to Canada. To them, of course, the girl at once bore the friendless Fanny, nor could she have chosen a better place. From Martha's story of her being a teacher from Connecticut, and named Fanny Hunter, the " gude wife" at once conjectured that she might be the daughter of the late Pastor of N——, and this thought redoubled their diligence.

A week passed before her fever abated, nor was her strange discovery by the road-side at all explained, except by the wandering sentences she uttered in her delirium. Meanwhile the camp had broken up, and Martha had lost all trace of Mr. Catlett and his family. They, however, as we have already seen, with Judge Stanton and Harry Chester, were in Lawrence, and immediately upon the dispersion of the army, commenced their search for the lost girl. This, in a small place like Lawrence, could not of course continue long, without leading to her discovery, but it was ordered that Fanny should not be restored to her friends in any such common-place way.

About dusk, the very day they commenced their efforts, Martha ventured out, and was strolling through one of the most unfrequented parts of the city, when in turning a corner, she came plump upon no less a personage than Harry Chester.

"Good lors! it's Mass' Harry!" she exclaimed, in a tone of joyful surprise.

The young man looked at her a moment, forlorn and ragged as she was, without recognizing her.

"Don't you know me, Mass' Henry? I's Marthy! Mass' Catlett's Marthy! You ain't agoin' to give me up to him, I know; but if you does, I must speak to you for de sake of de dear missus, dat's sick and all alone here! O! Mass' Harry! you used to know her on de prairie, and like her, too, I reckon; dar's a chance now to be a friend to her. Dar is so."

"Who is it, Martha? Speak quick, girl! Who do you mean?"

"Lors, Massa Harry, who should it be but Miss Fanny! I'm thinkin' you don't reckon on her as much as you did, or you would n't forget her name so quick."

"Forget her! Where is she? Can you show me the way? Is she well? Forget her, indeed!"

"Dar now, you begins to talk. Yes, yes. I'll take yer to her, and mighty glad she'll be to see you, I reckon. She, dat's been callin' for yer when she was ravin' 'stracted."

"Calling for *me?* O, Martha, has she been so ill?"

The pleasure he felt at the first announcement, was almost counterbalanced by his pain at the last.

"Well, I reckon you'd think so, Mass' Harry. O lors, to think what would hab happened if I had n't found her dat ar night, wid de rain beatin' on to her poor head. Here 'tis, Mass Harry. Dis yer's de place. Now you jest stand here a crack, while I go tell Miss Fanny who's come."

Fanny was sitting bolstered up in her arm-chair. Her face was paler than when we saw her last, and the little hand that supported her head was very thin and white. She raised her eyes, which were bent in anxious thought upon the fire, when Martha entered, and inquired where she had been. Martha had grown wonderfully prudent since her attendance upon the invalid, and determined to be cautious and not break the good news too sudden like. She gave some trivial answer, and was thinking how to commence, when the door opened, and a tall figure stood in the entrance.

Martha had just time to cry, "O, Mass' Harry, Mass' Harry! go back! you spile it all," when Fanny sprang from her seat with a faint scream, and the next instant the young man was at her side.

"Fanny! Fanny! have I found you at last?"

What reply Fanny made is not known. Indeed, Martha declared that of the whole of the long conversation that ensued, she "could n't hear de fust word." Harry Chester did the most of the talking, and at the conclusion of one of his long harangues, he seized the little thin hand, and dared—notwithstanding the direful consequences that once before followed this presumptuous act—to press it to his lips. This time it was not withdrawn—perhaps Fanny, in her present feebleness, lacked strength to do it. and when she raised her eyes to his face, those eyes that on that other occasion flashed upon him with angry pride, they were suffused with tears.

"Mass Harry tire Miss Fanny all out," Martha said at last, approaching, and Fanny herself bade him leave her, yet followed him with her eyes to the door, and when he returned again and again, to say a parting word, somehow did not grow angry at his repeated disobedience.

The young man did not sleep that night, until he had informed all her friends that the lost girl was found, and the next morning bright and early, Mr. Catlett and his wife, Nanny and Bob, with the judge and Harry at their head, came in a body to welcome her back to life again.

"You are a noble girl, Fanny, and I'm right glad your Yankee purpose saved the judge and Harry," said Mr. Catlett. "If they'd hung them, I would never have lived in Missouri or Kanzas a day."

"Somebody else helped," said Nanny with a blush, throwing in a good word for Bob, who stood rather in the background.

"Yes, indeed," said Fanny, "we could have done nothing without him. You should thank him quite as much as Nanny or I."

"Well, young man," said Catlett, "mebbe now's as good a time as any to tell you, that wife and I have n't quite known your worth. We have thought Nan might do better, but I reckon now you 've shown so much pluck, you can have her for the asking."

"Then I 'll take her," said Bob, seizing Nanny's hand.

Dave and Tom Walton here made their appearance. "Miss Fanny," whispered Tom, as he shook her hand, "I 'm mighty glad you 've come to life, though you did make a fool of me."

The company waited a week longer for Fanny to regain her strength, and then the whole party set out for La Belle Prairie. They made the journey in safety, and Mrs. Catlett at once ordered Viny to bring her pipe and a shovel of coals, while she took time to recover herself. The young housekeeper welcomed them joyfully, and declared that she thought they never were coming back, but intended to stay at Dave's place forever.

"Dave's place no longer," said Mr. Catlett. "He must settle down in Missouri for all that I see; for as to interfering with that woman's land agin, or letting any body else that, I can hinder, I sha'n't do it. She's earned it, and she shall keep it."

'Ria also declared that Madam Hester had been saying dreadful things all the time they were gone, and that one night particularly, about two weeks ago, all of a sudden she gave an awful scream, and jumped clear out of her chair, and then she jabbered away about trouble and sorrow for two or three hours. It was the very night that Fanny wandered out into the wild.

The time for parting came at length, and Harry and Judge Stanton left for St. Louis.

CHAPTER XLI.

"Shake! shake! shake! Dear! dear! what can the matter be? A roaring hot fire in the chimney, shawls and blankets in abundance, and poor I huddled up in the corner, shaking and shivering. Was the breeze that just lifted yonder curtain indeed from the arctic regions, or have the fleas and musquitoes so thoroughly drained my system as to leave it henceforth incapable of warmth?

"Chatter! chatter! There it is again; that cold sensation that now and then comes creeping over me, making my flesh all ' goose-quills,' as the children say, my limbs to shake with extraordinary energy, and my teeth to beat time most merrily. O dear! how dreadfully I feel! What does it mean? Am I bewitched, magnetized, have I got the St. Vitus' dance, that I sit here shaking away against my will, or have I in some way merited the fate of that wretched man whose teeth, ' through summer's heat and winter's cold, did chatter, chatter, chatter still.' Shall I make a stand against this rude assault? Shall I determine, in the very depths of my soul, to shake no more? Alas! what does it avail? Even as I make the resolve, another fit seizes me, and trembling, shivering, shaking, I bow like a bulrush before it. Yes, Viny, I give it up. Put me to bed directly, pile on the clothes, blankets, coverlids, old coats; any thing to infuse warmth; for I am certainly perishing with the cold. And, Viny, tell your mistress to send for the doctor immediately."

"Lors, Miss Fanny, it ain't nothin' but a chill. We all has 'em, you know. You'll be hot 'nuff by-and-by, when de fever comes."

"Nevertheless, Viny, that makes me no warmer at present. If before that time arrives, I become a solid lump of ice, what then?"

"De fever thaw you out mighty quick, Miss Fanny."

This was Fanny's first experience of a chill. Others followed in quick succession, and she soon found to her sorrow, that among the ills that flesh is heir to, a "Western shake" is by no means the least. Every other day for a fortnight, this tormentor laid his iron grasp upon her, and when at length the little German doctor, who was called in, succeeded by his huge doses of quinine and blue mass, in throwing off the chills, they left poor Fanny so thin and pale, as to be a shadow of her former self.

"Yes, yes," said the doctor, in reply to anxious inquiries as to whether they would return, "dey come back some day, den you take some dis, take some dat, send dem off. So now you come to dis countree, you get what you call *seasoned.*"

"Yes, doctor, but suppose I die in the seasoning," said Fanny, dolefully.

"Shaw, Miss Fanny, nobody dies with the chills," said Mrs. Catlett. "I reckon I've had hundreds in my day."

There was one friend, however, who had taken the alarm, and was coming to the rescue. Uncle Peter had lived long enough at the West, to know that a succession of chills was no such light matter, and the thought of his little Fanny away off there on the prairie, shaking off all her bloom, troubled him not a little. So arranging his business as expeditiously as possible, he made his prepara-

tions for starting for the East earlier than usual, and took
La Belle Prairie in his way.

He came one evening just as the family were taking
supper, and with a scream of delight Fanny rushed into
the arms opened so cordially to receive her. With tears
of joy running down her cheeks, she kissed him again and
again, and forgot all her past troubles in her present happiness. Uncle Peter was very grave, taking long, anxious
looks at his niece, and observing every thing about the
establishment with an air of curiosity and surprise. His
ill-concealed look of amazement at some of Mrs. Catlett's
household arrangements, struck Fanny so ludicrously,
that two or three times she could hardly keep from laughing. His horror all burst forth the first time they were
alone.

"And you 've lived here so long," he exclaimed. "You
poor child! no wonder you got the shakes. I am only
surprised that you are not quite dead."

"Why, Uncle Peter, it 's pretty comfortable here."

"Pretty comfortable! I should think so. I wonder
you had n't frozen to death. Why, see here, there are
chinks in this wall where I can put two fingers through."

"Yes, but this is the parlor, you know. The other room
is where we live. It is much tighter, and then they keep
up roaring fires."

"Worse and worse. I want to know if you are all
huddled up in that one room, babies and niggers and all.
O Fanny."

"Hush, Uncle Peter, I 'm afraid they will hear you."

"I can't help it. Whoever supposed we were sending
you to such a place as this. I thought I knew something
of western life, but this is coming ' up the country' with a
vengeance. I'm sure I thought they were well enough
off to live in a house, and not in a barn."

"Well, so they are," said Fanny, a little mischiev ously. "Only look at the silver on the side-board! Can we make any such display at home?"

"Stuff!" said Uncle Peter. "You might as well put a Brussels carpet on my store-room, in among the greasy barrels. It would be just as appropriate. Look at the tobacco stains on the hearth, and the cobwebs in the corners. I tell you, Fan, your mother's back shed is in better order this minute than this parlor."

"O, uncle! you are too observing. Your old bachelor eyes spy out every thing. Mrs. Catlett is so fretted, and over-worked, and the servants indolent and careless. You don't know how difficult it is to teach them any thing. I used to long to take hold and show them myself, but of course this would n't do, and so I have tried to get accustomed to their ways. You have n't the least idea, uncle, of the difficulty of managing these black servants."

"No, I thank my stars I don't know any thing about it. My lot has been cast in a free State, and I mean it shall be. Why in the name of common decency don't they stir round and fix up things?" said Uncle Peter, with sudden indignation. "The idea of putting a man to sleep in a room with half the glass out of the windows. I got up twice last night to move my bed out of the rain, and in the morning there was a puddle of water in the room large enough to sail a small boat."

"O that's nothing!" said Fanny, laughing. "You should have been here before the roof was mended. You see during that long dry spell it got very leaky, and Mr. Catlett thought he could n't spare any of the hands to mend it, and so one night there came up a terrible thunder-storm. Such times! It makes me laugh to think of it. We moved, and removed, and moved again! but still the floods descended, and it is hardly exaggerating to say that before morning we were all afloat. However the next day they set about mending the roof."

"I should think so," said Uncle Peter, gruffly. "And they thought you were as tough as they, and could paddle round in the water like the rest of 'em, without taking your death of cold. I wonder you ain't dead and buried long ago. Well, that's your school-room, I suppose, shall we go and see it? It's a trifle larger than the niggers' huts, ain't it?"

"O, yes, it's quite a room. You see there's a cellar underneath, where they keep the potatoes and other vegetables. There's no cellar under the 'big house.'"

Uncle Peter stepped round in his spry way and looked down the steps.

"Why it's half-full of water!" he exclaimed.

"Yes," said Fanny, peeping over his shoulder. "It always is after a rain. There, you see, they keep the vegetables in barrels on a shelf in the corner, and poor little Tom has to wade in after them every day. I pity him these cold mornings. We can hear him overhead when we sit in school, scolding and shivering, till Tibby, that's the cook, pushes him in with her long stick, and he makes a great rush, and splashing, and comes out presently with the basin of potatoes on his head, looking like a little drowned rat."

"You don't mean to say," said Uncle Peter, who was looking down the doorway, and had paid little attention to what she had been saying; "you don't mean to say that you have been teaching school here all summer, over a cellar half-full of stagnant water?"

"It was unpleasant at times," said Fanny; "and I felt afraid that it might be unhealthful, so I spoke to Mr. Catlett, and he had it cleaned out once or twice, but it was of no use, for it filled up again the next rain. Besides there are times when it is perfectly dry."

Uncle Peter gave a sort of groan. "No wonder they have chills and fever, and every thing that's bad. They could n't have contrived a better place for breeding fevers, if they had tried."

They passed into the school-room, Uncle Peter stopping to examine the door.

"What's the matter here?" he said, as he vainly endeavored to close it.

"O, that door!" said Fanny, "it has been out of order ever since I came here. There's no use in trying, Uncle Peter, you can't shut it tight."

"No, I see not. Has it been in this condition all winter?"

"Yes, but we stuff old carpets into the crack, and keep out the cold as well as we can."

"As well as you can? Why did n't you have it fixed? The door has swelled a little. It only wants planing off. Half an hour's work would make it all right."

"So I told Mr. Catlett, but he had n't the tools, nor any one to do it. Maud and I tried to hack it off with an old hatchet, but we did n't succeed very well. However it is a good thing at times, for the fireplace smokes so badly when the wind is east, that we are obliged to keep the window or door open to breathe."

"Humph!" said Uncle Peter, "well, what next? What do you call this yellow powder, that keeps sifting down between the boards upon a man's head?" and by jarring the floor he brought down a fresh supply.

Fanny laughed. "They keep the corn-meal up there in the loft, and Tibby scatters it all about. We have quite a shower occasionally, especially when the wind blows."

"Agreeable ?" said Uncle Peter. "It must improve the hair."

"I have worn a sun-bonnet in school all summer," said Fanny, "and this winter I quilted me a little hood on purpose. It is excellent, and keeps me from taking cold, I have no doubt."

"I wonder you are not in a settled decline. The old red barn at home would be a deal more comfortable place to keep school in than this old shanty," and Uncle Peter surveyed the little room with its low window and rough benches, with great disdain.

His contempt of her domain roused Fanny's pride, and she entered warmly upon its defense, pointing out the recently swept floor, the new rush-bottomed chair—a present from Uncle Tim—the clean curtain before the window, and the pretty prospect from the open door.

"Indeed, Uncle Peter," she said, "I have spent a great many happy hours in this room, cheerless as you appear to think it. One gets along very comfortably with these little inconveniences, after one makes up one's mind to it. You don't know how much less I mind them than at first. I am getting toughened, you see."

"You look very much like it," said Uncle Peter. "I'll tell you what, Fanny," he continued, as they were crossing the yard, "you may pack up your duds as soon as you please, for I'm going to take you home with me to Connecticut."

"O, Uncle Peter!"

"Yes I am. Do you think I am going to leave my sister's child on this place any longer? I don't know what possessed us to ever let you come here. Why your mother would cry her eyes out, if she had the least idea of the hardships you've suffered the last year. Why what ails the girl? She looks as if I had told her some bad piece

17

of news, instead of that she should see her home and her mother in a couple of weeks. Come, have n't you seen enough of high life in Missouri?"

"O, uncle," said Fanny, with tears in her eyes, "I do long for home, but—"

"But what?"

"It seems to be my duty to stáy here. I am earning a large salary—something of a consideration, certainly, to a poor minister's daughter—then my scholars are improving very fast, and if I leave them now before another teacher could be obtained, they would lose all that they had gained. It would be a great disappointment to Mr. Catlett if I should go."

"It would be a great disappointment to your friends, Fanny," said Uncle Peter, gravely, "if by remaining in this unhealthy spot, without any of the comforts to which you have been accustomed, you should ruin your constitution, and either fall a victim to this Western fever, or come home two or three years hence, all broken down by the chills, a confirmed invalid for life. That would be very poor economy in the long run. No, no, my little Fanny must n't come to such a doleful end as that; we 'll take her back to old Connecticut, and see if we can't get a little pink into those pale cheeks; and there she shall teach school, and lay up money to her heart's content, like a little miser as she is."

Still Fanny looked grave.

"Now, Fanny, there's no use in arguing the matter. I reckoned as soon as I heard that you had the shakes, that you would have to go home; and when I came to see how you were living, I made up my mind at once. I know just how they work. A few tough old customers like me get along without much damage; but in nine cases out of ten they ruin the constitution, and take away every spark

of life and energy there is about one. Fanny, yo have
no right to sacrifice yourself, and I won't let you ither.
I don't care how much good you are doing, and I believe
you are accomplishing something here; I'll say that for
your comfort; but it's a little too much to lay down your
life for them. No, no, I'm your lawful guardian, and you
must make up your mind to obey me. You are not of
age. I shall speak to Mr. Carlett this very morning, and
you shall have none of the trouble and vexation of that.
So now make up your mind to get ready, and go with me
like a sensible girl. You are not leaving a lover behind,
are you, that you look so sorrowful about it?"

Fanny made no reply, and so it was decided. She could
not but acknowledge that Uncle Peter's reasoning was just,
and that she would be throwing away her health by remaining. True, the chills had left her, but there was no
certainty of their not returning, and she possessed less
physical energy to oppose the second attack.

Uncle Peter went directly to Mr. Catlett, and informed
him of the turn affairs had taken, resting Fanny's removal
entirely upon the ground of her failing health. Mr. Catlett argued the case strongly, fretted and fumed not a little, and told Uncle Peter that he had better be at home
minding his own business, than to come there and get
away their teacher. Yet, on the whole, he received the
intelligence better than Fanny expected.

"Tell ye what," he said, taking Uncle Peter by the
button-hole, "I don't blame you for takin' good care of that
little girl. There ain't many such in these parts. She's
done the young ones a powerful sight of good, and if she
has n't taught the old ones a lesson or two, it ain't her
fault. We'd like to keep her right well. I was tellin'
my wife there the other day, that there was religion
enough in her to carry us all up, if she stayed here long

enough. But if she must go, she must, only don't you let nobody look down on her, rich or poor, do you hear?"

It was more difficult to gain Mrs. Catlett's consent to the new arrangement, and Fanny, upon whom that task devolved, almost gave up in despair as the lady continued her tirade of lamentations and grievances. She sat down, however, with her that evening, and planned it all out. Nanny had promised to hear Joy and Johnny recite an hour or two every day, and the girls might continue their studies under the direction of Mr. Mack, Mr. Turner's teacher, who would be glad of two or three more scholars through the winter. It was troublesome to send them so far, but better than that they should idle away their time at home.

All this time, however, she had a deep-laid plan in her heart, which she at last disclosed with fear and trembling. They might not be able to secure another teacher at present, and then, perhaps, not a permanent one. Changing instructors was always injurious, now why not send the girls to some good boarding-school in New England, to go through with a thorough course of study."

"Mercy!" interrupted Mrs. Catlett, "think of the expense."

"It would be more expensive," Fanny said, "but the advantages were greater in proportion. They would never regret giving their children a good education. Would they think of the plan? She would take the oversight of their studies, and be a sister to them in every respect."

She looked anxiously at Mr. Catlett, but he remained silent. His wife, however, declared it to be impossible. "It would cost all they were worth to send three great tearing girls to a boarding-school. It was hard enough to raise money now, without any more pulls on the purse-strings. It had been a dreadful year, too. The wheat crop was very small, and the tobacco about as bad. Then they had lost the girl, Martha and the expenses of the

Kanzas folly had footed up to a large amount. O, no! it could n't be thought of for a moment!"

Fanny looked discouraged, but a pair of pleading eyes were gazing in her face, and a little hand pressed hers so convulsively, that she commenced again and talked so earn· estly, addressing herself to Mr. Catlett, that that gentleman promised to think about it.

"You see, wife," he said, in talking the matter over with that lady, "it 's worth a hundred dollars a year to have the young ones under that girl's influence, I tell you. I 'll think about it."

"Well, Mr. Catlett, 'Ria can't go anyhow. She 's too old to go to school, and Nanny 'll be stepping off before long, and I want 'Ria for oldest daughter at home; but if you are a mind to foot the bills, I don't care·if Cal and Maud were to go for a year or two. As you say it 's a good deal to have somebody to see to 'em, and I really believe they *do* love the girl."

"Why, Maud, child," said her father, as she whispered something in his ear, "you don't want to go way back there to Connecticut, away from every body, do you?"

"Yes, I do."

"What for, chick? What do you expect to learn there?"

"O, pa, if I stay with Miss Fanny, I know I shall learn *how to be good.*"

The grief felt by the whole family at the prospect of losing Fanny, was soon in some measure forgotten in the bustle of preparation for Dave's wedding. It may astonish our readers, as it did most of the people on the prairie, that the young man should end his bachelor days so suddenly After this wise was it brought about.

Madam Gamby one day came riding over on "Old White," and requested Mrs. Catlett to send off the young ones, for she had a little business to talk over with herself and Dave. The old lady was heartily ashamed of her treatment of poor Fanny in Kanzas, and even conde-scended when the family first returned to the prairie, to ride over and make an apology to the young lady herself.

"You see I had n't nothing particular agin you, Miss Fanny," she said, "except your helpin' off them fellers, and I should have felt different about them, if I 'd known they was the squire's friends. I just wanted to scare you a little, that was all; but I 'm sure I never thought you 'd go tearin' off inter the woods at the rate you did. You might have known I had n't had time to tell the governor of you, for the fellers had n't been gone above half an hour. Come, now, let by-gones be by-gones, and shake hands and be friends."

This Fanny was quite ready to do, and though Mr. Cat-lett was but half-reconciled to the "old hag," as he called her, she resumed her former footing with the family. On the present occasion, the room being closed, Madam Gamby stretched her feet upon the hearth, and thus opened her business.

"Neighbor Catlett," she said, "I 'm a plain-spoken woman, as you all know. It ain't my way to be hangin' round and waitin' to see which way the wind blows, or how things work themselves. I like to get my paw in and give 'em a shove. Well, you know my claim over the border? I find it wants 'tendin' to, the balance of the time. You see those rascally free-soilers are pouring into Kanzas as thick as fleas, and if you ain't on the ground pretty much all the while, they work heaps of mischief. Well, I can't be in two places at once, and what I want is to get a manager for my place over here, so that I can walk straight to Kanzas, and get my place there into good shape. Now, then, I 'm comin' right to the pint. There 's a chap from over the river settin' up to my Boss. He seems likely enough, and I can't say as I see any particu-

lar objection to him, but the gal herself seems rather to
take a shine to your Dave, and I've noticed he's been
rather sweet on her for quite a while. Now thinks I to
myself, they are old neighbors, and I reckon I'll give 'em
the first chance. So that's my business to-day. If the
boy's a notion to step in right off and be head-man on as
pretty a farm as there is in Missouri, now's the chance;
if not, the other chap stands ready, and we'll settle matters with him. What do you say, young man?"

Dave had turned all sorts of colors during this speech,
and at its conclusion rose and walked to the window.

"He's quite overpowered at the good news," whispered
Mrs. Catlett, "being unexpected, too. He's *so* fond of Boss,
but Dave is naturally bashful, and apt to be despairing."

"Nonsense!" said Madam Gamby. "I want an answer
right off. What's done, must be done in a hurry. If it's
the funds you want to know about, all I've got to say is,
that whoever takes one of my daughters, will have a good
livin' and half what's left, when I step off. Come, speak
quick if you want the gal."

"I'll take her," said Dave, with a kind of a gasp.

"Very well, that's settled, then. Now I've got to be
over on that claim by next Friday week, sure. So we'd
better get the wedding over with by next week, certain."

"So soon?" said Dave, faintly.

"Bless you, yes! There's nothing like doing such
things up in season. I've sent to town for the gal's
fixin's, for a weddin' I'm bound to have next week."

And a wedding there was. Madam Gamby rode home
on her "Old White" to acquaint the bride elect with the
result of her negotiations, while Dave prepared himself
for the occasion, by two or three drinking frolics, after
which it was observed that he appeared to be perfectly
resigned to his fate.

CHAPTER XLII.

DURING the last few weeks of Fanny's stay on the prairie it was evident that Aunt Phebe was failing very fast. For a long time she had only left her arm-chair by the fireside for her bed in the corner of the room, and at length even this exertion was too much for her, and so partly because it was difficult for her to breathe in a reclining posture, and partly because she was so averse to the change, they bolstered her up in her arm-chair, and let her remain there.

"No, no," she said earnestly, when Mrs. Catlett proposed removing her to the bed, "jest let de Lord find me up and waitin' for Him. 'Pears like I could n't watch no whar else nigh so well."

Fanny took her little Bible down every day, and read a chapter or two to the old woman, and it was affecting to see with what eagerness she drank in those precious words, many of which she had never heard before. It was seldom that Fanny did not find Maud there before her. The child's affection for her old friend, always earnest and strong, seemed just now to engross every other feeling of her nature. Ever since they had told her that Aunt Phebe would not live to see the leaves come again, Maud had given up her long rambles on the prairie, and the greater part of each day was spent in the cabin.

There, sitting on her low stool, her large, serious eyes

resting alternately upon her teacher and her old friend, she would listen to the chapters that Aunt Phebe loved the best to hear, privately marking passages in her own little Testament for future reference. "Dar, now, honey, go run awhile," Aunt Phebe would say, "'t ain't nat'ral for sich as you to stay penned up 'long an old woman all day; ain't a bit lon'some, you see, jest thinkin' ob de glory to come."

But the child would not leave her, and Aunt Phebe seeing that to urge her only gave her pain, suffered her to come and go as she pleased. There had been no gloom in the sick room. The old woman's soul seemed so full of bright anticipations, and ardent longings to be gone, that it was impossible to wish her further from the heaven to which she was approaching. "Going home" was the chorus of one of the hymns she sang, and her whole demeanor was like one who, after long wandering in some distant land, receives a summons to his father's house. Even Maud held long and cheerful conversations with her, about her expected departure, and if at some near approach to death, a sudden chillness crept over the child, and the tears *would* come, Aunt Phebe's hopeful words would soon drive away her sorrow. It therefore surprised Fanny very much one morning as she entered the cabin with her usual smile, to meet no answering token of welcome on the old woman's face, but in its place a troubled expression that she had never seen there before.

"Miss Fanny," she said, in answer to Fanny's anxious inquiries, "it's all dark. De Lord's been givin' me a sight at my sins. 'Pears like I should n't get dar, arter all."

"But you hope he has forgiven you your sins, aunty?"

"I did, child, I did! but I's never 'pented of 'em as I ought afore. I never see how black dey was. O, chil'en, you don't any one on yer know what a sinner I be! Miss Fanny, I'm one ob dem foolish virgins you read about t'other day, goin' to meet de bridegroom widout any oil in dar lamps.. Thar ain't de fust drop in mine, and it's all dark! dark!" She seemed in great distress, wringing her hands, and rocking herself back and forth.

"Aunt Phebe, we are all great sinners, but God's forgiving mercy is greater than our sins. He says, 'Though your sins be as scarlet, they shall be white as snow.'"

"I know it, I know it, I ain't got a word to say agin the Lord! but there don't none ob dem promises mean me! I's been agoin' on like I was a Christian, tryin' to make out I was better 'n every body else, and I's de bery worst ob all. O! what ken I do? Chil'en," turning with streaming eyes to two or three fellow-servants at the door, "don't let this yer turn you back. You keep right on, 'pent ob your sins, and trust in de Lord, and He won't cast you off in your dyin' hour. Chil'en, I's been cheatin' you all along, but I did n't go to do it. I thought I was on de road to glory, sure enough. You keep right on, I want to see you all dar if I be cast out."

"And why need you be cast out, aunty? Not because you are a sinner, for Christ died for just such sinners as you. O, Aunt Phebe, have you forgotten all those bright promises that used to cheer you so?"

"Dey are all gone, honey. Dar ain't nothin' left but dark. Satan's done got de victory dis time."

And in this hopeless strain she continued. It was in vain that Fanny talked to her of the forgiving mercy of God, of full salvation through Jesus Christ, the free invitations of the Gospel. They seemed to bring no comfort to her mind. A deep overwhelming conviction of sin shut out every ray of hope. Fanny tried to treat her like an unconverted sinner, entreating her to repent and believe in the Lord Jesus Christ. Aunt Phebe cried out with sobs and tears that it was too late. Then Fanny took the other course, recalling to her recollection all the bright evidence she had given that she was indeed a child of God. Her consistent life—her love of prayers, and religious conversation, and her constant efforts to bring others to Christ. It but plunged her into deeper despair, for she counted it all as hypocrisy, declaring that she had been a wretched deceiver all her life. Her self-righteousness was all gone; she looked upon herself as the vilest of sinners, and with tears and groans deplored her doom.

Hours and hours Fanny spent with her in reading the Scriptures and in prayer, but no effect was produced. The cloud was not lifted. No ray of light penetrated her soul, and as this constant agitation of mind was fast wearing out the body, it seemed as though she must soon die in gloom and despair. "O, Miss Fanny," Maud would say again and again, "do comfort aunty! It just breaks my heart to see her so."

To her fellow-servants this sudden change from sunshine to darkness was unaccountable. They had always looked upon Aunt Phebe as a saint upon earth, a pattern of all that was good and excellent, and as for her religion, why, as Uncle Cæsar expressed it, she "had enough to toat her dry-shod clar ober Jordan." For years they had witnessed her exemplary life; had seen how her whole heart was in her religion; listened to her exhortations with the deepest reverence, and borne the severest reproofs from her lips. As far back as most of them could remember, Aunt Phebe had seemed on the very borders of Canaan, waiting the Lord's time to take her home, and now when she was "mos' dar," and the Lord had stuck by her thirty years, for Satan to get the victory at last. "O!" said Aunt Tibby, "it's enough to make us all shake

to tink what He ken do, and who's agoin' to get clar if
Aunt Phebe don't, hey?"

"Well, dar's one ting," said Viny, pertly, "mebbe it's
bad, but I do say, if the Lord throws off Aunt Phebe arter
all she's been adoin' for Him dese thirty years, I don't
tink dar's much use in the rest ob us tryin' to be good,
I do so."

Some one repeated this speech to Aunt Phebe, and it
almost broke her heart.

"Dis yer's de wust ob all," she cried. "'Pears like I
could bar to go down alone, but to drag odders along, too.
O, chil'en, don't you talk dat way! Don't you get sot
agin de Lord. It's all jest right, I'll be whar I belong,
but if de Lord will jest let me look ober inter glory, and
see you dar a tunin' your harps, and singing His praise,
?pears like I could most feel happy. O, chil'en, it ain't de
Lord's fault dat I'm goin' down to torment, and I'll
praise Him if He does send me dar."

"Aunt Phebe," said Fanny, one day, after she had
made use of some such expression, "an unpardoned sinner
does n't talk that way. If God was as angry with you as
you think, you would n't love him like that. The blood
of your precious Saviour—"

"No, no, Miss Fanny, not mine! not mine!"

"He is yours, Aunt Phebe, unless you refuse to trust in
Him. If you expect to get to heaven any other way than
through His righteousness, you are under a dreadful mistake, and if you will think so much about your own sins,
as to shut out all love to your Redeemer, and faith that
He can save you, in spite of them all, I don't know but it
must be as you say, and you be miserably lost at last."

"O, Miss Fanny, don't *you* say dat!"

"You have been putting too much trust in your own
goodness, and now that God has taken away this prop and

showed you how sinful and vile you are, these very sins
serve you as an excuse. You fall back upon them, and
put your Saviour out of the question. You put no trust
in Him, and so He never will be yours."

"I know it! I know it! O! what shall I do? Whar
shall I look?"

"Where can you look but to Jesus Christ, aunty! to
' the Lamb of God who taketh away the sin of the world!' "

"Miss Fanny, I *will* look to Him! Mebbe 't ain't no
use. Mebbe He won't hear to me, but leastways I'll
try."

That afternoon Fanny was called down to the cabin to
see Aunt Phebe die. The paleness of death was on her
face, but the old smile was there, too, and Fanny saw at a
glance that all was peace. She was in a kind of stupor,
but when they told her that Miss Fanny had come, her
dim eyes brightened, and she beckoned her to approach.

"He *is* mine!" she whispered. "O, Miss Fanny, He's
my Lord! my Saviour! I's found Him! Dar can't
nothin' part us no more. I'm goin' to see Him face to
face!"

"I knew it, aunty," said Fanny, her own face beaming
with joy. "I knew you would find Him again. He
never forsakes those who put their trust in Him."

"It ain't me!" said the old woman, earnestly. "I's
done wid dat. I ain't *nothin'! nothin'!* De Lord Jesus
He's done saved me! You tell 'em," she whispered,
pointing to a group of her fellow-servants, who, with awe-
struck faces, stood gazing in the corner; " tell 'em not to
trust in dar own goodness. De Lord He'll gib 'em de
victory. Mass' Jack, Miss Car'line. O, I want to meet
'em all up yonder! Tell 'em dey *mus'* come. De Lord
dat died for 'em, He'll let 'em in. Dey must lub Him.
O, dar ain't nothin' in dis world worth gibin up de Lord

for. I can't speak it, *you* tell 'em." She gasped for breath.

"Aunty, have n't you one word for me?" said Maud, pressing forward. She was deadly pale, but her large eyes were tearless.

"Lord bless you, honey, and comfort your poor heart. You'll be lonesome like when old aunty's gone, but de Lord he'll make it up to you somehow. O, honey, tink ob de time when you and I'll meet up yonder. You've promised, you know. I shall be a waitin' for you. You won't forget."

"I *will* meet you up there, aunty. If God will help me I'll begin to be a Christian this very day."

The old woman closed her eyes with a smile. There was a moment's silence, and then Fanny's voice broke the stillness of the chamber of death:

"Let not your heart be troubled; ye believe in God, believe also in me.

"In my Father's house are many mansions; if it were not so I would have told you. I go to prepare a place for you.

"And if I go and prepare a place for you, I will come again and receive you unto myself, that where I am there ye may be also.

"Yea, though I walk through the valley of the shadow of death I will fear no evil, for thou art with me; thy rod and thy staff they comfort me.

"And I saw a new heaven and a new earth, for the first heaven and the first earth were passed away, and there was no more sea.

"And there shall be no night there, and they need no candle, neither light of the sun, for the Lord God giveth them light, and they shall reign forever and ever.

"And God shall wipe away all tears from their eyes.

and there shall be no more death, neither sorrow nor crying."

"Most dar," whispered the old woman, and with the smile yet lingering on her lips, she passed away.

"Thanks be to God who giveth us the victory through our Lord Jesus Christ."

The same evening, a little before sunset, Mr. Catlett, who had been gone all day to Cartersville, a town, some nine miles from the prairie, returned home, and leaving his horse at the stable, walked up the lane at the back of the house. As he passed Aunt Phebe's cabin, he remembered that he had left her worse in the morning, and it occurred to him to look in a moment and see how she was getting along.

As he opened the door, a ray of sunshine streamed into the room. It fell upon Aunt Phebe's empty chair, upon the bed with its white covering, and upon the bowed head of a child, kneeling at its foot.

"How—what!" Mr. Catlett suddenly started back. Why did a chillness creep over him, as the stark, motionless form met his view, and he felt in that room the visible presence of death? Whence comes the mysterious feeling with which the most thoughtless of us look upon the remains of our fellow-mortals, after the spirit has taken its flight? We tread softly, and speak in whispers in the chamber where the dead one lies, even though that one in life was the meanest and most insignificant of his kind. There is a certain dignity in death that all must acknowledge, and he who pays respect to no living person, with bowed head does homage to the dead.

"Maud," said Mr. Catlett.

The child looked up, and pushing back her hair, displayed a face bathed in tears, but with a look of calm happiness shining through them, that seemed strangely at variance with the time and place

"Maud, how came you here? Who left you all alone?" said her father, glancing at the bed.

"Nobody, pa; that is, I mean, I wanted to stay. Don't scold Viny, please. I begged her to let me just a little while. Indeed, pa, I couldn't go away," said Maud, bursting into tears.

"Why not, child? What use was there in staying here?" said her father, in a softer tone than was usual to him.

Maud struggled to repress her tears, and then, looking timidly up in his face, said, "Pa, I stayed here to *pray*."

Mr. Catlett stared at her, but made no reply.

"You see, I promised her just before she died," said Maud, her voice faltering a little, "that I'd begin this very day to be a Christian, and I knew if I asked God here to make me one, he would, and oh, pa"—the same bright look returning to her face that it had worn at first —"I do believe he has."

"Pshaw!" said Mr. Catlett, "they've turned the child's head with their Methodist talk."

"Pa," said Maud, too much absorbed in her own thoughts to heed the interruption, "I'm glad you've come—I want to ask you something. I've wanted to before, but I was afraid. I want you to forgive me. I've been a bad girl times. I've done things you and ma told me not to. I'm sorry, and I've asked God to forgive me, and now I want you to. I'm going to try and be a better girl. Will you, pa?"

"Don't ask me, child. I've nothing to forgive. We are bad enough, all of us, the Lord knows," said Mr. Catlett.

Maud looked at him wonderingly, and then said, in a low voice—

"She said she wanted to meet you in heaven, pa."

" What makes you think she 's got there herself?" said Mr. Catlett, carelessly, though he turned away from the child's earnest gaze.

" I don't think; I *know*. That is n't aunty there, pa, Miss Fanny says so. Aunty's in heaven. O dear, I never shall see her any more," said Maud, with a fresh burst of grief.

"There! there! Come away, child, you'll fret yourself into a fever. They'd no business to have left you here alone," said her father.

" Pa," said Maud, " I never felt so happy in all my life. Thinking about aunty do n't seem to make me at *all* sorry. I thought it would. I thought it would be dreadful to have her die, but now I feel so sure that I'll see her again up yonder."

This was said with all Maud's characteristic energy, her eyes sparkling, and her cheeks glowing with excitement. They stood gazing at each other a moment—the man of fifty winters, who had grown gray in the service of this world, and the child whose treasure and whose heart were already in heaven. It was but a moment, and Mr. Cattlett turned away with a tear in his eye.

" Well, well, child, have it your own way," he said ; and taking her hand he led her out of the cabin.

CHAPTER XLIII

"It's the last time," said Maud.

They were walking slowly down the shaded path lead·ing through the woods to Aunt Phebe's newly-made grave.

"We never shall walk here together any more, Miss Fanny. O, it's hard to go away after all."

Fanny squeezed the little hand that was clasped in hers.

"Of course *you* want to go, Miss Fanny, because it's your home, and I s'pose you are a great deal happier in that beautiful place you've told us so much about, than you are 'way out here on the prairie, but it seems as if Cal and I were leaving every thing but you. I don't know what makes it all look so dark to me to-night."

"It isn't strange, Maud, that you should feel a little sadly about leaving home. I expect you will feel very home-sick at first in a strange place, but you must try to look on the bright side of things. See now how dark it is down in the woods, while the tops of the trees are all full of beautiful golden light. The sun is certainly shining, though we can not feel it."

Maud made no reply, but ran forward a little way, and stooping over a grave she laid a few evergreens at its head, and stood silently by until her companion came up. Then sitting down side by side upon a flat stump, they talked softly together about the dead, Maud once or twice springing up to gather some bright berries she descried in the distance to add to the little offering upon aunty's grave.

"She loved every thing bright and beautiful when she was alive, Miss Fanny, and I think there always ought to be flowers on her grave," she said. "Did you ever see any body so cheerful and happy as aunty? and yet she had n't the first thing to make her so, only religion. She had heaps of sorrow, you know."

"I never heard her speak of it," said Fanny.

"No, she did n't ever talk much about it, but she told me. O, Miss Fanny, she had two beautiful little babies that they stole away from her in the night, and sold 'em, 'cause she would n't let 'em have 'em in the daytime. She said for years and years she could n't never get to sleep without hearing 'em cry and scream just as they did that night."

"She never told me," said Fanny. "Was it long ago?"

"O, yes, years and years, when she belonged to Grandpa Whately. You see, first, her husband, he belonged to another man, that moved 'way off down river somewhere, and took him with him, and before poor aunty had time to get over that, they sold her two babies to a trader, and she just went crazy for ever so long. She said she did n't get no comfort till she found religion, and then she see that it was all right. But I don't think it 's right, Miss Fanny. I don't believe God likes to have such things happen. Do you?"

"No, Maud; I think they are all wrong from begin ning to end."

"And you do n't have 'em where you live, Miss Fanny?"

"No, I thank God that we have no slaves in New England."

"Then I wish I was going to live there, too, or else

I wish pa would send all the people there, or somewhere else where they would be free. I would, if I could."

"He would be a poor man then, Maud, like Tim Jenkins over the creek, who you all despise so."

"I don't care. I had rather be 'poor white folks' all my life than to have such things happening."

"Why Maud, you are getting quite excited."

"Miss Fanny, I've been thinking heaps about it lately. I used to talk to aunty, but she didn't like to hear me. But I know what I mean to do, Miss Fanny, when I grow up. When pa gives me my share of the people, I'm going to set 'em all free, every one, and I'll study real hard and know heaps, and then I can get my living teaching school like you do. That's just what I mean to do."

Fanny smiled at the child's enthusiasm; but she kissed her heartily, calling her her own brave girl.

It was a sorrowful day at La Belle Prairie when Fanny and her two scholars went away. From Mass' Jack and Miss Car'line in the "big house," down to Aunt Tibby and the little piccaninnies in the kitchen, all regretted their departure.

Dave was to drive them down to Belcher's to take the stage, and while big William was gearing the horses, Fanny slipped down to the quarters to bid the servants good-by. It was about sunset, and the field hands were just returning from their day's work. They all gathered around her, men, women and children, and while she passed from one to another shaking hands, and speaking a few parting words, there was plenty of sobbing among the women, and one or two of the men wiped their eyes with their shirt-sleeves.

"Don't see what on airth we's goin' to do widout her," said Aunt Tibby. "'Pears like a streak ob sunshine was goin' off de place."

"It does so," said two or three.

"Leastways dar won't be no 'ligion left," said Viny, "Aunt Phebe and Miss Fanny both gone."

"Miss Fanny don' forget me," said a little squeaking voice, and black Jake pressed forward with his apron full of berries which he thrust into Fanny's hands, while Patsey brought her baby in the little dress and apron Fanny had made for it, holding in its chubby hand an egg for a parting gift.

"Bless her heart," said Patsey, "she's cryin' her own self," and with a few earnest words of advice, interrupted by their sobs and ejaculations, Fanny took her leave of them.

The parting words were all said at last, and the farm-wagon containing the travelers, wound slowly over the prairie. As they approached a curve in the road that would soon hide the house from view, Fanny turned to take one more look at her late home. The sun had set, and upon the golden hue in the west the evening shades were fast settling. The house looked white and ghastly against the evening sky, and two or three trees in front seemed waving their long arms in silent adieu. Fanny gazed till a turn in the road hid it from her sight, and with a tear in her eye, and a feeling of sincere regret in her heart, she bade farewell to her home on La Belle Prairie.

CHAPTER XLIV.

WHAT! no wedding? Have we followed the young people through all their doubts and difficulties, and are we not to see them comfortably married off at last? It's too bad! Well, dear reader, what could we do? It was only last winter that our lovers plighted their faith. We can only inform you that they are in earnest correspondence, that the young man is pursuing his theological studies, and that they are unitedly bent upon a mission to Kanzas. In their fresh enthusiasm, "hoping all things, believing all things," they will go hand in hand to their work. May God go with them and make them the apostles of a pure Gospel.

Jack Catlett still occupies the old family mansion, though he feels decidedly poor, for the war in Kanzas, and the loss on the claim, have taken several thousands from his estate. Mrs. Catlett still frets at the servants, and calls oftener than ever for her pipe and a shovel of 'coals. Maud, the brave, enthusiastic Maud, is in Connecticut, and declares that as " soon as ever she is grown, she will go out to Kanzas and help Miss Fanny to do good." It would not be strange if she should carry out her resolve, for she possesses energy and perseverance enough to accomplish any thing she proposes, and in spite of Uncle Peter's prediction, that the ghost of the " grand-daughter of Governor Peters, of Virginia" would rise in indignation from the grave, if one of her descendants should teach school for a living, we expect one day to hear that Maud Catlett has become a missionary teacher at the West.

That old sprig of Virginian aristocracy, Madam Hester, was found one day dead in her chair, and the dust of the "grand-daughter of Governor Peters of Virginia" has mingled with that of our common mother earth at last.

Tom Walton spends much of his time in St. Louis, and it is whispered that he has bestowed his blighted affections upon the beautiful daughter of Judge Stanton, who has kindly consented to make him happy.

Bob Turner, and Nan also, expect to be married in the fall, and as Dave, with his bride, are settled on Madam Gamby's old place, that lady being in Kanzas the greater part of the time, we may expect gay times next Christmas with three young couples on the prairie.

The widow and Zi occupy their rightful claim in Kanzas, and Jack Catlett frequently declares, with a terrible oath, that nobody shall disturb them if he can help it.

Tim Jenkins had found, by conversing with free State men in Lawrence, that he could find schools there for his child, and having made a little sum as a soldier, he determined to take a claim, and remove his family upon it. So immediately after the siege of Lawrence he became a citizen of Kanzas; but, strange to say, votes steadily for the introduction of slavery, so blind are men to their true interests. Though good men there hoped at first that the change in location would work a reformation in this shiftless man, yet it became soon manifest that as the Ethiopian can not change his skin, nor a leopard his spots, so next to impossible is it for one in years to reform the habits of a lifetime. Tim Jenkins is Tim Jenkins still, but his little daughter attends a school near by, and is a promising scholar. The removal to Kanzas may prove an infinite blessing to her.

As for Martha, she had retreated from Lawrence, as

soon as she knew that her master was there. She need
not have done so. Jack Catlett made little effort to recover the fugitive. He did not wish to sell a hand to
Texas, and the whole family stood in great fear of the
girl, Mrs. C. particularly, declaring that she would rather
do half the work herself than to have her round again.
After the family returned to the prairie, Martha came
back to the city, where she is an industrious laborer for
wages, and does exceedingly well, so long as the lull of
the storms which visit that distracted country leave her
unexcited as to her wrongs. But when she snuffs the
battle afar off, she seems like a fiend of darkness, and
wanders about, working mischief to both sides.

Uncle Tim and Aunt Lina are living together in one
cabin as the hands of Dave, Mr. Catlett having given this
faithful servant to his son. They are superlatively happy
in their union, but Uncle Tim has never been able to forgive himself for getting that saw for " Miss Fanny."

The future of this beautiful country where our scene
has been laid, is, at the time of our completing this history, all enveloped in darkness. No human eye can look
far enough adown the vista of time, with the vision of
prophecy, to unroll its destiny to men.

What trials and struggles may await Harry Chester and
Fanny, with Maud Catlett, in their efforts to give true
Christianity, with a Bible education, to Kanzas, will depend very much upon the solution of the question of
liberty and slavery there. Full of great results is the
problem of the freedom of this Territory. The history of
the State will unfold itself in the moral power of such
citizens as Gamby with her slaves, or Harry Chester with
a free Gospel.

THE END.

LIST OF NEW BOOKS

PUBLISHED BY

JOHN E. POTTER.

MAILING NOTICE.—Any of these Books will be sent to any address, free of postage, on receipt of price. Address JOHN E. POTTER, PUBLISHER, *No.* 617 *Sansom Street, Philadelphia.*

THE HORSE AND HIS DISEASES: embracing his History and Varieties, Breeding, and Management and Vices: with the Diseases to which he is subject, and the Remedies best adapted to their Cure. By ROBERT JENNINGS, V. S., Professor of Pathology and Operative Surgery in the Veterinary College of Philadelphia; Professor of Veterinary Medicine in the late Agricultural College of Ohio; Secretary of the American Veterinary Association of Philadelphia, etc. etc. To which are added, Rarey's Method of Taming Horses, and the Law of Warranty, as applicable to the purchase and sale of the animal. Illustrated by nearly 100 engravings. 12mo., cloth. Price $1 50.

CATTLE AND THEIR DISEASES: embracing their History and Breeds, Crossing and Breeding, and Feeding and Management; with the Diseases to which they are subject, and the Remedies best adapted to their Cure. To which are added a List of the Medicines used in treating Cattle, and the Doses of the various remedies requisite. By ROBERT JENNINGS, V. S., Author of "The Horse and his Diseases," etc. etc. With numerous Illustrations. 12mo., cloth. Price $1 50.

SHEEP, SWINE, AND POULTRY: embracing the History and Varieties of each; the best modes of Breeding; their Feeding and Management; together with the Diseases to which they are respectively subject, and the appropriate Remedies for each. By ROBERT JENNINGS, V. S., Author of "The Horse and his Diseases," "Cattle and their Diseases," etc. etc. With numerous illustrations. 12mo., cloth. Price $1 50.

THE LADIES' MEDICAL GUIDE AND MARRIAGE FRIEND: a plain and instructive Treatise on the Structure and Functions of the Reproductive Organs in both sexes; the Diseases peculiar to Females, and the Diseases of Children, with the appropriate Remedies for each, and valuable Directions and Recipes for the Toilet, Beautifying the Skin, Cultivating and Arranging the Hair, &c. &c. By S. PANCOAST, M. D., Professor of Microscopic Anatomy, Physiology, and the Institutes of Medicine in Penn Medical University, Philadelphia. With upwards of 100 illustrations. 12mo., cloth. Price $1 50.

THE FAMILY DOCTOR: a Counsellor in Sickness, Pain, and Distress, for Childhood, Manhood, and Old Age; containing in plain language, free from medical terms, the Causes, Symptoms, and Cure of Disease in every form, with important Rules for Preserving the Health, and Directions for the Sick Chamber, and the Proper Treatment of the Sick; the whole drawn from extensive observation and practice. By Professor HENRY S. TAYLOR, M. D. Illustrated with numerous engravings of Medicinal Plants and Herbs. 12mo., cloth. Price $1 25.

OUR BOYS. The Personal Experiences of a Soldier in the Army of the Potomac. A very readable book by A. F. HILL, of the Eighth Pennsylvania Reserves. 12mo., cloth. Price $1 50.

THRILLING STORIES OF THE GREAT REBELLION: comprising Heroic Adventures and Hair-breadth Escapes of Soldiers, Scouts, Spies, and Refugees; Daring Exploits of Smugglers, Guerrillas, Desperadoes, and others; Tales of Loyal and Disloyal Women; Stories of the Negro, etc. etc. With Incidents of Fun and Merriment in Camp and Field. By a DISABLED OFFICER. With colored illustrations. 12mo., cloth. Price $1 50.

THRILLING ADVENTURES AMONG THE EARLY SETTLERS: embracing Desperate Encounters with Indians, Tories, and Refugees; Daring Exploits of Texan Rangers and others, and Incidents of Guerrilla Warfare; Fearful Deeds of the Gamblers and Desperadoes, Rangers and Regulators of the West and Southwest; Hunting Stories, Trapping Adventures, etc. etc. By WARREN WILDWOOD, Esq. Illustrated by 200 engravings. 12mo., cloth. Price $1 50.

FANNY HUNTER'S WESTERN ADVENTURES. What Fanny Hunter Saw and Heard in Kansas and Missouri. Illustrated. 12mo., cloth. Price $1 50.

3

THE LIFE OF STEPHEN A. DOUGLAS: to which are added his Speeches and Reports. By H. M. FLINT. With a portrait on steel. 12mo., cloth. Price $1 50.

LIFE OF KIT CARSON, the great Western Hunter and Guide: comprising Wild and Romantic Exploits as a Hunter and Trapper in the Rocky Mountains; Thrilling Adventures and Hair-breadth Escapes among the Indians and Mexicans; his Daring and Invaluable Services as a Guide to Scouting and other Parties, etc. etc. With an account of various Government Expeditions to the Far West. By CHAS. BURDETT. 12mo., illustrated, cloth. Price $1 50.

EVERYBODY'S LAWYER AND COUNSELLOR IN BUSINESS: containing plain and simple instructions to everybody for transacting their business according to law, with legal forms for drawing the various necessary papers connected therewith; together with the laws of all the States, for Collection of Debts, Property Exempt from Execution, Mechanics' Liens, Execution of Deeds and Mortgages, Rights of Married Women, Dower, Usury, Wills, &c.' By FRANK CROSBY, Esq., of the Philadelphia Bar. 12mo., law half sheep. Price $1 50.

THE AMERICAN TEXT-BOOK: containing the Constitution of the United States; the Declaration of Independence, and Washington's Farewell Address. 32mo., cloth. Price 25 cts.

MODERN COOKERY, in all its branches: embracing a series of plain and simple instructions to private families and others, for the careful and judicious preparation of every variety of food, as drawn from practical observation and experience. Embracing upwards of Twelve Hundred recipes, appropriately illustrated. By Miss ELIZA ACTON. The whole carefully revised by Mrs. S. J. HALE. 12mo., cloth. Price $1 50.

WAY DOWN EAST; or, Portraitures of Yankee Life. By SEBA SMITH, the original Major Jack Downing. Illustrated. 12mo., cloth. Price $1 50.

TUPPER'S COMPLETE POETICAL WORKS: comprising Proverbial Philosophy, a Thousand Lines, Hactenus, Geraldine, Miscellaneous Poems, etc. etc. With portrait on steel. 12mo., cloth. Price $1 50.

FEMALE LIFE AMONG THE MORMONS: a Narrative of many years' Personal Experience, exemplifying the old adage, that "Truth is stranger than Fiction." A truly startling work. By MARIA WARD, the wife of a Mormon Elder. Illustrated. 12mo., cloth. Price $1 50.

MALE LIFE AMONG THE MORMONS. A work of great and unusual interest, which will be eagerly read as a companion volume to "Female Life." By AUSTIN N. WARD. Illustrated. 12mo., cloth. Price $1 25.

THE YOUNG LADY'S OWN BOOK. An Offering of Love and Sympathy. By EMILY THORNWELL. 12mo., cloth. Price $1 50.

GREAT EXPECTATIONS. By CHARLES DICKENS. Complete in one volume, illustrated with steel engravings. 12mo., cloth. Price $1 25.

THE EARLY DAYS OF CALIFORNIA: embracing What I Saw and Heard There; with Scenes in the Pacific. By Col. J. T. FARNHAM. 12mo., illustrated. Cloth. Price $1 25.

NICARAGUA; Past, Present, and Future. By PETER F. STOUT, Esq., late United States Vice-Consul. With a New and Improved Map of the Country. 12mo., cloth. Price $1 50.

SUNLIGHT AND SHADOW; or, the Poetry of Home. A very readable volume. By HARRY PENCILLER. 12mo., cloth. Price $1 25.

THE PET KEEPSAKE. A Token of Love. Illustrated. 12mo., cloth. Price $1 25.

THE RAINBOW AROUND THE TOMB; or, Rays of Hope for Those who Mourn. By EMILY THORNWELL. 12mo., cloth. Price $1 25.

A Catalogue including all our Books, Albums, and Bibles, with prices, may be had on application to

JOHN E. POTTER, Publisher,
617 Sansom Street, Philadelphia.

www.ingramcontent.com/pod-product-compliance
Lightning Source LLC
Chambersburg PA
CBHW030814110726
47900CB00006B/1622